PRAISE FOR HER WICKED ROOTS

"*Her Wicked Roots* is a stellar, genre-bending debut from Tanya Pell. It's a full-fledged **gothic, creepy as hell and full of yearning, soaked in dread and mystery.** I can't wait to see what Pell does next!"

—Christopher Golden, *New York Times* bestselling author of *The Night Birds* and *The House of Last Resort*

"Tanya Pell is a horror horticulturist who has cultivated a manic botanic gothic that grafts Silvia Moreno-Garcia to Daphne du Maurier, and what sprouts out is absolutely beautiful. ***Her Wicked Roots*** **reaches in and rummages through the reader's subconscious until there's no weeding it out.**"

—Clay McLeod Chapman, author of *Wake Up and Open Your Eyes*

"Tanya Pell's *Her Wicked Roots* is a winding, creeping ivy, a nighttime garden bursting and blossoming with rich texture and dark, sinister bouquets. Beautiful flowers can, however, be deadly. **A richly gothic and lush retelling.**"

—Cynthia Pelayo, Bram Stoker Award–winning author of *Vanishing Daughters*

"*Her Wicked Roots* is a true treat, sure to delight and thrill in equal measure. **A must-read for fans of queer gothic novels.**"

—Johanna van Veen, author of *Blood on Her Tongue* and *My Darling Dreadful Thing*

"Lush and languid . . . A full-blooded and enchanting gothic that, much like some of the flora it features, is beautiful and lethal in equal measure. **Nothing short of spectacular, Pell's latest is twisted, twisty, full of queer longing and chlorophyllic menace. . . .** There's a quiet dread that Tanya Pell has clearly mastered. "Rappaccini's Daughter" meets Silvia Moreno-Garcia in this claustrophobic, botanical beast of a book that is indeed as exquisite on the inside as its cover suggests. Thorny, horny, and full of tension."

—*FanFiAddict*

"**Darkly enchanting,** *Her Wicked Roots* is haunting, propulsive, and as hypnotic as the poisonous blooms at the novel's heart. Truly a bewitching sapphic delight."

—Francesca May, author of *Wild and Wicked Things* and *This Vicious Hunger*

"This gorgeous, haunting story coiled tight around my heart and refused to let go. **An intoxicating tale of secrets, desire, hurt, and bravery,** rooted in the fear of losing the ones we love. Tanya Pell is such an exciting voice in horror, and this gothic mystery is truly unforgettable."

—Josh Winning, author of *Heads Will Roll*

"**Tanya Pell skillfully brews a gothic Victorian horror novel that's equal parts *The Secret Garden* and *Midsommar*.** . . . Like the belladonna plant that populates Edenfield, *Her Wicked Roots* is deceptively approachable—but beware of the poison just under the stunning surface."

—*BookPage*

"Eerie . . . **It's easy to sink into the spooky atmosphere, and an impressive final twist will catch even the most genre-savvy unaware.** For readers seeking fun queer gothic horror, this delivers."

—*Publishers Weekly*

"Perfect for fans of Silvia Moreno-Garcia's *Mexican Gothic* or Kit Mayquist's *Tripping Arcadia,* **the book features a *Gone Girl*–esque twist that will plant this story's wicked roots deep into readers' souls.**"

—*Booklist*

"Tanya Pell cultivates a world that is both beautiful and unnerving in *Her Wicked Roots,* a gothic novel that blends horror, mystery, and queer romance into one darkly enchanting read. **Blooming with gothic atmosphere, Pell's debut novel is truly magnificent.**"

—*Capes & Tights*

HER WICKED ROOTS

A GOTHIC TALE

TANYA PELL

GALLERY BOOKS
New York Amsterdam/Antwerp London
Toronto Sydney/Melbourne New Delhi

Gallery Books
An Imprint of Simon & Schuster, LLC
1230 Avenue of the Americas
New York, NY 10020

First Gallery Books trade paperback edition August 2026

Interior design by Kathryn A. Kenney-Peterson

Manufactured in the United States of America

10 9 8 7 6 5 4 3 2 1

Library of Congress Control Number: 2024952050

ISBN 978-1-6680-8729-9
ISBN 978-1-6680-8730-5 (pbk)
ISBN 978-1-6680-8731-2 (ebook)

For the women who grow in defiance

Chapter 1

CORDELIA'S HEAD BANGED AGAINST THE side of the carriage and she startled awake, fingers clawing reflexively at the small bag in her lap, pulling it closer. For one terrifying moment, she thought the jolt was the carriage being forced to a halt. That at any second the door would open and rough hands would reach in, drag her from her seat, and force her back to the Barrow and the horrors that would await her there.

But it had only been a lurch as the carriage wheel bounced through a pothole. Cordi heard the driver cursing the roads with language that might have made a fainter heart blush but only made her exhale a shaky laugh.

"Are you all right, dear?"

The only other passenger was an elderly woman with a lapful of yarn and knitting needles poised like tiny spears in her hands that had been *click*ing and *clack*ing since the driver had helped her settle into her seat. Those needles were finally still as she watched Cordi with concern.

Cordi gave a wan smile, trying to keep her features hidden behind the uneven waves of her hair. "Yes, ma'am," she said meekly, hating the attention she had drawn. "Just startled."

The old woman clucked and went back to her knitting. "Bad dreams?"

Are there any other kind?

But the woman didn't seem to need an answer. The door to conversation had been opened and she was apparently happy to fill the quiet while her thin fingers, the skin wrinkled and sagging with age, returned to her nimble knitting and purling. "I sleep like the dead myself. Suppose I'm getting practice in," she said with a little chuckle. "Not too long till the grave for me. But I simply cannot sleep without a proper bed. Was never able to. And certainly not on a dusty road, jostling about like a package."

"Yes, ma'am," Cordi said again, not wanting to be rude.

When she had first boarded in the city, she had imagined the eyes of the other passengers on her, scrutinizing her face even as she tried to keep it turned casually away. Surely they were memorizing her so they might later tell the constables what they knew. She had been certain at each stop that she would be arrested, and so had waited with bated breath and a pounding heart as each passenger disembarked and their luggage was handed down, pressed into a corner of the carriage in an effort to make herself as small as possible. She did not breathe until the wheels had begun moving again.

In these moments of uncertain limbo as she waited for the lurch of the carriage, Cordi's hand would sink into her pocket and clutch her beloved talisman. The treasured fox, a gift from her brother carved from linden wood, offered her some small measure of comfort. Her thumb would stroke its smooth belly as a penitent's fingers might slide over prayer beads.

When she had been forced to clamber down herself at the stops in order to make water or burst, she had shuffled through the people milling around the station. Men stood about in dark hats and coats, reading papers, checking watches, and guffawing at bawdy jokes. Ladies attended small children or tried to revive wilting feathers in their hats, noses turned up at the scent of horses and tobacco. Cordi had done her business and kept her head down, her collar turned up, forcing her gait to be steady as she wove through the crowd, her face a mask of casual annoyance. Just another passenger eager to be on her way. Just another poor, wretched girl among thousands. She willed all eyes not to linger upon her, retreating to the safety of the coach and the quiet, dreary passengers within.

No one had spoken to her, nor to each other for that matter. Everyone had kept to their own business. It made her wonder about their own secrets. If they were all running from something, just like her.

No, she scolded herself. No. She was not running from something. She was running *toward.*

"Dear?"

Cordi reflexively straightened against the carriage seat. Years of harsh school inspections gave her a straight spine and folded hands on cue. "Ma'am?"

The older woman's lips pinched together, eyes narrowed behind tiny golden spectacles, sweeping over Cordi's poor clothing, lingering on her hands, dotted with scars from a hard life lived. Upon her seeing these, her lips turned at the corners into a tender smile, something warm and comforting. "I said you were much too young and too pretty to be having bad dreams. That's all."

Kindness was a gift Cordi had not known for some time. Something she had almost forgotten how to acknowledge. "Th-thank you," she stuttered. "Ma'am."

The woman nodded and resumed her knitting, the sound of her needles tapping together filling the small space.

Cordi allowed herself to look out the window and found her eyes dazzled. Green fields and hillocks stretching into the distance, marred only by the occasional fence or copse of trees. Sheep, their wool stained with fresh mud rather than the muck of the city.

Cordi pressed her nose against the frosty glass, fogging it with her breath as she tried to crane her neck, looking for any glimpse of crowded buildings and the life she'd left behind. A world of black and gray and death, the early morning sun choked behind low clouds and smoke from chimneys coughing out soot, ash, and brick dust to corrupt the recent snow.

There was only the lush pastoral scene passing hastily beyond her window. Days and miles separated her from the cruel city and the crimes committed there, both her own and others'. With each mile traveled, she felt a link in the chain tying her to her old life crack and fall away.

The driver cursed again before pulling up the reins, the carriage rolling to a stop.

"Oh," Cordelia breathed at the sight of a meadow carpeted in an early spray of bluebells.

The purple and blue flowers dipped their heads lazily, heavy with dew yet to burn away, sparkling and twinkling in the changing light. A field of stars.

The coach swayed as the driver hauled himself out of his seat and down to the ground. He rapped quickly on the door before it swung open on her side. Instinctively, Cordi pressed farther back into the seat, one hand clutching her bag. "Why have we stopped?"

The driver pushed his hat back on his head, revealing clean, pale skin beneath, a clear line separating his scalp from his face, dusty and tanned by years in the sun. "That dip we took. One of the team is pulling to the side. May have picked up a stone or I may need to adjust his straps. But you might as well stretch your legs if you've a mind." The driver was a genial man; though curt, he treated her and the other passengers with nothing but respect. His nose was red from a chill even early spring could not quite vanquish and paired splendidly with his red beard peppered with stiff, gray hairs. More of those same hairs sprouted like weeds from his ears.

He backed away from the door and she heard his thick boots on the road as he went to attend to his horses.

"You go right ahead, dear," the woman offered. "Will do you some good to see some sun. Too pale. I'm staying right here with my work. If I disembark, I'm likely never to make my way back up again."

Cordi considered staying put, tucked into her corner. But she was tired of sitting and the air wafting into the carriage from the open door was so sweet. She slung her satchel on her shoulder and climbed out, blinking in the bright sunshine.

As she stepped down, knees adjusting to the feel of solid ground beneath her, she had to choke back happy tears even as she drew a deep breath into her lungs. She shut her eyes, half convinced she would open them to the squat wall covered in black frost that marked the path between the stone steps of her former prison and its iron gate. But when she lifted her lids, the flowers and trees were still there, not muted and leached of all color by soot and sorrow, but dazzling and alive, as far a cry from the frozen wasteland as she might ever find.

Had her brother, Edward, seen it like this? Had he marveled as well?

Cordi walked through the tall grass, sweeping her hand across the stalks, letting them tickle her palm and dampen her skirt and ankles. She was drawn to the blue flowers, some the same color as the pure sky above her—the color of Edward's eyes. Others were rich indigo, as dark blue as her own. They put her in mind of the last time she had seen her brother, standing at the gates of the Barrow, wearing his school-issue coat, threadbare and black and not at all suitable for the winter days that loomed. Gray fingerless gloves he had found in the charity basket, fraying and riddled with holes she had tried to stitch together, covered his hands for all the warmth they would offer. He had held his hat, and a dingy, stained canvas bag was tossed over his shoulder.

On those steps they had parted for the first time in their lives. Before he disappeared into the city streets, she had reached under her shawl and pulled out a length of knitted wool. The scarf was several different colors, the fibers salvaged from pieces beyond repair and lengths of wool she had scrounged or begged for. Some she had even stolen from Mrs. Clark's knitting basket when it was her turn to clean the head teacher's suite of rooms. Those pieces she had used for the tassels, for they were the brightest: pale blue and deepest indigo. A reminder that they were family. A plea not to forget her.

Did you knit this with your eyes closed? She had slapped at him as he had known she would, and he'd ducked before hugging her to his heart, laughing into her hair, the sound bittersweet. *I treasure it and you. Now, promise me you'll learn to knit a straight line by the time I come for you. And I* will *come for you, Dee.*

It was the last she'd seen him before he set off down the walk, scarf tucked beneath his collar, hat pulled down over his head, hiding his curls. Just another young English boy in black and gray on another black-and-gray English morning.

Here, though, was all the color in the world. She gathered some of the flowers, breaking them off along their crisp stalks, the tips of her fingers numbing with the damp chill. She took only a few, enough to chase the darkness of the carriage away, to remind her she was free. Turning back to the road, she glimpsed another splash of color: a taller flute of a plant, dotted with small amethyst flowers, that rose over the bluebells, their heads bowed like supplicants before a god. The pink-purple flowers were thickly clustered together, their trumpets open mouths inviting bees to dine upon the sweet nectar within.

Cordelia approached, intending to add it to her small bouquet, the color striking and alluring. She extended a hand—

"Stop!" the driver shouted.

She snatched her fingers back, nearly strangling the bluebells as her grip tightened.

"Don't touch that one, missy. That there's foxglove."

"Foxglove?" she said dumbly.

Whether he heard her faint reply or not, he carried on. "Poison, it is. Pretty to look at, but best be leaving it alone. Could kill a horse if eaten. Would probably spare your life if we were quick enough, sure, but wouldn't likely spare you pain."

Like so many things, Cordi thought, giving the flower one last look before she trudged back to the carriage.

The driver nodded at her good sense to listen, adjusting the strap on one of the horses. "Funny how nature protects itself. How some of the loveliest things are also the deadliest." His eyebrows plummeted and he turned back to the meadow, shaking his head. "Strange to see foxglove this early. Though I don't mind telling you I've seen queerer things growing this close to Farrow."

Cordi's heart pounded in her chest. "Are we so near?"

"That we are, missy. This is the edge of Rutland. Quick stop at the crossroads ahead and then we'll head on."

She looked around again, the magic and wonder of the place making sense. This was where she was meant to be. This was where she would put down roots and find her home.

With the horses secure, they could continue on, and Cordi found herself fidgeting, eager, almost giddy. Her companion noticed the change. "The fresh air seems to agree with you," the woman said with a laugh.

Cordi did smile then. A true smile. Plucking a bluebell from the bouquet, she offered it to the woman, who took it with thanks. "How sweet. I loved gathering flowers when I was young." The woman clucked again. "And I loved having them gathered for me when I was your age. How the boys brought me flowers! Oh!" She giggled, face crinkling with delight, but the wrinkles were of a life well lived. Different scars than Cordi carried. Lines carved with love by time.

A knock sounded from above—the driver signaling a stop. Obviously for Cordi's companion. The woman began to gather her knitting, shoving the bundles of yarn and needles into a thick carpetbag, tucking the bluebell into the buttonhole of her own coat. "Where are you off to, love? Will you be departing with me? On the way to Babford, perhaps? I think I heard they'd been advertising for a new schoolteacher. Would that be you, then? A small class you'll have, to be sure, but, oh, they will keep you on your toes. Especially those Pratt boys, my goodness. But a young thing like you will have the energy for their mischief. The walk isn't far, blessedly. You gather your things and I'll—"

"No," Cordi interrupted, almost laughing at how eager strangers were to talk once the opportunity had arisen. So unlike the city. "I'm bound for Farrow. I'm—"

"Farrow."

Cordi's mouth snapped shut. Stupid of her to say where she was going to anyone. Careless.

But the older woman only stared, the eyes behind those tiny spectacles lost as the sun streaming in from one window reflected off the glass, turning her eyes into glowing white moons.

"You're going to Farrow." The woman's voice, previously warm and grandmotherly, had turned cool, chilling the very air.

"Yes, ma'am."

"I see." The woman inhaled a slow breath as the wheels slowly rolled to a stop. The carriage swayed as the driver jumped to the ground to assist his passenger. As the door opened, the woman remained in her seat. Though her eyes remained obscured by the golden lenses, Cordi felt the stare behind them, hard and severe.

"I don't understand," Cordi said, confused at the sudden change in demeanor, gripping her bag as if the woman might launch herself across the seats toward her.

"Perhaps not." The woman's hands shook as she tugged her shawl around her shoulders. "But ignorance won't keep you safe. Ignorance has never kept a woman safe. If you've any brains in your head, child, you'll not stop at Farrow. There's nothing there for young girls, no matter what promises serpents make. Nothing."

Then she was gone, so quick out of the carriage she didn't even take the hand the coachman offered. Cordi leaned forward before the door could shut to see her shuffling down the road, back bent, head bowed, at a pace that might send her sprawling if she was not careful on the uneven terrain. The bluebell Cordi had given her drifted to the ground and was crushed by the woman's heel into the dust of the road.

The sun dipped behind a cloud and the world turned bleak. "All right, miss?" the driver said, but he seemed wary himself.

Cordi nodded and he closed her in, the carriage suddenly feeling like a tomb.

Chapter 2

ALONE, SHE FORCED HER FINGERS to release their stranglehold on her bag and pulled at the cords holding it closed. She mentally took stock of every item she carried: a threadbare shirt, a gray homespun skirt, an oversize jumper full of holes, the hem ragged beyond repair. There was a pair of thick wool socks, a small kerchief filled with what was left of her coin, and a bundle of letters tied with her old hair ribbon.

It was the coin she removed first, unfolding the bits of cloth holding them. She listened to them clink together merrily, as happy to be free as she was. She counted them carefully, biting her lip as she did sums in her head. Not nearly as much as she would have liked to present to her brother and host family. But it would have to do. Proof she could take care of herself, that she would not be a burden. She reknotted the kerchief with extreme care before placing it at the bottom of her bag. All her wealth in the world and precious little of it.

She pulled her precious fox from her pocket and ran her thumb over the groove she had worn in its belly, staring into its features and willing it to speak to her. To guide her. As usual, no response came, but she was comforted just holding it in her hand. Edward's parting gift to her.

For eight years they had been at Barrow Charity School together. After their parents' deaths, none of the extended family had come forward to offer the then ten-year-old Edward and eight-year-old Cordelia a home. So they had instead been shuffled off to an orphan school on the outskirts of the city where they could be educated and sheltered. Where they would be berated and hungry. And unloved.

They had endured together. But when Edward came of age, he was turned out like all the rest. He had too long protected his willful little sister, bribing her bullies and charming her teachers when possible, and he was dismissed with little more than the clothes on his back, a letter of reference, and whatever he might have claimed from the box of donations reserved for those aging out of the system.

He had left her with the fox, intricately carved in linden wood by his own hands, and the promise he would come back for her. Close now to her destination, she returned the trinket to her bag and took out the bundle of letters, toying with the edge of her hair ribbon, no longer restraining her ashen waves, and a small smile of triumph appeared on her face unbidden.

She had sworn that when she left the Barrow, she would cut off her accursed braid and hang it from the birch rod like a flag. And Cordi *always* kept her promises. She had indeed cut her braid away, leaving her blond tresses short, falling just against her jaw. Then she had broken that wretched switch against her knees into splinters, saving the thicker end Mrs. Clark always held in her gnarled grip to deliver the blows. This piece she had tied her braid to and planted it like a flag in the garden where it had happened. A flag not of surrender, but of victory. They would see it and they would know she had bested them in the end.

She ran her fingers across the pages, finding the indentations left by the pen. Edward always used a heavy hand when it came to writing, even while those same hands and fingers were utterly nimble when he held carving tools.

As promised, he had written every day, though the letters had come only twice a month to keep as much money as possible in his pocket, his letters filled from top to bottom, the writing cramped to preserve both ink and paper. A few lines a day. Each dated.

His letters, detailing his search for work, his travels farther from the city in search of steady income, his determination to bring her to join him, had spurred her own industry at the school. She could not leave the grounds, and chores were a regular part of her duty—nothing she was paid for—but she had been resolute she would find a way to help gather coin. And wouldn't it be a surprise for Edward when he did fetch her? To have extra money to offer the household? She'd convinced the gardener—a foolish drunk named Mason—that he needed her assistance. And for a ha'penny a week, she'd turned soil, dug up rocks, and pulled weeds.

But it had cost. Bile came to her throat as she thought of it; then she saw the scars on the backs of her hands—old and new—and remembered the fresh ones on her back, and she notched her chin higher. She would not be ashamed.

Edward would have been proud of her. They had tried to break her, but she had not broken. God, how they had tried in those last days. . . .

She did not want to picture them. Mrs. Clark with her sneer as she held the bloodied birch, a twisted and perverse light in her eyes. And Mr. Mason watching from the corner, his face perspiring, a self-satisfied smile on his face. They thought they had won. They had taken their pound of flesh, true. Cordi would bear those scars forever, as she would bear the weight of the memories that precipitated her abuse.

She looked out the window to the blue sky and green fields. She did not want to think on her suffering. She wanted to think about her liberation. Of her reunion with Edward.

Cordi tugged the topmost envelope free from the pile and slid the letter out with reverence. It was so different from all the others that had come before it—so short and strange—but it was the one that had given her the most joy upon its arrival. It had been the last, though, making it a bittersweet reminder of what was meant to have happened. She read it again as they lurched down the road, though she knew it by heart.

My darling one,

I swore to you your freedom. Be patient a bit longer. I'll come for you. And I will steal you, if I must.

Love always,

Edward

After its arrival, Cordelia could scarcely contain her happiness. Her brother was coming! The wait was almost over after he'd had steady employment for some time in the village of Farrow, working for a very kind man, a trade carver with a family. He had been impressed with Edward's skills and had offered him work, such as it was. He couldn't pay much, but Edward was given a small room over the workshop and took his meals with the man's family. A Mr. Starling who had a wife, Rebecca, and three daughters, Ann, Agatha, and Alice.

She thought Mr. Starling would eventually agree to let her stay with the family. Perhaps they needed an extra set of hands to help with the girls and the house in exchange for lodging. She didn't care if she slept by the fire, curled up like a dog, so long as she was free of the Barrow and with a family again. Her family.

Cordi had waited. And waited. But no more letters came. And neither did Edward.

Days and then weeks and then months without word. Still she waited, watching the calendar change over, somehow too slowly and too quickly together. And finally, Cordi's time had come to leave the Barrow. And she would have! She had waited so long for that moment when she would be free to walk through those gates and never look back. Only, how would Edward know where to find her? Her only family in the world. All she had left that was hers.

With too little coin to get as far as Farrow, she'd done what she had to do to stay, though she had been loath to do so. Her industry in the garden was not enough, so she'd had to do more. Assisting Cook between lessons, marking for teachers, and, worst of all, asking Mrs. Clark if she might stay on working for nothing but her room and board. Oh, how it had galled her to ask. To beg. And how she'd had to bite her tongue again and again at every ridiculous order and petty punishment.

I want all the guest silver polished, Miss Beecher.

The fireplace in my room needs a good scrubbing, Miss Beecher.

I found a hole in my new stockings, Miss Beecher. I told you to launder them, not take scissors to them, you useless thing!

But she'd done it. Endured every harsh word and harsher beating and gritted her teeth through it. The stubborn, willful Cordelia Beecher turned meek servant. Each night her hands and back ached and her heart the worse, but she stayed on. She'd made herself more than useful. She'd made herself indispensable to those she hated. Because she'd had faith her brother would come back. He had *promised*. And they didn't break their word. Not them.

Cordi put the letter away again, not wanting to return to those dark days when hope was hard to cling to. When Mrs. Clark had relished Cordi's pain as she'd doled out the daily mail, dragging out Cordi's torment with a sly smile. *No mail again, Miss Beecher. Tsk.* Thoughts of those days would lead to other thoughts. And none of that mattered. Not now. If Edward could not come to her, she would go to him.

She had tried to wait. Had tried to be patient.

But her hand had been forced after . . .

After what they did.

So she was headed to Farrow.

It was over two days' journey by mail coach to the rural county and her ticket only went one way. But the fare for passengers was cheaper than by any other means, though it had eaten into her coin well enough. She didn't care. All that mattered was reuniting with her only family.

The carriage slowed to a stop and Cordi looked out the window to see that they had made it to another inn, smaller than any of the previous waypoints. The building was narrow, and Cordi could hardly imagine it had more than two rooms for travelers.

"All right, missy," the coachman said, opening the door. "This be Farrow. Your stop."

Her heart leapt and she shoved her letters deep into her bag, fingers clumsy as she tied it tight and hitched it onto her shoulder. The driver extended his hand to help her alight and she had to force herself not to recoil deeper into the carriage away from that hand, callused and large and so like another man's hand. It was not him, she assured herself with a quick glance at the driver's face, red from cold rather than drink. She had left *him* in the city. Still, she could not quite keep her fingers from shaking as she took the offered palm, shuddering as she descended the small step and onto the beaten earth of the road.

"Cold, missy?"

The fresh air was still crisp with the echo of winter. She wore her only other skirt, a coarse black sack that hung on her hips, and her shirt of linen, grayed with age, under her school-issued coat at least two inches too short in the arms and waist. She had let down the cuffs long ago, but still the skin of her wrists lay exposed. The collar of the coat was down, leaving her neck naked and vulnerable. She reached up a hand to smooth what was left of her shorn hair, sure she looked an absolute mess from both the blind haircut and the days of travel.

"A little," she said, hoping she didn't sound nervous.

The shadow that crossed his face suggested she did. "You'll forgive me, missy, but, being a father myself . . . well . . ." He rubbed at his beard with a hand red from the ride. "You're not any real weight, little thing that you are, and I never get no passengers here. I can take you on to the next stop. Bigger town. Won't be any trouble. No charge. Strange stories come out of this place. Not anything I believe, but it don't feel right leaving you in this place. Not with the things you hear."

The old woman's warning tolled in her heart like a bell. "What things?"

He pulled a face. "Ah. Gossip and rumor is all. And I'm no washerwoman fond of telling tales. But I don't like the feel of it and that's good enough for me. My daughter might be all grown up now, but I'd not want her left in such a place as bloody Farrow with its strangeness. Not without knowing she'd be safe."

Cordi glanced about cautiously, suddenly feeling quite foolish and more than a little uneasy. Yet to give up here when she had come so far and was so close was unthinkable. She had no one else but her brother. Nowhere else but Edward. Clearing her throat, she offered a grateful smile. "Thank you. But I'm expected."

The coachman looked kindly on her, concern touching his eyes. "You have family in these parts, then?"

"Yes." She hoped, immediately hating herself for even that little weakness. Hope was the kinder sister to doubt, but hope was not belief.

Her answer was said with enough confidence, and the driver seemed relieved. He gestured to the inn. "Well, you be getting inside and warming yourself. You'll likely have a bit of a walk ahead of you and night comes dark in these parts."

His concern was touching. "Thank you." Surprising herself, she offered her hand in friendship.

He took her hand in both of his, squeezing gently, and she liked to think he was a good father. That his daughter was well loved.

A small flame of envy lit within her chest, and she dropped his hand awkwardly, stepping away toward the inn, eyes lifting to the sign for the Fox and Fawn. Her steps slowed and what began as a smile widened into a grin.

The sign was a newer addition, judging by the condition and color of the wood and the paint. It hung in stark contrast to the rest of the inn, weather-beaten and worn. The namesake creatures had been carved in relief into the wood, the fox on one side and the fawn on the other. And she would know the hand that had carved it anywhere. For the fox was the twin to the one she carried in her bag.

Cordi nearly flew up the short set of stairs and across the floorboards to the door of the inn.

She stepped into a dimly lit room littered with a handful of tables, a fire smoldering in a small brick hearth. She hurried quickly to the bar where the innkeeper stood, a ledger spread on the counter in front of him. He'd probably heard the coach arrive and was readying the books for any mail deliveries, but Cordi wanted to speak to him before the coachman could rightfully gain his attention.

"Please, sir," she pleaded, almost out of breath with anticipation, "might you tell me where I can find the home of Mr. Starling?"

The innkeeper was tall, with sloping, narrow shoulders and a wiry frame. His face was all sharp angles and he was smoothly shaven, displaying a pointy chin and a prominent Adam's apple. Long fingers tapped across the bar with nervous energy and he shifted back and forth on his feet, obviously a man who rarely stood still.

"Starling? His place is maybe a quarter of an hour straight up the road from here. Would you be family, then? Not knowing them to have family beyond Mrs. Starling's sister."

Cordi forged ahead, hands clasped to her heart to keep it in her chest. "Thank you, sir. How shall I know it?"

The innkeeper shrugged, head bobbing on his neck, putting Cordi in mind of a heron. "His shop and storefront are next to the house. Piles of lumber along the side. One of the only homes you'll find this far out. Just walk straight down the road. You'll come upon her." He reached for a book. "Be needing a drink or something to eat before you—"

But Cordi was already wheeling around, headed for the door just as the coachman shouldered it open, mailbag in hand.

"Did you say you was family?" came the innkeeper's call after her.

No, she thought, but the word *family,* as precious as the word *freedom,* caught in her heart like a fishhook pulling her down the wooden steps again and onto the road.

Chapter 3

CORDI MIGHT HAVE RUN THE entire length of road to the Starling home had she been wearing shoes suitable for anything beyond the scrap pile. But even when the heel peeled away from one and the toes of the opposite foot felt the brisk, barely spring air through the holes that widened with each step, she hurried on. She told herself that comfort meant little. Comfort—if it could be called such—had delayed her too long already.

If she had insisted they leave together . . . If he had come back . . .

It didn't matter. What was done was done and she was going to see her brother again.

The Starling house, as the innkeeper had said, was distinctive. The lumber that lay in great piles against the side of the shop was already stripped and ready for its master's hand. Edward had told her that Mr. Starling was the only true craftsman in the surrounding counties and had plenty of work filling orders on everything from doors to furniture for those who didn't want to pay the price of shipping from the city. Edward said Mr. Starling was as good a master craftsman as any to be found in the city and it was only in name and notoriety that he was at a disadvantage.

Cordi had known that Mr. Starling would eventually offer Edward a partnership. She had just known it. The tone of Edward's letters was always humble, offering any number of ways he might improve whenever he wrote of a customer's satisfaction or Mr. Starling's compliments, but she had read them enough to know the pride Edward had taken in his master's praise. She could *feel* his excitement in every stroke of the pen. His belief that he would be able to collect her sooner than he expected. A promise of reunion.

Then nothing.

Mrs. Clark had been stealing her mail. Cordi was sure of it. Certainly the woman was vile and loathsome enough to do such a wicked thing. And how she must have delighted in Cordi's hurt and humiliation. She might have been eager to see the back of Cordi when she was a charge, but as cheap, dependent labor? No, she must have been stealing the letters, hoping to keep more coin in her pockets and Cordi under her thumb.

Of course, it had occurred to her that something had happened to Edward. An accident. An illness. Something that kept him from coming for her or writing. But she'd written to Starling herself and received no reply, cementing her belief that Mrs. Clark was behind it all.

She didn't allow doubt to slow her as she ran up the hard, beaten road to the workshop. Behind the structure, she could make out the merry sound of a child's skipping rhyme and she smiled, stilling to listen as she recognized the ditty, knowing it was the Starling daughters and tearing up thinking how lovely this life was.

"Mary, Mary, quite contrary
How does your garden grow?
With silver bells and cockleshells
And pretty maids all in a row."

Her lips moved in time with the words, but the next stanza was not as she expected, and her smile faltered.

"But what's planted in the Garden
Will grow where it is laid.
Your only hope is to avoid
The breath of a pretty maid."

A biting breeze swirled around her, and she shivered in her thin clothing, disturbed by the haunting words repeated without inflection in a tiny chorus of children's voices. It was all rather macabre. But children loved scary stories, didn't they? It was assuredly all in good fun.

The sound of a hammer falling steadily brought the grin again to her lips as she pictured her brother looking up and seeing her framed in the doorway. Imagined how happy he would be to see her. It was his blue eyes and golden hair—features he had inherited from their mother and now the only way she could remember her mother's face—she sought as she pulled open the door to the workshop and stepped inside.

But it was not Edward who looked up.

A man stood behind a workbench littered with smooth wooden pegs that looked to be the spindly, intricate legs of a table he was working on. The man's face was covered with a well-trimmed beard, the same salt-and-pepper color as his full head of hair. His eyes were warm and brown, and Cordi had the absent thought that they were a proper color for a woodcarver.

He cocked a brow at her sudden appearance, but he smiled, showing a set of white teeth, as he brushed at his sawdust-covered apron. "Can I help you, miss? You seem to be in search of something to come rushing in so." His tone was teasing, but not unkind.

"Are you Mr. Starling?" Cordi lifted one hand to her chest, fearful her racing heart would beat right out of her, and found she was shaking. She half hoped Mr. Starling might recognize her, though she looked little like Edward, who favored their mother, while Cordi shared their father's sharper features. She hoped that perhaps Edward had spoken of her regularly. Surely he had.

Surely.

Mr. Starling placed his hammer aside and set to rolling the cuffs of his shirt back down his arms to rebutton them at the wrist as he appraised her, taking stock of her poor, crumpled clothing. He would know immediately she was not a customer. "I am indeed, miss. What can I help you with? Is it a work order you've been sent to deliver?" His hands stilled and he scrutinized her once more, smile weakening. "You don't come from the house."

It was not said as a question, but she could feel his uncertainty and his unease as he shuffled back from the bench and farther away. The house? Cordi didn't know what house he was referring to, but the mention of it disquieted him. She held the flowers out in front of her, surprised to see him flinch as if she'd brandished a sword. She raised them higher so he might see them for what they were: not sinister, but an innocent gift. An offering, however small. "No, sir. My name is Cordelia. I'm here to see my brother, Edward."

Mr. Starling's smile fell away completely and his face paled to match the white birch trees that grew up and down the road outside. A muscle twitched near the corner of his eye and he lifted a hand to banish it, the other slowly reaching for the counter as if to steady himself.

For one terrible moment, Cordi was suspended, certain he was going to tell her that Edward had been in some kind of accident. The thing she had never allowed herself to believe—that he was gone—was going to be real. She would be free, but alone. Her knees threatened to buckle and the blood rushed to her ears so she might ignore the sound of his voice when he spoke her worst fears. *Accident. Terrible. Gone.*

She was not prepared for what he did say.

"Edward, miss? I'm afraid I've no idea who you'd be referring to."

The inner workings of Cordi's mind could not make sense of this statement. So she tried again, speaking slower and more clearly. "Edward Beecher. Your assistant. I am his sister. Could you please call him in?"

Mr. Starling recovered himself somewhat and tried to regain his smile, though he didn't quite manage and it came out more as a grimace. "I can't very well call to someone that isn't to be found here. I've not heard of an Edward Beecher and I've certainly never had one as an assistant."

"But you have!" Cordi could hear the hysteria in her own voice, panic threatening to overwhelm her when mere moments before she had been so blissfully happy. She tugged her bag around, dropping her paltry gift of flowers in her hurry, and reached inside, pulling out her precious letters, handling them roughly in her distress. "He wrote of you! Of your family! Of the work you did together! I—I wrote to you myself! Oh! But you didn't get those either, I suppose." Her lip quivered and she tried to steady it with her teeth, fingers curling tightly over the bundle in her hands as if it were her only tether to the shore as a storm in her breast threatened to sweep her away. "Our headmistress, you see. She—Edward would have told you of her. She would have stolen my letters and yours. Edward will tell you. My brother. Edward?"

Mr. Starling looked at the letters and then back into her face, something almost fearful in his expression. "My dear girl," he said slowly, "there has been some mistake. I'm sorry. But your brother is not here."

"He *is*!" she insisted. She had not come so far to be met with lies. "You are Mr. Starling, Edward's master. He boasts of your talent in every letter! He tells stories of Ann and Agatha and Alice, *your* daughters. Of how darling and precocious they are. He writes of your wife, Rebecca, and praises her kind nature and her glorious cooking! I know how well you have treated him and how generous you have been with your praise and how stern with your criticism. He told me all! And I've *seen* the sign at the inn! I know his work and would bet my last breath upon it! If that is not enough, all his letters are sent from Farrow! He is here!"

Because he was. He had not moved on. He was still there somewhere. She knew it deep in her heart. But she would not have even needed such certainty with the evidence of guilt written all over Starling's face.

"He isn't." Mr. Starling's voice was harder now, tone insistent. He squared his shoulders, standing taller behind his bench, but she could see his fingers shaking ever so slightly against the counter. Cordi missed little, as Edward had often told her, and she did not miss this. "Now, I must ask that you—"

"John?"

A woman entered from a side door, chestnut hair swept back into a low, braided bun against the nape of her neck. She brought the scent of baking bread with her, streaks of flour on her cheeks and the apron she wore over a simple blue dress. Cordi knew her immediately, for Edward had described her in detail: *She has round, pink cheeks and eyes lined with laughter, for she laughs often. She teases Mr. Starling so about finding sawdust in his beard and he says he must match her for she is always speckled with flour and it is how they will know each other when they are old and blind, by touching each other's faces and finding sawdust and flour.*

"John?" she repeated. "I heard raised voices. Is something wrong?"

"You are Mrs. Rebecca Starling," Cordi said quickly. "Please, can you help me?"

Mrs. Starling smiled tentatively, looking her up and down as Mr. Starling had, lingering on the state of Cordi's shoes, and pity came to her face. "I hope I might. Do you have business with my husband?"

"Rebecca," Mr. Starling murmured in warning, coming round the worktable.

"Yes!" Cordi plowed ahead, stepping forward, hands still grasping the letters from Edward. Now she held them out in front of her, both weapon and shield. "My brother—*Edward Beecher,*" she said, drawing the name out so there could be no mistake, "was living here, working under the eye of your husband. I have come a long way to find him. Please."

It was Mrs. Starling's turn to pale, but unlike her husband, who had mostly managed to keep his composure, Rebecca lifted flour-dusted fingers to her lips in surprise. "Oh!"

"*Rebecca!*" her husband breathed, moving to her side and taking her hand in his own. Cordi saw his fingers flex upon hers in warning.

Mrs. Starling gathered herself, though her eyes seemed redder than they had before, as if she was quite close to crying. "I'm sorry, dear," she said, voice faint. "But I'm afraid you have us mistaken. We have no one by that name here. Nor has there been. My husband hasn't had an apprentice in quite some time. Years and years."

Cordi stared in amazement, letters fluttering in her hands like frightened birds. She found she couldn't feel her legs and had to look down, strangely possessed of the idea that they had turned to wood—and wouldn't that be funny? To be so strangely changed. And she might have been relieved if they had, for then she could chalk the entire exchange up to a dream. A strange dream she was having as she rode toward Farrow and to the only hope that had kept her going day after day. But her legs were there, dust-covered boots against the wooden planks of the shop. She tried shutting her eyes and opening them again, willing herself to wake.

Had he done this, Edward? Had he convinced these people to lie for him? Perhaps he didn't want to be saddled with his troublesome little sister, relishing his own freedom. Freedom from responsibility. What was she but another mouth? A burden? He had been free of the yoke of her for so long, why would he want to chain himself again? So he had left her there in that place and never come back. He didn't love her, didn't—

"Stop," she told herself, the word hardly more than a movement of air, a tiny bird caught within the cage of her mouth, denied flight. It wasn't true. None of it was true.

Promises made were promises kept.

"Miss," Mr. Starling attempted, voice calm and rational, "I'm sorry you have been led to believe that Ed—your brother was here. But you can see that he is not. You can seek him in the village if it pleases you, but my advice is that you return . . ." His voice trailed off, and that was all the proof needed to damn him.

"Home, Mr. Starling?" Cordi said, her voice as wooden as the trappings of the shop as she lifted her head. "As I'm sure you are well aware, Edward and I had no home."

Mrs. Starling looked away, but Cordi didn't afford Mr. Starling that privilege so easily.

She held his eyes, daring him to lie again.

He didn't, and in the face of her righteous dignity, he dropped his gaze.

There was movement at the window in the back of the shop. Just a quick flash and then gone, but Cordi was sure she had seen a head of brown hair and small fingers releasing their grip on the sill before moving away.

Cordi tried to think of something else to say, but there was nothing. Defeated and suddenly unfathomably weary, she dropped her hands. With numb fingers, she fumbled to put the letters back into her bag and turned without a word, crushing the blue and purple flowers beneath her feet just as the old woman had in her flight, back bent, head bowed. The small bell above the door tinkled merrily at her departure as if already celebrating her absence.

She was alone.

Chapter 4

SHE FOUND HERSELF WALKING DOWN the road in the direction she had come, feet scraping along the dirt, kicking up dust. Mr. Starling had effectively carved and hollowed out both her head and her chest. Her satchel was heavy and she swayed on her feet, feeling as if the very life was draining from her. And it might well have been. For what had been sustaining her for years if not faith in Edward's promise?

They were lying. They had to be. She could tell by their faces and their tiny tells—the shaking hands and wire-thin voices. She had Edward's own words, and he would not have lied to her. Nor could he have managed to send every letter from Farrow if he had not been *in* Farrow.

Mr. Starling had suggested she inquire about Edward in the village. He had said it like a challenge, and Cordi could guess well enough she would find much the same story no matter how many doors she knocked on or how many faces she looked into. They would all lie.

But Edward would not have.

She didn't know what to do or where to go. It had all been so simple in her head after her flight from the city and its cruelty. She would find him. She would find shelter. She would find work. They would be a family again. It would be easy.

Now . . .

Now she saw it for the foolishness it was. Reckless and impulsive rather than clever. How stupid and naïve she had been to think the task so simple as arriving upon a doorstep with nothing to offer save a poor bouquet and spare coin. Yet how discourteous the Starlings had been to deceive her so! But what could she do?

Cordi tried to consider her circumstances. She had paid for her ticket to Farrow but had precious little money left to her name. She needed to think quickly, but she could only conjure up Edward's face and his letters and his promise. She had no idea where to go or how to follow him, and she had waited so long without word. Was she now to be left without hope?

It was some time before she realized she was being pursued. "Miss?! Wait!"

Slowly, as if she had aged a hundred years in the past few minutes, Cordi turned and saw a little pink-cheeked girl running after her. She was perhaps seven, her brown hair loose and flying behind her. She wore a blue dress the same color as Mrs. Starling's. A hand-me-down, Cordi knew, noting the hemline that had been altered multiple times and the tidily stitched holes in different shades of blue thread. She carried a small bundle and a pair of boots, gray with dust, tied together by their laces.

Though she had been running on short legs, she was barely out of breath as she reached Cordi, who watched her approach with a flicker of recognition. One of the Starling daughters. Alice, if she were to guess.

"Thank you, miss. Mama asked me to bring you these," she said, holding out the boots. "She said that your own shoes were in no state to carry you far. These are Mama's old pair. She asked that you take them since you looked to be about the same size. And she said you were too thin and should take some food as well."

Cordi, numb and distant from her body, saw her hands reach out almost blindly even as her lips moved to form the words she hardly felt. "Thank you."

The girl passed her the shoes first and Cordi sank to the side of the road, tugging off the tattered leather of her own shoes. They lay discarded in the dirt, fallen in on themselves without her feet and ankles to give them shape. Cordi felt much the same, deflated and ready to collapse in upon herself now that she had nothing to look forward to. Automatically and without enthusiasm, she pulled Mrs. Starling's boots on one at a time. They were not high-quality, but they were sturdy and well-oiled, though Cordi could barely appreciate this distinction. In fact, once the laces were tied, she did not even make to rise from the road, too bewildered and lost to do little more than sit in the dirt. All she had lived and suffered for, the faith that had sustained her, had been taken.

The little girl passed her a small bundle. Cordi smelled the bread within and could feel how soft and warm it was even beneath the cloth. She remembered Mrs. Starling's flour-dusted hands and realized the loaf was freshly baked. Gifts indeed.

Bribes, her brain corrected her. Guilt-given. Bread and boots for her brother. At the thought, Cordi had the urge to throw the bread away from her and rip the boots apart with her bare hands. Better to walk barefoot on the stony ground than to take offerings from liars.

"Are you the one Edward was always writing to, then?"

Cordi's head whipped up so quickly she nearly toppled over backward. The little girl stood studying her, head angled to the side, scrutinizing her face.

"I am," Cordi whispered. "You . . . you know Edward, then?"

"Of course I do. He made me a toy duck, you know. I could pull it on a string and it would kick its feet between the wheels. Agatha broke it, though she says it was an accident. I don't quite believe her. I think she was quite jealous of it because she had asked Edward to carve her a toy bear and found she liked my duck better." The girl paused. "Papa promised to mend it for me, but he still has not. He does not like us to talk about Edward. I think he has perhaps forgotten him. Grown-ups forget, you know."

Alice. She was sure of it now. Edward had said that Alice was the most precocious of all the girls, and that even at such a tender age she suffered fools little. *She is stubborn, that one,* Edward had written. *Her father says she will turn her husband's hair gray before his time as she has already turned his. She does as she pleases and, though quick to learn, she is not quick to change if it does not suit her.* He'd said she bore a striking resemblance to Cordi herself in this way.

Cordi glanced quickly back down the road, making sure Alice was not being sought.

"I do know, Alice," she said lightly, hoping to sound like a confidante. "Grown-ups often forget things or simply do not know them at all. But I can see that you do. Edward spoke of how intelligent you are."

Alice preened.

Licking her lips, Cordi asked, "Do you know what happened to Edward? Where he has gone?"

The little girl shook her head, brown hair sliding back and forth across her back. "No. He left without saying good-bye. It was quite rude, and I am not sure I shall forgive him after all this time."

Even though the answer stung, Cordi refused to let this seedling of hope wither. Not yet. "Do you remember when you last saw him?"

"A long time ago, in his room. He was always writing letters. I suppose they were for you. Some he would give to Mama to post in town. Others he hid, though I did not see where. He would always catch me spying." She gave a cheeky grin. "Well, not always. I saw him sneak off to Edenfield even after Father's work there was done."

"Edenfield? What is that?"

Alice turned up her nose. "Perhaps you *are* a grown-up if you don't even know that." The resemblance Edward boasted was becoming clearer.

See? She could almost hear Edward's voice. His chuckle.

Holding back a smirk, Cordi tried to look contrite. "It's not that. I'm simply not from here, but from far away. Like Edward was when he first came, so I'm not yet familiar with this place. If you could tell me where Edenfield is, I would be grateful and it would confirm Edward was right about how remarkable and clever *you* are."

A pout touched Alice's lips as she considered. "I suppose. It is not a secret after all, though secrets are delightful things. It is the way you are going. You had to pass the road to its gates on your way to our house and it is the only road on the right. It is a far walk, so it's good Mama gave you her boots. Yours would not have lasted." She quieted, little lines pulling together between her brows as she puzzled something through. "I might have said that Edenfield is not a secret but is very much *like* a secret. A strange sort of secret that everyone knows—at least here—but nobody will speak of. Like Mrs. Brooks and the boy who comes around to trim her hedges when her husband is away. Edenfield is a secret like that. And the gardens. And the ghosts."

"Ghosts?"

"Of course! Everybody knows that Edenfield is full of ghosts. Mama was most distressed about Papa working there, but he and Edward came back hale and whole every night. And Edward seemed to grow happier by the day during that time. He was quite queer later, after they were finished. He was sick and I thought he might have seen them. The ghosts. That they had done him a turn, but he did get better. Some of them don't, you know? That's what Agatha said. So maybe the ghosts didn't hurt him."

Ghosts? Such nonsense. But why should ghosts not be the reason for a child's dear friend to suddenly go missing? If her parents had told her Edward was gone and not given her an explanation, why would she not dream of a reason? Ghosts made as much sense to a child as anything and were certainly a better alternative to being abandoned by someone she trusted.

She wanted to ask more, ask about how Edward was sick, but feared that Alice would soon be sought if she did not return quickly. And she had a clue now. A place to start looking for a sign of her brother at least. Edenfield. She had real hope again and she smiled broadly at Alice. "You *are* clever. And I thank you. But I do think it would be best if you didn't mention Edenfield or Edward or our conversation to your parents."

"Why?"

Cordi hesitated, not wanting to ask the child to lie—but hadn't she been lied to herself? "Because," she said with a shrug, "they're grown-ups."

Alice nodded wisely, as if there was no other possibility. "Yes. You're quite right. And when you *do* find Edward, tell him that I expect him to apologize very formally for going away as he did without a good-bye."

"I will. I promise."

Chapter 5

IT WAS ONLY A HANDFUL of minutes before Cordi found the turn off the main road that led toward this Edenfield. The road was wide enough for two carriages and both sides were bordered by tall hawthorn trees whose branches reached for each other over the road, shaping themselves into an almost natural tunnel akin to the vaulted archway of a church. Beyond the hawthorns were more of the silver birch trees so prevalent in the area, their white trunks disappearing as she passed one hawthorn only to reappear again, a forest of ghosts marching alongside her, yet forever standing still.

It was a densely wooded area. No wonder Mr. Starling did so well there.

Her stomach soured as she thought of him. Of his lies and deceit. Though his wife had given her the boots and bread, which she supposed was a kindness in a way, it was a far cry from what she had truly come for.

What she could not rationalize was how Edward could become so fond of people who would so openly and brazenly deny his very existence. How could they have cared for him at all if they purged their house and memories of every trace of him? Neither had they written to tell her Edward had fallen ill, though they had known of her. Alice knew who she was. Had insisted her mother posted Edward's letters regularly. How could they have carried on a charade as a kind, loving family for so long for Edward's benefit?

Or had it been? Had they been just as Edward had told her? Perhaps there was something more sinister at work than simple lies. A conspiracy of some kind? Perhaps the school had discovered where she had gone and sent word ahead. Edward could have told the Starlings to lie, hoping to drive her off before she could be caught and dragged back to face punishment.

Again.

But that made little sense. They would surely have given her a note from Edward or he himself would have left some kind of sign. And it certainly didn't explain the reaction the Starlings had to Edward's name. How their faces had gone ashen, their eyes haunted, features far more fitting to the Barrow than to the happy home and pleasant country Edward had written about. No, they had most certainly been lying to her. Hiding something.

She chewed on various theories as she nibbled on the bread—its crust perfect and crisp and its center warm and soft—as she walked, hardly noticing the passage of time and the gradual slip of the sun in the sky. Nothing seemed to fit, and it all began with the last letter from Edward. The one that had been so brief and strange. And how he had ended it . . .

I will steal you, if I must.

Why would he have had to? At the time of writing, he could have presented himself as a legal guardian. And now she was grown herself. Even if Mrs. Clark wanted to object to losing her favorite whipping animal, there was nothing she might have done to protest her leaving. Mercy, if she had left sooner . . .

At that errant thought, the muscles of Cordi's back spasmed, and she clenched her jaw against the memory of the pain and—worse—the pleading. She pushed it aside, concentrating instead on the road ahead, which seemed to stretch on and on, though she fancied she could just make out the end of the line of trees in the distance. She needed to stop thinking about what was done and decide what was next.

She couldn't very well walk up to the house and ask after her brother.

That strategy had proved useless with the Starlings, and they were supposed to have been such wonderful people. And Alice said the house itself was akin to a secret. So the odds were low that she would get a direct answer from its inhabitants.

Very well, she decided. She needed to be *indirect.*

But what could she say? She didn't even know who the inhabitants of Edenfield were, so it was unlikely she could simply walk up to the front door and—

Just then, from seemingly out of nowhere, the gates lay before her, set into a thick stone wall that ran off in both directions farther than Cordi's eyes could see. They were wrought iron, tall and black. The bars of the gates had been shaped into the trunks and branches of trees, each one unique as it stretched upward. The decorative gate arched at the top in a spray of branches and individually wrought leaves. At its center, where the halves met, was a heavy bolt molded into the shape of a rose in full bloom.

A plaque was mounted to one side on the stone wall and Cordi pushed aside some bracken so she might get closer. " 'Edenfield,' " she read aloud. And beneath that, " 'With the fruit of her hands, she plants a vineyard. Proverbs 31.' "

Cordi looked through the gate and her jaw slackened. Beyond the iron branches lay a path of white stone, wide and long and twisting around elegant fountains and topiary. Both sides of the drive were marked with hedgerows, meticulously trimmed and beautifully formed and leading the way to the front of the house.

If *house* was the proper word. Alice had called it a manor, and even that seemed almost too insignificant. *Castle* was the word that came to Cordi's mind, conjuring up old stories of princesses trapped in towers her mother used to tell them when they were little. Cordi thought on them now and wondered if it might be so bad to be trapped in such a beautiful place, warm and safe. But the thought died quickly. She knew what it was to be imprisoned, though she knew little of warmth and less of safety, and there was no price for her freedom. And now that she had it, no glittering palace could wrest it from her.

But if Edward was trapped within, by God she would rescue him.

She leaned on the rose bolt, pressing her face against the cold iron branches as she looked about, hoping someone might allow her entry, but the rose shifted in her hand, lifting and allowing the gate to swing inward. Still, she hesitated on the border between the woodland tunnel and the lawn of Edenfield. Though nothing barred her way, something kept her from taking that first step beyond the gate. From somewhere deep within—some primal sense of urgency and self-preservation—came a dawning awareness, and Cordi found her feet rooted to the ground. Something urged her away from this place and back to the safety of the trees and beyond to the road and on to . . .

But there was nowhere else. There was only *here* because *here* was her only tie to Edward.

It was only the reaction of the old woman from the carriage and Mr. Starling's strange behavior when he had thought she was from "the house." Only Alice's talk of ghosts and the mystery of Edward's disappearance that had her so silly. She was tired and angry and maybe a little frightened, but she was not leaving Farrow without her brother. Cordi gritted her teeth and planted her booted foot on the white stones of the drive, crossing the threshold of the estate's grounds. Then again, till she was once more walking, striding forward, her bag on her shoulder. The stones crunched underfoot and seemed to glow brighter with each step as the sun sank lower in the sky, turning the grass and hedges that surrounded her into dark shadows. Dual fountains splashed, and she noted they were filled with plants she had never seen before. Large pads of green floated upon the surface, their stalks sinking below, and tall grasses seemed to sprout from the water.

Rounding the fountains, she saw her first unobstructed view of the house, and she took a deep breath as her head tipped back farther and farther to take it all in. She had grown up in a gray, cramped, cold city with tall, narrow buildings that fought for space along even narrower roads.

Edenfield sprawled in all directions: left, right, up, and—she had little doubt—down into cellars and basements. The facade was a marvel of beautiful stone, crowned with spires and steeply pitched roofs, all flowing into one another in exquisite lines and curves. Downspouts were capped with statuettes of women holding jugs that would pour water during heavy rain. An elegant porte cochere extended from the main entrance, casting a large, heavy door into the deepest shadow. Two remarkable towers flanked either side of the house and the builder had managed the illusion of a gnarled trunk twisting in on itself with a false balustrade, likely mirrored within by an actual spiral stair to the top of each tower. The columns and walls of the manor were covered with ivy, creeping up and over and across the tops of windows and winding around any surface it could claim, shrouding the entire structure in a natural cloak.

With the sun setting behind the house, again the sense of foreboding overcame her.

Alice's words about ghosts returned, and she fancied the manor the sort of place that would easily attract such spirits, if there were such things. Certainly it would conjure up such images in the minds of children! But Cordi herself could not help but feel as if the house watched her every step with countless dark eyes set in its stone face.

Something gathered and took shape behind a window on the south side of the house where the shadows were the deepest and the ivy the thickest. Something that stared steadily at her without moving. It was unsettling, as if Cordi's imaginings had conjured a phantom. And yet, Cordi found herself staring back into the unknown, chin raised in defiance, daring it or the house to cage her.

Chapter 6

CORDI SHIVERED IN HER OLD coat and forced her eyes away from the knowing darkness behind the glass to find lamps lit within the northern side of the house. Several windows now glowed golden in the dim light. Beckoning with the promise of warmth and answers. Or at least with possibility.

She ignored the prickling along her neck warning her she was still being observed and tried to focus instead on what to do. Someone had lit the lamps and someone watched her approach, so all that remained was for her to gain entry. The front door would not do for one of her station. The servants' entrance, then, for there must be one. Not daring to look back at whatever watched her from darkened windows, Cordi stomped across the gravel, rounding the north tower in search of another door.

It was easily spotted at the back corner, a staircase with a wrought-iron railing that descended below ground level to an unremarkable door flanked by windows, light spilling from within. A kitchen, most likely. A coal hole was set into the ground right at the stairs so the collier might come and dump the black bricks directly into a vault below.

Licking her lips, Cordi stepped quietly down the stairs, hugging tight to the supporting wall away from the windows. Her senses were assailed by the smell of cooking food from within, by spices and herbs she had never known before. At the Barrow, the food had been tasteless, scarce, and often inedible, in the form of burnt porridge, stale bread, and—occasionally—a watery stew of hard potatoes, moldy onions, and the poorest cuts of meat the butcher could sell.

A man dressed as Father Christmas had once visited the Barrow when she was perhaps ten or eleven and each child had been given a small peppermint. Cordi had made hers last for as long as she could, wrapping it in a bit of stolen paper and hiding it behind the loose baseboard in the girls' washroom, where she hid all her meager treasures. She had taken it out each night for a taste, finding that its flavor reminded her of Christmases long gone, when she had had a mother and a father and she and Edward had been warm and loved. It had reminded her of a home.

Reading Edward's letters from the Starlings had made her grateful he was warm and safe and—she had thought—loved. Cordi had delighted in her brother's good fortune, and any resentment she felt for her own empty belly and threadbare pillow was reserved for the calculated cruelty of those at the Barrow. Never at Edward, because she knew she would share in his happiness.

How wrong she had been. . . .

The Starlings. Mrs. Clark. Mr. Mason.

No. Not here. Not now. She would not think of them. Of *any* of them. She had a job to do and she needed her wits about her, not her ghosts. Squaring her shoulders, she knocked politely on the door.

A moment later, a face moved about in one of the windows, peering out and trying to discern her shape in the darkness of the stairwell. The door opened a fraction and a tremulous voice spoke from within. "Who are you?"

"I—I—" she stammered, thinking quickly, trying to remember what she had planned to say on her long walk through the hawthorn tunnel. "My name is Cordelia. I—"

"What do you want?"

"I'm looking for work. I've traveled a very long way, and I heard of Edenfield and thought with a house so big—"

"Stella?"

Another voice, this one firm and authoritative, sounded from deeper within the kitchen. The door shook as if its guardian had taken a start.

"Who is it at the door, Stella? It is far too late for any deliveries."

"It's a young lady, mum," said the first speaker, her head turning back into the room and her voice barely over a whisper. Stella, apparently. "She—she says she's in need of work."

Heavy footfalls sounded and Stella scrambled backward as the door opened wide and a heavyset woman, face stormy and lined beneath a white linen cap, glared out at Cordelia. "Name?"

"Cordelia, ma'am," Cordi said, dropping her hands to her sides, adopting the posture she might have for a surprise inspection at the Barrow.

The woman looked her up and down, missing nothing, eyes narrowing on the short cuffs of her coat and the state of her shirt and skirt beneath, wrinkled beyond hope from the long carriage ride and walk. She sniffed at the condition of Cordi's hair, and Cordi's fingers trembled with the urge to smooth it behind her ear, suddenly self-conscious of the haphazard hacking she had done.

The woman clucked. "Well, come along in, then. I've no mind to be standing in the doorway and letting in the night air. If we will be speaking, we will be doing it indoors." And she turned away.

Cordi exhaled a ragged breath. Could it be this easy? She carefully stepped over the threshold into the warmth of a kitchen, a fire crackling in the hearth and chasing away the chill of trepidation in Cordi. Quickly she eased the door closed behind her, worried that if she made too sudden a movement or too much noise, she might be cast out again.

Stella had retreated several paces from the door and stood with her head down and away, putting Cordi in mind of a frightened rabbit. Cordi knew many like her at the Barrow. Girls—and several boys—easily manipulated and taken advantage of by older or bigger children.

Cordi had been like them once when she was young and desperate for affection, thinking in her wide-eyed naïveté that the older girls who insisted she share—or more often hand over—her pitiful portions of potato or bread would grow fond of her if she did so willingly and with enthusiasm. They would tell her she was good and sweet and be pleased with her and she would have friends.

It was only when she realized Edward was going hungry sharing with her the food he had pocketed from his own dinners that she had managed to find the strength of spirit to say no to the next bullies. For that was what they were. Bullies and not friends. Users. Her first refusal had earned her a black eye along with an empty belly. Her second, a split lip. There had not been a third because Cordi had leapt upon one of the more notorious girls in the washroom, climbing upon her back like a cat, spitting and clawing and yowling. She had been disciplined harshly for fighting, but nobody had tried to steal her food after that, her tormentors moving on to easier prey. To more submissive children who needed to learn such a lesson for themselves.

Cordi lifted a hand in greeting and to show she meant no harm, and the girl darted a fast glance up at her, affording Cordi a look at her face. She was young, with dark hair and light eyes. Or eye. One eye was so pale Cordi couldn't discern its color in the glow of the fire. The other—her right—was obscured by a sagging, drooping eyelid that seemed to cave inward, as if nothing at all was behind it. Jagged lines and old scar tissue crisscrossed over her eyebrow, the lid, and the thin skin beneath. Cordi hoped fervently her shock didn't show in her face, but before she could muster a smile, Stella had looked away again, turning her face farther from view.

"Return to your place, Stella. And you, wash your hands and sit," said the stern woman, motioning toward a seat at a low table already set for five. Three of the seats were occupied and Stella sat quickly at a fourth. The head of the table had a chair pushed out, a bowl of something hot sitting at the place, a spoon out of order.

Cordi went to the sink and washed her hands well, making sure to scrub under her nails vigorously out of habit. Turning back to the table, she took the empty seat at Stella's left, placing her bag carefully by her feet but not shrugging out of her coat, for she had not been told to. She could not help but notice how pretty Stella's profile was, though Stella's eye remained fixed on the bowl in front of her. Across the table were three other women and girls, ranging in age from perhaps only a year or two younger than Cordi to a woman well into her advanced years.

The woman who seemed to be running things—the housekeeper, Cordi guessed—placed a bowl and spoon in front of Cordi. "We have already said prayer, but I'll ask that we say it again for your sake before we begin our meal a second time," she said, taking her own seat at the head of the table. She sat with a grunt, folding her hands at her chest and bowing her head. The others did the same without hesitation. Cordi mimicked their posture, ready to hear a version of the familiar words so often used at the Barrow before meals as thanks to God.

"We thank you, Ladies, for your bounty to nourish our bodies. We thank you, Ladies, for your breath to redeem our souls. For your gracious gift, for your deliverance from evils beyond the walls, and for the hope of life eternal in the Garden."

As one, the others seated at the table chimed in. "Thanks given to the Garden, for the Garden is right and good."

Ladies? Garden? Curious.

Cordi slowly lifted her head as the clinking of spoons on bowls began in earnest. A plate was passed around covered with pieces of crusty, aromatic bread dotted with butter and speckled with herbs. Cordi took one with a quiet "Thank you," placing the bread on the edge of her bowl as the others did, and waited to be spoken to. She did not dare eat until instructed to do so.

She did not wait long. "After you've eaten, you will wash up and I will take you to Lady Evangeline. We'll see what can be done to make you presentable."

"Yes, ma'am. I can—"

The woman waved her away, chewing on her bread before swallowing. "It is not me you need tell your story or your references. What you can and cannot do is not my concern until Lady Evangeline has taken a look at you and determined if you are to be *made* my concern. Now, eat up. You look half-starved and I'll not have the Lady believing I have been inhospitable."

Bewildered, she lifted her spoon to her lips in obedience. The moment the broth touched her tongue, her stomach yawned eagerly. She took another bite, the second full of bits of root vegetables and greens, flavored to perfection. Unable to help herself, she exclaimed, "This is delicious! I've never tasted something so wonderful!"

One of the ladies across the table—the eldest, her hair gray under her cap—sat up a little straighter, a ghost of a smile tugging at the edge of her lips so her wrinkles deepened, but the housekeeper only nodded solemnly. "We are quite blessed by the Garden."

Cordi ate with vigor, careful not to scrape her spoon or appear ill-mannered, finding it difficult not to drain the bowl to the dregs. The bread proved to be just as delicious. Its smell was divine and its taste sharp, foreign and strange to her tongue. She let it melt in her mouth, identifying the almost forgotten flavor of butter. *Real* butter.

"Thank you all, ladies," she said, meaning it, momentarily afraid she might begin to cry, her emotions raw and head still reeling from the day. "For inviting me to your table. I don't think I imagined such kindness in the world."

The three across the table blinked at her with haunted expressions, though the eldest's lips were touched again by that almost-there smile. Beside her, Stella kept her head down, eating slowly, each movement careful as if she was afraid to spill her supper or make too much noise.

Her own meal finished, the housekeeper pushed back from the table. "Call it kindness if you will, but it is our duty to ensure that no daughter be sent away without her voice heard and her belly full. Come along now. Wash your face and do what you can about your hair—there is a little mirror there by the inner door—and I'll take you to see the Lady."

Cordi gathered her bag and stood.

"You may leave your things by the back door."

A pain in her chest. "No, ma'am," Cordi said without thinking, clutching the satchel with its dear letters and carving within. "I cannot. I—I must keep it."

The woman either did not notice Cordi's trepidation or did not care. "Suit yourself."

Small victory bolstering her confidence, Cordi did as instructed under the housekeeper's eye, cleaning the dust from her neck and face. It was a bit of a shock to see her face in the mirror: her features were drawn, her eyes hollow and sunken, her lips chapped and torn from her worrying teeth. She tried not to let the surprise show as she touched damp fingers to what was left of her blond hair, knowing now was not the time to mourn a vanity.

A few moments later, Cordi was following the housekeeper up a set of dark stairs, pinching her cheeks to give them a bit of color and trying unsuccessfully to smooth the waves of her hastily cut hair, half wishing she had left it long enough to be pulled back. She kept close behind the housekeeper, a darker shape amid many dark shapes as she moved with purpose down hallways and passages. Cordi did not look around, afraid she might lose her way in the vastness of the house and become trapped forever among the shadows. The errant thought made her shoulders hunch forward, the walls—their distance difficult to discern in the dark—closing in. Cordi tried to breathe deeply, reminding herself that this was not the Barrow. She was not a prisoner.

The housekeeper abruptly stopped in front of a door, a warm light spilling through the gap at the bottom, and lowered her voice to a murmur. "You will be presented to Lady Evangeline. You will stand straight and speak when spoken to. I will go in first and you will just wait here. You will not move from this spot until I fetch you inside."

Cordi found herself nodding dumbly.

The woman took a long breath in through her nose, gaze sweeping over Cordi once more, and then she knocked. A calm, low voice called from within: "Enter." The housekeeper turned the knob and obeyed the command, back straight as any Barrow child's, closing the door behind her.

The end of the hall was lit by only one wall sconce that hissed and clicked, the flame dancing within the glass bulb. A dull ticking noise accompanied a white moth hitting the bulb, searching for the light within, not realizing that to reach it would mean death. Cordi looked back the way they had come, or at least the way she thought they had come. As daunting and huge as the house had looked outside, it was even more so inside in the dark. She could make out nothing beyond the small circle of light. For all she knew, the hallway stretched on forever, back toward the south of the house and whatever had been watching her from the window. Cordi stared into the darkness, eyes wide and watering as she tried to penetrate the gloom, wondering if whatever it was had crept unseen and unheard along the passages, watching her even now.

The door opened and the housekeeper stepped back into the hallway. "In."

Chapter 7

THE SITTING ROOM WAS OPULENT and extravagant in ways Cordi could little have imagined. Solid oak walls gleamed and glowed in the golden light cast by the fire and the lamps. Thick rugs of greens with ornate floral patterns in both blushing and vibrant pinks put her in mind of strange carpets of flowers and covered large sections of floor under heavy seating gathered together in groups, inviting confidantes to rest and laugh together.

The furniture, brilliantly crafted and so beautifully made, was all polished, dark, and stained in a way that best accentuated the grain of the wood on each piece. A couch and divan were covered in deep-green damask patterned with leaf and frond, while two high-backed chairs were more subtle, their hues deep purple in velvet. A heavy desk sat in a corner, upon which rested a silver-gilt candelabra and a marble statue of a woman's form wrapped in a sheath of cloth. Both low and high tables littered the room, and every available surface seemed to be covered with potted plants. Baskets hung from the ceiling holding jugs with long, trailing ivy. There were pots and bowls filled with every shade of green, and each seemed unique in leaf and form. The room smelled clean and fresh, like a spring day in a garden after an early rain.

It was a most splendid room and Cordi found her lips parting as she took in the grandeur. The air was so fragrant and not at all stifling, and Cordi might have believed she was outside. Something tickled her cheek and she reached up to find the curling edge of a vine, its leaves both pale and deep green and striped with purple. It was a lovely plant and she traced the veins along one leaf with her finger.

Preoccupied by the trappings, it took her a moment to notice the figure of the woman by the darkened window. Half-hidden by a giant plant nearly as tall as she was, its leaves enormous and brilliant green, she held a tin watering can, tilting it carefully into the pot. Tall and fair with long, pale hair, looped and braided and coiled about her head and set with silver pins, she wore a floor-length cream-colored gown, the cut exquisite and tailored to perfection, the hem of the skirt and the neckline stitched with white and silver flowers.

A small sound of surprise escaped Cordi's lips before she could stifle it and she dropped quickly into a pitiful curtsy that would have earned her the birch at the Barrow. "Good evening, my lady," she stammered, hating the weak and frightened sound in her voice.

The Lady stepped from behind the plant, stroking the leaves delicately with long fingers as if it were a beloved pet as she moved to yet another pot spilling over with green fronds. "Miss Eliot tells me you have come looking for work."

"Yes, ma'am."

A hum sounded at the back of the Lady's throat as she attended the fern, caressing it with affection. She inspected it carefully before setting aside her little watering can and crossing to the couches and chairs stationed nearest the warm fire. She arranged herself with practiced grace on the divan, her back straight and chin high, hands folded in her lap. "Well, we shall see. Come along and let me have a look at you."

Cordi sucked in her lower lip, feeling broken skin snag on her teeth as she walked deeper into the room, skirting the chairs and dutifully avoiding touching or disturbing anything with her movements. She thought of the strict etiquette and manners drilled into the minds of all the children of the

Barrow, even those who had resisted as Cordi had, and was grateful in that instance for their thoroughness as she stopped in the center of the rug where the Lady could see her properly.

"Introductions first," the Lady said, her voice filled with quiet authority. "I am Lady Evangeline, mistress of this estate. And your name?"

"Cordelia—" Cordi hesitated. Could she use the name Beecher? What about secrecy? Finding Edward? And what if they were searching for her out of the Barrow?

Her hesitation went on too long. "Ah. I see."

Cordi felt a flare of panic she knew was reflected in her face, but before she could utter a word in her defense or ask about Edward, Lady Evangeline gave her a forceful look. "Come. Sit," she demanded, patting the cushion beside her.

Again, Cordi's body urged her to back away rather than move closer, but she obeyed the gentlewoman's instructions instead, hoping her new-to-her boots did not leave dust trails across the splendid rugs. She sat stiffly, woodenly, submitting herself to close examination, keeping her eyes trained on the door, afraid something in them might betray her.

Lady Evangeline tapped a finger on her knee as she regarded Cordi. "You are not the first girl to appear at my door who wishes for discretion. And I pray you will not be the last. Edenfield is a haven for girls like you."

Girls like me?

"Girls like you," Lady Evangeline repeated, as if reading her mind as one might read a book, "that the men of this world have subjected to harshness and undeserved cruelty. You have the look of a creature fleeing a hunter. The state of your hair, your ill-fitting clothes, and the marks on your hands give you away, if nothing else."

Instinctively, Cordi covered one hand with the other, though scars marred the backs of both, and ducked her head. But to her surprise, the Lady gently unfolded her hands and lifted them for inspection. She turned them over, tracing both thin and thick lines of raised tissue with her thumbs and then the calluses on Cordi's palms with all her fingers. She sniffed in derision, and when Cordi meant to pull her hands away, thinking she had offended her somehow, the Lady only squeezed her fingers harder, jaw tightening.

"You need not be afraid here, little sister. Not of men or their fury or their wicked passions."

At this, Cordi felt her lip tremble as the painful memory caused too many sensations to assail her all at once. The foul stench of stale breath and onions and alcohol. Fingers digging into her wrists and thighs as she fought and cried. Blood on her tongue. The birch on her back.

Lady Evangeline nodded, her mouth thinning and eyes sparking with anger. "Brutal. All of them. They rip and tear at the earth and its keepers, never mindful of the flowers they trample. But we are strong. Stronger than they could imagine. And we grow and thrive and reach for the sun despite them."

Up close, Cordi could see Lady Evangeline was not as young as she had first supposed, but certainly not in her twilight years. Pale hair Cordi had thought simply blond was streaked through with gray and white. Her eyes were crinkled at the corners and her thin lips set in a permanent line that might only narrow further or turn down, for she did not seem happy despite her opulent surroundings and exquisite dressings. Something fundamental within her had withered long ago and been replaced with iron and steel.

"I alone am master and mistress here. And you will find no men in my employ, save for the few contractors I hire out of necessity from time to time."

Edward!

Before Cordi could say something foolish in her eagerness, the Lady continued, "But even they are forbidden access to the house except under the strictest of conditions and you need never be burdened with their presence.

Any that come looking for you will be turned away at the door, for you are no one's business but your own and mine if you are under this roof." She looked again at Cordi's hands. "I see no ring nor the pale brand of one upon your finger. You are not married, then?"

"No, ma'am."

"That is good. Better never to have been shackled in such a way. Now, with my assurance of safety, I would have your name if you are to remain here."

Cordi almost gave the truth willingly, but she forced a lie instead, for Edward was still her priority, no matter the goodwill of this woman who seemed to know her deepest secrets. She thought of the bleak, gray world she had come from; that would serve. "Cordelia Grey, my lady." And because she felt she owed the woman's kindness at least some truth, she added, "I've no husband or betrothed looking for me, though others might. I—I ran away after . . ."

A gentle pat of Lady Evangeline's hand on her cheek. "There is no need to speak of it again. Now, the rules—of which there *are* many—will be explained by Miss Eliot. A trial period of two weeks begins tomorrow, for though I strive to help every flower, I will not have my garden overrun with weeds. You will receive food, lodging, livery, and safe haven. A salary of thirteen pounds a year will be granted to you should you prove capable to the satisfaction of myself and Miss Eliot. For this, you will be required to work. And we must work hard, for there are few of us and the estate is vast."

"Yes, my lady."

"I can tell by your hands that you are used to tending the soil. Such a delight. My garden is the source of my pride and practiced hands are of such value, so I have a mind to—"

"No!"

Lady Evangeline looked aghast at the outburst and Cordi felt abashed.

"Apologies, ma'am," she said, voice mild. "I should not have spoken. I will do any work you ask."

When Cordi dared look, Lady Evangeline's eyes were sparking like coals from the fire. "Explain yourself. What fear do you have of my garden? Village gossip and scurrilous lies meant to wilt the flowers I have cultivated through long and arduous—"

"No, my lady!" exclaimed Cordi, frantically interrupting again. "I've heard nothing of your garden in any village. I meant no disrespect. I—I am familiar with gardening. It was only a fear. Of another garden. Another gardener." She swallowed hard, throat tightening. "I would be glad of any work you gave me. I should not have spoken."

Lady Evangeline's features remained hostile for a moment as she deliberated the implication and weight of Cordi's words. Slowly the hard clench of her jaw eased, but the storm did not pass from her eyes. "A gardener. One who would sow the earth and crush a flower in the same breath." She gave a mocking laugh. "I should no longer be surprised by the depth of depravity and arrogance of men."

The Lady again tapped a finger on her knee, considering. "Well, we will put you to use in the house for a start. Miss Eliot will prefer it as some of the maids have . . . taken ill. But you will have a chance to see and to learn to love my garden. To know it as paradise and safe refuge. My Eden as it was meant to be. You will see things in a new light."

She reached for a small silver bell on the table at her elbow, the merry tinkle resonating through the room. The door opened and the housekeeper returned before the sound had faded, and Cordi realized the woman had been waiting in the hallway the entire time.

"Miss Eliot, Cordelia will be requiring a maid's livery. A two-week trial, I think."

"Yes, m'lady."

"After you have her settled in the servants' quarters, I'll go over particulars with you regarding the duties she will begin tomorrow. I will go and say my good-nights and retire to my room."

Her good-nights? Surely she did not bid the servants good night each evening. "Yes, m'lady."

"That will be all, my dear," Lady Evangeline said, effectively dismissing them from the room.

Chapter 8

"THE RULES OF EDENFIELD ARE many, but they are of the utmost importance. I expect you to pay strict attention to each rule I impart to you."

"Yes, ma'am."

Miss Eliot's tone was as curt and void of nonsense as her stride. Cordi had to quick-step to keep up as the woman led her back down the labyrinth of dark hallways, a candle held before her, sheltered by her hand as if she wasn't so much worried about the flame sputtering as about disturbing the shadows that had settled for the evening.

"Can you read?"

"Yes, ma'am."

"Good. It will be easier on you, for the rules are displayed with prominence in each of the bedrooms and perhaps I shall not be forced to repeat myself as often for you as for others. Though I doubt it. Young girls these days and their lackadaisical attitudes . . ."

Miss Eliot trailed off as she turned yet another corner and they began descending a stairwell. Cordi threw a hand out to the wall, afraid she might trip on one of the narrow boards and plow directly into the poor housekeeper, who seemed so sure of her own footing even in the poor light and walked with quick, confident strides. Her hand sank into darkness so complete, she might have believed the appendage lost, severed at the wrist by the dark. She snatched it back, tucking it under her chin.

"The first rule is the most important," Miss Eliot said as she reached the bottom, rounding on Cordi so quickly that she nearly fell back to the step above. The candle cast the woman's plump, lined face into strange shadows, her eyes appearing sunken and the deep crevices bordering her lips becoming fissures of black. "No. Men."

Men was said with such venom, Cordi felt its sting land, the poison in the words slipping below her skin.

"Men are strictly forbidden except by order of Lady Evangeline herself, and even then they are not welcome, merely permitted out of necessity. There are no exceptions. This is for the good of us all. If this is not to your liking, then you may as well go now."

Cordi shook her head. "Yes. I mean, no. I understand. I've no—"

"Good." That word again, clipped and without inflection, as Miss Eliot spun on her heel and continued down another narrow corridor, this one of blank, pale walls and no trappings to cast shadows. The servants' wing, marred only by doors set into the walls facing each other, lined up like soldiers.

As they passed through, Cordi heard gasping coughs and a dreadful wheezing from behind one. The poor occupant sounded as if they were struggling for air. Lady Evangeline had mentioned that the odd maid or two had fallen ill. Cordi hoped it wasn't anything too serious, or contagious for that matter.

Miss Eliot noticed her slowed step and hurried her along. "Pay no mind. The Ladies and the Garden are kind and what will be will be." The housekeeper stopped in front of a door almost at the end of the corridor and knocked sharply. "Stella?"

There was the soft sound of feet and then the door opened. "Yes, mum?" came the quiet voice of the pretty young maid.

Miss Eliot stepped aside and addressed Cordi. "You will be rooming with Stella for your trial at the very least. We do not permit new girls their own rooms, and the Garden knows I've little enough hands to keep yet another chamber clean. I'll leave you to settle while I go and fetch your livery. Stella, show Cordelia where the linens are kept so she may make up her bed. I'll return shortly." Taking the candle, she departed, leaving Cordi standing on the threshold of the small bedroom.

Cordi shuffled awkwardly, wondering if she should step inside or wait to be invited into the girl's room. Well, her room as well, she supposed. Still, it felt like an invasion and—

"You can come in," Stella said, face down and angled away from the light of a lamp within.

"Thank you." She stepped in, turning her head to absorb these new surroundings. The room was close and friendly in the warm glow of the single light. It reminded her in some ways of the girls' dormitory of the Barrow, but more intimate and less gloomy. The lamp sat upon a small table between two beds, one bare, the other made up with white sheets lined with embroidered flowers and a good, heavy blanket. Each bed had a trunk at the end, presumably for any personal items. A basin and pitcher stood ready on a table by the door. Hanging above, a beautiful cross-stitched verse behind glass was flanked by hooks. One was hung with a smart, clean maid's livery and apron, sensible shoes standing at attention beneath, stockings rolled up inside, ready for the next day.

Stella quietly backed farther into the room, shuffling to her bed. Her hair was down and braided, though she pulled it over her shoulder to toy with the end of it as if it brought her comfort. Cordi recognized the gesture, and her own fingers longed to stroke the belly of her fox. Again, Cordi considered how Stella would have fared at the Barrow. A quiet, timid thing who flinched and hid from the next unkind word, the next blow. After discovering she could either be punished with food in her belly or without, it mattered not, Cordi had learned to fight rather than flinch. But she'd had Edward and her stubborn pride, while others had only their fear. Thus, she resolved to be gracious to her roommate. To win her over as a friend. "Thank you for sharing your room with me. It's lovely."

Stella remained perched on the edge of her bed. "Only the Ladies deserve gratitude."

Cordi wasn't sure how to respond to this recurring reference to the Ladies and resolved to ask when they were better acquainted. "I'm sorry we weren't properly introduced earlier. My name is Cordelia. Cordelia Grey. But most just call me Cordi."

"I'm Stella. Stella Luthland."

"Have you been employed here long?"

Stella continued to play with her braid. "Five years."

Five years. Then she would likely have knowledge of Edward in one fashion or another.

Cordi knew she could not risk questions so quickly, though her chest burned with the need to know anything at all.

"That's your trunk," Stella said, gesturing. "Your bedding is within and you can put your things in there. I—I know you didn't want to part with them at dinner, but they'll be safe. This is a safe place for us." This last was said with a sort of reverence that Cordi wondered at.

Cordi was used to hiding away pieces of herself where others might not leverage them against her. The same was true of her few, precious belongings, typically squirreled away where they would not easily be found, and the trunk felt as open and exposed as the roots of a vegetable freshly pulled from the earth, but there was no way to argue without arousing suspicion. Still, she promised herself she would check the floorboards and baseboards for a spot to stash her letters and beloved carving as soon as the opportunity arose. She knelt on the floor, shifting her bag out of Stella's line of sight. She pulled out the sheets and blanket, lifting them over the lid to the mattress. Withdrawing her few clothes from her satchel, she folded them carefully, laying them within the trunk. Then, as surreptitiously as possible, she spread the cloth that had held Mrs. Starling's bread out on the floor and laid her letters and fox on it, wrapping them within. Shrugging out of her too-small coat, she stuffed the bundle into one of the arms and folded it; this she placed beneath her clothes, with her bag atop. She laid the cord that cinched the satchel shut just so across the top of the burlap so she might know if anything was disturbed.

She had just risen when there was a now familiar rap of fingers on wood and Miss Eliot entered before either could open the way for her. She came in bearing an armload of clothing, pressed and folded, and a pair of shoes. "Try these. They look to be your size."

Cordi took the shoes and sat on a squat wooden chair in the corner. She tugged off the precious boots she had been given just that afternoon—two new pairs of shoes in one day!—revealing socks riddled with holes. Flushing with embarrassment, Cordi slid her feet into the new shoes, which were well padded but sturdy. She stood, testing them. "They're perfect, Miss Eliot. Thank you."

Miss Eliot clucked, dismissing Cordi yet again, and deposited the new clothing beside the linens. "Thanks are pretty words, but know that all we are given is a gift of the Ladies. Your gratitude is best directed to them, though your manners do you a service. Now, it is late and I've a mind for bed with so much extra work to be done now." She cleared her throat. "I expect you up early and ready for a day's labor. You will be cleaning the lower living rooms of the north wing from top to bottom. Dusting, polishing, sweeping, and the like. Stella will help you prepare in the morning. And she can show you the rules. You may even do her a service, for though she knows them well enough, you can read and may be a good influence in that regard."

Behind the housekeeper's shoulder, Stella ducked her head farther in shame. She couldn't read.

"I'll bid you both a good night."

"Good night, mum," Stella said softly.

"Good night, Miss Eliot."

As the door shut firmly, Cordi's shoulders slumped with exhaustion, as if the days of travel and long walks had finally caught up with her. "I have so many questions, but I daresay I should keep them to myself tonight. I'd no idea how late it had gotten. I'll make up my bed quickly. I don't want to disturb your own rest."

Stella didn't answer.

Cordi hoped she might prattle on, gossiping as so many girls in the dorms had done in whispers. She wanted to know more of the house, its peculiar mistress, and the Ladies they were meant to thank. Most importantly, she wanted to know of Mr. Starling's time on the estate with his young, handsome apprentice. But Stella did not speak, leaving Cordi with only her thoughts racing through her head.

Had she made a mistake in coming to Edenfield? It certainly appeared to be pleasant enough. Miss Eliot was obviously stern, but Cordi did not find her disagreeable. A sense of dignity in her position was to be expected. And Lady Evangeline had shown Cordi a cool benevolence Cordi had not anticipated. Her terms were most generous, and she spoke of her house as a haven for women less fortunate than herself. She had recognized hurts in Cordi and tried to assuage her fears. She had offered a kind touch rather than a birch rod.

And yet . . .

Cordi could not ignore completely that feeling of unease. Just a seedling nestled in her heart. She told herself it was the Starlings who'd planted it there. Alice had watered it with her talk of ghosts. Cordi would have to be careful not to tend it, though she would not ignore it completely.

She resisted the urge to fill the silence. Instead, she went to the bed and reached for the new clothing, only to stop and stare in wonder at what lay atop the pile. With a curious smile, she lifted two beautiful pieces of cloth, one black and one white, each embroidered with the most delicate and life-like flowers. The white was covered with orange marigolds and bluebells, while the black was stitched with lilac blossoms and white flowers shaped like stars. Each cloth was marked by two loops; holding them up, Cordi realized they were masks meant to fit over the nose and mouth, the loops set to wrap around the ears.

"What are these for? They're lovely!"

Stella's fingers twitched over the petals embroidered on her sheets. "For the south wing. For the flowers," she whispered, and pointed to the framed cross-stitch before burrowing under her coverlets and turning to the wall.

Brow furrowing, Cordi inspected the delicately stitched writing, still holding the masks, fingers absently tracing the beautiful flowers as Stella's had. She'd assumed they were the Commandments—and so they were, though not the Commandments Cordi had learned by rote, but rather the rules previously mentioned. Cordi's lips moved silently as she read, growing more and more confused by each carefully embroidered edict.

1. It is forbidden that a man enter herein
without consent of the mistress of the house,
for man is designed for mischief and deceit.

2. Thanks given to the Garden,
for the Garden is right and good.

3. She is to tend to her sisters as she would herself,
for what is reaped must first be sown.

4. She is to tend to the Flowers when called upon,
for to tend to the Flowers is to tend to all.

5. She is to cover her nose and mouth and hands
when tending the Flowers and
for the sake of her sisters.

6. She is to cleanse her masks and gloves with vigor
and take care not to touch bared skin
without having done so.

7. She is to honor the Flowers, for theirs is
the breath of life for the Garden.

8. She shall forsake earthly attachments
for the earth of the Garden.

9. She is called to the Garden in her time.

10. What is planted in the Garden,
grows in the Garden.

Chapter 9

THE FIRST TWO DAYS FLEW by in a frenzy of chores and hasty but hearty meals. For every repast, they thanked the Garden and the Ladies for the table's bounty, and while Cordi had not had time to ask about the latter, the former she heartily gave her gratitude for such abundance. Roasted garlic, crisp beans, the sweetest peas, and greens mixed with dandelions and other edible flowers Cordi had never seen. She could not resist asking about the herbs and learned of rosemary paired with lamb, mutton with gingerroot, and eggs cooked with an assortment of wild mushrooms.

Cordi collapsed into bed each night, shoulders and fingers aching from vigorous scrubbing, polishing, and the beating of rugs, pillows, and tapestries, but with the satisfaction of feeling full and useful. She'd spent two entire days in the manor, cleaning the seemingly endless rooms on just the lower floors. The house was so large and there was so much to do that she never saw any of the other servants except when she was fetched or during meals.

There was Sarah, perhaps in her early thirties, who had very straight and long equine features and was one of the tallest women Cordi had ever seen. Her hair was pulled back harshly from her brow and set into a knotted bun so tight it hurt Cordi's neck to look at it too closely.

She took care of Lady Evangeline's needs as her personal maid. Severe in both her countenance and her manner of speech, she reminded Cordi a bit of Mrs. Clark, though she certainly didn't seem cruel. Only rigid and stiff as an old oak.

Faustine, the youngest at seventeen, was from Haiti, her skin and eyes dark as turned earth, her head covered with tight curls under her maid's cap. She was the only one of the maids who laughed easily, hiding her wide smile with the back of her hand. She spoke a version of French she called Creole. She was pleased Cordi could speak passable French even if she giggled at Cordi's accent, which she said was "typically British." She had come to England when she was just a child with her "*maman*" after they had caught the eye of, as Faustine put it, "a doddering *cochon*." She spat when she said this, voice full of acrimony, and Cordi had been afraid to ask more. She, like Cordi and Stella, was an undermaid, tending to whatever duties Miss Eliot doled out.

Moira, the eldest of them all, took charge of the kitchen. She had endless energy even at her advanced age, both preparing and cooking meals. Though it seemed to Cordi she cooked far too much for the meager company the manor housed. Cordi had never seen any visitors, but she had seen more than one tray being prepared for breakfast the second morning there. Surely the thin—though certainly not waifish—Lady Evangeline could not eat so much in a sitting?

There were at least two other house servants Cordi did not see. But she could hear them in their room coughing violently and sometimes moaning. Miss Eliot seemed little concerned whenever she heard a rattling cough echo from down the servants' quarters.

"There was such sickness in the city during the cold months," Cordi said sadly at breakfast one morning, thinking of how many of the younger, sicklier orphans had passed year after year from too little heat and too little nourishment. "We called it winter fever. They said it was like a fire in your lungs and head. Does it flourish here too?"

There was silence, and everybody seemed to look at each other, except Stella, who kept her gaze dutifully down. Miss Eliot cleared her throat. "No."

Nothing more was said on the subject.

It seemed she was not the only one who harbored secrets. Indeed, Edenfield and its inhabitants, as Alice had said, did feel very much like a secret. A puzzle box for Cordi to master. But Cordi had never been one for puzzles, for they required mindful patience. And while Edward had lectured her on such virtues, all the patience she possessed had been occupied in waiting for him to return and free her.

Hickory is the most difficult of woods to carve. It is hard. Stubborn. Only the most skillful and patient can find what they seek in the wood.

Her third day in Edenfield found her in the main entrance of the manor, where the grand staircase climbed to the second level before branching off in two directions. The floor was inlaid, a massive tree lying at the foot of the stair, its branches covered in beautifully executed leaves in a dizzying array of greens. Miss Eliot had set her the daunting task of cleaning both the entrance and the vestibule behind the stair so they sparkled.

Left to her thoughts, Cordi once again considered how she might find information regarding Edward's visits to the house. Stella had so far proved a dead end. Her roommate was still wary, though Cordi nurtured hope she might be able to entice her into speaking freely.

Faustine seemed the most likely to speak openly and frankly, but they were never alone together.

As Cordi polished each baluster with a cloth, she tried to find Edward in every spiral of wood. In each room she cleaned, she looked for evidence of her brother's handiwork and fabricated possible excuses to see more of the house. She would offer to work more, work harder, if it meant looking in more rooms. She had no keys, as Miss Eliot kept them on her person, so there was no way to open any of the locked doors and no opportunity to snoop.

The study mocked her. Cordi had passed the open door once and glimpsed Lady Evangeline seated at a desk, head bent over a ledger. The heavy books looked like the type Mrs. Clark had kept as logbooks of bills and payments. If she could get a look at them, and they were clearly dated, it would be easy enough to trace back to the time when Edward had still been writing and determine when Mr. Starling had been hired and what he had been working on. And if a man's presence was so carefully monitored, she might even find evidence that Mr. Starling's apprentice had been on the grounds as well.

Then there was the south wing.

A door off the landing at the top of the stairs led to the other half of the house. The one evidently referred to in the rules of the house. The one for which masks and gloves were reserved. It was not hidden, not a secret, but another peculiarity that seemed very "like a secret."

It was not remarkable, yet its obvious relevance to the way the house ran made it so. It called to her, begged her to open it and expose any mysteries it might be hiding. But Cordi had tested it and found it locked, a hindrance to her search. Denied knowledge like the fruit of Eve.

Cordi had never been so tempted by the forbidden.

More than that, she had been so sure she had seen someone watching her from the windows on that side of the house, but who could it have been? Not the servants. And Lady Evangeline had been told of her arrival by Miss Eliot.

She had already concluded it had not been Edward. That stare had felt foreign rather than familiar. Curious. And certainly he would have opened the window and called to her. Or knocked to gain her attention. Not that he would have been allowed in the house at all! Unless he was a prisoner.

It is forbidden that a man enter herein without consent of the mistress of the house, for man is designed for mischief and deceit.

She scrubbed harder in frustration at her lack of progress. Till she might gain the trust of Stella or another or get a glimpse at the ledgers, she would have to carry on praying for a miracle. For another sign of Edward. It galled her: Why had he come back in secret, as Alice had said? Men were not welcome on the estate, so why had he returned? It would not be for theft!

I will steal you if I must.

The words from Edward's last letter came back to her, but she brushed them away. That had been different. A turn of phrase meaning he would liberate her from the Barrow. Her brother was no thief any more than she was.

She recalled her flight with a wince. Because she *had* stolen, hadn't she?

No, she reaffirmed for herself, setting her teeth and glaring at the stripes of scar tissue across the backs of her hands. No. She had kept what she had earned, and what she *had* taken she had paid for in flesh. Her only regret was that the other orphans would likely suffer empty bellies while Mrs. Clark relined her pockets with money meant for the school in recompense for what Cordi had taken as payment.

Casting evil thoughts aside, Cordi returned to her cleaning and the riddle of Edward. If he was not welcome, his job was finished, and his intentions were not to steal, what would he have come back for?

The hand-polishing halted and she blinked over and over at the obvious answer. Edward had been visiting someone in secret. Or at least hoping to catch a glimpse of them. But who? She dismissed the older ladies for reasons of age and countenance that would not have appealed to her brother. Stella or Faustine, perhaps? She could hardly imagine Stella wishing to be the object of attention even if Cordi thought her particularly pretty, no matter how she might hide her face. Cordi, who understood scars better than most, had watched Stella out of the corner of her eye brushing her hair that morning in the light coming through the window, the bristles moving through long, dark strands. Stella might easily have caught her brother's eye, but she would have avoided him at all costs.

Faustine? The girl was young and lively, and was certainly lovely with her dark skin, wide eyes, and tightly coiled hair. Her smile was infectious and her accent so singular Edward might have been smitten. Perhaps she had teased him as he tried to converse with her in French and he had given her one of those disarming grins that had made him so popular at the Barrow. The one that had gotten him—and her—out of trouble time and again. Could he have become enamored with the young Haitian mademoiselle and met her in secret?

Could Edward's charm have earned him the favor of one of Edenfield's inhabitants, regardless of the rules? Edward was young and, with his blond curls and easy smile, had always had little trouble finding girls eager to slip into a dark corner with him for a kiss. More than one Barrow girl had feigned a friendship with Cordi in an effort to get closer to her brother. When Cordi scolded Edward about them, he had laughed, telling her they were just silly things and he would have none of them for more than a moment's distraction.

They are too eager, mistaking infatuation for love.

Eager for anything resembling love herself, she had not understood her brother's heart on the matter. She barely knew her own, so it was just as well. She dearly wished she had prodded more now, however. If she knew the type of lady he fancied, she might know where to focus her attention. She chewed on her lips. Who did that leave? The other servants she had not yet been introduced to—the two who had taken ill.

Whoever it was who had drawn her brother's attention, she was at least confident now it had been a someone. And if that person had spoken with him . . .

Hope flared brighter in her breast. Another trail to follow, another lead. Something to cling to that might lead her to Edward. She found herself smiling as she rounded the grand staircase to continue cleaning in the vestibule. Lifting her eyes, she pulled in an awed breath. The vestibule opened upon a drawing room in the rear of the house, its doors thrown open to reveal a back wall of windows running floor to ceiling. Beyond, in the full light of the afternoon, was a garden unlike anything Cordi might have imagined.

Without conscious thought, she moved forward through the darkness of the foyer and toward the light of the windows, a moth to a flame. Early signs of spring were everywhere, from the new grass in a brilliant shade of green and buds and shoots just beginning to sprout and open. Within a week or so, Cordi could imagine a sea of colors shifting with the breeze like ripples atop a lake. An enormous back patio lay beyond the glass and, down white and gray stone steps, a path led between two massive walls of hedges that might have been the beginning of a labyrinth, for she could see other hedges and walls within.

Edenfield's garden. Beautiful and alive. Cordi's fingers itched to feel the soft brown earth and to trace the delicate petals of flowers again. And this was an unspoiled garden, rich and fragrant. This was not the Barrow. This was a garden of joy and life, not sorrow and death.

Cordi started to turn away, but from the corner of her eye she saw a flash of bright color dart across the opening of the labyrinth and she looked back, tilting her head this way and that as if she could see beyond the hedge walls. It had only been for a moment, but she was sure. A woman or a girl dressed in a lavish pink gown trimmed with lace, for she had glimpsed the skirt. Definitely not a servant. And not Lady Evangeline—because she had also seen a head of hair, and it had not been the pale tresses of the Lady, but strawberry.

In the distance, beyond the window, she could hear laughter. Light, musical laughter.

There *was* someone else living in the house.

"Ahem."

Chapter 10

SHE BARELY CONTAINED A SCREECH as she spun to find Miss Eliot, hands folded at her waist, staring at her from the entrance, her upper half in shadow.

Behind her, the ghostlike, retreating form of Lady Evangeline glided down one of the dark passages like a wraith, heels clicking, their echoes like the pitter-patter of a heart.

Cordi listened to the Lady's steps fade, almost forgetting Miss Eliot entirely. Rousing, she gave a nervous laugh and pressed a hand to her frantic heart. "You gave me quite a startle, ma'am. I've just finished the entrance and the stairs. I was about to—"

"Come with me."

Miss Eliot turned on a heel and hastened away, leaving Cordi no choice but to follow, frantically grabbing the cleaning supplies she'd abandoned in the vestibule. She trailed after the housekeeper as she hurried down the winding corridors back to Cordi's shared room. She did not knock but barged in.

"Put those down," Miss Eliot barked impatiently, gesturing to the bucket filled with rags and brushes slung over Cordi's arm. She moved to Cordi's trunk and yanked it open, and Cordi had to fight back a scream of protest at the invasion of her privacy. Or had Miss Eliot already discovered the letters from Edward? Was she being turned out? Had Mrs. Clark found her out?

Cordi could feel the Barrow far in the distance, its great black shape like a spider in the web of the city. The scars along her back and hands grew taut; she was going to be drawn back into that web, bound and devoured until she was an empty husk. Already she felt the cold of the Barrow's corrupted, gloomy halls seeping into her veins like a slow poison. But the housekeeper only snatched the long, gray gloves and one of the masks from the top of her belongings before snapping the lid shut again. Cordi might have sagged in relief had it not been for the serious countenance Miss Eliot bore. "Wash your hands thoroughly," she instructed, indicating the basin.

Cordi did as she was told, then dried her hands. All the while, Miss Eliot stood—rigid and fierce—and Cordi knew from her posture that she was to listen and not speak.

"This manor is large, and we are short-staffed at the moment. Typically, we do not permit girls in their trial time to take on duties in the south wing, but we cannot shirk the responsibilities of certain rooms there any longer. Sarah must attend the Lady, first and foremost. Faustine is, as you are aware, in the village collecting various sundries. Stella is more suitable, in my opinion, but there were protests and . . . well . . ."

Cordi could hardly imagine Stella protesting an order.

"It doesn't matter," Miss Eliot rushed to say. "The Lady has given her blessing for *you* to act as chambermaid for the day."

Miss Eliot watched her carefully, as if judging her reaction to this news. Cordi read the woman's face and body language quickly, knowing that to offer an objection or to question at all would be a mark against her. So she stood, hands folded, and nodded without speaking.

A sniff of approval from Miss Eliot, and then the woman was holding up the gloves and the mask, the white one, its orange and blue flowers so bright against the fabric. "You have read the rules." This was not a question, but Cordi's head bobbed again. "You will wear these *at all times* within the south wing. You will not remove them until you have reentered the foyer and scrubbed vigorously at both gloves and mask. I will show you where and how this is to be done. After, you will wash your hands and face."

Without waiting for a reply, Miss Eliot marched out the door again, expecting Cordi to heel. "You will be responsible for cleaning two bedchambers and their baths. You will change linens, dust and polish, scrub, and air out each room. The day is warm with a breeze and the Lady wishes this to be done immediately. The rooms have been neglected. You will stay to those rooms and *only* those rooms. You will not wander. You will find the doors on the second floor marked with ribbons and new linens already waiting for you. Soiled linens and towels will be placed in a large basket waiting where I leave you."

She led Cordi to a small powder room off the main stair. Inside was a stack of towels next to a sink with taps of running water. She mimed as she explained in painstaking detail exactly how Cordi was to scrub her gloves and mask upon the completion of her duties. How she was to place the wet garments within a towel and fold it before she washed her skin. How she was to take the folded towel and place it in a basket beside the door, to be laundered and pressed before the gloves and mask were returned to her.

Cordi's tongue burned with questions, but she knew they would be neither appreciated nor answered by the stern housekeeper. Miss Eliot was not needlessly harsh like her teachers from the Barrow, only flinty, but still Cordi could not bring herself to speak when given such precise, direct orders with the heat of the housekeeper's gaze keeping her in check.

Did you know ash bends with heat? Even something so sturdy will fold if it is too hot.

She pulled the gloves on, sliding them up her arms, where they clung like a second skin beneath her sleeves. She pulled the mask over her nose and mouth, the small loops fitting around her ears. Miss Eliot pulled at them and had Cordi shake her head vigorously, assuring herself of the fit. Satisfied, the housekeeper guided her up the stairs to the second floor, pulling a ring of keys from her hip pocket. Striding down the carpeted floor to the door to the south wing, she selected one key, longer and darker than the others, and fitted it into the lock.

In the whirlwind of instruction and worry about her belongings, Cordi only now realized she was being granted an opportunity. She had needed to know what lay within the closed section of the house, and here she was, being invited inside. Her heart beat rapidly, both in anticipation and in trepidation. For there was something else to consider. What was behind this door that she needed protection from?

Pulling the door open, Miss Eliot stepped back, staying on the other side of the wood, and gestured for Cordi to enter. A short passage led to yet another door, but this was where she was to be left. Once she crossed the threshold, she would be alone.

"Remember, the Lady is putting her faith in you to do as you are told and nothing more. When you have completed your task, return to this room, shutting the door firmly behind you, and pull the cord hanging on the wall."

She could bear it no longer, for the woman had finally made Cordi fear what lay beyond the opposite door. "Is there a danger, ma'am? Is that why I must wear the mask and gloves?"

Miss Eliot's face didn't change, but her eyes shuttered. "Precautions do not necessarily mean danger. Regardless, what we do, we do for the sake of the Flowers and our sisters."

The phrase from the cross-stitch. But Cordi still did not know what any of it meant and it seemed she would not yet. Not without finding out for herself or having first been accepted into their fold. Part of her wanted to refuse, to leave, but here was all she had. Here was the only place that might hold the information she needed.

And so she walked through.

Almost before she was fully beyond the threshold, the door was shut behind her, casting her in total darkness. Her heart leapt into her throat, and she felt a surge of panic. Her breath came fast and hot behind the mask, heating her skin, and her eyes opened wider as if she might be able to see better. When she heard a *click* behind her, she nearly screamed.

She was locked in.

It was too much, too close. She couldn't breathe in that small room. Locked in this tiny prison alone. With tears in her eyes and a shaking hand, she reached forward for the next door, the knob turning easily. Steeling herself, she pushed it open, suddenly a child again and certain a monster lurked beyond.

What she found was only a hallway. Paneled with wood like the rest of the house, doors on the west side and windows to the east. A lovely floral rug ran the length of the corridor. At the end, the hall turned to the left toward the front of the house.

Keeping her steps light, Cordi walked forward, the plush carpet absorbing any sound her footfalls might have made. She looked east to gaze out the windows and saw the grounds in front of the house. There she saw the sparkling fountains and white gravel path she had followed to the door of the servants' quarters on her first night. She could just make out the gate and the birch and hawthorn forest beyond.

The quiet was disquieting, and she was tempted to clap or stomp or yell just to break it. The wing was cloaked in a silence that felt ominous. Cordi found herself turning about, searching the shadows for some unnamed horror. Something monstrous that must be locked away. Something that would bear her down to the ground and rip at her with teeth.

Which of course was ridiculous. It was simply part of the house. Nothing dangerous or sinister lurked there. Only . . . who occupied the bedrooms she'd been sent to clean? She had glimpsed someone out in the garden beyond the vestibule. Did they live here on this side of the house alone? And why? She looked down at her gloved hands, fingers fisting and unfisting at her sides. Why did she need these here? Flowers and sisters and Ladies. None of it—this place, these people—made any sense. But the world had not made sense for some time. Not since she left the Barrow. Everything was so different from what she expected, even freedom.

She glanced back. She was not to wander however much she longed to. But lingering in the hall wasn't wandering, certainly. To her right, she could see the ribbons hanging from the doors of the two rooms she was meant to clean.

Licking the beaded sweat on her upper lip, Cordi crept silently down the hall, following the floral rug. At the end, she came face-to-face with a large painting of a garden, exquisitely rendered. Cordi could see each individual petal and leaf. Could almost imagine it was a window if it hadn't been for the way the light fell in the landscape, as if the painter had been sitting with the light behind them. She leaned close if only to assure herself that it was indeed a painting.

To her left, there was a short passage that led to the landing of a spiral stair. Cordi judged it was one of the twin tower stairs she had seen upon her arrival. It went up and down, and she suddenly realized there was no connecting door to this wing in either the entryway or the vestibule on the ground floor. Yet another strangeness.

To investigate this new piece and see where it might fit into the greater puzzle of Edenfield was tempting, but she had to be patient. Miss Eliot had not afforded her this chance without urging from Lady Evangeline. Cordi was not a member of the inner fold. Not yet. Which meant she had to be cautious. She had to prove herself.

She is called to the Garden in her time.

Cordi had no real understanding of the house rules as yet, but she assumed that particular commandment was meant to be a lesson in patience, and how pleased Edward would have been by it. She had to be patient. What else was there to be?

Besides, what better place to start looking than in the very rooms she *had* been granted access to? A sly smile on her lips behind the mask, Cordi turned back and entered the marked room closest to her.

It was a marvelous bedroom fit for a princess or other noble lady. A huge four-poster bed dominated the space with gauzy curtains floating down from the canopy. The pillows and coverlets, satin and silk, were all in disarray, thrown about or shuffled in sleep, and the sheets rumpled. A beautifully carved wardrobe stood against one wall and a vanity, draped in pale-pink fabric worked in ivory, took up one large corner. Two white settees, one tucked beside the door and the other at the end of the bed, made the space feel lighter against all the wood paneling.

Someone lived here. Someone Cordi was not supposed to see. And it stood to reason the other room she had been charged with cleaning was similarly occupied.

She stripped the fine sheets and coverlets, their quality evident even with her sense of touch dulled by the barrier between them and her fingers. She started to pull them to the center of the bed, when she noticed the giant window, its shades drawn. More light. And she was meant to air the room as well. It was then she perceived—only very faintly—a sweet, but slightly cloying scent. She couldn't identify it, only barely discernible under her mask as it was, but it was there. Something floral and rich. If she removed the mask, she might know it better, but she resisted the inclination, still unsure as to the mask's purpose.

Rounding the bed, she threw open the curtains with a sweep of both arms and blinked rapidly in the brilliant sun through the glass. It wasn't a window, but double glass doors leading to a balcony overlooking the back of the house and the magnificent garden she had glimpsed from the drawing room. Cordi pressed down on the latches, letting the doors swing wide, and fresh, cool air flooded the room and the sun warmed her skin.

The sheets and coverlets lay forgotten in a heap as she stepped into the full light of the sun. She tilted her face up, closing her eyes, still able to see the golden glow as it kissed the sensitive skin of her eyelids. She took a deep, cleansing breath as the gentle breeze swirled about the room, wondering if she had ever known a sun as warm or a sky so clear.

"Oh."

The voice was so soft with surprise that Cordi hardly registered it at all. She slowly lowered her chin and turned her head, blinking as if waking from a happy dream, only to wonder if she might still be in one.

Chapter 11

FRAMED IN THE DOORWAY, WITH one pale hand on the knob, was a princess. At least, she seemed a princess, for Cordi was confident she had never seen a girl as perfect and lovely as this. Her hair was long down her back, falling in a waterfall of reddish-gold curls and pulled back from her lily-white forehead. Her skin was remarkably clear, free from either blemish or freckle, and so smooth Cordi might have mistaken her for a life-size porcelain doll under other circumstances. Her high-waisted dress with its capped sleeves only accentuated her full figure, ample breasts, and soft skin. A healthy blush colored her cheeks as she stared at Cordi, her perfectly pink mouth an O of surprise. And her eyes . . .

Her eyes were violet. Even from across the room, Cordi could see them, wide as they were and framed by dark lashes. The same color as the brilliant irises growing on the border of the garden and rimmed by a deeper shade as rich as a plum.

Edward had once sneaked a plum from the kitchen as they prepared a Christmas dinner for the school trustees. They had shared it in an alcove, passing the plump fruit back and forth. But he had allowed Cordi the first bite. She would never forget her teeth puncturing the soft flesh and the spill of sweet juices into her mouth that she licked off her fingers long after the fruit was gone. She had carried the pit in her pocket and planted it on the outer edge of the garden, hoping it might one day sprout a secret fruit.

This girl, with her full curves and rosy cheeks and purple-toned eyes, was another secret, forbidden fruit and Cordi couldn't move under that gaze, staring back, wondering when and if the vision would vanish. The girl stood similarly transfixed, though not for the same reasons, Cordi was sure. Behind the mask, Cordi found it hard to catch her breath.

A small volume bound in red leather was held in the girl's other hand. "I'm sorry," she said. Taking a few steps inside, she casually placed the book on a shelf behind several others, fingers tapping along the spines nervously. "I'd no idea someone was in here. It was so quiet."

"No!" Cordi squeaked behind her mask, coughed, and tried again. "I'm sorry . . . miss. I'd no idea anyone was even—"

"Briar," came a voice from the hall. "Am I going to be waiting about for you all day?"

Another young woman appeared behind the first, just as stunning, but as different as night to day. This one had long, dark hair falling in loose waves like a shawl around her shoulders. She was thinner than her sister, with a narrow waist and slender arms. Rather than pink, her lips were darker and redder, her skin all the paler for it so she glowed like a pearl, dark shadows against snow. Her eyes, however, were the same as the other's: purple jewels set ablaze.

Though where the first looked at Cordi with fascination and surprise, the second scrutinized her with far more calculation.

Cordi dropped into a curtsy, recognizing without being told that neither of these glorious ladies was a servant. "Apologies. I was airing the room and changing the linens."

"Finally!" the second girl said, moving into the room like a gale-force wind, something like a smile about her dark lips. The blue-black waves of her hair shimmered, iridescent and lustrous. A haunting and haughty beauty. "Briar and I had begun to think that we would never have fresh sheets again."

Briar, still standing near the door, hands now crossed over the front of her pink gown, shook her head lightly, setting her curls in motion. "You're being particular, Prim. It hasn't been so long."

Prim rolled her eyes. "You're just trying to seem coy."

"And you're trying to seem clever."

Cordi watched the exchange in fascination. Sisters, she realized. They had to be, with their peculiar and distinctive eye color. And there was something about Lady Evangeline in each of them, though the one called Prim seemed to have much more of her bearing.

"You're the new girl, then?" Prim said, throwing herself down onto one of the white settees, tucking bare feet stained black with soil under her deep-green gown so as not to mar the fabric. She propped her elbow on the sofa and leaned her cheek on the back of her hand. "Mother told us of a new girl in the cloister."

"The cloister?"

She hummed. "That's what we call it."

"That's what *you* call it," Briar corrected, gliding into the room and taking a seat on the couch at the end of the bed, leaving tracks of dirt in her wake. She wrapped her fingers around the bedpost and offered a smile. "Don't mind my sister. She's just needling you."

Cordi desperately hoped the mask hid her furious blush, but, to be sure, she remained framed in the window, backlit by the sun. Her face felt hot and it had little to do with either the mask or the bright sunlight and all to do with the young woman with strawberry curls watching her with jeweled eyes.

Shaking herself, she moved back to the bed, keeping her distance from Briar seated at the end, and reached for the linens. "I—I suppose I should finish. I am sorry if I surprised you. I didn't even know that you—that you . . ." She wasn't sure what to say or if it was even appropriate that she speak.

"That we even existed?" Prim finished for her.

Cordi nodded hastily.

"Yes, well, that's *Mother* for you," she said with a sniff.

"Prim," Briar cautioned, but Prim disregarded the warning.

"Oh, don't be a goose. What will Mother do to me? Send me to my room? We never leave, dearest. Or have you forgotten?" She tsked, pursing those dark lips over her teeth, lids lowering in a coquettish manner. "This is rather intriguing, though. Typically Mother doesn't permit anyone new to come to this side of the house. But I'm glad it's you and not one of the others. A fresh face is such a rare treat. Eliot puts on too many airs, if you ask me—"

"We didn't," Briar countered.

"—and Faustine prattles so. And that other one. Stella. She's as meek as a mouse."

"You leapt at her from behind a curtain and frightened the poor thing nearly to death! She doesn't want to come, and one can hardly blame her! You treated her very poorly and she does work so hard."

Prim snickered and lay back against the couch. "It just gets so *dull,* and I was bored."

"You're terrible," Briar admonished before turning back to Cordi. "She's terrible. But not cruel."

"I am, though," Prim purred.

Briar ignored her. "It's true Mother never allows anybody new to attend us. Poor Jane and Irene must be terribly ill."

Jane and Irene. The sick servants. Briar looked so sad, and Cordi found herself wanting to comfort her, but she had no words to offer. She had never met either Jane or Irene or even knew what illness kept them so sequestered.

"Oh, don't be like that, Briar," Prim said, rising from her couch to lay a comforting hand on her shoulder. She looked truly contrite then, as if she too hated the sight of her sister in pain. She leaned down and hugged her around the neck, pressing her dark head against Briar's bright hair and petting her gently.

The day and the night. Two halves of the same whole.

Seeing them made the longing for her brother all the more acute, like a wound being freshly opened so that you realized the sting had never really gone away, only dulled.

"I'm sure they will get better soon!" Cordi said, attempting to be cheerful.

The sisters looked at her, their violet eyes watching her curiously, then at each other.

Prim's mouth set into a grim line, but Briar tried to muster a smile. "Yes. Yes, I do hope you're right."

"What's your name?" Prim asked, straightening, but keeping one hand on Briar's shoulder, her long, elegant fingers curled protectively over the satin sleeve of her sister's dress. Her tone was formal and not a little suspicious.

"Cordelia," Cordi answered, fumbling to execute another rather awkward curtsy, feeling stupid and graceless next to these two otherworldly beauties. "But everybody calls me Cordi."

"Cordi," Briar said wistfully, her pink mouth turning the first syllable into a kiss. "I'm Briar and this is my sister, Primrose. But Mother and I call her Prim."

Bobbing another curtsy, Cordi twisted her gloved fingers. "You're Lady Evangeline's daughters. I'd not realized. It is very kind of your mother to take me into her employ. It seems all of us—the other servants, I mean—had need of . . ." What could she say that was neither a lie nor too revealing? ". . . hope."

"And what is it that you hope to find at Edenfield?" Prim countered. She looked down, petting a hand down her sister's mane of hair and lifting a curl, individual strands catching and clinging to the spiral in an interlocking web. And Prim was the spider in that moment, Cordi the fly. But she would not be caught so easily.

She shoved all thoughts of her brother away, pushing them down—deep down—where they would smolder in her heart like a coal awaiting the chance to spark anew. But patience. Patience, or they would be snuffed out and never have a chance to burn properly.

She dared a look at Briar, whose eyes flashed in the sun briefly before she lowered them to her lap. Cordi turned her eyes back to Prim, who was still studying her sister's hair. "I think I've only ever hoped for two things my entire life: happiness and freedom. Maybe this is where I find them."

Prim froze for a moment, still not looking at her, then dropped her sister's hair, her face shuttering. When she spoke, her voice was low. "Happiness and freedom. Two things you will find in short supply here." She turned, calling for her sister to follow, and swept out of the room.

Briar stood dutifully and walked to the door, pausing briefly before looking back over her shoulder. "It was lovely to meet you, Cordi."

Then she was gone down the hall after her sister, headed toward the stair. Neither sister's feet made any noise.

Chapter 12

"I HOPE THAT THE FRUIT OF your labors is indicative of how much time you took completing your task."

The words spoken so loudly in the dark startled Cordi and made her head spin. Miss Eliot had opened the passage, key ring in hand, allowing Cordi to walk through, her head strangely light. After the sisters had left her standing alone in Briar's room, Cordi had felt energized. Here were two pieces to the queer puzzle of Edenfield. But her adrenaline eventually began to lag, and even though she had tried to hurry through her duties, knowing she had dawdled too long, she found herself moving slower and slower.

As she'd worked, changing linens and towels, scrubbing tubs and polishing mirrors, she'd compared the rooms. Briar's room was as she seemed herself: light and full of colors that invoked joy. Primrose's room was—as Cordi had expected—darker, though hardly malevolent. More mature. Heavy fabrics in green and purple damask and velvets so dark indigo they might appear black in low light. And all of it had required cleaning and airing. She'd handled their laundry, hauling heavy baskets to the hallway to line up with the basket of stripped linens. By then, she had been exhausted and had to steady herself with one hand against the wall as tiny black spots appeared in her vision. It seemed forever before she was finished, and she realized it must have been some time since someone was in to attend to the sisters' chambers. It stood to reason that the two ill servants—Jane and Irene—must have fallen to the same malady at the same time.

Miss Eliot snapped her fingers in Cordi's face, and Cordi blinked wearily. "Apologies, ma'am. Did you say something?"

The woman gestured to the stairs. "Down. Scrub your gloves and mask as I have shown you. Then wash your face and hands. Hurry, now. I need you in the kitchen immediately."

She stood waiting. Cordi shuffled toward the stairs, not nearly as sprightly as she might have been, and descended one careful step at a time, legs leaden. Miss Eliot hovered at the door to the powder room for a beat or two, assuring herself Cordi remembered how to correctly wash the garments, before she headed off to the kitchen.

She is to cleanse her masks and gloves with vigor and take care not to touch bared skin without having done so.

When Cordi arrived in the kitchen, there was a cup of tea sitting on the table, steam rising in coils and spirals from the top. Miss Eliot motioned for her to sit and then to the tea, so Cordi sank into the spot apprehensively and lifted the pretty, flower-etched cup to her lips. She took a tentative sip, mindful of its heat, and pulled a face.

Catching Cordi's grimace, Miss Eliot placed a jar of honey next to her saucer, the dipper clacking against the tiny pot. "You may wish to take it with something sweet. It can be an acquired taste, but it will refresh you."

Cordi did just this, stirring some of the thick, golden syrup into her cup and finding it far more palatable, though it certainly wouldn't be her first choice of drink. She wondered if the leaves were perhaps a local blend. She took another few sips and found herself feeling fortified. She was used to hard work, but certainly not without pause. Still, it was preferable to the Barrow.

"Forgive me, Miss Eliot. I cannot understand why I came over so queer."

The housekeeper hummed noncommittally.

The fog around Cordi's thoughts lifted slowly, a thin veil being drawn back so she might see the world clearly. With this newfound clarity, she could think about the possible ramifications of her meeting Briar and Primrose when she had not been meant to do so. If she were to tell the housekeeper, would she be turned out? But if she kept it to herself, and Miss Eliot learned of it on her own, she could be in more trouble. It seemed to Cordi that honesty—in this case—would serve her better and might earn her credibility.

"Ma'am," she said, placing her cup on the saucer. "I think it best I tell you, two young ladies found me while I was cleaning."

From the corner of her eye, she saw Miss Eliot stiffen and almost immediately deflate. "So, you've seen them? Spoken to them?"

"Yes, ma'am. They introduced themselves. They said they were Lady Evangeline's daughters."

A heavy sigh, and Miss Eliot moved to sit at her spot at the head of the little kitchen table. She'd poured no tea for herself. Her face was unreadable for the most part, but a flash of irritation lit her eyes. "I had suggested to the Lady the girls be sequestered to the garden while you worked. I suppose it doesn't matter, though I shall have to speak to her. She is very protective and will not want it kept from her, especially if they disobeyed. You were right to tell me." A pause. "What else did they say?"

Cordi shook her head. "Nothing of importance, ma'am. They were quite kind to me." Even if Prim had been somewhat cool. Should she not have been to a servant in her own house? "Oh! And they expressed concern for Jane and Irene? The two maids who are ill?"

Miss Eliot smoothed her skirt in her lap. "Yes, well, what can be done for our sisters is being done. Their concern is touching and will be relayed. I'm sure it will be a great comfort."

Sisters. Like a cloister, just as Prim had said.

"Ma'am," Cordi began hesitantly, wondering how far she might press for answers, "are Lady Evangeline's daughters ill?"

The housekeeper looked shocked. "Why ever would you think such a thing? Did they appear so?"

"No, ma'am!" she hastened to assure. "Only, the masks one must wear, and they said they never leave. I thought perhaps—"

Miss Eliot shoved back from the table. "Miss Primrose and Miss Briar are the picture of health. Now, you will finish your tea. All of it. I must go speak to the Lady."

It was only after the housekeeper was gone, as Cordi was sipping her tea and thinking of the two violet-eyed beauties in their castle, that she realized she very well might have discovered the reason—or reasons—for Edward's secret visits.

It was hardly a surprise to Cordi to find herself standing in front of Lady Evangeline only a short time later. She'd drained her teacup as instructed and only just had time to finish her lunch before Miss Eliot had returned, instructing Cordi to make herself presentable before they were hurrying yet again down corridors and hallways in the housekeeper's quick, efficient fashion.

This time, Cordi was led up the back stairs to the study on the second floor, the room she had so longed to investigate. Though she was certainly not being granted the occasion to snoop, she still took the opportunity to look about. Like the sitting room from the first night, the room was filled with plants of all kinds: ferns and ivy and pots full of swollen buds, their flowers ready to burst forth at any time. However, unlike the sitting room, this was not a place meant for company and genteel talk of the weather or polite political discourse. This was a room meant for dedicated study and research. A large drafting table was pushed against one wall and a heavy secretary desk topped with a glass-plated hutch stood opposite. The shelves behind the glass were crowded with various jars and covered domes containing bulbs and dried flowers and other curiosities. Cordi could see a stained mortar and pestle, glass vials filled with what might have been seeds or coarse dirt, peculiar bundles of herbs tied with different colors of ribbon, and even a skull marked by pins, words tattooed into the yellowed bone. There were other bones as well, black cracks shooting across their bleached surfaces like dark lightning. She might have been shocked if she had not been so curious, her most terrible vice.

The desk's lid was down and Cordi could almost picture precious account books within, hear them mocking her with their nearness. If she could just get a peek, maybe . . .

She didn't know what might come next. She only knew she needed some proof of Edward or risk falling to pieces. For so long, their reunion had offered all she had in the way of hope and she didn't know what it meant for her to have even that gone.

The rest of the room was lined with bookshelves bursting with ledgers and thick tomes and rolls of paper, a heavy apothecary cabinet squeezed in tight by the window, its rows of tiny drawers labeled in elegant script. Cordi couldn't imagine how much knowledge had to be contained within the study's walls.

And standing in the center of the room, backlit by the sun beginning its slow descent, was Lady Evangeline. She was clad in an afternoon dress of white dotted with tiny bluebells and a long, blue jacket with capped sleeves and pearl buttons on top. Her hair was gathered and arranged in a braid along the crown of her head.

"I hear you have met my daughters."

"Yes, my lady."

Lady Evangeline shifted to the windows to gaze out at the garden. "Willful girls. And I'd not have it any other way. A woman should do as she pleases and I have raised my daughters to obey no hearts but their own, but these they must guard and keep. No part of them should belong to another, though I understand well enough the affection they have for each other."

She did not mention herself, and Cordi wondered at a mother who did not care if her children loved her.

"The world of men is an unfit place for a woman, and I'll not have my daughters subjected to it as I was. If God created man in his own image, I have done it and better, for I did not deny my creations knowledge. The flowers of my Eden grow and thrive in the paradise I cultivated for them. And one would think it enough. But if one cannot even learn from the mistakes of the God of man . . ."

It seemed to Cordi that Lady Evangeline had ceased talking to her and was only musing aloud, for her gaze was distant and she tapped one finger against the top of the opposite hand absently.

She sucked in a breath and turned again to Cordi. She studied her closely from beneath long, pale lashes with eyes that—though not Prim's color—held the same sharp and steady calculation as her daughter's. "You have been to school."

It was not a question, but Cordi answered all the same. "Yes, my lady."

"A charity school, if I guess right. What did they teach you?"

"I had regular lessons in mathematics and history and French. We were instructed in the Christian faith. The girls were also schooled in knitting and embroidery and music, though I admit I am not accomplished in anything."

"And you were taught to garden."

Cordi could feel the lunch of cold roast and carrots and greens in the pit of her stomach. "I assisted in the garden, yes." She would not think of Mason as a teacher. Not when his true lesson had been barbarism.

The Lady hummed and took a turn about the room, her hand running across the backs of books as she strolled, orbiting Cordi slowly. "I shall grant you the courtesy of speaking plainly, Cordelia. I never desired a marriage nor children. I would have devoted my life to science and botany, not parlor rooms and a marriage bed, if this world were better suited to a woman with dignity and a curious mind. Do not misunderstand. My daughters are my pride and joy, my most perfect flowers. I cultivated my children with extreme care, and they have blossomed. And with their father gone, I have lived quite contentedly. Still, I cannot help but notice a certain restlessness has entered my daughters' lives. They've quarreled more of late. Gotten into mischief. I see now they might benefit from a distraction. I do not engage with society, and neither will they. Governesses were out of the question and so were playmates from the village. They have had each other for commiseration. Now . . ."

Lady Evangeline completed her walk around the room and stood before Cordi again, once more taking her measure. All her years at the Barrow had her standing straighter, face impassive, reminding herself, as she had always done, that she must not let anyone see the most secret chambers of her heart.

"I will speak to Miss Eliot. From morning through midday, you will be a companion for my daughters. Someone for them to converse with. Play games with. For picnics and walks and whatever other frivolity they might find amusing when they are not to their studies or work. I'm sure we can find something suitable among Prim's old dresses; you're more her size, as malnourished as you are. Should your trial period result in an invitation to stay on at Edenfield, we will have a small wardrobe commissioned for you for your duties as a lady's companion. Afternoons and evenings, you will attend to duties such as Miss Eliot requires. You will take your meals with the other servants and your tea with the girls, but only outside on days when the weather is fair."

Cordi was nearly struck dumb. A companion? To such striking and elegant creatures? She would be given smart, fashionable clothing? "Yes, my lady," she managed.

"Very well. You may return to your responsibilities."

As Cordi curtsied to her benefactress's back and made to leave, the Lady's voice stopped her.

"And, Cordelia?"

"Yes, ma'am."

Lady Evangeline did not turn again from the windows, only stared out into the green sea of her garden, tracing a line of condensation on the glass with the tip of one finger. "I shall insist that the mask and your gloves remain in place when you are within the walls of the south wing. For now."

Chapter 13

"STELLA, DO YOU THINK YOU could fix my hair?"

Cordi stood at the end of Stella's bed in her nightdress, holding a pair of scissors in her hand. Stella was seated on her bed, toying with the end of her braid as usual, legs drawn up under her blanket.

At her words, Stella looked up in confusion, hugging her knees tighter. "What?"

Cordi ran her fingers through the uneven locks. She would begin the next day as a companion to Primrose and Briar. She would wear a lovely blue-green dress, but without a maid's cap to cover her hair, she felt self-conscious and wanted to be made presentable. "I couldn't really see what I was doing when I cut it," she said, remembering how she had pulled the braid over her shoulder and hacked at it with Mrs. Clark's sewing scissors till it had fallen at her feet. "I know I look a mess. Do you think you could help clean it up for me?"

She is to tend to her sisters as she would herself, for what is reaped must first be sown.

Stella's voice was quiet as she answered. "I don't know how to cut hair."

Pointing to her head, Cordi laughed. "Me neither. And you certainly can't mess it up any more than I did."

After a brief hesitation, Stella pushed her blankets back. Cordi took this as agreement and retrieved the small wooden chair from the corner of the room, placing it by the table holding the oil lamp before taking a seat. She offered Stella the scissors with an open palm and the girl took them with wary fingers. Cordi folded her hands neatly in her lap and looked forward, her head straight and still. "I don't mind it being longer on the one side. I kind of like it. But I know the back must look horrid."

Stella made a sound that wasn't quite agreement, but certainly wasn't an argument. After considering: "You really won't be mad if I make mistakes?"

"Of course not!" Cordi assured her. "It's only hair. You can obviously see how much I care about it. Though your hair is particularly beautiful."

She could almost hear the sound of blood rushing to Stella's face behind her, but Cordi didn't look, knowing by now that Stella avoided eye contact. Given time, it might change. Cordi liked Stella's quiet nature and wanted them to be friends almost as much as she wanted to probe for information. *Almost,* she had to tell herself. Still, she could not deny the yearning she had long harbored for a friend. Cordi's only real experience with friendship was as a transaction, such was life at the Barrow. But now . . . she wanted something real. Besides, friends helped each other, didn't they?

She wondered if it made her wicked to consider how she might use someone to her advantage. Already the lies and little deceits ate at her, knotting her nerves. But was there any reason she could not be Stella's true friend in the end, once she had what she needed? Once she had found Edward? She could confess all. Yes. That made it easier. She could promise herself to be truthful later. *Patience,* she cautioned herself, as Edward often did.

It may take three years for a seed to become a sapling.

I do not have three years, Edward. But she could be patient. For him, she could.

A moment later, Cordi felt the bristles of Stella's brush along her scalp. It felt so nice, she almost regretted her hair not being longer simply to make the strokes last. There was only the whisper of the sound for a time, and Cordi imagined Stella was deciding how best to approach the hastily cut and uneven curls she was faced with. Then the brush was set aside, and Cordi heard the first snip and the gentle kiss of falling hair on the back of her neck.

"I'll just try to even it out a little on the left and in the back," Stella said, her voice suggestive of concentration. "I do like the longer waves on the other side. It is very bold. Why did you cut it?" Before Cordi could open her mouth to answer, Stella was apologizing. "I'm sorry. That's . . . that's not any of my business. I shouldn't have—"

"No, it's all right! I don't mind. I—well, I ran away from . . . not my home, but the place I grew up. It wasn't . . ." She let the sentence drift away, not sure how best to continue without saying more than she wanted and more than might be good for her.

"Safe?"

The word floated from behind, hushed and full of sorrow and knowledge, and just the tone of Stella's voice made Cordi swallow hard. "Yes," she whispered. "It wasn't safe. And I was always getting in trouble for my hair, you see. It was never right. Never behaved. Like me, I suppose." This was said with a wet little laugh, and she thought she heard an answering sound behind her. "Anyway, I swore that I would cut it off when I left."

"So you did."

"And then I ran. And I came here." She hoped Stella wouldn't ask more. Lying soured her stomach and she already felt wretched enough for those lies she had told.

But Stella didn't ask more, only resumed the crisp cuts along Cordi's waves. "I ran away too," she finally said. "I ran and ran and I will never go back. If the Ladies be willing, if I am good and serve faithfully, I will pass my days here till I am called to the Garden."

She is called to the Garden in her time.

Cordi could feel the determination in the girl's voice. Stronger than she had ever heard it. Blindly, she reached a hand up and over her shoulder. An offering.

Fingers clasped her own and Cordi squeezed gently. "I'm glad we ran. And I am glad of a place that offers such safety." The hand squeezed back—just once—before letting go, and Stella returned to the slow, careful cuts and there was only the sound of the scissors slicing through the fine tresses.

"We are safe here. But only from those who would wish us harm. There is still peril, but only if we do not follow the rules. The rules keep us, the Flowers, and the Garden safe. It is vital for our salvation. Our obedience and devotion are rewarded."

"I can hardly think of greater reward," Cordi said, keeping her tone light and conversational. Inviting Stella to confide in her. "Lady Evangeline certainly seems quite generous! She took me in when others turned me away. We have lovely food, warm accommodations, and companionship. What greater reward *could* there be?"

The next snip of the scissors was slow, the hiss as the blades severed the strands long, reminding her of the grass snake she had found in the vegetable patch of the Barrow once. A warning she should not venture too near. Even those without venom may lash out if cornered.

Stella's voice when she answered was not angry, but sure. "Service to the Ladies is itself a reward. But you will see. We keep the Garden and help it grow. There are greater blessings still if one is patient and dutiful."

Cordi bit her tongue. She wanted to probe for answers about the Ladies and the Garden. About what it all meant. But she held back, accepting this small victory as the first of many. Stella's trust was hard-won and Cordi needed to be content for now, so she continued to sit quietly under Stella's ministrations.

"There." Stella took up the brush, moving it quickly through Cordi's hair. "I did my best and I think it is a bit more even. There is a mirror in the drawer under the basin if you'd like to see it."

Cordi reached up and felt along the back of her neck. The hairline did feel even again. Shorter, yes, but even. She pulled open the drawer and found a small mirror on a chain. One meant to be hung up. Likely, Stella had taken it down. Cordi looked at her face within and gave a wide smile. "It's lovely!"

Stella had indeed done a wonderful job with the almost impossible task she had been given. It no longer looked like Cordi had taken a serrated knife to her hair, which was a vast improvement in and of itself. Stella had shortened the left side so the waves fell close against her head and behind her ear. She'd managed to even the haphazard tendrils across the back. The right side she had left longer, only cutting the ends at a rather jaunty angle that brushed along Cordi's jawline, sweeping from the crown of her head. Cordi ran a hand through her ashen hair, noting how long her neck appeared. It was—in her opinion—a very flattering and daring cut.

She wondered if Briar might think so.

She chastened herself for the inappropriate notion and beamed at Stella. "It's perfect!"

There was a hesitation before Stella lifted her face and looked at Cordi directly, not hiding her drooping, scarred eyelid. And she smiled. It was small, but it was real and it was a first. Cordi's own smile widened, and she shook her hair out, letting the longer side bounce across her cheek, and giggled. Stella laughed too, putting a hand to her mouth as if she was surprised the sound could come from her. She sobered, but Cordi could see her good eye alight with happiness. "I'm glad you are pleased."

"Thank you. You've all been so kind to me." She looked at the floor and the shorn trimmings of her hair that littered the planks. Taking up a candle from the table, she lit it with a long lighting stick from the lamp. "I'll get a broom to sweep up. I'll hurry back." Barefoot, she slipped out the door and closed it gently behind her, making her way quietly down the hall so as not to disturb any who might already be asleep.

After a moment searching in the dark of the broom cupboard, Cordi found the small brush and pan used for sweeping the steps and started back down the hall on tiptoe, halting when she heard hushed voices. A faint glow shone on the stones through the gap below the door of the quarantined servants' room. Jane and Irene. If they were better, she might bring the sisters pleasant news as a surprise gift! Wouldn't Briar be so pleased? Shielding her candle with the pan, she held her breath and listened.

The sound of muffled weeping came from behind the door and then a gentle shushing before Lady Evangeline's voice, low and gentle, could be heard. "Do not despair, my dear. She is not gone from us. It is a blessing. I know it is hard, but you must be strong for her sake and for your own. Come now, come," she said, as the other occupant of the room cried harder before her body was racked by a cough. "Drink deep. There you are. All will be well. Remember, what is planted in the Garden, grows in the Garden. Say it. Let it bring you comfort."

A raspy voice, exhausted and filled with tears, repeated the phrase. "What is planted in the Garden, grows in the Garden."

Cordi felt the blood in her veins freeze at the words, recalling them from the cross-stitch in her room and from Stella's quiet hope that the Garden would welcome her one day. Was it just a prayer or benediction? Why did it fill her with such a strange sense of dread and apprehension, a tight fist wrapped around her heart? Stella had told her the house was safe, but she had also mentioned peril from within. What if that untold danger had claimed Edward? What if it was going to take her too?

Shivering, more from the unknown than from cold, Cordi curled closer around her tiny candle. Part of her wanted to press her ear to the door and listen, to learn. Secrets, as Alice had said, were marvelous things. And often useful. But the risk outweighed the reward, in that moment. That was what she told herself. It was the risk of discovery and not fear that saw her pivot, moving swiftly and silently down the hall back toward her room and the safety of her ignorance, the words of the old woman in the carriage chasing her in the dark.

Ignorance has never kept a woman safe.

Chapter 14

"YOU'RE HERE!" BRIAR EXCLAIMED, RUSHING forward as Cordi opened the interior door to the south wing. Prim stood in the center of the hall, her face guarded as she watched her sister dash ahead.

"Good morning, Miss Briar. Miss Primrose," Cordi said, dipping into a far better curtsy than her previous attempts. She had forced herself to practice till she felt at least adequate at the gesture.

"Oh, please, no titles. Just Briar and Prim. We are friends now!" Briar said, her lovely face rosy with excitement. "And what wonderful friends we will be! I've thought of little else since Mother came to give us the good news! And you look lovely in the dress Prim chose for you. It was one of hers. She has such an artist's eye!" She gazed at Cordi for a moment as if enraptured. "And your *hair*!"

Cordi touched the waves self-consciously.

"It is so fresh! And it looks so fine with the shape of your shoulders and the cut of the dress. I can't imagine being so bold. Nor can I imagine it of Prim, and she is the bravest person I know!"

"Yes, well, the number of people you do know makes it rather a moot point, doesn't it, Briar?" Prim said, voice as cool and smooth as ice over a frozen lake. "Still, it is quite smart, I have to say. Is that the way the girls wear it in the cities?"

"Oh, not really." Cordi laughed nervously. "I mean, no. I actually . . . I cut my hair poorly and asked Stella to fix it. I gave her very little to work with."

Briar was circling her, the skirts of her own cream-colored dress printed with tiny red roses nearly brushing against Cordi's. "It suits you perfectly! You must sit for Prim sometime! She is wonderful at portraiture. Landscapes too. But she captures people so impeccably. She doesn't even need me to sit for her anymore. Nor Mother. She can draw us from memory. You could be a new subject. Don't you think so, Prim? Wouldn't Cordi make a charming model for you to capture?"

Too afraid of what Prim's answer might be, Cordi attempted to steer conversation away from her. "You paint?"

Prim's violet eyes turned wistful. "I do. Do you have an interest in art?"

"An interest, I'm sure, but no talent. I had no instruction. Though I find myself admiring many of the paintings in the house. I marveled at the one at the end of the hall yesterday," she said, gesturing over Prim's shoulder to the framed landscape. "It's beautiful. Is it one of yours?"

"Yes," she said, a note of pride in her voice.

"It's perfect, isn't it? Prim is not only the bravest person I know, but the most talented. Hush!" Briar scolded her sister, who had opened her mouth, likely to bring up the number of acquaintances they had again. She rolled her eyes. "She's always needling and lecturing and scolding."

"You always need needling, lecturing, and scolding."

Briar pouted, and Cordi's heart beat a strange cadence in her chest. But Briar burst into a laugh, running at her sister and enfolding her in a tight embrace that was immediately returned. Cordi couldn't help but notice, however, that Briar hugged her sister with abandon as a child might, while Prim bent over her sister with a protective air, a shield between the innocent young woman and the world.

There were more than stone walls and locked doors that guarded the princess, it seemed.

Minutes later, Cordi found herself following the pair down the winding staircase, windows cut into the stone at even intervals painting perfect rectangles of light along the inner walls. She moved in and out of shadow as the girls did ahead of her, watching the way the early light played on each sister's hair. Prim's dark locks shimmered like a raven's wing and Briar's strawberry curls burned.

They led her to a large parlor in the front of the house, sunlight flooding in from the east. Like so many of Lady Evangeline's rooms, this one was filled with plants of all shapes and sizes and shades of green. Here again, buds were beginning to form, and Cordi could imagine the room awash with color soon enough.

Briar made straight for the windows, flipping the tiny latches to open them. A cool breeze wafted in and Cordi was grateful for the long sleeves of her dress and her gloves, for she did not own a shawl and could not bring herself to wear her moth-eaten jumper or poor excuse for a coat.

"There," Briar said, breathing deeply, her face bathed in the pale sunlight of early spring. Dust motes danced about her, swirling in the gently moving air and sparkling like tiny fairies vying for her favor. And there it was again: Cordi's heart beat that strange rhythm and she frowned under her mask, looking down at her hands. Beneath the gloves, thin scars were raised. On her back, the same, leaving crisscrossing ropes of raised tissue across her flesh. The price of someone else's lust and lies. She did not want to taint the innocence of Briar with her own.

Cordi was no stranger to such things. She'd seen the looks between the older boys and girls at school, lingering stares and shy smiles exchanged across the dining room or the yard. The casual brush of hands in the hall. And everybody knew the different alcoves and shadowed corners some pairs sneaked into despite the severe punishment that might follow. And while a few boys had offered her a sly smirk or a wink of interest, she had never responded in kind. She felt no stirrings at the sight of even the handsomest boy from the Barrow. For some time, she'd wondered if it was simply because she had grown up among them. But the arrival of Anne when Cordi was about thirteen changed that.

Anne had been . . . beautiful. She was broader and healthier than most of the other girls, having spent her childhood without an empty belly. Cordi loved the rosy glow on her plump cheeks, the smattering of freckles on her nose, and her long, chestnut hair, always tied back in a perfect braid. They had become something akin to friends, Cordi immediately engaging the girl in conversation if only to have an excuse to look at her.

And when Anne had kissed her, just once, behind the laundry as it flapped and snapped in the wind where they were hanging damp linens, Cordi knew why she had never felt the same yearning as the other girls. Because she yearned for something very different.

It had shattered her heart to see Anne pressed against one of the most loathsome bullies in the Barrow a week later, the two hidden in one of the darker alcoves. A boy, no less. His fingers tangled in that perfect braid, ruining the careful plait. She had never spoken to Anne again. Better a lonely heart than risk betrayal by a false one.

Her eyes again strayed to Briar, and she felt that same flutter in her gut, only deeper and sharper, and she quickly looked away to find Prim staring at her, head cocked to the side. Cordi willed herself not to blush with little hope of success. Eager to take attention off herself once more, she made a point of admiring the floral wallpaper. Coupled with the army of plants, it created the effect of sitting within an ornate rose garden. "I should thank you, Miss Primrose. For the dress. It is quite lovely. I've never worn something so fine."

She shrugged an elegant shoulder. "It's nothing. And Briar's quite right. You don't need to address us formally while you are out of livery. Prim is fine."

Cordi's chest eased a bit. "I'm grateful all the same. To you and your mother. It was quite kind of her to offer me such a position, especially given my circumstances."

"What circumstances?" Briar asked, taking up a seat next to her sister on a lovely pale-green couch.

With both sets of eyes on her, Cordi fought the urge to twist her fingers together. She conjured up the image of Lady Evangeline the night before and notched her chin just a bit higher as she began to stroll about the room, measuring her steps and hoping she appeared confident. "Well, I'm certainly not accustomed to rooms and clothes as splendid as this."

"Mother said you went to a charity school. What was it like?" Briar asked, leaning forward, eager for a story.

Cordi gave a short cough behind her mask. "Nothing like Edenfield. It was cold and dark. There wasn't light like this, bright from a clear sky and generous with its warmth. Too much smoke from too many chimneys would choke it before it reached us."

"It sounds horrid," Briar breathed, but she also sounded excited. Fascinated by a world she had never seen.

"It was," Cordi acknowledged. "For me, at least. I'm glad to be free of it. Glad to know I won't ever have to go back."

"You have no family, then?"

Cordi felt her heart stop in her chest.

"*Briar!*" Prim scolded, obviously scandalized by her sister's question.

"I'm sorry," Briar rectified, and she sounded so contrite that any sting that might have spread from such a question was easily dismissed.

"There's nothing back there for me," Cordi said. Which was the truth. Wherever Edward was, it wasn't there.

Briar reached out a hand and clutched at Prim's where it lay on her lap. "I can't picture life without the sun or Prim. I don't know what I would do."

Prim looked at their joined hands for a long moment before she laid her other hand atop her sister's. "You'll never have to."

"Thank the Garden," Briar sighed, pulling her sister's hands to her cheek.

Thanks given to the Garden, for the Garden is right and good.

Cordi had been wrong about the sting. Seeing siblings and their obvious affection for each other brought it back, sharper than before. But she wouldn't let it sow doubt within her. Would not allow herself to lose hope. "So, what does a lady's companion do?"

"We hardly know," said Prim. "Mother was rather brisk about the entire arrangement."

"We aren't used to *company*." Briar said it as if the very word were exotic. "Only the servants."

"She is still a servant," Prim said casually, draping herself back against the cushions, hands over her head, long hair spilling over the arm of the sofa.

Briar shot her a look. "Must you?"

"It's all right," Cordi said, not wanting to be the cause of an argument on her first morning. "I am a servant. I only hope to make a suitable companion for you and do Lady Evangeline's faith justice. I've no intention of forgetting my place, though it is flattering you did for a moment, Briar, and on that I shall cling to the hope that I might be a friend as well."

The smile Briar offered lit the room and Cordi had to look away if only not to be blinded. Prim, too, had a tight-lipped smile, one eyebrow raised in approval. She seemed pleased, though in the way a cat is pleased, so that you are left to wonder if it is happy, content, or waiting for a chance to strike. Briar had said she was terrible, but not cruel, so perhaps this was just her way. She *had* tried to steer her sister away from asking too many personal questions. Cordi considered whether perhaps her perception of Prim's cool demeanor was only exaggerated when compared to her sister's innocent exuberance.

"I think I *would* like to sketch you, if you don't mind."

Cordi could feel the heat on the back of her neck as a blush began to rise. "I suppose." Briar leaned into her sister, cupping a hand over her mouth to whisper something in Prim's ear.

Cordi coughed. "Where should I sit?"

Prim and Briar both smiled now, their violet eyes twinkling. "Not here. In the garden."

Chapter 15

"It's all settled!" Briar came almost skipping into the room. "I've told Miss Eliot we'll take our tea outside."

Cordi plucked at the ends of her gloved fingers. "I could fetch the tea. I don't expect Miss Eliot would be very pleased to be serving me."

"Miss Eliot can sit on a pin," Prim said with a yawn, no venom in her words. "Besides, she won't let you into the kitchen without the *ritual cleansing." She is to cleanse her masks and gloves with vigor and take care not to touch bared skin without having done so.* Prim's last words were accompanied by an eye roll so severe that Cordi was concerned that her eyes might get stuck in the back of her head. "So I'm afraid you will have to simply become used to being pampered on occasion."

That's what Cordi was worried about. She didn't want to overstep her boundaries or cause harsh feelings between her and Miss Eliot, who could very well decide she wasn't fit for the household. Who was she to share tea and conversation with such fine, elegant ladies?

"Oh, please don't feel uncomfortable, Cordi. It is only tea, after all." It was Briar, her face full of compassion.

"See? Even Briar can be sensible," said Prim. "If you're worried that you will appear to be putting on airs, don't be. For one, you were instructed to entertain us, were you not? And for another, it is not as if anybody else relishes our company."

Something dark flickered across Prim's face. A hurt she very obviously resented. Cordi thought of the locked doors and the secrets and the rules and wondered if there was merit to her princesses-in-a-tower theory, for at least one of the princesses seemed restless.

She had little time to dwell on her thoughts because Briar was already pulling Prim up from her spot on the couch, demanding she retrieve her sketchbook at once so they didn't lose the light. "One would think you were the painter."

Briar pulled a face. "No, thank you. I will stick to my embroidery, which doesn't smell of turpentine."

As Prim left them alone to gather her things, Cordi motioned to her own mask. "Did you embroider these? And the cross-stitches and sheets?"

A faint blush. "Yes. I hope you like them."

"They're lovely!" Cordi exclaimed. "I've no talent at all. For anything, really, except—" She'd wanted to say *gardening*, but the word had stuck in her throat the way her screams had that day against the crumbling back wall of the Barrow where the onions grew like weeds. She was suffocating, a too-great weight pinning her down.

"Except?" Briar's voice roused Cordi from her thoughts, eyes focusing once more on Briar, staring, a little frown between her drawn brows.

Cordi forced the word out. "Gardening."

Briar's reaction was immediate delight. "Why, that's wonderful! Mother is a botanist without equal, you know? She taught Prim and me, though Prim is much more skilled. How marvelous that you have come to us! That there will be another set of hands encouraging the garden to flourish! I can show you all my favorite flowers and plants and—"

She stopped abruptly, pulling her hands to her chest before hastily taking several steps back. It was only then that Cordi realized Briar had been approaching her steadily and had gotten quite close. "And?" Cordi pressed, unsure what had cut her off so suddenly.

Briar gave a trill of nervous laughter. "I'm sorry. I just get overly excited. Prim finds me silly sometimes." She twisted her fingers in front of her dress and bit her lip with small, white teeth. "Mother would prefer I was more like my sister. Not prone to fancy, but strong and fearless. Devoted to study rather than dreaming. I lack discipline. I prattle on when I should be quiet. But I don't like the quiet. It feels lonely."

Cordi's heart ached for this charming girl, barely a woman, just like herself, with beauty and wealth and title, who seemed to suffer for it. Who also felt the pang of loneliness. Why were the girls sequestered so? Because of their mother's disdain for men? Surely it couldn't be so awful as that.

A slow roll in her belly reminded her that it could. A remembered scent of spoiling onions and foul drink. *Not now,* she insisted, wanting to tear out the roots of those memories but knowing she might only hope to smother them in darkness. She forced a slow breath in and out through her nose, the inside of the mask hot as her breath hit the fabric, and tried to lighten her voice. "I don't think you should feel silly. I think it is wonderful to find such joy in life as you. Few do. Prim is obviously capable and fierce, but who is to say you are not simply because you show delight rather than control? I see nothing wrong with exuberance and I am certainly not one to lecture anyone on discipline. It is a skill I have been told my entire life I lack."

Briar smiled at that, a shy smile this time, slow to appear, like the sun rising over the horizon. Cordi knew she would see that smile when she closed her eyes for some time.

She wanted to draw nearer to the warmth of that smile, to the warmth of the girl it originated from. Cordi had been so cold for so long, the fire inside her reduced to mere sparks, her faith and hope nearly reduced to ashes. Meeting Briar was like feeding that dying flame oxygen.

From where she stood, Cordi saw Briar's throat work as she swallowed, her chest rising as she took in a shuddering breath. She was watching Cordi, that smile slipping into something else. Could . . . ?

"Are we going?"

Both Cordi and Briar quickly turned to the doorway where Prim was standing, a linen bag speckled with paint and smudged with charcoal in one hand, her other hand fisted at the waist of her dress. She looked back and forth between the two women, jaw set, eyes searching.

Whatever spell had been cast was broken.

"Yes!" Briar squeaked, voice pitching almost nervously.

As they made their way down a hall toward the back of the house, Cordi noticed cobwebs. She found the same neglect in the salon they entered facing the back of the house. The air hung heavy, like stale mist. The dust had settled here too, and tiny clouds wafted from the rugs as they passed through. How long had their maids been ill?

As if reading her mind, Prim cleared her throat, whether from dust or to draw attention, Cordi wasn't sure. "Forgive the lack of housekeeping. Obviously, not all the rooms are suitable for receiving guests."

"Oh, you needn't worry about me!" Cordi assured her. "But if you like, I could put in a request with Miss Eliot and see if she would permit me to tidy if you are wanting the room."

Prim thought it over, her dark hair flowing over one shoulder as she regarded the space. "Yes. That would be splendid. It gets so close in here without adequate airing. And one can hardly expect Briar and me to attend to the cleaning with our obligation to the garden as well." She hummed, making for the door leading out onto the lawn. "I've told Mother she should look to hire more staff, but so few outsiders come to Farrow. And even fewer to Edenfield. What brought you here from the city, Cordi?"

And there it was. The first confrontation that would necessitate a reason for choosing Farrow as a destination. Lady Evangeline and Miss Eliot had seen her as another lost lamb and not questioned further, and she had stupidly imagined herself safe.

"I suppose," she began, "the same thing that brought the others."

Reaching the door, Prim turned, barring their exit, and looked at Cordi with knowledge beyond her years. Not with suspicion, but curiosity perhaps. Someone like Cordi who saw things others didn't. "I mean, what is it that brought you to Farrow?"

Cordi wrestled with the guilt of adding yet another lie. "I ran away. I got on a postal coach and went as far as I could on what little money I had." Not exactly a lie. "I didn't even know Edenfield was here when I stepped off the coach. It was a blessing, really, finding this place. With no money, no references, no—" She would not allow herself to say *family*.

"Oh, you poor dear." Briar reached a hand out toward Cordi's gloved wrist but pulled back before she could touch her as if afraid whatever sorrows Cordi carried were somehow contagious. A chasm yawned in Cordi's chest at that rejection, no matter how little it *should* have mattered.

"It's all right." Drawing her shoulders back, Cordi met Prim's unforgiving stare head-on. "I did what I had to do. I'm not sorry for running. I'm not sorry for anything I did if it meant surviving." *If it means finding Edward,* she added silently.

She couldn't fault Prim for questioning her. Not after seeing how protective she was of her sister. This was someone who would do anything for the one she loved, and Cordi found that admirable. It was something they shared.

Prim's mouth quirked, lips puckering. "You're not like the others, are you?"

"What do you mean?"

"All our broken and bruised and suffering ladies. Victimized by the world outside. You don't strike me as a victim, Cordi." She clicked her tongue and caught it between her teeth. "I don't believe you, you know."

Cordi felt the floor drop out from under her.

"*Prim!*" Briar hissed, reprimand evident in her voice.

"Don't misunderstand," Prim continued. "I mean no offense. I just don't believe you ran away. Oh, you might have run, but not at first. You fought and you fought hard. I see it in you, that strength, that fight. Whatever happened to you didn't break you."

In a way, it was a blessing in disguise. Because this didn't require a lie Cordi was reluctant to give.

"I can't speak for the others," she said, voice quiet and even. "I don't know what they suffered. I don't know what *you* suffer. Your sister. Your mother. I only know what *I* suffered. But you're right. I won't give them any more than what they already took."

The smile never left Prim's face, but there was a darkening to her look as her eyes dimmed. "What I suffer," she repeated quietly. "I think I will like you, Cordi. I didn't expect that." Then she turned and opened the door into the garden.

Chapter 16

AS THE TRIO STEPPED OUT into the light, Prim and Briar tilted their faces up to the sky in unison, eyes shut, the tiny veins behind their thin eyelids visible as they basked in the sun's glow. Cordi did the same, sighing happily, invigorated most heartily after moving from such a stale room into spring.

"You may take your mask off," Prim said. "You have no need of it out here. But best your gloves remain."

Cordi reached up and tugged the loops from her ears, drawing a deep breath of country air into her lungs as she gazed upon Edenfield's gardens, no glass between her and their magnificence. The wind moved the tall, slender stalks of the newly green grass like ripples along a still lake. Everywhere were pockets of shoots ready to explode into color, some already beginning to peek open, teasing her eyes with flashes of red, purple, pink, and yellow. The air was fragrant and both familiar and strange. Honeysuckle she knew, but another delicate scent struck her, and her feet moved to the edge of the patio and the steps that led down to the stone walk. Along the small wall, running in both directions, were bushes of lovely green leaves growing in clusters, and she could see strange shoots, eager to flower.

"What is this plant?" she asked.

Briar came forward, looking at Cordi's face rather than the plant.

"Lantana. Mother fought for years to get it to grow. It blossoms with the most gorgeous domes of tiny flowers—each like a star—in a beautiful array of colors. Orange and pink and yellow. A sunset you can hold in your hand."

"Beautiful," Cordi repeated, looking back at Briar. This time, neither of them looked away.

"Let's give Cordi the grand tour, shall we?" Prim asked, moving forward to loop her arm through Briar's. "We can find the perfect light for a quick sketch or two."

Briar hummed, turning to grin at her sister, and the two descended the steps leading into the hedge maze. Two life-size statues of elegant white marble shot through with gray veins flanked the entrance, matched by two others just within the maze. Cordi stopped to admire one on the inside, her face angled down to the earth, one hand touching her heart, the other holding a plump fruit. The sculptor had rendered her form to such perfection that she looked to be a living, breathing woman painted white, clad in a gauzy gown that clung to an hourglass figure, her wide hips and full breasts, nipples peaked against the sculpted fabric. She was lovely, her face kind and wistful.

"Persephone," Briar remarked. "Goddess of spring. Her mother—Demeter—is on the outer side of the maze."

Cordi looked across at the other inner statue, again of Persephone. This one had her veiled, her face shrouded, her expression sad. Cordi supposed she would feel much the same if she were trapped in marble. Or trapped at all.

A prickling on the back of her neck made her glance around. The girls were just ahead, their backs turned and heads close together. Cordi turned her head to look up at the house and saw the dark outline of a figure staring down from one of the upper windows. Even at this distance, Cordi could make out the sharp, distinguished features of Lady Evangeline. She gazed down, face impassive. She might have been looking out upon her garden, so beloved, or been drawn to glance out at her daughters by some stirring of maternal affection. But Cordi could not shake the feeling that the Lady's eyes were trained on her and her alone through the window, as if Cordi might be one of the specimens she kept under glass in her cabinet.

She thought of the two Demeters, standing guard before the labyrinth, hiding their twin daughters, and could not help but draw a comparison between the two Persephones and the two sisters with their mother's shadow looming in the house. Nervously, she slipped into the maze and behind the hedge, hurrying to catch up with the sisters.

"We used to spend hours in the maze when we were little," Briar said over her shoulder, delicate shoes kicking at the stones of the path as they began to walk. "Playing a sort of hide-and-seek, though we were usually giggling or running so loud, so it was more like a game of tag."

The walls were tall and thick, twisted ivy and brambles. Several walls had small "windows" cut into them so you could peer through and look down another path. It was some moments before Cordi realized she had not been paying any attention and would certainly be lost if she weren't being led.

"We still play occasionally," Prim admitted. "You probably think us silly, pampered children."

"Pampered, yes," Cordi admitted, seeing no reason to deny the logic. "Not silly. And certainly not children."

A sniff. "Mother would disagree."

"Then I am happy to tell you so."

"You say what you are thinking, don't you, Cordi?" Briar asked, glancing back. "I have always been told it is one of my less endearing qualities, saying whatever errant thought that crosses my mind."

"Not to me."

There was no hiding her blush this time, Cordi knew, but a matching color was in Briar's cheeks.

"Nor me," Prim added as they came to the end of the maze, and Cordi had to catch her breath in wonder.

The path continued on, open on either side and bordered by seemingly endless garden beds full of tall, proud stalks or low, spreading ground cover or shaggy ferns, their fronds waving as if in greeting. Ivy crept up elaborate archways and trellises. Moss and lichen covered eerily beautiful statues—weathered and worn—as they stood in fantastic pools of water. Everywhere Cordi looked, buds were taking shape and trees were beginning to blossom in pink and white, tiny petals falling like snow when the wind gusted. Near enough to them stood a small building, framed in wood stained black, its walls and ceiling made of glass. The glass was not like anything Cordi had seen before—not clear, exactly, casting everything within into gray shadows. The door was a deep green and mottled. She couldn't quite make out the pattern from the distance.

"That's Mother's greenhouse," Briar said proudly. "She had it specially commissioned."

"Did she?" Cordi asked, eyes raking over the wooden structure. Was this the project Edward had been on the grounds for?

"Mm-hmm. She's very proud of it. She cultivates her—"

Prim cleared her throat.

Cordi turned just in time to see a look pass between the sisters before Briar recovered with a brittle smile. "—her favorite plants there. Some of them are quite rare!"

Rare meant expensive. So, the Lady of Edenfield had ordered a special greenhouse built to hold them. She would have required the hands of a master craftsman and his apprentice for such a project, surely. "Might I see?" Cordi asked, taking a step onto the paving stones marking the way to the door.

"No."

Prim's voice was clipped and tight, the tendons at her neck rigid. Her eyes flicked over the roof and a tic pulled at her eyelid, nose wrinkling in obvious displeasure.

Briar shrank back, trying to make herself small even as she tried to lighten the mood with a laugh. But it was too nervous. Too wary. "Forgive us, but no. Mother would not approve. And besides, the door is locked."

If the plants held within were so rare, it only made sense to guard them, of course. But Prim's reaction and Briar's anxiety at Cordi's not-so-innocent question made her wonder what other secrets the greenhouse might be protecting. Prim was already striding away, Briar hurrying to catch up. Red-gold curls bowed toward black tresses and, though she was too far away, Cordi knew the sisters were speaking quietly.

The wind blew gently across the back of Cordi's exposed neck, bending the stalks of the flowers and grasses, sending ripples across the greenery like a stone dropped in water. She cast a last look at the black-and-glass structure, willing it to speak to her, but it remained silent.

But its very existence told her enough. She was getting closer.

Spirits lifted, she ran after the sisters, wincing as the gravel bit through the soft soles of her pretty shoes. By the time she reached the duo, Prim was no longer sneering, and Briar no longer looked so contrite. Cordi panted, strangely out of breath for such a short sprint. Perhaps country air took some getting used to.

"I can hardly imagine the royal gardens being finer than those of Edenfield!"

"Do you play chess, Cordi?"

"Hmm?" Cordi looked about to see Prim pulling a box from her bag and placing it upon a small iron table between two chairs. Prim sat in one of the chairs and flipped the clasp atop the box, from which she extracted a checkered board. With her free hand, she gestured for Cordi to join her at the table.

Taking the seat opposite, Cordi watched Prim set up her side of the board with the carved black figures. Cordi was to be white, then. She lifted a piece from the box, surprised at its weight. Not wood, but something like wood. Ivory, perhaps? She turned the piece in her fingers. "I've never played. You'll have to teach me."

Prim made an amused sound in the back of her throat. "Perhaps I will win for once. Briar is far too good at this game. I don't even like to play her anymore."

Briar ducked her head with a frown. "That's because it is the only thing I can actually beat you at!"

"Oh, don't be so silly," Prim teased.

Her sister's mouth gaped, and she began ticking things off on her fingers. "Art, astronomy, cricket, botany, maths, history, music . . . You're better at all of them than I am. Chess is one thing I'm good at."

"Embroidery, dear. You've the loveliest embroidery," Prim insisted with an eye roll. "And you could be perfect at everything you just listed if you only applied yourself a bit more. You've an impeccable ear for languages, for instance!"

"For all the good it does when there is no one to speak to. You will not even bother conversing in the Romance languages."

It was Prim's turn to wrinkle her nose. "They all sound the same to me." She offered a teasing smile to her sister. "Do not sulk, dear sister. Mother finds enough faults in me as well."

Cordi smiled, watching them bicker about their little differences, thinking of how she and Edward were much the same.

Edward.

Guilt twisted in her belly like a sour breakfast. Here she was, making friends, earning a fine wage, wearing lovely clothing, and *enjoying* herself while she still had no idea where he might be. Was that what had happened to

Edward? Had he come here, found something—someone—precious and forgotten her? Maybe he wasn't there after all. Maybe his heart had room only for a lover, not a sister. Maybe—

"Are you all right, Cordi?" Briar asked, head tilting so her long curls caught the light, turning individual strands to gold. "You look quite dour all of a sudden."

Cordi hurried to think of something to say. "I don't mean to. It's just . . . you two have each other and maybe I'm feeling a bit envious. I am sorry. Now *I'm* being silly."

Briar pouted and tutted gently. "Not at all! We understand, don't we, Prim? I dare not consider a life where we were parted!" Prim said nothing, only looked longingly into the trees beyond the garden, perhaps pondering that very thing. "You're here now, though! And we can be like family!"

The enthusiasm of this beautiful girl and the sincere desperation in her eyes to make Cordi feel welcome was almost too much to bear. Tears threatened, hot things she had always loathed lest they make others think her weak. She believed her. She *felt* Briar's need for Cordi to be happy with them, and she was touched beyond measure. Not just because she found Briar so alluring and the sisters both intriguing, but because she hadn't imagined how wonderful it could be to feel wanted. To feel cared about.

It had been so long since she had felt wanted. Edward's letters could offer only so much hope, especially when read in the gloom and melancholy of the Barrow. She had read each letter with pride, knowing she would be free to join him eventually. But she couldn't deny the worm of jealousy that had burrowed a tunnel through her heart, feeding it poison. Edward talked of sunshine and laughing children and butter while she suffered the cold and sneers and the birch. When his letters had stopped entirely, she had been left with a heart already begun to rot.

Prim turned back to them, her face once again impassive, all trace of melancholy gone. "Chess," she reminded her. "A game not so much of pieces on a board, but of learning your opponent and how they think. You want to be one, two, three steps ahead at all times. You want to anticipate their moves in order to steer them in the direction of your choosing. Chess is a game of manipulating the outcome in your favor." She lifted one of the smaller pieces with a domed head and held it up to the light. "Some people underestimate pawns. So often they are the first sacrificed, but they can win you the game as well as a queen."

Something about the way she said it put Cordi in mind of a snake coiled to strike. And she wondered if they were really talking about the game.

Prim went on, explaining each piece and how it moved. How the point of chess was to corner the king so he could not escape. After a bit, they began their game. Cordi tried to remember everything Prim had said and watched her closely, trying to decipher where she might move, and which tokens she favored. But she became so wrapped up in what Prim was doing, she realized too late she had forgotten to cover her own tracks.

"Oh dear," Prim said, swooping in with her knight. "I'm afraid you've lost your queen. And that would be checkmate." Prim dangled the white queen from her fingers in triumph as she tipped Cordi's king to the side, where it rolled back and forth, defeated.

Without intending to, Cordi glanced at Briar, her face again tilted to the sun as if she were a flower herself. Sitting like that, among the flowers in the garden, she put Cordi in mind again of the old nursery rhyme. *With silver bells and cockleshells and pretty maids all in a row.*

There was the snap of a lid and Cordi jumped. Prim had swept the pieces off the board and into the box, shoving the game back into her bag. "Are we ready?" she said, her tone even and almost too casual. Briar stretched like a cat, gracefully flowing to her feet to take her sister's arm. Cordi laid her hand against the back of her own neck, willing the heat away.

Beckoning her on, the sisters led Cordi deeper into the marvelous gardens, pointing out each plant with alarming precision. They seemed to know everything! The name of each plant, where it originated, its "genus and species" . . . This last Cordi had no knowledge of, but Prim and Briar explained things so patiently and with such fervor (even Prim!) that she didn't feel foolish asking questions.

Near the edge of the garden, Prim bade her sit along the path, framed by long green and pink stalks of something the girls called cordyline. Briar found it delightful that all three of them had names inspired by plants, and even Prim's lips twitched as she instructed Cordi to tilt her head this way and that, focusing her gaze, while Briar babbled on about how divinely inspired their meeting was.

Beyond the cordyline stood tall shoots adorned with the familiar, trumpetlike flowers of the foxglove, their amethyst coloring almost identical to the eyes of each sister. From the corner of her eye, she saw Briar lean down with a small pair of shears in her naked hand, cutting a few of the poisonous plants, humming softly.

"You mustn't!" Cordi said, throwing a hand out in alarm. "Isn't that foxglove?"

Briar's brows dipped together, and she smiled at Cordi in confusion. "Yes. Whatever is the matter?"

"But," Cordi began, thinking of the coach driver's words, "isn't it a poison?"

"Oh," Briar said with a little laugh. "Well, yes, but don't worry. I've no intention of eating it. But it is good of you to be concerned for me."

The jeweled bouquet in Briar's hands looked so harmless. So beautiful and perfect and not at all something to fear. And the sisters knew so much more than she did about plants.

"The pink and green are striking with your hair and eyes in that dress," Prim said, sketching on a large pad of paper with sure, quick strokes. If she had been listening at all to the exchange, she gave no indication of it. "I hope I mix the proper colors later."

"You always do," Briar insisted, taking a seat nearby. She laid the freshly cut flowers in a basket and began weaving a crown of daisies.

"You'll remind me, won't you, dear?" Prim said absently, her charcoal sweeping down the page. "Of exactly what I require to capture our new friend?"

Briar lifted her eyes to Cordi, and they held. Cordi watched Briar's throat flex, the heave of her chest as she took a rallying breath, and the hooded look that came over her eyes. Cordi held her own breath.

"Yes. I'll remember."

Chapter 17

THE SMELL WAFTING FROM THE kitchen was enough to make Cordi's mouth water and put a bit more spring in her step. After her morning with Briar and Prim, she'd again felt peculiar, as if her head were spinning or the floors were uneven. Her stomach, too, was angry and cramping, though it was not her monthly. The tea Miss Eliot had brought her helped again, settling her stomach and clearing her mind, though Cordi wasn't sure she would ever get used to whatever bitter root or leaves were used in its making. But she'd been well enough to see to her evening chores. Still, the smell of the dinner waiting for her made her realize she was famished.

"Good evening!" she called, stepping into the tidy, fragrant kitchen.

The women already seated around the table paused their conversation and looked up at her as one, their voices stopping so abruptly, Cordi knew she had been the topic of talk. Her step faltered and she felt suddenly out of place. Was this it, then? The rejection she had already begun to fear?

But Stella patted the chair next to her. "Come sit down, Cordi. You must be tired and hungry." Her voice was quiet but kind, and Cordi wanted to embrace her as a sister. Let them all gossip if they would. She was obeying orders. And she had not come to make friends, she told herself, even if it stung. Even if she thought she might have found them. She had come to find her brother.

With renewed purpose and with all the grace she could muster, she sat, folded her hands in her lap, and opened her mouth to inquire about everyone's day, when she saw a new face, opposite Miss Eliot's seat. The woman was young, yet she looked haggard and ancient, staring at Cordi with dull eyes, the whites mapped and marred with broken blood vessels. Her light-brown skin was yellowed with jaundice. Her cheekbones were sharp and pronounced, her eyes sunken and shadowed by dark, purple crescents underneath. She held one hand up to the white collar of her own livery hanging about her like a shroud, and Cordi was startled to see her nailbeds blackened as if with some disease.

Cordi forced herself not to gawk and instead inclined her head in greeting.

The woman only stared, nostrils flaring as if scenting the air before she grimaced and turned away, fingers moving to scratch beneath her cap before she remembered herself and let them fall, fluttering down to her lap.

"Ah," Miss Eliot said, bustling into the room with her clipped step. "I'm sure you're all famished, so we will say our blessing and I will go over the itinerary for tomorrow while we eat, since you all need rest." She gave the girl at the end of the table a severe look before taking her seat.

Miss Eliot led them in the same prayer Cordi had now learned by heart. *Thanks given to the Garden, for the Garden is right and good.* For a few beats after there was silence, save for the clacking of dishes and utensils as bowls were passed and plates were filled.

"Now then," Miss Eliot sighed after everyone had been served. "Cordi, it is only proper you be introduced to Jane. She has been indisposed for some time now, but we are grateful to have her with us this evening."

Jane only stared at her plate, face closed and hearing nothing.

Miss Eliot continued as if this were enough of an introduction. "As you all know—save you, Cordi, and I request your respectful silence, as this matter does not yet concern you—Irene has been called to the Garden as we all hope to be one day."

She is called to the Garden in her time.

Heads bowed and lips moved, whispering tiny prayers around her as Cordi recalled the conversation overheard the night before. Lady Evangeline's voice and the hacking cough from the sickroom. Cordi observed Jane through the bars of her lashes, seeing her tense. Horrified, Cordi watched her bite down hard on her lip and saw blood, dark and oily in the low light, trickle down the corner of her mouth. She wiped it away with the back of her hand, smearing it across her mouth like paint. She spoke not a word, her throat working silently. Whatever pain or grief she felt, she swallowed with the blood.

"Though Irene will be missed at this table, she is not gone from us. The ceremony will be held tomorrow at Lady Evangeline's request. Cordi, as you are still on trial, you will be excluded from the . . . service. You will attend to your duties in the house."

Alone? Excitement flared in her chest. "Yes, Miss Eliot," she said, hoping she didn't sound too eager. As curious as she was to know exactly what kind of ceremony she was being excluded from, it was more important for her to look for confirmation that Edward had been at the house. Besides, it was probably only a funeral. She had attended enough of those at the Barrow, standing beside too-small graves, furious at the dispassionate words spoken over the tiny, moldy wood coffins by staff who were probably grateful there was one less mouth to feed. Though she doubted such was the case here. These women seemed to care for each other. Recalling Briar's own concern over the two servants, Cordi knew she would certainly be weeping at the graveside.

There was quiet for a moment and Cordi perked up, afraid her errant thoughts had caused her to miss something important. But Miss Eliot tapped her fingers on the table, obviously weighing her next words. "I realize the workload has been especially difficult of late, which is why so many rooms are being ignored. Thankfully, the true work has not been interrupted and the Garden is cared for. As grateful as we are, I have broached the topic with

Lady Evangeline of inquiring for temporary or even permanent help. She is taking the matter under consideration." She spread her hands. "Well . . . we do as we must for now." She cleared her throat and motioned to the table. "I realize I've talked too long without giving you permission to begin. See to your dinners, ladies. That is all."

At first, nobody moved, but eventually there were tentative grips on napkins and the soft tearing of bread. The scrape of a knife and then quiet chewing. Moira looked relieved and Cordi made a mental note to tell her again how wonderful her food was. She would tell her after dinner and offer to do extra washing so that Moira might not. She needed the others to know she would not forget her place among them or risk losing any little confidences. Sarah ate quickly, as usual, so she might rush away and clear Lady Evangeline's and—Cordi guessed—the girls' trays. They might leave them in the little corridor. Faustine was trying her best not to stare at Jane, for once as quiet as Stella.

Jane remained frozen, staring past her dish and through the table, through the floor. Cordi reached for her own fork and began to eat, more edible flowers with thick gravy over some kind of chicken dish. Yet she could hardly focus on what was on her plate, her head filled with the knowledge that tomorrow she would be alone in the house and have her first real opportunity to search.

She wasn't even aware of the onion until she bit down and the pungent vegetable crunched between her teeth.

Cordi shoved back away from the table, holding a hand over her mouth as she began to retch and sweat, fighting the urgent need to expel the onion. She was distantly aware of the others talking, someone speaking to her, but the room felt too close, too hot, and the food was poison on her tongue. She fled, hurtling away and out the back door, running up the darkened steps and to the corner of the house, where she was violently sick into the pristine grass.

She sank to her knees, all the contents of her belly being purged, and with it came the tears, finally, scorching a burning trail down her cheeks, lashing them till all she felt was the fire. She wrapped her arms around herself and squeezed, trying to stop their flow, to still the shaking.

"Cordi?"

Stella. Her gentle voice was at odds with the turbulent storm of Cordi's thoughts. She could hear her teeth rattling, even as she tried to spit the last bit of bile.

"Here."

A cup of water appeared over her shoulder, and she took it, greedily pulling cool water into her mouth and spitting again, rinsing the sick and offending onion from her palate.

"Are you all right?"

Cordi's first instinct was to nod, but instead she shook her head and sniffed, hard, the tears coming anew. "I hate onions. I can't—" Another sniff. "He—"

And she was back at the Barrow, working in the garden. Mason had her helping him tow away the grass clippings. He'd already bundled them up into their burlap sacks, but he wanted her help in dumping them, he'd said. Back behind the garden wall where they threw the rotted or frostbitten vegetables and weeds. His back was sore that day, he complained, and he'd stooped more like an old man than ever before. Making himself smaller. She'd remembered that later. Something he'd used to trick her, to make her feel sorry for him, to make her want to help.

So she'd agreed, hauling two of the heavy bags in her arms, grown strong from the months of laboring in the garden, Mason paying her small wage. She'd made herself indispensable to him *and* Mrs. Clark, she'd thought proudly. And with Edward's letters having gone quiet, she needed the money more than ever to go find him.

She'd dropped the bundles amid the refuse and leaned down to open the first sack to dump its contents when he'd grabbed her from behind, taking her to the ground so quickly she thought he had fallen. But then she'd felt his hand on her ankle above her boot, trying to pull up her dress, and her mouth had opened to scream. He'd shoved his hand over it, the filthy fibers of his rough gloves pressing against her lips and scratchy against her tongue. She tasted dirt.

Now, you and I both know what you're about. Bendin' over when you know I'm lookin' and takin' my coin for the service. He had grunted, trying to force her legs apart with his knee. *So be good now or I'll be tellin' Mrs. Clark what a little whore you've tried to play.*

And for a split second, she'd wondered if it had been her fault. If she had made him think—but, no, she had not. Had never. And he knew it; it was a lie! A lie just like all of them lied. Nobody cared for her. Nobody cared for any of them. They took and hurt and he was just another one. And she'd fought harder as he finally got a hand up her skirt and pawed at her thighs. She'd bucked and kicked but hadn't been able to dislodge him.

Finally, she'd quieted. Stilling. Thinking. Drawing harsh breaths in through her nose, the smell of molding, spoiled onions strong. He'd taken her down in the rubbish pile and all around her was the smell of rot and him: foul breath and filth.

Patience, she'd told herself.

And she'd not moved as he removed one of his gloves, touched her thighs and fondled her backside with his callused hand, rough, torn skin scraping over smooth. Not moved as he'd pushed up her skirt and reached for his own belt. But as he'd cooed at her, lifting just enough of his weight off her and loosening his grip, lulled by her compliance, she'd gritted her teeth and slammed her head back into his face, hearing the crunch of bone and feeling her scalp light on fire.

He'd fallen off her and she'd run. Run for her life. She'd made it inside and run straight for the washroom, shaking like an unwanted kitten tossed into the snow. She'd peeled off her filthy apron and smock and bathed herself in freezing water, scratching at her skin—at everywhere he had touched her—till she nearly bled. She'd tried telling herself he'd not gotten what he was after, but any relief she might have managed at her escape was totally eclipsed by fear and cold fury.

And if she had thought the horrors were over, she had been mistaken.

Mr. Mason, wanting to preempt any attempt she might have made to report him, had gone straight to Mrs. Clark. He'd labeled her a thief and a whore, claiming she had robbed him and when he had caught her, she'd tried to seduce him. Apparently, Mrs. Clark was not concerned with Mason's broken nose or chipped tooth, or the bleeding at the *back* of Cordi's skull where, if one felt around, one might have detected a puncture wound very much like what a tooth would leave.

No matter her protests. No matter her own accusations. No matter the tears finally dragged from her by the *crack* of the birch rod against her skin—her hands, her back—Mrs. Clark would believe none of it. Only struck more, harder, demanding Cordi admit her faults and tell her where Mr. Mason's money was hidden. Only after the wicked strip of wood began to spray blood on the backswing and Cordi's knees had buckled did Cordi realize what her headmistress was about. She hated Cordi, true enough. But she hated them all. It was that the woman believed her. Knew she had told the truth about receiving payment for helping with the gardening, and Mrs. Clark wanted the money. What little there was of it.

After Cordi's wounds had been treated—with little attention and even less compassion—she had forced Cordi to lie on her stomach in the infirmary with all the girls of the Barrow brought in as a procession. Cordi was made an example for those with lofty ideas. *See what whoring does to you. See what thieving does to you.*

It had taken days for the wounds to scab over and not break open with every movement she made. Longer still for them to heal enough for hard scar tissue to form. But as soon as they had, as soon as she had seen her chance, Cordi had run. She had taken her precious savings, her beloved fox, and the money stolen from Mrs. Clark's room. And she had not looked back. As she left, she had considered burning Mason's shack around him. Considered letting him die screaming and writhing as flames licked at him as they most certainly would in Hell when he got there.

Absently, she lifted a hand to the scar on the back of her head, hidden beneath her hair, where a tooth had dug in and broken. Mason had ultimately taken nothing but her own ignorant delusions of safety, but she had paid for the lesson in flesh and blood and tears. And she still couldn't stomach onions.

Stella was kneeling next to her, her hands fisted in the skirt of her dress. Slowly she laid a hand atop Cordi's where it rested on her knee. The young woman looked at her with her one good eye, the other eyelid drooping, its long lashes kissing her cheek. "I hate the sound of a cart."

Cordi blinked stupidly, sniffing hard.

Stella licked her lips, her eye wet, but no tears fell. "If I hear the sound of a cart—the creak of wheels on stone?—I think he's come home. Even though I know it is impossible. And it will start all over again. The fists and curses. Blows I can't dodge." She took a deep, steadying breath and looked out toward the back of the house and the garden beyond, into the growing dark. "He took my pride, my eye, and would have taken my life if I had not found the courage to run. I know I am safe now, but I forget sometimes. We all do."

What was it Prim had said about all the servants? They were all broken somehow. Suffering and victimized. She had praised Cordi for her strength. Yet, sitting in the grass with Stella, only yards away from where she had thrown up her dinner, Cordi didn't feel strong, and she suddenly resented

Prim for her comments. What did Prim know of the kind of hurt they had suffered? What did she know of real-world pain? How could she look down upon them—any of them—for the cracks in their hearts or the scars on their bodies? They were weeds, growing in defiance, but still growing, still determined to cling to life no matter the odds.

"We follow the rules and we are rewarded," Stella continued. "We do what we are told and here, at least, we are rewarded. We reap what we sow in the Garden." Without warning, she tugged, cradling Cordi's head on her shoulder, causing a surge of new tears.

But Cordi allowed them and wasn't ashamed as Stella stroked her short hair as she did to her own braid at night, comforting Cordi the way she comforted herself. Cordi held tight, latching on to Stella's smaller frame as she cried and let herself be held when she had not known reassurance in so long. She missed Edward even while she hated how he had left her with people who could so hurt her. Still, she wanted her brother, but this kind girl—someone who understood—would do for the moment.

Chapter 18

OUT OF RESPECT FOR WHAT was obviously a solemn occasion, Cordi kept her head bowed as the other servants filed out after breakfast the next morning. Miss Eliot gave Cordi strict instructions to tend to Lady Evangeline's private salon and to air out the laundry by the back door to the kitchen. She was ordered to—under *no* circumstances—touch the Lady's plants beyond shifting the pots to dust or polish.

The salon was next door to the study, and Cordi could hardly believe her luck. "Ma'am, I forgot to mention last night that Miss Primrose and Miss Briar would like me to tidy and air their back salon as well."

Miss Eliot studied her reflection in one of the large saucepans Moira kept so pristine and adjusted the hat she had pinned onto her head. "Very well, but wait till we come in from the service. I'm sure I will need to take a peek first. I imagine the curtains will need taking down to be pressed too." She sighed heavily. "Always so much to do. This is most inconvenient, but we are at the mercy and grace of the Ladies."

Cordi nodded as if she understood, but she certainly didn't. She'd puzzled over the rules and rituals: the prayers, the gloves, the scrubbing, the locked wing. If the girls had a poor constitution, it would make sense, but they were so healthy and radiant! She considered that their mother might just be paranoid. A woman concerned not only about losing her precious daughters to society or marriage, but about losing them to illness. She must worry about them terribly.

And there *was* illness at Edenfield. She'd seen that herself. Heard the horrible hacking sounds from Jane and Irene's room. Irene had succumbed, but Jane looked like she had only narrowly avoided such a fate. Lady Evangeline might have reason for her concern, for as generous as she was to her staff, she was a mother and a mother would surely put the safety of her children at the forefront.

Edward had been ill after working there. That's what Alice had said. But he had gotten better.

And he had come back.

But not for you, the dark, wounded part of her mocked before she could steel herself against it. There was no time for petty jealousies. She needed to take advantage of the house being empty. Soon she was alone and began gathering cleaning supplies as fast as she could, hoping to have as much time as possible to snoop before she tackled the salon. The ledgers had to contain something. A house so orderly and strict could only be kept so if the mistress was the same.

Buckets filled to the brim with supplies banged against Cordi's knees as she all but ran down the halls and up darkened stairs. She was out of breath by the time she reached the salon and opened the door, unceremoniously depositing everything at the edge of one of the beautiful rugs with a *clang*. Quickly she went to the windows and opened them, letting the air circulate in the space, and leaned out, looking every which way in hopes of catching a glimpse of where they might be holding the funeral, ultimately seeing nothing. She hadn't seen a graveyard yesterday during her tour of the garden. She supposed it made the most sense to keep a family plot in a more secluded space out of respect for the dead.

Satisfied, Cordi moved quickly from the room and to the study, holding her breath at the door and hesitating. To cross the threshold was to absolutely and without question break faith with the kindness she had received, and she was loath to do so. But then she thought again of the quiet whispers, the cryptic comments and furtive glances, and the blatant lies of the Starlings. No. She would not be given information. She was on her own. If she wanted to find him, she had to be ruthless.

"Ignorance never kept a woman safe," she reminded herself, feeling quite sure she was learning such lessons the hard way.

There was nothing but the faintest creak of the hinges as the door opened. The curtains were still drawn, shadows lingering in every corner, turning the jars and specimens behind glass to ominous shapes, and Cordi swallowed. Her shoes were pristine, but still she toed them off, choosing to investigate in her stocking feet. If she needed to rush from the room, she wouldn't want the sturdy soles of her new shoes to give her away. She went straight for the beautiful secretary desk, its lid dropped down, and tugged at the handle.

Locked.

"No!" she barked, the sound shattering the quiet. She tried again, shaking it gently, hoping it was just stuck, but it was locked tight. Her fingers drifted over the small keyhole as she let loose a string of hushed curses. Her one chance. This was her *one* chance. And she was being thwarted by an accursed lock!

She slammed her hand against the lid, the sound and sting in her palm both satisfying. Fine—if the desk refused to give up its secrets, she might still find something. Certainly all the house ledgers couldn't be held within. Maybe they were cataloged! She hurried to the shelves, fingers sliding over folios, looking for books large enough and heavy enough for the house accounts. She found some, but their tops were coated with fine dust and the closing dates were before Edward had left the Barrow. No. The newer ledgers *had* to be in the desk.

Drawing her tongue between her teeth, Cordi returned to the desk. Kneeling, she looked beneath, feeling along the underside, hoping to find a spare key, but the wood was smooth. She went from plant to plant, checking each pot while doing her best to disturb the dirt as little as possible, wary of leaving any trace. As each minute ticked by, she grew more and more discouraged. A locked wing. A locked greenhouse. A locked desk. Secrets buried or hidden away. Edward was among those secrets somehow. Her brother might be counting on her to solve this mystery and she was failing.

Failing him as he'd failed her.

I'll come back.

Cordi dropped to the floor in a heap, a child again wanting to throw a tantrum, angry at the lock, angry at Edward. She was angry and tired of being thwarted at every turn. Her eyes narrowed on the keyhole in fury, the dark eye mocking her. She couldn't try to pick the lock. She had no idea how such things were done, and she couldn't risk breaking it. Maybe she could go back to the Starlings, confront Mr. Starling and tell him she knew he was lying because Alice had—

Except she didn't have the heart to get the little girl in trouble. Not when she had been the only one honest with Cordi.

Cordi's head dropped back as she took in the room around her. A room filled with words. Whole worlds bound inside leather and packed on shelves. The mistress of the house had forsaken the real world after her husband passed for those on the page and the garden she had grown. Locked herself away as she had her daughters. Content.

Could that be enough? She thought of Stella and thought perhaps it could. But then she thought of Prim's quiet bitterness and wondered. For herself, Cordi knew she needed more. Fine things and grand houses were well and good, but what did it matter if you weren't free? A cage was a cage, no matter how gilded.

She stood, resigned, and brushed off her skirts, her eyes falling on the mantel over the fireplace, cold, its ashes swept clean. Plants and flowers crowded the space but were flanked by two ornate busts, something about them familiar.

Cordi stepped close to the first one and knew the lost gaze and face etched with want. Persephone. The fair goddess of spring from the garden. Briar and Primrose had told her the story in turns. How the beautiful and beloved child of Demeter had been stolen and dragged off to the underworld by the dreadful and frightening Hades. How he had tricked her, trapping her with him for six months of the year with a pomegranate, Persephone's ignorance of the forbidden fruit sealing her fate. The rest of the year she was permitted to return to her mother, who so loathed Hades and his theft that she tormented mankind with winter and scarcity till her precious child was again beside her.

Truth be told, Cordi had thought the tale sad, sympathizing with the gentle Persephone. The poor goddess was trapped no matter where she was, whether in the underworld or beside her mother. She wasn't free. She hoped the pretty goddess was happy with her husband and her crown. She hoped—at least—she was loved.

The other bust was just as beautiful, but the face cruel in its beauty. Determined. Righteous.

"Demeter," she whispered, recognizing the likeness from the statues outside barring the way to the heart of the garden, keeping watch over her child. The mother who guarded her hearth and home and had been betrayed.

Carefully, Cordi tipped the statue to the side, Demeter's empty eyes watching yet another betrayal. A set of keys.

A huff of air escaped Cordi's lungs. With her free hand she slid the keys from under the hollowed base and settled Demeter exactly as she had been before, the goddess's face disapproving. She carried the ring to the desk, searching as she went. She fitted key after key into the hole with no luck, till finally one long, slender key twisted, and the tumblers of the locking mechanism fell away.

An exclamation of triumph flitted over her lips, swallowed up by the plush room. The rolling lid slid up and away, exposing the beautiful, polished surface of the desk. Everything was orderly, the fountain pens and blotting paper and ink bottles. And stacked in the back, the ledgers.

Cordi pulled the top ledger onto the desk, opening it wide, being careful to disturb nothing else. She flipped back till she found the most recent dates and then further, searching for the time when Edward's letters had stopped arriving. Nothing. No mention of Mr. Starling. No mention of her brother.

She chewed on her lip and grabbed another book, flipping back faster now, frantically scanning the notes and figures, all in crisp, clear letters. The Lady of Edenfield wrote as she kept house, orderly and with painful precision. Orders from towns and cities Cordi vaguely knew for garments and cloth. Unfathomable sums paid for bulbs and saplings. Bills from the village grocer. And then finally she saw the name almost too late, fingers frantic and eyes straining.

Starling.

Mr. Starling. Greenhouse. She'd been right.

He had been paid the final amount for his services with the greenhouse. Which meant the work had met with approval. Cordi moved her finger up through columns as if tracing the path the craftsman had taken. If she knew his destination, she could find his beginning and perhaps . . .

All materials have arrived safely. Starling and apprentice (Beecher) begin work on new greenhouse. A first deposit for labor has been paid in the amount of . . .

Cordi's finger trembled over the word, the name. *Beecher.* Edward Beecher. Her breath was ragged with relief and indignation. He *had* been there and worked for Starling, and here was proof. But what to do?

She couldn't take the book, but neither could she leave the only real evidence she had. Ripping it wouldn't do. She grabbed the beautiful letter opener—pure silver—and carefully, as close to the binding threads as she dared, cut away the page showing Edward's name. She wanted to look more, but the knowledge of time marching ever on was heavy in her mind.

Paper in hand, she restacked the ledgers, assured herself the desk was tidy, and secured the lid, relocking it. Placing the keys back under Demeter and meeting the goddess's glare of disdain with a self-satisfied smirk.

Back in her shoes and the salon, Cordi went about her chores, the comforting rustle of paper in her apron pocket. It had Edward's name. It proved his existence in Farrow. At Edenfield. What it meant beyond that she didn't know, but she had something real. Not a promise or a desperate wish. It was one more piece to the puzzle. One she could see and touch and knew for certain.

She left the salon with renewed purpose, dragging her cleaning supplies behind her. The heavy curtains she had taken down to be laundered were draped over her shoulders, but she kept her head high, as if the little piece of paper gave her strength. She stacked the baskets of linens, heaving them up and opening the door to the kitchen, and found herself humming, pleased with her discovery, all guilt she might have felt at her subterfuge disappearing with so little a thing as a piece of paper.

Cordi wrangled the baskets to the lines, dropping them to adjust her bonnet where it had gone askew, tucking her hair back into place, and rolling her shoulders. She'd felt odd for days now. Not sick, but alternating between exhaustion and vigor in strange waves. She supposed it was just the work and the exhilaration she felt at the possibility of learning more.

And being close to Briar . . .

Warmth spread in her chest as she began hanging the damp laundry and she allowed herself to daydream of her last—and only—kiss. Anne's lips against hers as clean sheets snapped in the cold air around them, hiding them from view. Only this time, it was Briar's lips she imagined, her pink mouth soft and perfect. Her lids slowly closing as their kiss deepened.

Cordi's own eyes fluttered shut and she pressed fingers to her mouth, laundry billowing around her, heat flaring under her ribs and lower still.

"Excuse me. I'm looking for Miss Eliot."

Cordi flushed hot, yanking her hand away from her mouth as if she had been burned, and pushed the sheets aside, her breath hitching in her throat and her eyes going wide.

Standing only a few yards away was Mrs. Starling, staring at Cordi, her face pale with recognition.

Chapter 19

THE TWO WOMEN STARED AT each other across no more than a few meters, but Cordi felt as if a gulf had opened between them, the earth rolling beneath her shaking knees, threatening to draw her under and bury her alive.

There was no hope of Mrs. Starling not recognizing her, even beneath her maid's livery and cap, with her face filling out and cheeks pink with health. The woman's eyes were sharp, her lips gone pale, as if she was more frightened than shocked.

"Wh-what are you doing here?"

Cordi blinked; the tremor in the woman's voice and the way her hands—one holding a sealed letter—fluttered over her breast betrayed her. She *was* frightened. Maybe there was some weight to Cordi's musings after all. The Starlings were afraid Cordi would uncover proof here. Which she had!

In a fashion.

Mr. Starling had a stack of elm delivered this week. The grain is so fine, Dee! He said it is good wood. Smart wood. Difficult to work with. He said the craftsman must be smarter and more stubborn still.

Cordi calmly reached for another linen, draping it over the line and fanning it out before pinning it in place, watched the wind lift it like a bride's veil. "Working. I'm afraid Miss Eliot is not in at the moment. She and the rest of the household are indisposed. May I help you, Mrs. Starling? Perhaps I can do more for you than you were willing to do for me."

The woman flinched, and Cordi clenched her teeth, all tender feelings she'd felt for the family through Edward's letters vanished.

"You shouldn't be here," Mrs. Starling hissed, an edge to her voice.

"Are you so sure?" Cordi dared, folding a coverlet across the line and hooking it in place.

"You little fool," Mrs. Starling snapped, and Cordi bristled. How dare this woman lie to her face, steal her hope, and then call her foolish! "What could have possibly possessed you to come *here* of all places?"

Cordi tugged on the coverlet carefully, straightening the wrinkles, trying to calm the inner storm. "Is there somewhere else you might suggest I go? You and your husband had little help to offer, though I thank you for the boots."

"You should have left Farrow. You've no idea what this place is! There is nothing for you here but—"

Cordi stepped closer, kicking the basket away, trembling with rage so long held just beneath the surface that would not stand to be condescended to any longer. "My *brother* is here and that is *everything*! You and your husband refused to help me. You *lied*. Did you expect me to turn tail and run? Run where? Back to the city and the life we knew there? Did he tell you about the Barrow? Did you read my letters to him after he stopped writing? At least when I had word of him I could be comforted. Someone still loved me. When his letters stopped, so did my world! All I had left was hope, and you and your husband tried to steal even that from me!"

The woman's lip trembled, but she tried to swallow, and Cordi could see the calculation. See she was trying to gather herself. "We didn't—"

"Don't you *dare*!" Cordi yanked the paper from her pocket, thrusting it up between her and Mrs. Starling. Her voice pitched dangerously low. "*Beecher.*

Edward. Beecher. My brother. *My* family. *Your* husband's apprentice. Dare to tell me he was not—did not sleep—under your roof or sit at your table and share his smile with your family, and I will swear a ruin that would make the Devil quake."

Mrs. Starling stared at the paper and her breath hitched, a ragged sob torn from her chest, her entire face crumpling. Her nose began to run, and she licked at the moisture there before wiping it with the back of her sleeve, voice tremulous and pleading: "You don't understand."

"Then tell me!"

If Mrs. Starling had looked frightened before, her face now took on all the wild terror of a snared rabbit and she shook her head frantically, eyes rolling, breath short. Her mouth opened and closed, voice cracking like the high whistle of the wind through a break in the eaves before sinking to a low rasp, words lodging in her throat before they could be spoken. Her lips mouthing the same words over and over: "I cannot."

Cordi bared her teeth as if she might tear into the woman's throat. "Then I will bring the law to your door." It would mean risking her own freedom, for she would be dragged back to the Barrow, but if it meant finding Edward or finding out what had happened . . .

The words seemed to shock Mrs. Starling out of her hysterics, and she gaped. "You don't understand at all, do you? You—" She looked behind, listening, then grabbed Cordi by the wrist and pulled her against the wall, hidden from both the empty eyes of the house and the lane.

"You have no ken what you've done by coming here, girl." Mrs. Starling spoke in hushed tones, and if she still sounded afraid, it suddenly seemed as if it was less for herself. "And if you think the law of man can stand against this house and the she-devils inside, then you've not the sense God gave you. Though not even God would tarry on these grounds. *Yes,*" she hissed. "Yes. Edward did work for my husband. We lied to you, and God forgive us for it, but we know only that he disappeared one night, taking nothing. Our girl—Alice—she had seen him sneaking off to this cursed place before and had said nothing. I daresay she told you as much?" Mrs. Starling shook her head. "I should never have sent *her* with gifts, such as they were. And poor tokens at that for a brother lost.

"But he *is* lost," she said firmly. "If he came back here, he is lost. I should never have agreed to let my husband work on the cursed soil of this tainted Eden. For that's what she would make of her garden if she could. I'll not allow it again. She sent another order, but now—" She tore at the letter she held in her hand, shredding it with fingers that shook before shoving it into the pocket of her apron. "I was against it, and seeing you is God's answer, true enough. Your poor brother . . ."

"Tell me what happened."

Mrs. Starling sagged, the fight gone out of her. Wearily she began speaking. "He came to work here, with my husband. They built her greenhouse. John didn't want to bring the boy, but he needed the help putting it together. Couldn't do it alone. He thought they were so careful. They brought their own water, their own—this place has a sickness on it and John didn't want it to infect Edward like it has infected so many others. But it did. Somehow.

"It was some time after they finished up work that Edward fell ill like the rest. Fever. Ravings. Couldn't catch his breath. If you live in Farrow long enough, you know it for what it is. The poison of this place."

A wind came from out of nowhere, sending clouds across the sun and darkening the yard. Cordi felt her flesh form goose pimples and her mouth go dry.

"We took him to the old cottage. The one we use for such things. She won't treat the men, you understand. Never the men. Only the girls or the women and only if it suits her. So we do what we can, which isn't much. The screams that come from the place . . . you can't imagine the screams. The sounds that wake our children and set them weeping. Most of the time they don't—" She shook her head and swiped a hand across dry eyes, too tired to weep. "We were sure we'd arrive one morning and find him dead. Another boy for her boneyard. But he was alive. Weak, but alive. After a time, we allowed him back in his room above the shop, but not back in the house and certainly not near the girls. Not till we were sure. We could not just turn him out. He was a good boy. We loved him." She held up a hand. "I know what you might think, but we did. The girls adored him. But one morning, he was gone. John searched for him but found no trace. He never came back for his things or his wages. He vanished. I don't know what became of him, but I've my suspicion. He was drawn back to this house. Lured here. He saw one. Saw one and was put under a spell." The woman crossed herself.

"Saw one what?"

Mrs. Starling's eyes flashed and her lip curled. "You already know. Didn't Alice tell you?"

"Alice only told a ghost story. There are no ghosts here. Just—"

Briar. Primrose. The ghosts of Edenfield. That silly skipping rhyme she had heard at the Starlings' house. That's what this was about? The princesses in their beautiful tower were the monsters of this place's fairy stories. It was . . . ignorant. Cruel. The sisters were generous and kind and lonely. Prim was rather abrasive, but she wasn't a monster; neither of them were! How utterly simpleminded and petty for the people of Farrow to turn them into horrors when their only crime was—

"Ah. I see."

Cordi found Mrs. Starling watching her carefully. Whatever the woman saw in Cordi's face had her stepping back.

"You as well." She huffed a laugh. "I'll say no more, then, but this. Leave. Leave while you can. We will do what we can to help you. God knows, we owe you that much. I have your brother's things and the money he was owed. I will leave them at the cottage. His possessions are yours by right and I'd not the heart to throw them away." She pointed. "Outside the gates, turn left into the woods. Follow the wall all the way to its end. The cottage is there, or what is left of it. The ruin needs burning to the ground and then this house with it; Hell's fire cleansing what the light of Heaven cannot. For what it is worth, I am sorry. He was a fine boy, your brother."

"Don't," Cordi snapped, her tongue thick and face hot. "He is not gone. He is *here*."

The woman looked at Cordi pityingly, disappointment and worry etched into every line of her face, as if she was already assured of what choice Cordi would make. "I'm sure you're right, dear. But not as you hope."

Then she was gone around the corner. Cordi listened to her steps running across the gravel drive till they faded. The skin around her eyes felt tight and her heart was beating with such ferocity, she was afraid it might burst from her chest. Her breath grew shorter and quicker, unable to pull air deep enough into her lungs. Her skin crawled and ice and fire flooded her veins simultaneously even while black spots began to appear in her vision.

Her shoulder collided with the stone masonry of the house as she crumpled, her knees refusing to support her any longer. The fabric covering her arm grated against the wall as she slid down, folding forward till her forehead rested on the cool grass there in the shade.

Lies. Lies. Lies. Lies.

She repeated the word over and over in her head, screaming it, trying to quell the panic and fear and doubt that had begun to take root. But no matter how hard she tried, she could not drown out the words of the vicious rhyme.

But what's planted in the Garden
Will grow where it is laid.
Your only hope is to avoid
The breath of a pretty maid.

Chapter 20

"DAMN!"

The curse slipped from between her lips before she could stop it, though she couldn't find the energy to care. Her head was throbbing, and Cordi pressed her gloved fingers to her temples, willing the pain away as she stooped to pick up the dustpan she had dropped, spilling its contents onto the floor she had *just* swept.

She sat on the edge of the carpet in the girls' back salon and gazed out into the garden. Cordi had managed to compose herself before the staff returned, shuffling in with shoulders weighed down by grief, but eyes shining with an almost rapturous light. Miss Eliot had instructed her to see to the salon after lunch, which was eaten in near silence. Jane had not eaten at all, though Miss Eliot had placed a bowl of broth in front of her and whispered quietly in her ear. The girl's dark eyes were as hard and cold as river stones. She'd turned them on Cordi several times over the course of the meal, but Cordi did her best to ignore her. She did not want to be swept up in another's grief for fear of losing herself to it. She needed to keep her mind sharp. There was much to consider. Mrs. Starling. The paper now tucked among her precious letters. The warning. And the suggestion. That most of all.

I'm sure you're right, dear. But not as you hope.

It meant the Starlings believed Edward was somewhere on the grounds, though they believed him dead. Possibly buried.

"What's planted in the Garden," she whispered, the words hot on her skin within the confines of her mask. The prayer and the children's rhyme and the rules. All the same. And now the words seemed ominous.

Edward had been to the house and had become terribly sick. But there had been no help offered because "she" didn't treat the men. Lady Evangeline, obviously. The mistress of the house who despised men. Cordi could well remember the coughs from the sickroom, the voice of the mistress of the house urging the crying occupant to drink. How kind she sounded, how encouraging. But she spoke of her daughters with a peculiar distance, and Prim regarded their mother with something rather like contempt. Though Prim regarded most things and people with an air of contempt. Briar spoke of her mother's intelligence, but not of her love.

The girls might be the ghosts of Edenfield, but it seemed their mother was something else. Something the people of Farrow feared. Mrs. Starling mentioned demons, devils, and Hell. The locals thought the place unholy, ever anxious of the shadow it cast over their small village.

Cordi stood, sweeping up the dust once more, trying to think of what she should do. She had proof Edward had been here, so she could go to the law. But she had little faith they would do anything; she believed that much of Mrs. Starling's story. She could confront Lady Evangeline, but she would have to reveal her deception and that would see her thrown out and then she'd have failed.

She could leave. Go as Mrs. Starling had suggested and start afresh somewhere—

"No!"

She spoke the word to the empty room. A promise to herself and to Edward. She was staying. She was going to find him. She was—

"No what?"

Cordi whirled to find Prim standing in the entryway, hands resting one atop the other in front of her skirts. She looked even more beautiful than Cordi had come to expect, her hair lifted off the nape of her neck but hanging in large, hot-ironed curls, crowned with green ribbons. The style drew attention to the sharp angle of her jaw, making her lips appear fuller, darker. Her dress was white, rather than funeral black, the bodice and overgown worked in a beautiful pattern of ivy.

She waited for an answer.

"Oh! I dropped the dustpan and had to sweep everything up again. I was sure I was about to do it once more." The lies fell easily now, and Cordi burned with shame.

Prim looked about the room and breathed deeply, a smile spreading across her face. It softened her sharp edges but did not dull them. "You've done a lovely job. And all by yourself too. Thank you."

It had been a lot of work to sweep away the dust and cobwebs and polish all the surfaces of the room. To beat the pillows and cushions. To wash the windows. But it felt nice to be acknowledged for her labors. And as much as she would have delighted in a kind word from Briar, it mattered more coming from Prim, who was direct and little interested in flattery. "My pleasure."

A trill of laughter. "I very much doubt that if you're yelling at dustpans."

And this poised, sequestered girl was supposed to be a villain? Prim's words were what Cordi needed to hear, banishing the doubt Mrs. Starling had tried to seed in her heart. Even if Edward had been under the spell of one of the sisters, it was due to no fault of their own. And they would not have done wrong to him, certainly. Prim was formal, true. Prone to speaking her mind and unapologetic, but that didn't make her wicked. And Briar was the sweetest, kindest, most—

He saw one. Saw one and was put under a spell.

"Cordi? Are you listening?"

Cordi started. "Yes!" she squeaked. But what had Prim said? "No. Sorry. I—I was far away. I'm listening now."

Prim regarded her coolly, weighing her apology. Then: "I'm afraid I must beg a favor of you, Cordi."

"Oh?"

"Yes," Prim said, perfect white teeth worrying her bottom lip. "Briar is feeling rather depressed after Irene's . . . after Irene. I hate to see her in so bleak a mood as this. Would you be willing to come? I think your companionship does her good. We might play a game. We've cards and chess or any number of distractions."

It was evident Prim was unused to asking for favors and that she found it quite an uncomfortable task, but here she was, asking rather than demanding. And again, Cordi could not help but feel Mrs. Starling's warning was fueled by vicious village gossip sprung from narrow minds and spouted by jealous tongues. Lady Evangeline had every reason to distrust men after taking in so many abused. She might only be trying to keep her daughters and household safe, as she had readily admitted. But the sickness? What had made Edward so ill?

"Of course! And how are you after today? It must have been hard on you too. To lose so faithful a friend."

Orchid eyes slipped away. "Thank you for your concern, but I am well. I do not hold too tightly to people. They so easily disappoint. Fragile things with fragile hearts. Much easier to be heartless."

Despite the strength of her words, Cordi could sense the hurt behind them. "I very much doubt you truly feel that way. I've seen you with your sister."

Those same eyes now flashed with warning. "My sister is another matter."

Cordi found herself shrinking under such a look. A reminder that a beautiful, ornamental blade could still cut deeply. "I apologize. I didn't mean—"

An imperial wave. "It's nothing. I am too sharp-tongued and stubborn to accept your kindness without a fight. So, let us leave it at that. You will continue to be courteous, Briar will continue to be naïve, and I will continue to be cruel. We all have our parts in this drama, don't we?"

They found Briar in her room, lounging lazily on her divan, her cheeks splotchy, eyes rimmed with red. She wore a dress similar to Prim's: white, but the pattern was one of bluebells and purple violets. Even in her distress, she was the most beautiful thing Cordi had ever seen.

"All right, Briar. Enough of this," Prim said promptly. "I've brought Cordi to cheer you up and you'll not mope any longer. We won't have it. Time to rouse yourself."

Briar jerked to a sitting position. "Oh! Hello, Cordi! I do wish Prim hadn't bothered you. I must—"

"You *must* stop pouting is what you *must* do. And I didn't bother Cordi. She was nearly finished with the salon and I'm sure she would much rather entertain you and tolerate me than argue with her broom and dustpan."

"I am sorry for your loss. I'm sure it has been quite a strenuous day for the household," Cordi said from the doorway, conscious of her wrinkled and dusty livery, the gloves streaked with polish and spotted with soap.

But Briar's smile bloomed like a flower emerging from winter's slumber. "You're so sweet to us, Cordi. So kind."

A corner of Prim's mouth lifted. "That's just what I was telling her." She tugged her sister to standing, tucking a stray curl behind her ear. "Now, I thought we'd play a game. Whist? Chess? Whatever you like, dearest Briar."

Dearest Dee.

Cordi's throat closed.

Two tiny lines appeared between Briar's brows and her lips puckered.

And then she rose up onto her toes and clapped her hands. "Hide-and-seek! We haven't played in forever! And it will be so much more fun with Cordi, since we always know where the other one is hiding."

Prim smiled indulgently. "Hide-and-seek, then. But only indoors today, I think."

"Marvelous."

"Shall I count first?" Cordi suggested.

"Yes!" Briar said, squeezing her sister's hand and tugging her to the door. "You must sit here and shut your eyes."

Giggles—most from Briar—fled from the room and down the hall before Cordi had a chance to begin to count. She smiled behind her mask, happy. Happy she was wanted. Happy to be playing a child's game if it meant she was included. As she counted, she felt the tension easing from her shoulders. It most certainly was only gossip and envy to think Prim and Briar sinister, and Cordi had resented it. Prim had said she was heartless, but she didn't really mean it. She had every right to be bitter. No matter how isolated, she likely knew what wagging tongues said about her and her beloved sister. Still, something ate at Cordi, planted by Mrs. Starling's account of Edward's illness. By Alice's insistence he had sneaked off to Edenfield on occasion.

A sickness, Mrs. Starling had said. A sickness on the house. Jane with her haunted, skeletal face and nails black as the grave. There was indeed a sickness that pervaded the manor, but how did it spread? Cordi felt fine. The other servants were well. The girls themselves hearty!

Cordi touched her gloved fingers to her mask, feeling her lips move as she counted aloud. She could not feel her breath, the fabric tightly woven. There had been the sickroom at the Barrow filled with little ones coughing and choking to death, their lungs filled with blood and water and yellow phlegm. The doors stayed locked and the doctor—if he even was a doctor, for all the care he gave—always wore a mask when he entered, as did the school's nurse.

Miss Eliot had insisted the sisters were the very picture of health and they did so seem it. But Jane. Irene. Edward. "Hmm." The vibration of her lips where her fingers pressed the mask against her skin tickled and Cordi was snatched out of her thoughts. What had she been doing? The game! Oh, she hoped she hadn't been idle long!

"Fifty!" Cordi called, leaping to her feet, listening for the titters of laughter that had marked the sisters' passage. She bit the inside of her cheek and toed off her shoes again, leaving them by Briar's door. She would move quietly as the girls themselves did and catch them unawares. She went to the stairs, intending to head down, but saw the staircase climbing to the third floor.

She hesitated for only a moment before slipping quickly and quietly up the steps, stifling a giggle. It had been a rare thing to play at the Barrow and she marveled at how her heart beat so quickly! How delightful to feel like a child! To abandon one's cares and heartaches for a moment at play.

The stairway ended in a door rather than a landing, and Cordi hesitated. The darkness of the stair seemed to gather there, for there were no windows. She took a step back down, eyes fixed on the dull knob and the black eye of the keyhole beneath. Perhaps she shouldn't. Neither sister had said anything was off-limits, though Miss Eliot had banned her from wandering. But that was before. And was it wandering or snooping when she was meant to be searching? It was a game, after all.

Better to beg forgiveness, she decided, reaching a hand toward the door. Anyway, it was likely locked.

To her delight, the door opened silently into darkness. The air was cool and musty and, peeking in, Cordi could see light filtering through small windows of thick, dusty glass. All the floorboards were bare, the room packed with items covered in dustcloths.

An attic.

The perfect place to hide.

Cordi listened, hoping to hear the sound of a foot shifting or a muffled laugh. She stepped inside on silent feet, the fox hunting prey with glee. "Come out, come out," she cooed, attempting to elicit a fit of laughter from Briar.

Her blood sang in her veins. How she hoped she'd find her first. And alone.

She twirled in the middle of the room, hands on her hips, hoping to catch the fluttering edge of a sheet, but nothing stirred in the room. She was about to return to the stairs when she looked down. There on the floor, just visible in the muted light, was a path in the dust. One that might be made by long skirts. It began at the door and Cordi tracked it with a fox's sharp gaze in its direct path to a dark corner where something—someone?—hid beneath a sheet.

Cordi felt her lips spread in a feral grin, stalking carefully, hoping the boards didn't creak as she made her way to the sheet, the object beneath as tall as she herself, though wider. Perhaps one of them was tucked beneath something or inside a wardrobe. Her tongue between her teeth, she reached forward and yanked the sheet up, the cry of victory strangling in her throat and cutting off her air when she saw the eyes beneath. Not amethyst at all. But blue as a summer sky and gazing into hers.

Edward.

Chapter 21

HE WAS THE SAME AS she remembered. Golden curls that were the envy of so many a girl in the Barrow and blue eyes filled with life and warmth and laughter. He was smiling. A small, secretive smile she was not familiar with, but one that suited his face.

"Edward," she whispered, tears springing to her eyes, coating her lashes till she had to blink them away to see him clearly.

He looked back at her from the painting, expression alight with something she would attribute to longing. Every detail of him had been rendered into a portrait worthy of a lord's gallery. He had been captured on canvas with such skill, she found herself half believing he might speak to her. Edward, his back against the trunk of a tree, the shadows of other trees behind, and another darker shape in the distance. A moment in time preserved forever in pigment.

And there was but one sister who painted.

Prim, whose tongue and wit were dagger sharp, but who carried an air of melancholy she hardly seemed aware of, like a shroud around her stiff shoulders. Prim, who was not silly or fanciful, but logical and determined, who would not likely mistake infatuation for anything deeper. She had painted this. And she had done it with love.

Even Cordi, who knew little of love and less of art, could see how each stroke of the brush had been infused with the kind of love Cordi herself longed for. How Edward had been painted with confidence, but with extreme care, as if it were a masterwork. As if the painter had been afraid of missing even the smallest detail, like the way he had a dimple on only one cheek and how his left ear was slightly lower than the right.

It was Prim he had been sneaking away to see. Prim who claimed to be heartless and cruel. Prim who had looked at the greenhouse with contempt and told Cordi how faithless and disappointing people could be.

Before she could stop herself, she reached forward and let her fingers brush Edward's painted cheek. There was no warmth. No life. Just the cool, rough texture of the canvas and paints beneath the tip of her gloved finger. But still she felt in her heart he was there and alive.

"I'm here," she whispered.

Be quick and smart, she thought. *Observe. Find.* Her eyes darted over the painting, searching for clues. The bark of a tree was clear against Edward's back, dark and cracked and broken. Not the smooth, pale bark of a birch, but it could have been any number of other trees. Pine? Ash? Oak? She stilled—the strange shadow in the background. That was different. *That* was singular.

She squinted in the low light, peering closer, trying to make it out. The angles were sharp, but strange. Broken in places. A structure. The greenhouse?

The derelict cottage!

It had to be, she was sure. And where might you hide someone who needed to be kept secret and safe, if not a cottage that nobody used? The bark of the tree must be one from the great hawthorn forest surrounding the manor.

A soft sound—distant, but loud in the silence—sent Cordi's pulse quickening. Someone was coming up the stairs.

Carefully, she threw the sheet back over the portrait, hiding Edward from sight. On her toes, she slipped quietly back to the middle of the attic, careful to stay on the clear path. A glance at the door showed a shadow along the wall, creeping slowly up the stairs. Cordi rushed toward a dusty corner of the attic and turned her back, pretending to peer over shrouded furniture as if she were still searching. Still playing. As if it were all still a silly game.

Someone set foot into the attic, slippered feet on bare floorboard, and Cordi had to force her body not to stiffen. Not to turn. She was not cornered. Not in a trap. She was playing a game of chess, not hide-and-seek.

A hand gripped her shoulder and she turned with a cry, lifting her arms as if to shield herself.

Briar leapt back with a startled scream of her own.

Cordi slumped, leaning her weight on the flat surface of what was likely a desk or trunk of some kind. "You *scared* me!"

"I scared *you*?" Briar gasped, one hand pressed against her heart, chest heaving up and down. "You nearly frightened me half to death!"

They looked at each other, panting, shaking in relief, and burst out laughing. Briar hid her mouth with one hand, laughing behind her fingers, ever the lady. Cordi guffawed behind her mask in a most unladylike manner, which only set Briar into a greater fit of giggles. "Your face!" Briar twittered. "Your eyes went so wide, they might have popped from your head!"

The light from the greasy windows was poor, but still enough for Cordi to see splotches of red across Briar's décolletage and neck from her own distress. "I thought I was meant to be seeking," she teased, tearing her eyes away from the expanse of creamy skin. Doors she had long slammed shut on her heart began to ease open, allowing light in. It was terrifying and marvelous.

Briar's smirk was almost wicked. "You will find I am not always so patient when—"

"What are you doing up here?"

Prim stood in the doorway, hands at her sides, body rigid, looking in on them. And though a fair distance separated the two, Briar took a step farther back from Cordi, as if she had been caught doing something her sister would not approve of.

But Prim was not looking at her sister. She was looking at Cordi. Body preternaturally still. Dust motes floated in the gloom between them, panicked, their peace shattered by the three invaders to their realm. Cordi could not see Prim's eyes but felt them, piercing and penetrating. Instinctively, she slammed the doors to her heart shut, terrified that look might flay her open and reveal her secrets.

The still-smoldering coals of her earlier rage lay in the pit of her stomach and Cordi had to fight to keep the fire banked. To not scream. She felt betrayed. Edward had not come for her but had come for this proud girl who had so enchanted him. Prim had stolen her brother from her. Had lied and hidden him from even her mother! Prim—

Had no idea who Cordi even *was.*

Cordi was a servant. Another broken girl in the cloister. Someone in service to the house. Her relationship to Edward was still a secret. And Cordi had to keep it that way or risk everything. She forced her voice to be steady and feigned confusion. "Looking for the two of you."

"You shouldn't be up here," Prim furiously spat, fingers curling at her sides into claws, something angry pooling inside her. Cordi fancied she could see it spreading across her perfect features like cracks in porcelain, but it had to only be the dim light. Still, here was evidence of something darker inside Prim. Something she tried to hide. Something cruel.

"I—" Cordi pushed herself upright, dust and cobwebs now clinging to her clothes, and she tried to wipe her smutty gloves on her apron. "I didn't know."

"Why are you being such a goose, Prim?" Briar said with a frown. "We were only playing a game."

Prim didn't answer, just watched Cordi, and then her eyes shifted toward the painting in the far corner as if reassuring herself it was still there. Still covered. Cordi resisted the urge to turn and check to make sure she had covered it properly. That she had left no trace. Instead, she tried to look contrite and wounded.

She would be wily. She would play, only the game was different now. But at least she knew who she was up against and the stakes.

Clearing her throat, Briar stepped closer to her sister. "Prim? Are you—"

"I'm fine," she snapped. And she was, her posture shifting from aggressive to royal in the time it took for Cordi to blink, her face warping from ferocious to cool indifference. "Let's go downstairs. Cordi will want to tidy herself, and I'm bored of this game." With a sweep of skirts, she turned, head high, and descended the steps.

"I'm sorry," Cordi whispered conspiratorially to Briar, who watched her sister's retreating shadow, body poised for flight as if she needed to stay within easy reach of that woman-shaped darkness.

Briar tried to muster a smile, but it died on her lips. "I'm sure Prim is just overtired. She didn't mean to be so abrupt. She's been so unsettled of late. Worried about me and the garden. I'm always in the way and it is such a strain on her. She feels so responsible for me. I do wish I were better for her. It has always been the two of us. And now . . ." Briar shrugged. "You?"

A long cobweb had caught in Briar's hair and Cordi closed the distance between them, reaching a hand up. Briar inhaled sharply, her eyes wide, her mouth opening the slightest bit. Cordi's hand hovered close to Briar's temple and then carefully pulled the strands of webbing from the curls, holding Briar's eyes the entire time.

Briar wet her lips with the tip of her tongue and, behind her mask, Cordi did the same. "I've no wish to come between you." The words came unbidden but were out before Cordi could pull them back. Briar blinked up at her, Cordi the taller of the two by scant inches, and blushed rose-petal pink. "I—"

"Are you two coming?" came an imperious voice from a level below. One that would not be denied.

Briar opened her mouth, but words seemed to fail her.

"Yes!" Cordi called, still holding Briar's gaze, wanting things she shouldn't.

Briar took a steadying breath and ducked her head, pressing the back of her hand to her heated cheek as she led the way out of the attic. Cordi wanted to grab her hand. To pull her back.

She thought of Edward behind the dustcloth, staring through it and into her back. *Find me,* he seemed to say. Find him. Edward was what mattered. Her family was what mattered. Everything else was a distraction.

The cottage. She would search there. She had hope beyond hope now. But she would need to be cunning. Mrs. Starling's warnings, so easily dismissed only a short time ago, suddenly seemed to have some merit. She would not soon forget Prim's face when she feared discovery.

So she would be wary. Careful. Even more now than before. But she was no longer preoccupied with guilt at her little deceptions. If a strategy of ruses was needed for this game, she would play it well. And if she was to be surrounded by liars, she would become a better one.

Lies were just the truths we wanted, after all.

Chapter 22

THE NEXT DAY PASSED AS only those when you wait anxiously for the arrival of something can. A birthday. Or Christmas. At least such as Cordi could remember from before the Barrow. In the morning, she fulfilled her role as lady's companion, another beautiful dress ready for her, this time in pale yellow the color of buttercups, and long, lilac gloves. A new mask awaited her, adorned with daffodils and moonflowers, and she touched the threads with reverence, somehow feeling as if Briar had made it specially for her.

The younger sister was hesitant to meet her eyes for the better part of the morning, and Cordi worried that either she had been too forward or Prim had chastised her sister, seeing what Cordi was beginning to suspect but dared not truly believe: that Briar might feel similarly. How could she? The fairy-tale princess and the . . . scullery maid? Just the thought made Cordi wince with shame.

But when she shut her eyes, Cordi could trace the curve of Briar's cheek, the bow of her lips, and the dip at her throat. She had memorized the smiles with which Briar was so generous and her doe-eyed expressions. But the look she had given Cordi in the attic? That was burned into her memory. There had been want there. Longing that went beyond the curious.

That look had distracted Cordi the entire morning, straining her determination from the previous day to the limits, and she had sought it again and again, though she didn't know if receiving it a second time would have pleased her or terrified her more. It was one thing to want what could not be yours. It was quite another to have hope. Especially when such hope only complicated matters. Cordi needed to be focused but found it almost impossible as she sat with the girls, knowing one was a liar and the other desire.

She had tried to engage Prim in conversation, both to spare herself and Briar embarrassment and to see if she might glean some insight into the girl who had so lovingly painted Edward's portrait and then secreted it away in the attic. But Prim answered only in clipped sentences, her body rigid, her mind obviously elsewhere. Eventually she claimed a headache and excused herself to lie down. She took Briar with her, her sister shadowing without protest.

Effectively dismissed, Cordi returned early to the kitchen. This time, it was Stella who met her. She had just finished preparing the tea. "Oh!" she said, jumping as Cordi tripped over the last step, nearly falling into the room. "Are you all right?"

"Yes. Of course," Cordi answered, voice rough. "Where's Miss Eliot?"

"Didn't you pass her on the stairs? She was summoned to the south wing," Stella said, indicating the intricate bell system along the wall, each bell labeled by room, those for the girls' chambers marked only with *B* and *P*.

"I must have been in the washroom," Cordi mused, settling into a chair. She kept her livery there to change into so she might put her companion clothes away with her mask and gloves.

Stella placed a full cup in front of her, the tea paler than Cordi remembered. "I told her I would prepare your tea. And I set your lunch aside in case you came back hungry."

"Dear Stella," Cordi said, wrapping her hands around the cup. "You're the sweetest soul."

The girl's face blushed, her lips tightening, and she shook her head. "Not at all. 'She is to tend to her sisters—' "

"'—as she would herself,'" Cordi finished with confidence, the words now rooted into her mind where they would likely never be torn free.

Stella gave an approving nod. "Drink up. I must see to the laundry." And she was gone, hurrying from the room.

The tea was not as strong as when Miss Eliot brewed it, but Cordi felt to say so might be a criticism and she did not want hurts between her and Stella too. Even after she finished, she felt weary, her head heavy and full of riddles, but there was work to be done.

The rest of the day had been spent beating rugs and scrubbing steps till Cordi's hands were red and raw and she'd weaved her way back to the kitchen, slightly nauseated. Miss Eliot had given her a salve before dinner, one Lady Evangeline made herself in her greenhouse from healing herbs. The smell was pungent but not unpleasant, and Miss Eliot said the Lady used something called eucalyptus and tea tree oil. She'd also been instructed to have another cup of the bitter tea under the attentive eye of the housekeeper. Cordi inhaled the scent of the salve, the perfume of the oils on her tongue and filling her lungs. It was clean and fresh, and the tea cleared the fog from her mind.

Allowed her to think again.

"Did you drink your tea earlier today, Cordelia?" Miss Eliot asked, staring with a stony expression into the teacup at the bits of tea leaves that clung to the sides.

"I did, ma'am. Stella kindly brewed it for me."

The housekeeper said nothing else on the matter.

Finally the hour had come for everyone to retire to bed, and Cordi could hardly stand it a moment longer. She lay stiff and silent in the darkness of the room she shared with Stella as the house stilled and the moon rose. She waited for what felt like hours for Stella's breathing to become steady and slow, and her mind would not quiet. She pondered the riddles of the girls, the strangeness of the rules, and her queer bouts of dizzy exhaustion. She could not stop hearing the skipping rhyme and found her lips shaping the words, the haunted, dreadful faces of Mr. and Mrs. Starling floating before her in the quiet dark like taunting phantoms.

Eventually she risked slipping from her bed as Stella slept across the room. As quietly as she could, she pulled her sad excuse for a coat over her white nightshift and padded silently to the door, Mrs. Starling's cast-off shoes clutched to her chest. She froze, her hand on the doorknob. She had been listening to Stella's steady breathing, timing her steps to the cadence. But Stella had gone quiet.

A small eternity passed . . . then a snore from the bed, and Stella shifted in sleep and Cordi breathed again, hurrying out. She tiptoed along the corridor, careful in the dark, for she did not dare bring a light and risk being seen. She stole out of the kitchen and up the stone steps. The grass was cool between her toes as she stepped out into the moonlight overhead, and she shivered both at the night air and in anticipation of her promised prize: Edward's belongings.

Yet, she hesitated.

Her feet flexed, toes moving through the blades of soft grass. She wanted to dig her toes in, feel the cold earth beneath her nails, and root herself to the spot. She could stay there all night and feel the sun burn the dew from her cheeks when it rose in the morning. She'd be safe and cared for and it could be all she ever wanted.

Cordi sucked in a breath, surprised to find herself in a half crouch. Had she intended to lie down? She couldn't quite remember, but the episode had passed and she quickly shoved her feet into the boots, hastily tying the laces.

She tried to cling to the shadows, avoiding the white pebbles of the drive where they glowed under the watchful eye of the moon, reflecting its stolen light. Luckily, there were shadows aplenty. She slipped through the gates and—truly hidden from view—began to run as quickly as she dared lest she trip over a root or a stone, one hand against the wall so she did not lose her way in the dark. As she ran, the singsong skipping rhyme refused to go silent in her head.

But what's planted in the Garden
Will grow where it is laid . . .

She raced through the dark and some part of her thought she might keep running.

The wall ended abruptly, and Cordi skidded to a stop, lungs burning, head heavy. The spots in her vision were back, now tiny bursts of light against the darkness around her. She stepped back and leaned against the wall for support, one hand pressed to her heart as she dragged cool night air into her lungs.

The cottage was meant to be here, but Cordi couldn't see a thing, the night having swallowed the structure and the trees with it. She withdrew a candle stolen from one of the wall sconces and the friction matches they'd given her for her room. Striking one, she had to squint at the sudden glow in the dark, shadows forming all around her and chilling her from the inside. It had almost been easier in the dark. But she lit the candle with a shaking hand, holding it at an angle to avoid hot wax dripping onto her fingers as the wick caught. A tiny white droplet fell to the ground, but not to grass. To old, decomposing leaves.

She held the candle aloft.

The ramshackle cottage—little more than four leaning walls and a slanting roof threatening to collapse at the first available opportunity—was so overgrown with invasive ivy and mushrooms sprouting along its rotted wood, it almost looked as if it were part of the greater forest beyond. The door hung crookedly in a warped frame swollen with damp. The windows were empty save for a few broken shards of glass.

This was where they had brought her brother in his infirmity? This was a haven for spiders and snakes. Even the Barrow was kinder to its sick than *this.* Or was this a trap? A trick? Cordi didn't want to go inside, but what if Mrs. Starling had told her the truth this time? Edward's belongings might truly be inside! Just the possibility had her feet moving, nearly slipping on the sodden leaves and the mud beneath. The trees overhead seemed to lean down, ready to overwhelm her. As she approached the door, she became agonizingly aware of her breathing. Quick and loud in a world gone silent. There were no night sounds at all save for the occasional *drip* of condensation from the trees to the forest floor.

There was something wrong about this place. That bell under her ribs rang an alarm this time. She should not be here. She needed to turn around. Leave well enough alone and go back to her ignorance or, better yet, leave Edenfield altogether.

But she had come so far and endured so much. She couldn't live her life not knowing the truth.

With her shoulder, she shoved against the swollen door and pressed forward into the gloom. The smell of decay and mildew and earth hung heavy in the room. The forest had taken over much of the space. Grass grew through the planks in the floor that had not fallen away, taken by termites or rot. Old leaves and pine needles were piled about, showing tunnels for mice and moles and hedgehogs. Ivy grew through the walls, a natural curtain reaching to claim more real estate. Spiderwebs glinted silver in corners, some sheltering heavy sacs waiting to burst open. Birds' nests clung to what remained of the rafters and support beams, still sheltered from the elements.

Nobody was there but her.

Her disappointment threatened to drop her. She had not even been aware of how she had dared to hope Edward might be there to greet her. She had been promised his belongings, not him.

Cordi wanted to scream. To rage. To tear down what remained of the horrid building with her hands till her fingers bled and splinters dug beneath her nails. How much longer did she have to pretend? How much longer was she going to be denied the only person she could remember who loved her?

Tears stung her eyes and slipped down her cheeks, but she wiped them away with the torn cuff of her coat. It had been a foolish hope for her heart to harbor. And Cordi was learning all too quickly that hope was more painful than doubt to suffer.

Then she saw it.

Pushed against a bare wall and so dark and misshapen she had taken it for another pile of leaves and debris. A horse blanket, if she had to guess, draped over something large, meant to conceal. Stepping carefully to avoid falling through what was left of the floor, Cordi approached.

She tugged the blanket away, dreading to see her beloved brother, face hollowed away and half-eaten by scavengers, ribs splayed open, his chest filled with dead leaves and the swollen heads of mushrooms. The vision was so real she almost screamed as she dropped the blanket. But it was only a sack beneath. Cordi fell upon it, wrapping an arm around it, holding it tight to her chest. She felt cloth inside, heard the crinkle of paper and the rattle of wood. She resisted tearing into the canvas bag, afraid to lose something in the dark, regardless of the moonlight.

Cordi climbed to her feet, holding the precious bundle close. She blew out the candle once safely through the cottage door, then made her way back to Edenfield and through the gates, trying to ignore the prickling along her scalp.

She felt exposed. Watched.

She waited for the feeling to dissipate, but it refused, leaving her to wonder if there were not creatures in the trees. Or ghosts. Or, worse, someone spying from the manor.

Once concealed in shadow, she took a moment to study the house in the moonlight, its ivy shawl drawn close over one shoulder where the sisters slept.

Upon her arrival at Edenfield, she had seen a shape in the windows watching her. Had it been Briar, Prim, or just her imagination so recently filled with thoughts of ghosts and bogeys? It seemed likely enough now it was one of the sisters. But which one? There was no way to be sure and neither of them had mentioned seeing her. What she knew for certain was that there were no ghosts. Only rumors and the memories haunting the women who lived and worked in the manor.

But there were obviously inner workings to the house Cordi didn't understand. The house and its inhabitants had grown infamous in the county. Enough people were afraid of it to conjure up monsters out of the unknown.

It was easier to think outside in the open air. Her mind didn't feel as muddled or foggy as it sometimes became in the house. A thought that displeased her. Had she somehow become ensnared to it? She couldn't deny the mystery of it anymore. Not now that she knew there was at least *some* credibility to Mrs. Starling's words. Something was wrong at Edenfield, and ignoring it no longer served Cordi's interests. She shivered, a curious sensation creeping along her spine. A preternatural sense of some kind of dread. The sooner she found Edward or information about his whereabouts, the better.

Or she might leave.

The thought paralyzed her. She could hurry inside for her things and never go back. Edward's wages were in his bag. Mrs. Starling had promised they would be, and Cordi believed her this time. The grief and pity on her face had not been false. There would surely be enough money to move on. To start somewhere else!

Edward had not come for her even after he promised; why must she continue to suffer for the sake of someone who had abandoned her?

She hated herself for the thought, for the weakness of it. How disloyal a heart. She was better than that. She was true and strong and she would not break.

Cordi again willed the darkness to conceal her from sight as she hurried back to the shadow of the house and around to the rear. She crept around the corner, scanning the windows for any glimmers of light, but the moon remained the only source of illumination. She held her breath as she snuck down the stone steps to the kitchen door, priding herself on her fox-like cunning and her stealth.

The pride was short-lived. Someone had locked the door.

Chapter 23

"NO!" CORDI GASPED IN DISBELIEF before she could stop herself.

She flung herself to the side of the house, out of sight of the windows and any eyes that might be watching. Though she had little hope if someone was inside, waiting for her return; she'd already betrayed herself.

She counted the seconds, expecting at any moment for Miss Eliot to open the door and toss her belongings onto the steps, banishing her. But nobody came. Nothing stirred inside.

Was it possible Cordi had thrown the lock as she left? Or had Miss Eliot woken to a noise and found the door open, locking it out of habit? If they had noticed her missing, certainly there would be lights within. But all the rooms were dark. It must have been in error. She might still get away with it.

Maybe she could wake up Stella. Knock at their window and ask to be let in. Would her friend keep her secret? And what would Cordi say about the sack? No, Stella would be a last resort, their friendship still in its infancy. She had to look for another way in, that was all. There were doors and windows aplenty, and she had to at least *try*.

Feeling like a thief in the night, her illicit treasures held tight in her arms, Cordi flitted among the shadows to the back of the house. A low mist had gathered, shrouding the garden in an eerie gray cloak of swirling fog. Cordi watched it twist and slip over the steps down to the maze where it wound around the hedges, making the statues there appear to burn with invisible fire.

Cordi.

She jumped, her shoulder scraping against the side of the house, the rough stone biting into her skin through her thin coat. Had she heard her name, or had it only been in her head? She pressed tighter against the house, hugging the bag closer, the feeling of eyes on her stronger now.

She needed to get inside.

Cordi swallowed hard and eased onto the patio, grateful the lamps lining the low wall and those dotting the path to the maze were unlit. She ducked beneath windows toward the first set of doors.

Crack!

Only some primal sense of self-preservation kept her from screaming at the sound of what might have been a branch breaking somewhere within the maze or beyond. The sound had been so faint, nearly swallowed by the fog, but she had heard it. She was sure. Someone—*something*—was out there.

Cordi . . .

Yes. She definitely heard it that time. Not with her ears, but she heard it all the same. A voice, sad and lonely, calling her. And something within her awoke at that summons.

"I'm coming," she whispered to the dark, her feet already moving across the open patio and down the path.

It was foolish, illogical, but it was also necessary. What if it was Edward?

Edward's things. They felt heavy in her grip, cumbersome. But she couldn't just leave them in the open. The scent of the lantana reminded her: the dense bushes grew against the wall leading into the maze. She could easily secrete the canvas bag between them. Kneeling in the damp grass in front of the fragrant plants and lifting the thin lower branches, she shoved the precious sack back till it hit the wall, carefully concealing it.

Pushing to her feet, she drew her thin coat tighter around herself and walked toward the hedge maze, avoiding the knowing stares of the twin Demeters, the silent sentinels, white marble glowing in the moonlight. She could feel the goddess's disapproval at an interloper in her realm, like the one who'd stolen her precious daughter.

She entered between the statues, the tiny rocks crunching under her feet. She winced at the sound. She had avoided the gravel till now, keeping to the grass and earth and smooth flagstones.

Come find me.

Yes, she said to that strange voice in her head. *I'm coming.* That was what she was here to do, wasn't it? The towering hedges seemed to close in upon her, the mist swirling about her legs, ready to pull her under. She felt faint, turning to brace a hand on one of the statues of Persephone. Persephone looked upon her, her expression sad and sympathetic, as if she would take Cordi's pain if she could.

Once again, Cordi's mind strayed to another spring goddess. . . .

But any fantasies that might have begun to take shape flickered and died as a pale golden glow appeared on the hedge that marked the opening.

Someone had found her.

Cordi stifled a gasp and pressed herself back and down, curling into the shadow cast by the goddess, fitting herself between it and the hedge as best she could. The voice was gone—perhaps it had never been there at all. Nobody had called her from the garden.

Whatever eyes had been upon her had been inside the house, someone peeking between curtains, watching and waiting. She had not been careful enough.

What would they do if they caught her?

The scarred skin along her back rippled and she stifled a whimper at the memory of the birch across her flesh and the spray of blood in her peripheral vision. How she had felt it land upon her cheek, hot and thicker than her tears.

No. They would never be so cruel or terrible, but they would certainly dismiss her. They might even report her to the police if they thought she was a thief or working for someone like Faustine's former lord. They would protect each other, and she would be cast out. She would lose Edward for good. And Briar.

The glow of a shuttered lantern entered the maze, then turned and moved down the path in the opposite direction from where Cordi hid, the gentle scrape of displaced stones as someone walked with slow, confident steps. From her hiding spot, Cordi was only just able to catch a glimpse of long, dark hair trailing down the back of a figure in a dark cloak.

Prim's hair shone under the moonlight, midnight blue like a raven's black wing. Brushed to a glossy brilliance, gathering in the folded-back hood of her cloak. She stood motionless, lingering at the first corner, head cocked, listening for something. Then her head jerked toward the center of the maze and she was gone, her light moving swiftly.

Cordi gripped the base of the statue and hauled herself up, eyes growing wide in the dark, desperate to keep sight of the tiny spark of orange flame from the lantern through the hedge. Her fear was overshadowed by a burning curiosity and renewed hope that Prim might lead her to her brother.

She tried to match the pace of Prim's footsteps, taking long strides to catch up, aware of every sound she made as she moved, rounding the first corner and then another, always looking for the faintest glimmer of light through the thick leaves. But Prim was too quick. Too sure, and Cordi suddenly found she could no longer see a light. Could no longer hear Prim's steps.

Stubbornly she carried on, moving as swiftly as she dared around bends and corners, always stealing a quick look first to make sure she didn't run into Prim. She had no idea what would happen if she caught Cordi. How she might react. But she remembered Prim's curled fingers and the near snarl on her lips in the attic, her perfect mask fracturing in her fury.

What might she do if they were alone?

But it was ridiculous. Prim wasn't dangerous! She was . . . "Lost," Cordi whispered to herself. *I am lost.*

She realized it too late. She could not orient herself, stumbling down paths and facing dead end after dead end. The low-lying fog had become so thick, it was yet another obstacle, disorienting, as if she were waist-deep in water. Hands would reach up at any moment from the gray mist and tug her below. She knew she should stop and calm herself, knew she should come up with some plan to make her way back to the house, but the knowledge that she had lost her quarry and her senses made her eyes sting with furious tears.

Swallowing a scream of rage and despair, she forced her feet to a halt and leaned against the hedge, her back pressed against the twigs and sticks, feeling them poke her through her thin coat. She ran a hand through her hair in exasperation and stared ahead at the opposite wall, where one of the many holes cut into the greenery showed her the other side and the paths beyond.

Movement darting across the cutout made her start. Prim. But she had doused her light and pulled up the hood of her cloak. Maybe she had sensed she was being followed or had heard Cordi's steps on the gravel. Perhaps she had forgone whatever undertaking had led her out into the garden.

Or maybe she had seen Cordi enter the maze and had been following *her* all along.

Cordi swallowed hard, praying her heartbeat wasn't going to give her away and that her own clumsy stumbling through the maze had saved her. She had floundered through, following the weak light of the lantern, and then only guessed. Prim would be far too sensible.

It was so quiet, Cordi could hear the blood pounding in her ears, painfully aware of the faint whistle of her breath. Clutching her collar at her throat, Cordi took a step toward the small hole in the hedge. Then another. She tried to float across the rocks, willing them not to rattle against each other. When she reached the opposite hedge and its window, she took in a deep breath of fragrant, familiar air, leaning forward to peer through.

The figure, the hood of her cloak now pulled over her head so her face was in shadow, stepped directly into the opening, her hands cupped near the bottom of her hood where her mouth might have been. And she blew a breath, long and strangely sweet-smelling, into Cordi's face.

Surprised, Cordi pursed her lips as she tried to form Prim's name, but only the *P* came out, a puff of air from numbed lips, her tongue clumsy and heavy, and her head filled with crawling ants. Her skin tingled and she realized she could no longer feel the ground beneath her feet, nor her feet at all. And then Cordi collapsed onto the pathway, the sound of the gravel shifting as she fell.

She lay on the ground, gazing up at the pale eye of the moon, the halo around its orb fuzzy and soft as if it were weeping. Her eyelids fluttered and her breath became shallow. She couldn't move and her lungs burned, and she was tired. So very tired. But before oblivion claimed her, a shape loomed above, blotting out the moon, staring down at her.

Prim, her hood pulled back, face lit by the lantern she held aloft, her hair falling over her shoulders. "*Damn,*" the raven-haired girl cursed. "*Damn it all!*"

Chapter 24

THERE WAS PAIN. EXCRUCIATING PAIN in her head, her chest, her abdomen, and her bowels. Her mouth felt like someone had lit a fire on her tongue and left it to smolder and blister while her lungs burned like the bellows of a forge. Her stomach and intestines were no better; searing, stabbing pokers of flame speared her from the inside, demanding she expel everything in her body, even though there was nothing left.

No food. No water.

In her more lucid moments—which were few and far between—Cordi wondered if her body held anything beyond the pain anymore.

She remembered little. She had been outside, following Prim. In the maze. Prim had done something to her. Had given her this pain somehow. But there was nobody to tell and no way to warn of the dangers anyway. Her tongue wouldn't work, her breath was too short, and she couldn't hold a thought in her head.

And, it seemed, Prim had become her nurse.

In her first moment of awareness, she had heard crying. Distant whimpering punctuated by stifled sobs. A clipped voice: "Get hold of yourself! You are not helping!" But then the pain had seized her and Cordi's entire body had spasmed till she was lost to the fire that burned in her brain.

Shapes and shadows had come from every direction, in all colors, but all with malice in their eyes and form. Twisted faces with the perverted features of those she knew—Mrs. Clark, Mason, Stella, Prim, Edward, Briar—and those she did not. Demons and regrets and anxieties she had long thought banished to the void surfaced and tormented her with her mistakes, her failures, her vanities. She saw Anne with that terrible boy, only his fingers buried in her hair had become twigs that tangled and twisted in her braid. Laughter fell from Anne's lips along with petals and she was laughing at Cordi. At her ignorance and innocence. At her otherness. She saw Edward, only he was the Edward from the painting, his face made of oils on canvas, his features melting and warping and spinning with color. Even if she closed her eyes, she could hear their goading and their whispers above the screams that tore her throat raw and burst blisters that had formed on her tongue, filling her mouth with acid and flame.

At some point, she had been restrained. Had felt blood and skin under her nails where she had tried to scratch her flesh open to let the fire out. She remembered hands gripping her arms tight, strength she could not fight, and then fabric wrapped around her ankles and wrists. Silks.

But they might have been iron cuffs covered in spikes, the way they burned both hot and cold. Everything hurt. Everything was pain on pain on pain.

She'd awoken several more times over the next hours, or days, or weeks. There was no time wherever she was, though light moved there, and breezes touched her feverish skin.

Touched but did not soothe, because she was only frayed nerves and flayed skin. Faces—real faces, she thought—were sometimes with her. Briar, her lovely features touched by fear and sorrow and something else that twisted her lips, but that Cordi could not name. Could not see. Prim, mouth thin and tight, eyes always focused. And Lady Evangeline, dignified and clinical as she bent over Cordi's prone form. When together, Lady Evangeline and

Prim spoke in clipped sentences, words Cordi could neither understand nor even truly hear. The world was muffled beyond the shallow wheeze of her own breath and the crackling of the fire within her skull, but she was aware of Lady Evangeline, masked and gloved, her hair too bright, pulling at Cordi's eyelids, checking her nails, touching her pulse, occasionally forcing a bitter draft between her lips.

Cordi would sleep then, whatever they were giving her laced with some kind of sedative. But she didn't care. If it offered reprieve from her personal Hell; she would have begged for it had she had the voice for such things. Under the sedative, she did not always see the phantoms of her folly. Sometimes she heard Edward's voice, far away and slow. Sad. Lonely. And afraid.

Dee . . . Dee . . . Run . . . The Garden . . .

"Hornets," she'd whispered once through chapped lips before a cough racked her body till she was quivering with exertion, her heart fit to burst. "There are hornets in my head. Let them out. Please."

A cool cloth was placed against her lips and water was dripped across her tongue and down her throat. A familiar scoff: "Do not be silly. There are no hornets in your head. The only thing held within your skull is a brain, though I may need to reconsider my opinion on that matter if you are determined to be foolish."

Prim.

She could make no sense of it. Prim had done this to her. In the garden. Why couldn't Cordi remember how? But Cordi had seen her, and she'd been so angry before Cordi lost consciousness. That she remembered clearly.

Didn't she?

It seemed to go on forever, the delirium and the pain and the weakness and the nightmare that was being awake and aware, even by halves. And the longer she dwelled in agony, the more she began to question what had happened to her. *Had* she been called to the garden? *Had* she ever chased Prim through the maze? *Had* Prim hurt her? It had seemed so real, but if it had been real, why would Prim be nursing Cordi back to health?

What *had* happened?

Eventually, the day came when Cordi opened her eyes to weak sunlight desperately trying to break through the clouds that cast the world in shades of gray beyond the windows. For a fraction of a second, she was back at the Barrow on the day Edward left, everything around her cold and waiting to either die or be born, and she wondered now which she was.

Remembering herself, she braced for the wave of pain that always followed consciousness, but it didn't come. Cordi held still, cataloging, sure that at any moment the pain would return with cruel calculation, but it didn't. No flames licked along her skin or burned within her veins. There was no buzzing in her head. No hornets with fire-tipped stingers.

She felt . . . fine. Weak—yes, oh so weak—and her throat was dry, but the fever was gone.

No monsters, neither real nor imaginary, hid in the corners of her room.

Wait . . . *not* her room.

It was not the chamber she shared with Stella. There was no second bed so carefully made up with not a crease in sight. There was no cross-stitch of the rules or small basin. This room was wholly and completely different.

The wallpaper was the deep blue of a sky just before dawn, when the sun begins to break the black of the heavens and reminds you of color again. A floral print of gold peonies wove across the blue, glinting here and there in the stray catches of light. There was a large vanity of rich brown wood that needed a proper dusting. Cordi could see swipes made in haste across the surface, which was littered with bottles and wrappings and what looked like needles of the type a doctor might use for injections. The mirror might have given her a better view, angled down as it was, but the reflection was hazy, the glass sheathed in yet another thin layer of dust. A settee against the wall was in disarray, pillows and blankets teetering precariously in lumpy piles. But the lamps were all clean, the windows sparkling, and few corners had cobwebs. A fine room, though not one used regularly, but an attempt had been made to tidy it.

Probably for use as an infirmary. For Cordi's infirmity.

She was alone in the room, and she tried to raise her head off the pillow but found she could not, weak as she was. She tried smaller movements. Her fingers first, then her hand, noticing how fine the sheets were beneath her. And she realized her hands and feet were free; she was no longer bound like a madwoman. She rolled her head to the side, and she looked down her body to her wrist, remembering the ties that had held her—then gave a small gasp.

Her nailbeds were black, as if she had been digging in dirt. Her veins were strangely dark, a spiderweb of purple cracks under her almost translucent skin, climbing up along the inside of her arm. The bruises made from the bindings on her wrists had faded to an unsightly yellow, but broken blood vessels were still visible.

How long had she been ill? Her gaze flitted to the window as the sun began to finally break through the clouds. What had—

Cordi shut her eyes as a beam of light struck her face, the sun framed by the panes like a portrait. It was warm and Cordi breathed in deeply, as if she could inhale the light, draw it down into her murky lungs, and let it fill her, heal her, nurture her. She felt it spreading through her body, brilliant and golden behind her thin eyelids, all the colors in the world dancing within the glow. She felt herself leaning into that warm touch, a caress like she had never known. One that was as comforting and gentle as her mother's kiss might have been if she could still remember how it had felt.

The door opened and there was a sharp intake of breath.

Cordi opened her eyes to see Stella, masked and gloved, standing in the doorway with a large basket. She stared openly, a strange marvel in the widening of her eye before she shut the door hastily behind her, rushing to the foot of Cordi's bed, but no farther.

A pang hit Cordi. She would have liked Stella to take her hand. To offer a word of kindness or to give her any sense of what had happened. She attempted to ask but found her tongue too heavy and dry. How she longed for water.

"I can't stay," Stella whispered urgently behind her mask, white and embroidered with violets and green leaves. "I'm only meant to bring in the fresh linens and take the old. But I've brought your things."

From within the basket, Stella produced Cordi's old skirt, and she peeled back a fold to show her the letters and carving. Cordi's eyes grew the size of saucers in her head, and she felt fear seize her heart. She had been discovered. But wait—Stella couldn't read. And if she had turned them in to Miss Eliot, why would she be hiding them?

Stella nodded as if she had read Cordi's mind. "Miss Eliot demanded your trunk be emptied and everything burned, just in case." In case of what, Stella didn't say. "But when I was emptying your things, I found these. I . . ." A pause as Stella wrestled with what to say. "I imagined they were precious to you if you hid it so."

Cordi wanted to embrace this girl, her friend. To tell her thank you. But all she could manage was a pitiful nod and a whimper. But Stella seemed to understand, her eye softening briefly before she bent, reaching one arm up under the bed. Cordi could hear the scratch of fabric and a dull thud before Stella straightened with a grunt.

"I'm sure you'll find a better place for it soon enough," she said softly, her voice muffled by the mask. "I'll be off and telling them you're awake. Lady Evangeline has been bent over her books for days, her tea sitting there, growing cold. And Miss Briar . . ." A tsk. "She's been in such a state. Even

Miss Prim is snippier." Stella hoisted the fresh laundry from the basket with her strong arms and then piled the mass of laundry on the settee in its place. "I'm glad for you, Cordi. So glad. Such a blessing."

Cordi attempted a smile, the corners of her mouth twitching, but it wouldn't come. The effort made her want to shut her eyes and turn back to the light again. She wished to retrieve her fox carving, to hold it and find comfort in its familiar grooves and contours, but she lacked the strength. At least it was close. The door clicked shut behind Stella, and Cordi let herself begin to drift, grateful for such a kind soul who had kept her secrets.

But a new buzzing began in her brain. Not painful, this one. Just a thought, rattling around, flitting from one corner of her mind to the next, stealing her peace.

Stella had been masked. Had been wearing gloves.

Cordi was in the south wing. And she was wearing neither.

Chapter 25

"ARE YOU QUITE SURE YOU can't manage another mouthful?" Briar said, spoon perfectly poised, raised as she leaned ever so slightly over Cordi's bed from her seat. The broth was clear and tasteless save for a slight sourness that lingered on the palate for some time after eating, but Cordi blamed the wounds on her tongue. It was a wonder she could taste anything at all.

She shook her head delicately against the pillow. "No. Thank you." She thrilled a little at Briar's pout as the girl dropped the spoon back into the bowl, the white napkin beneath sprawled across her lap so she did not spill anything on her dress. Pink that day, her favorite color. Pink with little orange blossoms stitched around the neckline and cuffed sleeves.

Briar placed the bowl on the table by the bed and sat back in her chair, hands in her lap, but Cordi noticed how her fingers clutched at the fabric. Nervous, then.

It had been several days since Cordi had gained true consciousness. Her bedroom had long ago been a nursery before the girls had grown and their toys and prams were relegated to the attic above, forgotten. Lady Evangeline had subsequently permitted the girls to decorate it themselves, Briar had told her, though she freely admitted it had been Prim who had really done the work. Picking out the wallpaper and the pieces of furniture with her keen artist's eye.

It was such fun when we were doing it. I think Mother meant it as a distraction for us. But when it was finished and we realized there was nobody to occupy it, it only made us sad, Briar had told her. *Or maybe it was just me. Prim's always telling me I'm too sentimental and silly about such things. That I feel them too deeply. I wish I could help it.*

I think you're wonderful, Cordi had thought. Did think.

The room had become Cordi's sickroom, as she'd suspected, though nobody seemed to want to answer her in regard to when she would be well enough to return to the north wing and her duties. She could hardly imagine such a fuss lasting much longer when there was so much work to be done and so few hands to do it.

And she felt fine! Splendid, really. As if her illness had made her recognize what a healthy body felt like. Had she always gone through her life without the awareness she had now? She swore she could feel her blood moving in her veins. The fine hairs on her body sensing lightning. She heard things more clearly. Smelled things with a sharper sense. And she *felt*. Strange, silent signals that reached her from someplace within, as if elsewhere a bell had been struck and the echo sounded in her belly.

She sat up a bit straighter against the pillows that had been bolstered behind her, feeling foolish abed while one of the ladies of the house waited on her. Briar didn't seem to mind at all, though. She had taken charge of Cordi's meals, while Prim had taken charge of her health, making sure she continued to show signs of improvement and monitoring her "vitals" in a manner most professional and courteous, which only continued to confuse Cordi more.

"Is the room to your liking?"

"Hmm?" Cordi asked, coming around. "Oh! Yes. It's divine! But you didn't need to go to all the trouble for me." On one of Cordi's "walks" up and down the hall with Prim to "build her stamina and keep her blood circulating," Briar had done her best to dust and polish and tidy as if *she* were the servant. She brought in fresh flowers every day from the garden, and their fragrance and colors were always a delight. As was the company.

"I'll not hear that again. You act as if you are a burden, and you are no such thing. We will get your strength back again, won't we? I won't settle for anything else." Her apple cheeks blossomed and she looked down, hiding her face. "I don't wish to cry over it anymore, so I won't. But I would have been very cross if you had died, Cordi. Cross and miserable and heartbroken."

Heartbroken.

The word struck her and something in her belly awakened, blossomed. Light spilled through her pores and drew the long-buried seeds of desperate desire from their beds of strangled weeds. Briar's words pulled Cordi as the moon pulled the tide. That so angelic and kind and marvelous a creature could care for her, wait on her, find her company meaningful, was at total odds to all Cordi had known. Mrs. Clark had always told her she was worthless, stubborn, and an irritation. And she had been headstrong. Obstinate. But she had wanted to be loved too.

"Briar?" She waited till those violet eyes lifted, surprised to see the earnestness in Briar's face. And Cordi allowed herself to be obstinate again and dared. "I would never want to hurt you. I—"

"And what a cozy pair you two make."

Cordi deflated inwardly as she turned to see Prim standing in the doorway, arms crossed as she looked in on them. It never failed how Prim was *always* there. As if she knew what Briar was feeling and when, and had to be there to either soothe or silence. As usual, Briar was mum, refusing to look at either her sister or Cordi, when only a moment before Cordi might have drowned blissfully in her eyes and been grateful for such a beautiful death. But Cordi rallied, determined to spare Briar any of her sister's venom. After what had happened in the garden and the clues tying Prim to Edward, Cordi was wary of Prim, even if she had kept Cordi alive. She could not trust her, of this she was certain.

She forced her mouth into a smile. "Your sister is refusing to let me carry on about lazing around in bed while you two wait on me and the rest of the staff work harder without me there to help. I promise I'm feeling perfectly well! Don't you think we should see if Miss Eliot is ready for me to return to work?"

Prim arched a brow and Briar bit her lip, standing and busying herself with tidying up the tray. Prim watched her sister's back for a moment before lifting a shoulder. "I'm afraid Mother hasn't given her permission yet. But you needn't worry. Mother has inquired for help beyond Farrow. Meanwhile she intends to close up a few of the rooms in the north wing that see little traffic. I've told her before there is no point in having all those bedrooms cleaned, but Miss Eliot has always insisted. And as for lying in bed, I've come to tell you to get dressed. We're expecting company."

"Company?" Briar and Cordi said in unison.

"Mother wishes to have an early tea and she has seen fit to have it with all of us," Prim said, her face betraying nothing, as if it had been carved from smooth, flawless marble.

"Mother?" Briar questioned, and Cordi could hardly tell if it was said with wonder or fear. Perhaps both.

"Yes, dear. Our mother. You know the one." Prim cupped her hands at her waist. "She's very eager to see how our patient is doing. And she believes a walk out of doors would do you both good."

Before Cordi could say anything, Prim was at the wardrobe, pulling it open and revealing a line of beautiful dresses in various shades; some Cordi recognized as those she had previously worn. Was this where they kept the clothes she borrowed rather than cluttering up the girls' own wardrobes?

Prim selected a dress of daffodil yellow with a pretty blue overgown the same shade as a robin's egg. She carried them to the bed and draped them across the bottom, careful to make sure the skirts didn't fall to the floor. She also pulled out a fresh set of stockings and delicate slippers, similar to those the girls themselves wore. "If these don't fit, you could always go barefoot as we often do. Mother will not mind. But they should do. Only please don't force them on your feet. It would be dreadful to have you healing so well only to be bedridden again over a blistered heel."

Was she teasing? It almost sounded as if she was being playful, and Cordi wasn't sure what to do or think. Still, she had to say something, and she pushed farther up on her hands. "I'm really allowed out today?"

"Mm-hmm," Prim said, distracted as she arranged everything on the bed to her liking. "Only don't tire yourself out or go too far from the house. It may rain again. We've had such damp weather the past few days, wonderful as it is for the garden. The ponds and fountains may be ready to overflow, however. And if Mother thinks *I'll* be dealing with her umbrella palms, she is mistaken. The last time I tended them after so much rain, she berated me ceaselessly for cutting them back too far even though they were perfectly fine." She seemed to think about this. "Briar? Be a dear and check the back pond. It quite slipped my mind. I'm sure the duckweed is out of control. Take Cordi with you. You can lead her through the maze so she doesn't get lost."

It was the first time the maze had been mentioned since Cordi's recovery, and she watched Prim carefully, trying to read her. But nothing crossed her smooth features. No hint they shared a little joke or a secret. It was as if Prim were simply making conversation and either could not remember Cordi following her through the maze and the injuries she had inflicted or had simply chosen not to care.

Or perhaps Cordi *had* imagined it after all.

And then she remembered. The sack! Edward's things! She had hidden them in the bushes before pursuing Prim. If the bag was there, it would confirm that Cordi had been in the maze. That something had happened to her. Unless it had been discovered. But Cordi didn't think it likely. Prim's inference that they had been confined indoors for quite some time gave little chance for discovery.

Satisfied with her selection, Prim straightened. "We'll leave you to dress." She beckoned to Briar imperiously. "Come along, dear. Let's give Cordi her privacy. You can fuss over her after she's dressed properly."

Briar flushed the same color as her dress, rising stiffly and avoiding both Cordi's and Prim's gazes as she turned and left the room. Prim followed, but as Cordi threw the covers off to stand, Prim shut the door and turned back into the room.

Cordi fought the instinct to retreat into the bed.

"You know," she began, "Briar made such a fuss when you fell ill. Not in front of Mother, of course; Mother suffers emotional displays the way I suffer stupidity or the way Briar suffers boredom." Prim tapped a finger to her dark lips, shaking her dark head. "She is silly, isn't she, our Briar? Sweet and tenderhearted, but silly. Tantrums and tears, that one. When she was only a sprout, she would cry and cry till she was red in the face if anyone denied her anything. And after Jane and Irene, well . . . I could hardly let her make herself ill. She does sulk so. I did my best to make sure you got better. And if you think convincing Mother to help is easy . . ." A pursing of her lips. "You were so, so sick. So quickly. So strange. Aren't you at all curious?"

An answer was not expected, so one was not forthcoming.

"Let me offer you some friendly advice, Cordi. We are friends, aren't we?" Prim asked, her voice pitched just a bit too high, her peculiar and fantastic eyes flat.

This was not the first time Cordi had been cornered by a bully. The Barrow was full of girls and boys who spoke sweet words before using their fists. And Cordi already had an idea of what was coming. School rules applied here as well, she decided. Tell-tale-tits would be punished severely. To point a finger of accusation at Prim would mean retribution. And what evidence did she have that her very savior had been the one to inflict such an injury? None. They both knew it. As such, she conjured up a smile to match Prim's tone. "Of course."

Prim's lips twitched at the corners, amused. It really was a game to her, wasn't it? She looked around the room with vague disinterest, but Cordi refused to be fooled. Prim did everything deliberately. She wanted to make Cordi uncomfortable before she made her next play. "Mother will want answers as to why you were out in the middle of the night skulking about the garden. I do hope you have a good explanation for her. For Briar's sake as well as your own."

With a tilt of her head, she left the room, shutting the door softly.

Chapter 26

AS THE GIRLS LEFT TO let her dress, Cordi deliberated over what she would say to Lady Evangeline's questions and how she would retrieve Edward's belongings. She had been foolish and rash, barreling ahead, and it had nearly cost her life. Prim was now on her scent, suspicious if she had not already been. And now Lady Evangeline would want answers as to why her newest addition to the staff—one who had already been rewarded with a new position—had been found lurking in her treasured gardens.

Was she to be thrown out? She didn't think so if Prim had warned her, a mystery in and of itself. More likely Prim realized Cordi had found the painting or made some other discovery, and she needed to make sure Cordi was properly grateful she had been revived at all so she would be less likely to reveal Prim's own secrets. And she was using Briar as leverage.

Of course Cordi wouldn't betray Prim to her mother. There was simply nothing to gain.

Cordi adjusted the sleeves of the dress, but as she slipped her feet into the slippers and turned toward the mirror to give her hair a quick brushing, she had another shock.

After being so ill, she expected to look drawn and gaunt, her eyes yellowed and the delicate skin beneath bruised and dark. She clearly remembered how poorly Jane had appeared, and she might have had a similar illness. But Cordi looked the picture of health. Her hair was glossy, her cheeks bursting with color. She might have been mistaken for a noble's daughter just returned from a holiday. She checked her nails. The beds were still dark, but deep purple rather than black. A few faint scratches still marred her throat where she had tried to claw her skin off, but otherwise . . .

Another striking difference as she leaned into her reflection was the color of her irises. Still deep blue, but was the center around her pupil not changed? More violet than blue? With the light from the windows behind her, it was difficult to tell, but it certainly seemed—

A knock on the door and an impatient Prim called out, "Are you quite finished?"

Cordi backed away from the mirror, dismissing what was likely a trick of the light. She had more important things to think upon. How to get Edward's belongings back to her room. How to learn what had really happened to her in the garden. Chief among them was still how to find Edward.

But all those thoughts slipped from her head like rainwater through a downspout as she opened the door to Briar, pink and flushed and almost vibrating with excitement. "Come on!" she urged, waving Cordi along. Prim stood at the opposite side of the passage, arms folded again, saying nothing.

Two could play this game of pretend, and Cordi chose to flash Prim a winning smile before she followed Briar. But she felt Prim watching, eyes on the back of her neck where her hair was shorter. Could feel the girl's gaze narrow in suspicion.

Whatever confidence she felt began to wane, however, with each step down to the first level. By the time they reached the doors of the terrace, Cordi found herself thinking, as she had done in the Barrow, of ways she might avoid punishment. The scar tissue along her back rippled and she unconsciously rubbed the shiny, raised skin on the backs of her hands.

"Cordi?"

Between her and the doors stood Briar, looking at her curiously. "You've gone quite pale. Are you sure you're fit to be out of bed?" Cordi opened her mouth, but all that came out was a breathy squeak. "Oh, dearest, whatever is the matter?"

Even the endearment was not enough to shake Cordi out of the spiral she found herself sucked into. How could she explain her fears without risking insult? Rationally, she knew Lady Evangeline was not Mrs. Clark, yet she made Cordi want to run.

Run . . . Deeeee . . .

Why hadn't she run sooner? Why was she not running?

Someone gripped her elbow from behind and Cordi wheeled around, arm lifted to defend herself, fingers hooked into claws so she might tear into skin and—

Prim was taken aback but did not release Cordi's arm. For a moment, Cordi considered what it might be like to rip the smug mask from the liar's face.

"Let me go," she said, no deference in her voice.

The young woman studied Cordi's face and then her hand, darkened nails ready to drag down flawless skin. She let go of Cordi's elbow, folding her hands at her waist, and clucked her tongue. "I apologize for startling you. I merely thought to take your arm, fearing you might be faint. Still, how marvelously violence suits you, Cordi. You were so pale and now your cheeks are roses in full bloom. One imagines how a scuffle might bring out the best in you."

"Are you sure she is quite well, Prim?" Briar said as if Cordi were not even there. "We can tell Mother she needs more rest."

"I'm fine!" Cordi snapped, more harshly than she intended, and dropped her arm. "I was, as you say, only startled." She might concede that much to propriety, but she would not apologize.

It seemed Prim cared little. "Excellent. See, sweet sister? She's almost perfect. Come along."

The older girl swept past, satin and crinoline sweeping the floor with the sound of leaves blown by an icy wind, her crisp, sharp steps the crack of branches. Cordi shivered as that wind whipped around her heart, threatening to freeze and kill whatever hope had begun to rise from the frostbitten ground.

"Is something wrong, Cordi?" Briar pressed, fingers plucking at her dress. "You can tell me. I'll listen."

Some of that hope grew green again, sparking with life at the sweet urging, and Cordi managed a shake of her head. "Just nerves."

Briar came to loop her arm through Cordi's and led her to the door. "I shall tell you a secret," she whispered, leaning in, her sweet breath stirring the air by Cordi's ear. "Mother makes me nervous too. Prim as well, even though she is the favored daughter."

There was a bitter edge to Briar's voice, a hurt that might have scarred over, but whose memory lingered. Emboldened, Cordi patted the redhead's hand where it lay on her arm. "I cannot imagine a soul who would not hold you in the greatest esteem."

Briar tutted but blushed all the same, and the sun that had begun to thaw the not-so-barren soil in Cordi's heart warmed her from the inside. She let herself be escorted by her beautiful companion out onto the terrace, where a fine tea had been laid. Lady Evangeline was already seated, her posture straight and perfect, face angled up at her elder daughter, who stood behind one of the chairs, sharing whispered words. Cordi did not believe it was her imagination, that Prim did in fact look nervous. It was a subtle difference, but there was a definite rigidity to her spine, a distance to her eyes, as if she, too, had been trained at the Barrow and expected a reprimand at any moment.

"Ah, Cordelia," the mistress of Edenfield said briskly, spotting her. "You appear to be much improved, my dear."

Cordi tried but failed to ignore the feel of Briar's hand on her arm, the edges of their hips pressed together beneath their day dresses. "Yes, my lady," Cordi said as she disengaged herself from Briar's hold with reluctance.

Lady Evangeline gestured with a wave to the other chairs. "Come along, girls. I fear the weather may turn again."

While Prim and Briar sank into their seats, Prim to her mother's right and Briar on the left, Cordi stood to the side, wondering if she was there as a servant or—

"You as well, Cordelia, though I expect you to only partake cautiously. We'll not chance rich foods yet."

With trepidation, Cordi settled in the empty chair opposite Lady Evangeline. Three sets of eyes watched her, and Cordi was not sure which pair unnerved her the most. She was not educated in fashionable conversation or high tea manners and feared she would embarrass herself.

Two teapots sat upon the table and Lady Evangeline lifted the larger, pouring steaming cups for the three girls. Setting this pot aside, she poured her own cup from the smaller pot. Cordi noticed how much darker her tea seemed. Perhaps the Lady preferred a strong brew. Cordi examined her own cup. It was not the tea Miss Eliot served, but it was quite fragrant. Loose tea leaves swirled upon the surface, spinning in a tight circle. Though it was still too hot, Cordi took a deep drink, suspecting she might need fortifying for what was to come.

Feeling she should say something, Cordi took in the table with its fine cloth and silver service. There were tiny sandwiches of cucumber and something creamy in pale bread, dainties in an array of colors, cheeses and jams, and vegetables and fruits cut in clever shapes: radish roses, carrot spirals, and others. "It is a lovely table. Thank you for inviting me, my lady."

Lady Evangeline nodded once, accepting. "And how are you feeling today?"

"Well, my lady," Cordi answered as a plate of the small sandwiches was offered her. She took one gently with tiny silver tongs, trying to keep her hands steady. "I am much improved."

"So it would seem." She took a sip of her tea. "Quite a remarkable recovery. But I admit curiosity and you'll indulge me. What were you doing before you were found?"

Beneath the table, Cordi squeezed her hands between her knees. She dared not look at Prim sitting straight and tall, eating a salmon sandwich with perfect manners. In her periphery, Cordi could see the sunlight glinting off the tiny cake fork Briar held. They knew she had been in the garden, so it was pointless to lie about that particular detail. So if she couldn't lie and couldn't tell the truth, she would have to find some common ground between them.

Cordi frowned into her lap. "I'm sorry, my lady. I shouldn't have been in the garden. I know that. I knew it then. I admit my curiosity is a sin. So often I was told that very thing by my teachers, but I'm afraid I couldn't resist looking into your garden again. I always loved the garden at school, such as it was. But yours is so exquisite! I couldn't sleep, and I thought—" She bit her lip as she had seen Briar do, hoping she looked contrite. "I didn't think, really."

"You need not apologize for love of the earth and her treasures." *Thanks given to the Garden, for the Garden is right and good.* The mistress leaned back and pursed her lips. "Do you recall the last thing that happened before you presumably fainted?"

Yes. "No."

She could almost hear a chuckle in her head. A throaty sound of delight as Cordi wrestled with her conscience. Something Prim would certainly relish, not having one herself. But if a lie was necessary, Cordi would tell one. What had this woman done to deserve her honesty, anyway? Cordi easily recalled the words of Mrs. Starling. About how Edward had fallen so similarly ill.

Fever. Ravings. Couldn't catch his breath. If you live in Farrow long enough, you know it for what it is.

The poison of this place.

The woman who sat so properly across the table, the very picture of society, might have very well let her brother die. But Edward had recovered, like Cordi. Mrs. Starling had said so. Cordi looked back and forth between Prim and her mother as they sipped their tea, looking down their oh-so-similar noses. If Prim had been enamored of Edward and her mother knew . . . Well, Briar had said in so many words that Prim feared her mother, if but a little. What would she have done to keep her secret safe?

Anything, Cordi felt sure. She would have done anything. Would *do* anything. Cordi might not have an advantage, but she still had pieces she might move.

"I apologize if my illness has put a strain on the household," she offered, carefully folding her napkin in her lap. "I would be most happy to resume my duties if you see fit. It isn't my intention to be a burden. Not when you've been so kind to me. To all the women here."

It would be a stretch to say Lady Evangeline smiled, but she did seem pleased. "It is good of you to say so, Cordelia. But I think you are serving a greater good where you are, at present."

The conversation moved slowly after that, talk of the garden and the weather. Of plant purchases being made. Of plans for the garden. Expanding, perhaps. Cordi and the girls were not required to speak much as they enjoyed the repast. Prim gave a few opinions and suggestions, most of which Lady Evangeline dismissed or countered. It did Cordi as much good as the sunshine to see Prim bite back retorts. More than once, Cordi found herself lifting her face to the sky, letting her eyes close, breathing in the day. It was as if she took more strength from the sun than she did the few, meager bites of food she allowed herself.

"Briar, why don't you take Cordi with you on a walk. I'd like to speak to your sister."

Briar dabbed her pretty mouth with her napkin and slid her chair back. Cordi hesitated, wanting to hear more, wishing she might slip into the role of servant again. "Should I stay and clear, my lady?"

A wave. "Not at all. Attend to Briar. Whatever she requires of you."

Cordi ducked her head as she too pushed away from the table, hoping her flush was hidden. "Yes, my lady."

Chapter 27

"IT FEELS *INCREDIBLE* TO BE out of the house!" Cordi exclaimed as she and Briar stood on the back patio, heads tilted skyward. Had fresh air ever felt quite so divine? It was as if Cordi could feel each individual pore and hair along her body breathing and soaking in the sun. She could smell the distant scent of rain and knew it was coming their way. Had she been cooped up for so long that all her senses were now heightened and desperate to be useful? She stretched her arms up to the sky, grateful beyond words to be alive and in this day.

"It's wonderful to see you like this, Cordi. Happy and hale. You gave me quite a fright and I'll thank you not to do it again," Briar said, walking down the stairs.

Me. Not us. A corner of Cordi's mouth lifted as she unabashedly watched the gentle sway of Briar's hips as she moved toward the maze, following slowly. Cordi bent low and feigned adjusting one of the new slippers, the longer waves on one side of her head hiding her face from any spying eyes at the house, and she looked under the bushes along the wall.

There. A dark shape just discernible if you knew where to look.

She stood and quickened her pace to catch up. As loath as she was to come between two siblings, perhaps she would have to play Prim's game a bit more strategically.

Cordi paced herself next to Briar, clasping her hands behind her back and committing each turn to memory. "I have not properly thanked you as I have your sister and mother and it speaks poorly of me. Dear Briar. My constant and stalwart champion through my infirmity."

There it was. The blush she wanted. That made her heart race. It spread up Briar's throat and into her cheeks even as she pushed a wayward curl back over her shoulder. She was wearing her hair down and free of ribbons or combs and it shimmered in the dappled light. She gave a shy smile, just the barest flash on her lips, but Cordi knew how pleased she was. "Oh, I didn't do anything. Prim and Mother deserve all the credit. I was probably in the way. I just didn't want you to wake up and feel alone."

The pillows and blankets on the rumpled settee. Had Briar taken to sleeping in there? Had it even been safe? Lady Evangeline had always attended her with a mask. Cordi looked behind them and lowered her voice by degrees. "Briar, can I truly ask you something?"

"Of course."

"Why are there masks and gloves, and why am I not wearing them now? Why do we only take them off outside?"

Briar's feet skidded to a stop, sending pebbles and rocks scurrying away in all directions. She looked frightened, and Cordi thought she had perhaps gone too far. Then Briar's face fell and she resumed walking, her hands rubbing at her arms as if she had taken a chill. She didn't say anything for some time.

"It's difficult to explain, actually. But, well, you know Mother is a botanist? Someone who studies and understands the nature of plants? Well, she is far more brilliant than people realize. I think people underestimate other people—especially women—quite a lot, don't you? And you know how women are treated out in the world. I mean, you know far better than I, I'm sure. I've never been beyond the gate."

Cordi shuddered inwardly but said nothing. Not then.

"Mother wanted to pursue her passion, but her father forbade it. Demanded she marry. She was forced to wed our father or lose her home and her family. And she might have willingly suffered such a loss if it hadn't meant losing her gardens and all her books, all her work. I wonder if she might have been happier that way. . . ." Briar looked a little lost then. Her eyes—following her thoughts—grew distant; perhaps she was wondering what she might have done or thinking of the ramifications of such a choice. Cordi found it hard to think of an innocent young woman like Briar alone in the world. What might become of her?

"I suppose it doesn't matter, does it? Mother married Father. Her parents died not long after—here, actually—and she and my father inherited Edenfield. Eventually Prim came along. Then me. But Mother wasn't satisfied with only a domestic life. She wanted knowledge. Still wanted to prove herself. Began experimenting with plants. Prim says Father found it all rather amusing at first, the way she remembers it. Plants and cuttings and seeds or bulbs arriving from all over the world.

"Mother discovered a way to cross-pollinate certain plants and flowers. The results were marvelous! But also rather terrifying if you didn't understand them. And she realized long-term exposure to certain poisonous plants could yield immunity." Briar was excited now, but Cordi also sensed nerves. As if she was tiptoeing around what she truly wanted to say.

"It sounds incredible," Cordi said reassuringly. And it did! To think of how important such discoveries might be. The good such knowledge could do.

Briar turned to Cordi as they emerged from the maze. "I'm glad you think so. I know Mother wanted to put you on a trial period first and then you fell so ill, but now things are different, aren't they? You're happy here?"

Something about her earnestness both delighted and unnerved Cordi. She felt cornered out in the open, a creature who sensed no immediate threat but knew danger was near. But how preposterous, with Briar of all people.

And how could she deny the truth? "I am happy here. I—I didn't expect that."

"Why?"

Cordi realized they were straying from the topic, but it was a fair trade. Answers for answers. They were drawing close to one of the pools. The placid water reflected a gray sky, clouds pregnant with rain. But underneath the surface, Cordi could see tiny creatures darting about near the shore. Tadpoles, perhaps. Long reeds and cattails grew in bunches around the far end where a moss-covered statue of a woman gazed into the water, one hand reaching for the surface, a crown of carved flowers around her hair, the stone dotted with fungus and black mold. She was beautiful like that, Cordi thought, weathered and draped in moss and lichen.

They stopped near the edge of the pond, the grass wet, the soil soft beneath their slippers, and Cordi kept her eyes on the statue, somehow comforted by the curious expression on its face that time had not been able to erode. "I know you think I know much of the world, Briar, but I know very little. We lost our parents young and were sent to a charity school because nobody would take us in. And I didn't see beyond its gates for years. I was surrounded by girls and boys, but it was more like a prison than a school. The older ones taking from the little ones. The staff cruel and heartless. Friendships were hard there. They were built on transactions. Alliances. I just wanted us to be free. I hated that cage as much as I hated the people who kept us prisoner."

"Us?"

Cordi flinched when she realized what she had said. Stupid. Not paying attention. But she found she did not want to pretend with Briar. She absently stroked the back of her hand, her fingers finding all the raised scar tissue. "My brother. He was older than me. They sent him away when he was old enough and I suppose I was alone after that."

"He left you? Your own brother?" Briar's voice was incredulous.

"He didn't want to!" Cordi explained, hating the inflection in her voice that betrayed her fear and then hating herself all the more for the suspicion. "He wanted to come back! He promised he would."

Briar shook her head, not understanding. "Then why didn't he?"

Dee . . .

The tiny hairs stood up again on Cordi's arms and she felt the distant thunder even before she heard it. She looked in the direction of the rumble, something inside her feeling an intense pang of anticipation at the sound. In the distance just ahead of where the storm clouds were gathering was the forest deep in shadow. Cordi tensed, wanting to run to it, to find some secret place and scream her anger and fear and hurt away, but her feet felt rooted to the ground. "I don't know. I wish I did."

"It must be hard on you, then. To be around Prim and me." Briar had taken up a long pole with a net attached and was using it to scoop small green plants from the pond where they had nearly obscured the water.

"Sometimes. But it isn't your doing." *But possibly your sister's,* she thought.

Briar kept scooping, stretching ever farther with the pole, but some of the plants eluded her. "Here," Cordi said, gently taking the pole. "I'm taller."

"Yes. My elfin friend. When I saw you for the first time, tall and lithe and bathed in sunlight, I thought of forest elves and fairy stories and—" Briar touched her fingers to her lips, trying to snare the words that had already escaped. She cleared her throat. "Have you read many fairy stories? Mother dislikes them, I think. Except 'Goblin Market' by Rossetti. She was quite eager we devour the wisdom of the poem. You can read it if you like! It's very good!" She laughed. "And I am rambling."

Cordi pursed her lips. With her extra inches, Cordi was able to just snag the cluster of plants Briar had been trying to collect. "Is this duckweed? These little tiny sprouts?"

"Yes. It grows so fast! And we don't get enough waterfowl that eat it. It will take over the pond if we don't pay attention. That's part of gardening, isn't it? Trimming back? Cutting away the parts of something that do not benefit it anymore. And— Oh! Cordi! What happened to your poor hands?"

Cordi jerked the pole back so quickly the net splashed in the water, sending the plants on the surface and the tadpoles beneath in all directions. Feeling so natural in Briar's presence, she had forgotten Briar had only seen her hands gloved. She again touched a scar, embarrassed by Briar's innocent curiosity and concern. She considered asking for Briar to forget all about it, to just ignore them. But she had told Stella the truth, and something in her had felt liberated by it.

"I was punished. At the school."

A gasp, and Briar joined her hands as if praying in front of her mouth. "A man did that to you, didn't he? That's why you came to us!"

"No. And yes. It was a woman who gave me these. The headmistress at my school. The man . . . he was the gardener and she liked him very little, but she liked me even less. He tried to hurt me. And I suppose he did, but not as he might have. Yet the headmistress blamed me." She felt her face flush, not sure how much she should say. Not even confident Briar would understand.

But the girl's face said she did. "Oh, my sweet Cordi. What a time you've had. It's barbaric! I'm going to make it up to you somehow. I want to make sure you're happy! And I've prattled on and I still haven't even answered your question, have I? About the gloves and the masks. Not really."

Cordi had almost forgotten. Being around Briar did that to her. Made her want to be selfish. Made her want to forget sad memories and painful truths.

The wind picked up, sending Cordi's and Briar's hair whipping around their faces. The sky was darkening quickly, but the rain would still hold for a time. *Not long,* something inside Cordi said. Something that wanted the rain desperately.

Briar looked toward the house, then motioned Cordi to follow, pulling a set of keys from her pocket. They knocked lightly against something in her skirt with a soft *thud*. "We have to hurry," she said, voice notched with something that might be panic or might be excitement. "It will be easier if I show you."

And she lifted her skirts, running across the lawn toward the greenhouse.

Chapter 28

THERE WAS SOMETHING OMINOUS ABOUT the greenhouse. Something subtly menacing that put her in mind of a witch's cottage, oppressive and frightening. She tried to convince herself it was the ever-darkening sky, casting it in such bold, sharp relief against the landscape. Edward had helped build it and it was the last thing he had done before he went missing. She looked for signs of his hands having worked or shaped the wood, but the flat, even beams, carefully measured frames for the many windows, and slanted roof yielded nothing.

But the door. The door was another matter.

As they got closer, Briar searching for the right key, Cordi examined the door. It had been stained a deep green and—at first—that was all she saw. But then she noticed the ivy pattern carved through the wood, up and down as if trails of vines covered the entire entrance. This, she knew, had been Edward.

Briar fitted the key into the lock, pushing her way in. Unable to resist, Cordi let her fingers drift over the carved leaves and vines, happy to have found yet more evidence.

"Quickly!" Briar whispered from the darkened interior. "Shut the door!"

Cordi snatched her hand away and shut them in. The heat in the room was oppressive and Cordi found it difficult to draw a regular breath, her lungs beset by thick, muggy air. But oddly enough, she also felt revived somehow. As if the pores in her skin were opening, drawing the water from the air. She'd read about bathhouses once in school and wondered if this was what one felt like. The air hung with mist, and she already felt moisture along her skin.

Briar plunged deeper into a room filled with plants lining both sides and running down the middle of the structure creating a bifurcated path, disappearing around the corner. There were enormous leaves in every shade of green. Some plants were tall, some squat. Some in large planters while others sat upon shelves in clear jars filled to the brim with water, their roots long, pale, and exposed. Some bore flowers, though few she recognized.

Except one. Thinking to impress Briar with at least some knowledge, she stepped toward a tall plant with offshoots of clusters of intricate and delicate white flowers. "Queen Anne's lace," she said confidently. "I'm surprised your mother would cultivate something so common and hide it under lock and key."

Briar returned and gave a huff of laughter. "That's not Queen Anne's lace! That's hemlock. It is a potent poison! See this?" She gently touched a purple bell-shaped flower, the head drooping gently as if in sleep. "Belladonna. It means 'beautiful lady.' "

"Belladonna," Cordi repeated, the word foreign. "It's lovely."

"It's deadly nightshade. Another poison." She gestured around. "They all are."

"All?" Cordi scanned the room, shocked at the multitude of plants and flowers, all dangerous and deadly.

"All. Everything here," Briar said with a touch of sadness as she backed up, her ample hips pressed against a worktable covered with cuttings in tiny jars, pruning shears, and long gloves. A small red leather-bound book lay on one edge of the table, reams of paper and pens at the other. Briar picked up the book absently. "Oh. This is Prim's journal. It shouldn't be in here. She'll be going mad for it, I'm sure. She writes everything in it. Things she doesn't share with even me, though we promised always to share everything and—"

"Briar," Cordi said, urging her on with her interrupted explanation even as her eyes focused on the book. Prim's journal. Prim's most secret thoughts.

Those pink lips pouted as she turned the book back and forth but did not break the spine. Did not break her sister's confidence. "I want you to understand, Cordi. I don't want you to be like the others. They think we're frightening or something of a miracle. And we know what they say of us in the village. How they cross themselves when we're mentioned. I don't want you to think that. I like the way you talk to me. Look at me. Like . . . like we're friends." She tossed the book down absently before she pressed her hands back, gripping the table behind her. It made her chest jut out and elongated her throat and Cordi wished she could blame her shortness of breath on the heavy air. "You see, Mother . . . well . . . she didn't just cultivate plants. She cultivated us too."

Cordi had no sense of what she meant, so she only stared dumbly, waiting for an explanation.

Briar made a sound of frustration. "I'm not clever enough to understand. Not like Prim. It makes me quite a disappointment. But *you're* clever, Cordi. Haven't you noticed that we're different, Prim and I? It is because Mother made us different."

A sense of cold dread swept through Cordi and her fingertips and toes numbed. She felt she might be falling, but the room didn't sway and neither did she.

Briar pointed around the room. "Hemlock? Peacock flower? Henbane? Nightshade? I can touch them all. Taste them all. Breathe them all. My beautiful, deadly sisters. They are as much my family as Prim and Mother, I suppose, for we are much the same. They helped Mother make me. My life's breath is their perfume. Mother grew us this way, me and Prim. Oh, I don't mean in a pot or flower bed, but through long exposure. Tiny doses here and there from the time we were little. She wanted us to be powerful and safe. She wanted to ensure no man could touch us. And they can't." She plucked at her skirt nervously before wrapping her arms around herself protectively. Armor and comfort. "Nobody can. We're toxic."

It was suddenly hard to breathe again, and Cordi wanted air, but she wanted answers more. "What do you mean?"

Briar laughed, but it was without joy. "You know."

She did. God help her, she did. The ghosts of Edenfield. The skipping rhyme. These beautiful, haunting girls who could never be seen because they could never be touched. Their mother had made sure no man could steal her precious daughters. Her spring goddesses.

Your only hope is to avoid the breath of a pretty maid.

Belladonnas, indeed.

"Jane and Irene," she said through lips gone dry. "Their illness? And—"

"And you."

The figure—Prim—face concealed by the hood of her cloak, the strange breath in Cordi's face through the window of the hedge. Prim had poisoned her with her breath!

"I thought we had been so careful," Briar said as if reading Cordi's mind, but her gaze was distracted. "But then you were sick! Somehow you must have had traces left on your skin. I thought maybe our dresses, the ones lent to you. Maybe they hadn't been cleaned properly and it had bled into your skin slowly. Or—my darkest fear—the last mask I made you. I wanted it to be so special! Something just for you, my darling friend. But maybe I wasn't careful. When Stella found you stumbling around outside, confused and in pain—"

"Stella?"

"Hmm?" Briar said, barely hearing. "Yes. Stella found you. She must have awoken and you were gone? Poor dear was so afraid to see you like that! So worried about you! As was I! And Prim, of course! Oh, Cordi—"

She still didn't know it was Prim.

"—I was sure you were lost to me. To us! But then you got better! So much better. And it is different now."

Cordi lifted her hands, trying to see through her skin. "Briar, why don't I have to wear the gloves or the masks?"

A long moment passed between them, Briar avoiding Cordi's concerned, questioning gaze. Her fingers danced along the spine of the red journal, pushing it back and forth across the table, the only sound the slide of its passing. A guilty blush rose up her white throat.

Briar licked her lips. "Because you're like us now."

Panic rose within her at this admission, stated so casually. There had been more than just men there. There had been children! Small skeletons with bones blackened by poison. Yet, Stella spoke of it as if it were sensible and right!

And if Irene wasn't there, where was she?

"Is Jane well? Is she as she was before?" Cordi prodded carefully, unsure if they had discovered Jane's disappearance.

A beat of silence. "I shouldn't be telling you this, but Jane left in the night. Took not a thing. Miss Eliot is in such a state. I don't know what Lady Evangeline will say." A sound of pity. "It was hard on Jane. The loss of Irene. She and Irene were very close, you see. *Very* close. And I think she must be feeling a bit of guilt for not following her. If only she had remained. They would be together again in time."

Cordi's gaping mouth and horrified expression must have spoken volumes because Stella followed with an exasperated sigh. "It's not like you think! This is a safe place. I worry you are fearful for nothing. This is why everyone must go through a trial period first. So their fears are put aside. What has been done is a miracle!"

There was no mistaking the awe in Stella's voice now, and Cordi knew she could not relay her true fears to her. She thought of what Prim had said about chess. How you had to know your opponent. Know what moves to make to guarantee your victory later. This was not a safe move. Some things she would have to keep to herself for a bit longer at least. Whatever spell had been cast over the women of Edenfield had them believing the Lady of the house was beyond reproach. A righteous and beatific goddess protecting her flock and rewarding the pious.

And she worried that her own remarkable good health and seeming turn of fortune were doing more harm than good. Wouldn't anyone look at her, knowing where she had been only weeks before, and be envious? Maybe she couldn't make Stella understand the danger she was in, not without revealing too much, but she could still get her help in another matter.

"Maybe," Cordi said, and just that small acquiescence made her ill. "Maybe you're right and I just don't understand it all yet. I don't know. I want to understand. I just . . . Everything has been so fast and so confusing." All this, at least, she could admit freely, easing the barbs of the lies that were beginning to fall from her tongue without much thought.

"Miss Briar said you found me outside. I should thank you for rescuing me."

Stella shook her head. "Thanks to the Lady and the Flowers."

"However did you find me?"

A moment of silence and Stella stiffened, head turning sharply to the door as if listening. "Oh. I woke up to make water and I saw you weren't in bed. I thought maybe you were doing the same. But then I saw the back door open. I knew you had been so upset before, I thought maybe you were getting some air, so I came to look for you. I didn't want to wake the others. I . . . heard something. And it was you!"

She was rambling, her sentences clipped and clumsy. She was lying, whether in part or whole Cordi could not tell. The back door had been locked, not open. Cordi's caution had been warranted, but it was a small consolation paired with the knowledge that she could not wholly trust anyone. Still, Stella was all she had. "Would you do something for me?"

Stella nodded and her face lit up behind her mask. As if it were not an inconvenience but a blessing Cordi was bestowing simply by asking. "Of course! Whatever you need!"

Cordi snatched the keys from the vanity and held them out as an offering. "Miss Briar dropped these. Will you return them to her? You could leave them in her room or say you found them." She did not mention that she had already removed the key to her own door.

Stella took up the ring, looking at the keys long and hard for a moment before closing her gloved fist tightly around them, iron grinding against iron. Cordi wondered if she had made Stella angry by asking her to lie. "I didn't take them! I swear!" Cordi sought to assure her friend.

"I believe you," Stella said, but her voice was flat.

Cordi tried to look gracious rather than afraid. Stella would not betray her. Stella wanted to help her. But she couldn't help but notice the fever that had settled into Stella's eye. A strange brightness and eagerness to please. "I trust you, Stella," she said, hoping she sounded both grateful and slightly authoritative. "I'm thankful to have a friend like you. I want us to be friends. I've not had many."

A softening in the girl's face above the mask. One that was far more familiar. The one that belonged to the girl who had comforted her and held her as she cried when she'd tasted the onion. "We are friends. More. We are *sisters*. All of us are sisters here. Made more than the women we once were."

We were women once.

Cordi offered a tremulous smile, thinking of Jane and hoping she was safe. "I would very much like a sister. I miss having a family."

As Stella began straightening the bedding, Cordi was grateful she had thrown the covers in place to hide the sheets now stained with soil. Hovering by the window, Cordi considered how best to proceed, given the opportunity at last to speak. But before she could, a firm knock came, and the door opened.

Prim, beautiful face set in such a way she might have been carved from the whitest marble, stood in the open doorway, one hand still on the knob. She gave Stella only the briefest glance, the girl dropping into a low curtsy, before she turned her gaze on Cordi.

"So popular, dear Cordi. Always with visitors or callers," Prim said smoothly, the honey in her voice accompanying the beelike sting of her words. "I'm to tell you to breakfast quickly. Mother would like a word with you."

"With me?" Cordi asked.

"Stella," Prim said sharply, causing the girl to startle. "If you've finished here, I would suggest attending to my sister. She's all a jumble with so many happenings in the house, and seeing a friendly, *consistent* face might cheer her."

Without a word, Stella curtsied once more, gathered up the laundry basket, and slipped past Prim into the hallway.

Alone again with Prim and her ever-changing moods, Cordi tried to look baffled at the summons. "Lady Evangeline wishes to see me, you said?"

"She does. In the greenhouse."

"Whatever for?"

Pursing her lips and lifting one shoulder elegantly, Prim answered, "I'm sure I don't know. Only do make sure you remember what I said about having the answers Mother wants to hear." Prim's long lashes kissed her cheeks as she blinked slowly. Once. Twice. "You do remember what I said, don't you?"

Cordi clenched her hands into fists, feeling the cut reopen and the wet ooze of blood on the tips of her fingers. The faintest scent of flowers rose to her nose, and she nodded.

Prim's lips twitched in a smile. "Of course you do. You're such a clever thing, Cordi. What fun it is to have you here."

With a whirl of skirts, she left, the door shutting solidly behind her.

After she was gone, Cordi couldn't eat. She only sat on the window seat, watching the blood slide down her arm while trying to ignore the memory of poisoned skeletons unearthed in the night and the feeling she was not as clever as she thought.

Chapter 33

IT WAS WITH A FAMILIAR dread that Cordi stood in front of the darkly stained door of the greenhouse. One she felt along each raised line of her back and hands. There had been no shortage of occasions for punishment at the Barrow, and Cordi had found herself on the receiving end of the headmistress's tongue—or birch—more than most. Facing the door, hand poised to knock, Cordi desperately wanted to run.

Despite all the pains and horrors and secrets she'd found at Edenfield, she'd not truly considered leaving without her brother. This, however? This terrible quiet that, in her experience, preceded what she had been told was discipline made her stomach turn to water and set her knees to trembling beneath her crinolines, the hiss of the fabric reminding her of the hiss of snakes.

Of serpents.

Of forked tongues whispering pretty lies.

If she had been sensible, something she had rarely been, she would have run. Or never have come at all. She might have listened to someone, anyone, who knew better than her. But good sense had never been a quality attributed to Cordi by her teachers. She was simply stubborn.

It was that stubborn refusal to listen to all her instincts regarding self-preservation that had her knocking on the door, mouth going dry at the imperious command from within.

"Enter."

The greenhouse was stifling already in the late morning sun, condensation trickling slowly down the glass panes to gather along corners. The air, so different from outside, was thick in Cordi's lungs, but still she found it pleasant. So pleasant, she imagined lying down on one of the benches, cheeks brushed by fronds, forehead kissed by delicate, deadly flowers as she slept among them. Her friends. Her sisters.

"Cordelia?"

Torn from her sleep-deprived mind's ramblings, Cordi jerked toward the voice coming from the back of the greenhouse. "Yes, my lady."

"Well, come along."

Skirting the center tables, Cordi followed the path to the rear of the room. Between tall leaves and peculiarly spotted or jewel-toned flowers, she could see the white-blond tresses of Lady Evangeline as she bent over something on the table Cordi had searched in the night. The sound of a spade in dirt and the rattle of pottery filled the space, and Cordi realized she had no weapon, no defense, having left the shears in her room. Prim had been her greatest fear till now. But the set of the Lady's shoulders, much like Mrs. Clark's, was enough to have Cordi stopping some distance away.

"How do you find yourself this morning, Cordelia?" Lady Evangeline asked without turning, her tiny spade shoveling dirt into a wide pot on the table. Her hands were encased in long, sturdy garden gloves and a rosette apron covered much of the front of her day dress, this one the color of a sunlit forest, and she wore a mask of the same color, no embroidery to be found. "You continue to improve, I trust?"

"I do," Cordi said, folding her hands in front of her dress in much the same way she had the first night and trying not to panic at the sight of the mask. Something she would not have thought necessary. But if she was turning like the girls . . .

"I am pleased to hear it. Very pleased." Setting the spade aside, Lady Evangeline took the rim of the pot in both hands and shook it. "Best not to pack the soil to start. Better to shift it and let it sink rather than force it down. Things can't grow if you don't give them a little wiggle room to start; did you know that, Cordelia?"

Such seemingly random questions had never been, in Cordi's experience, random. The wariness she had felt at the first summons was now a screaming alarm in her head, but she found her feet planted. A learned experience to stay small and quiet and not move and maybe things would be over quickly.

"Roots have to work too hard if the soil is too tight," she answered, deciding feigned ignorance on this issue would not serve. The hard, packed soil of the Barrow had taught her this lesson as much as the harsh conditions had. She wondered if Lady Evangeline considered her own question, however, when it came to her daughters.

The pot thumped solidly on the table. "Just right! Come join me. I have more to fill yet."

Cordi settled herself at the other end of the table, a burlap bag of black soil between them. The Lady passed her another small spade and a pot, but did not offer her gloves or apron, so Cordi did not ask for them. Nor did she mind. The dirt she had so dutifully cleaned from her hands that morning again filled along her nailbeds and into the lines of her palms, sticking greedily to the edges of her torn wound. And this was a strange comfort.

They worked side by side, the slice of the metal spades through the dirt the only noise at first. But such silence is heavy and not meant to last.

"You have heard Jane has left us."

It was not a question and Cordi did not pretend it was, so she did not answer, only waited.

"I wonder if perhaps you might have spoken to her."

Again, not a question, but something probing. How much could she say, or should she say? Prim had advised her again to give her mother the answers she wanted. Somehow, this was to Prim's benefit, but Cordi had yet to puzzle out how. But while she considered this, the Lady only waited, and Cordi saw no use in lying this time. "I did, my lady."

The Lady hummed. "And when was this?"

"Last night," Cordi answered, watching the dirt fall from her blade into the pot. "Outside in the garden," she volunteered before the next question could be posed.

"I see. And is there a particular reason you were skulking about the garden in the middle of the night? Again."

This was, of course, the real test. Denying something Lady Evangeline clearly suspected would serve her no better than it had at the Barrow with Mrs. Clark. What Cordi needed to do, as Prim had so *graciously* suggested, was provide adequate answers, not necessarily the truth.

Though not necessarily lies either. Cordi was beginning to see how the two could intertwine like a plant's root system to keep the plant alive.

"I am . . ." She paused, considering how best to frame what she might say. Shaking the pot as she had seen Lady Evangeline do, she tried again. "I am hearing things. I'm not sure how best to describe it, Lady."

No response was forthcoming save the sifting of soil and the metallic *snick* of the spade.

"I need to be outside. I don't know why. I don't know what draws me from my bed. But I hear something. Or perhaps I only feel it. Still, I find myself in the garden, looking for something. I was here last night when Jane found me. I think she heard it too. She said as much, but I don't know if that makes me feel better."

The Lady's hands had gone still, resting quietly on the lip of the pot. "What did Jane say that disquieted you?"

Cordi picked up her own spade again, holding it casually, but finding comfort in the weight and the brown-tipped point. "She didn't make much sense. I couldn't quite understand what she was telling me, but she said she 'heard them' too. She asked me to go with her, but when I refused, she said I was too much like 'them' now." Cordi turned confused eyes to her mistress, hoping to appear properly contrite and sincere. "Who did she mean?"

Ageless eyes set in that cold, inscrutable face probed Cordi's own, looking for deceit. But Cordi was now playing the game properly by telling the truth inasmuch as it mattered, and she recognized this in the slow upturn of the Lady's mouth beneath the mask, a smile that pulled the skin around her lids tight. One Cordi was sure mirrored her raven-haired daughter's own.

"Fascinating. I knew it would be different, but I'd not imagined . . . Oh, Cordelia." Lady Evangeline chuckled. "I did tell you that you would grow to love my garden, didn't I? And to see how fond you have become of my flowers—and so quickly. Blossoming with them. Yes, dear. I do believe you were meant to be with us. And your faithfulness deserves some reward, I think." The Lady held out one gloved hand and took up Cordi's own naked palm, twisting it gently around to show the slice along her finger and tutting.

"I know Briar told you some, but not all. Now, don't fret. I'm not angry," she said when Cordi involuntarily tensed. She squeezed Cordi's finger till droplets of blood appeared along the wound, and while Cordi winced, she did not pull away. Together, they watched the red rivulets join with the dirt, becoming darker, blacker pools that dripped to the floor between their feet.

"Not all," Lady Evangeline repeated, a too-bright gleam in her eyes as she watched Cordi's blood fall and burst into flowerlike patterns. "But perhaps soon."

Releasing Cordi's hand, she gestured to a small basin and a pitcher filled with clean water, and Cordi dutifully cleaned her hands while Evangeline hovered nearby. "Briar is impetuous, but I don't really fault her for prattling in this instance, though I do wish she'd show a bit more restraint. Still, I find I am not quite willing to curb her little rebellions. Girls will be girls, after all."

Cordi stayed silent, ignoring how the Lady spoke of her daughters as simple children and trying to disentangle the meaning behind Evangeline's words, searching for any implication that she knew of Cordi's entanglement with her youngest. But if Evangeline suspected or cared, she made no further mention.

"You know by now the reason for my daughters' seclusion. And while you may initially believe me wrong for the part I played in the physiological changes of my own children, I ask you to consider your own experiences with the world beyond Edenfield. You know better than most, judging by those scars you bear, how cruel the world can be for a woman. What kind of mother would I be if I had the ability to protect them from such harm and chose to let nature take its course, so to speak? What if someone had been there to protect you, Cordelia?"

The question had been meant to wound, and Cordi was in no position to fight off the poison of such words. The crisscrossing lines on her back felt fresh again, her neck and face hot, and she found she was angry. Angry not at Mrs. Clark or Mr. Mason for what they had done, but with Edward for what he had not. He had promised to protect her, but he had not returned. He had chosen Prim over her. And even if he truly meant to return, he had still put Cordi in second place. Yet here she was, looking for him. Keeping *her* promise, at least. Putting him first as he should have done for her.

"I protect what is mine. And also what is not. Girls and women who might in other households be dismissed or unwanted. I welcome them. My late husband," she said as if the word tasted foul on her tongue, "was quite put out when I would no longer allow him into my bed. I'd always found marriage an inconvenience and the marital act unrewarding. Did this deter his own passions? No. And when he was gone, his bastards came to me. The boys for money, of course, for all the good it did them. The girls for protection. Several through the years. Jane was one. Stella another."

Stella? Stella was Prim and Briar's *sister*? Yet there was a resemblance, wasn't there.

Stella's pretty profile with her high cheekbones and her thick hair like Prim's.

"I can protect you, Cordelia. You and all the women and girls who come here." Lady Evangeline reached out her gloved hand and gently tucked a strand of hair behind Cordi's ear. A motherly gesture. An offering. "How you'll grow and blossom here, Cordelia. How pretty a Flower you will make."

Despite herself, despite all she knew and the warning bells clanging in her heart, Cordi found she was smiling.

Chapter 34

"WOULD YOU LIKE TO PLAY, Cordi?"

Briar sat at the gaming table, the chess set already arranged in front of her. Her face was eager, full of health and something more. Hope. Desire.

Cordi had not stopped glowing. Even after her restless night, her talk with Lady Evangeline, and the knowledge that Prim was in the room, harboring secrets and resentment behind a façade of propriety and sophistication, seeing Briar's face light up as she looked at her made her want to forget all about what she should be doing and concentrate only on what she wanted. On *whom* she wanted.

It could be as the Lady had said. Cordi could have a home here where she would be safe. More than safe. Where she might be happy and thrive. A home. And wasn't that what she had always wanted? Yet Cordi could not give up the hope of finding her brother. Not yet, even if that hope was beginning to wither and die in her chest, denied the sun it needed to thrive, the soil poisoned with anger and hurt. Nor could she simply ignore the danger Prim still posed. When would she strike again? For she would.

Cordi had no doubt about that. Whatever leash held her back would not hold forever. She needed to find Edward before it snapped. Then she might have a chance of convincing Briar to come with them. With her.

"I'm no match for you," Cordi admitted, sitting opposite Briar, the white chess pieces in their neat rows. "I'm not sure I will be enough to keep the game interesting."

"Oh, don't underestimate yourself, Cordi dear. I'm sure Briar finds you quite stimulating." Prim yawned from where she lounged on a low green couch, the now familiar red volume in hand.

The urge to upend the table and lunge for the journal was so strong, Cordi's weight shifted in her seat, but she held. She was so focused on the book, she hardly heard Prim's dig, giving it little mind.

Briar, on the other hand, gave the slightest intake of breath and flushed straight to her roots, sitting up straighter and dropping her shoulders as if she had been corrected by the birch against her back. Just the thought of that thin rod marring Briar's perfect skin made Cordi want to snarl. "You're horrid," Briar said.

"Am I?" Prim responded, tone bored.

"Yes. And we're going to ignore you if you're going to be rude. What's come over you? You're in a sour mood this morning and you are taking it out on us."

"Who else is here, darling sister?"

Briar shook her head. "Prim, please. I only asked Cordi if she fancied a game."

Prim hummed. "I think I know exactly what Cordi fancies."

Ignore her, she mouthed, gesturing for Cordi to make the first move.

Yes. Best to ignore Prim, or at least let her believe she was being ignored. She did not want to risk Prim catching her coveting the journal. Cordi chose a pawn, and the game began. The one on the board, at least. She rather felt like she had been playing her game with Prim too long already and she was no longer sure where she was on the board or whose turn it was to move.

Prim had no such qualms. "As if you could just ignore me, Briar," she said as if Briar had spoken aloud. "When I know all there is to know about you? When I'm the one who has taken care of you and shielded you and treasured you for so long? Now that you have a new toy, you don't want to play anymore?"

Briar huffed and made another move on the board, shifting one of her own pawns. "Stop acting as if you are so much more worldly than I am," she said, a note of defiance in her voice that Cordi could not help but admire as she played a bishop. "Maybe I'm tired of your little insults and mean-spirited jokes. And I seem to recall you telling me more than once these past two years that you rather resented always having to play at entertaining me. How bothersome it could be to have a little sister who constantly needed your attention and protection."

The piece in Cordi's hand trembled as she placed it on a square. Had Edward felt much the same? Exhausted by his little sister who begged and pleaded for his return in each letter? He had always looked after her in the Barrow, protecting her from the trouble she found. Possibly she had been too much trouble. She'd certainly managed to find it when he was gone, hadn't she? Was that why he had chosen Prim over her?

Unaware of how her words affected Cordi, Briar went on, pink lips thin. "I thought I would let you have your wish. Cordi doesn't find me a bother."

"Yet," Prim mumbled.

Briar paled and the piece she had picked up to play shook in her fingers. She shot Cordi a look as if trying to read her face, uncertainty settling on her pretty features. Cordi gave her head a firm shake. "Never," she said with confidence, one little sister to another. One *pest* to another.

The smile showing her small white teeth was second only to the pleased expression that banished the doubt in Briar's eyes.

A howl of laughter from the couch. "Please," Prim snapped, tossing her book to the far cushion and facing them. Cordi forced herself not to glance at it, the shiny red cover gleaming, a streak of blood in her periphery. "You've been here, what, Cordi? A matter of weeks? And you can promise with such confidence you will never tire of us? For we are a package, Cordi. That *I* can promise. Never one without the other, is there, gentle sister?"

Briar stared at the chessboard, an unreadable expression on her face.

Prim slid from the sofa and spread her arms wide, spinning in a circle. "Never grow tired of this? Of four walls? Is that what you hope for, *Cordelia*?" she spat. "A lifetime of parading around in our castoffs in our grand home? I suppose it is much improved from whatever street you walked in the city."

Cordi leapt from her chair, nails digging into her palms where they would leave marks. She had so rarely fought at the Barrow, but she *had* fought. And she would fight dirty. It was the only way she knew how. "How dare you? You think you know so much? You don't know anything about me."

"No. I don't. You've been so careful, haven't you? But you don't need to be, dear Cordi. I can read you perfectly." She held up her hand and started ticking off points on her fingers. "You arrived with no money and no references. You weigh your words ever so carefully and haven't seen fit to tell us anything even remotely revealing. You've no idea how many of you there have been through the years, and yet you think yourself special because you've been taken into a little of our confidence? What are you *really* after here, Cordi, hmm? You sneak about and ask such innocent questions. And you bat your eyelashes at my terribly gullible sister, who obviously falls all over herself for a charity case as long as it can be brought to heel when she coos and simpers."

"*Prim!*" Briar shouted, standing as well.

"I admit, Cordi, you're amusing to watch. That, at least, has been a role you have fulfilled. And you're spirited. Not like the others, as I've already told you. Oh, Faustine is lively in her own way. I think she'd be a bit of a challenge, but she doesn't want to play our games. What was it she called us, Briar? Witches, wasn't it? Something like that. She's not a true believer, is she? Not like the other one. Your little mouse pet, Stella."

Briar shot her sister a venomous glare. "She is not a pet. She is as dedicated to you as she is to me and you are pointlessly cruel to her."

The laugh Prim offered made Cordi shiver. "But she'd never dare to be alone with me. Too close for comfort, I suppose. I remind her of what she might have had. Might have been. You, however, give them hope, don't you? Just like Irene. Oh, it really was too bad about Irene. Such promise, that one. But then Jane arrived. And they didn't need us. Nobody ever needs us for long. They had each other, didn't they, dear?" she asked, cocking her head at Briar. "Though not anymore, of course. What with Jane gone too."

Briar started. "Jane?"

"Oh, didn't I tell you? Vanished in the night, I'm afraid. Isn't that right, Cordi?" Cordi didn't dare look away. "They went to rouse her this morning and her bed was empty."

Briar's nostrils flared as she took quick, frantic breaths. "What if she—"

"She won't," Prim said, preempting her sister's question and showing no concern. "Besides, who would believe her?" Her dark brows lifted, and she feigned shock. "I thought you would be so happy, dearest, considering how sulky you were when you learned of her after Irene snub—"

"Stop it!" Briar hissed, her apple cheeks blooming red, irises darkening.

Prim licked her lips, just a pink flash of tongue, barely concealing the coquettish smile. "Why should I? Are you afraid Cordi will think less of you when she learns she is not the first pretty thing to catch your attention?" A shrug. "At least she has held it. You so often grow tired of playthings."

Cheeks burning, Briar said nothing.

"One less to bother with. Don't sit there and fret about her. She's made it on the streets before."

"How can you be so callous?" Cordi said quietly, unable to stop herself, thinking of Jane's grief and the struggle she faced, deranged and penniless and unwelcome in Farrow.

Prim giggled like a debutante at her first ball, pleased by the attention. "Practice."

Her sister turned away from both of them, hiding her face. Cordi went to her, placing a hand on her shoulder, the edge of her pinky just brushing the skin of Briar's collarbone. Skin she had tasted. There were words she might have said if they had been alone, but those were not for Prim's ears. She would not give her any more weapons to use against either of them if she could help it.

"Oh, you do look like the knight in shining armor, don't you, Cordi?" Prim sneered. "See, Briar? It truly doesn't matter. Cordi is here now. Someone who doesn't scare easily. You don't scare easily, do you, Cordi?"

Cordi was scared. Terrified. She knew only too well what Prim was capable of and had seen the bone garden. Though the hornets in her head had flown, faded to fog, the memory of the pain lingered. Prim spoke of the other servants the way a child might talk of dolls. Broken dolls. And children broke their toys all the time, didn't they? Yes, Cordi was afraid, but she wasn't a coward. "Why would you want to scare me, Prim?"

A flash of pleasure behind Prim's hooded eyes. A spark of interest. As if Cordi had passed a test. "It's always more fun that way. More fun to break the ones who don't think they have anything to lose."

She was wrong. Prim didn't know her at all. She had so much to lose. And too much to gain. She tried to think of Edward, to put his image at the forefront of her mind, but her eyes shifted to Briar of their own accord.

Briar saw, meeting the stare with her own, and Cordi felt the heat between them. Saw the flash of memory of the previous day behind Briar's eyes as she lifted a hand and cupped her throat where Cordi's lips had been.

Prim saw, too.

She laughed. Low at first. Then loud and long. Doubling over and clutching at her belly, tears leaking from her eyes as she laughed at them. When she straightened, her face was wet and splotchy, and Cordi was no longer sure if she had been laughing or sobbing. But Prim gawked at her sister. "You little fool. I warned you what it means to give your heart away."

Briar denied nothing. And neither did Cordi. What was there to say? The move might have been Cordi's, but Prim had steered her where she wanted. As if to emphasize her point, she stepped to the chessboard, studying it carefully, one finger grazing her upper lip. She moved the white and black pieces in quick succession, playing both sides, till—once again—the white queen dangled between her fingers.

"You're not very good at protecting your queen, are you?"

She dropped the piece to the floor, where it landed with a dull *thud,* and then turned on her heel, snatching up her journal and striding from the room.

Chapter 35

THAT EVENING, CORDI ONCE AGAIN found she could not settle. She paced the floor back and forth so many times, she worried she might wear a hole in the rug. She had wanted to throttle Prim after her little tirade in the salon but had opted instead to throttle the pillows on her bed. She'd sulked, had a long bath, sulked some more, and then retired to her room with a dinner tray, too afraid she would use her utensils on Prim's face rather than her food.

She flopped on the bed for the hundredth time, trying to force herself into a state of calm. But Prim's words had hit home. Even if she was wrong, she was also right.

Cordi was a liar.

She *was* a liar. She *did* sneak. She *did* try to glean information from Briar, the more approachable of the two. But it wasn't like Prim painted it. She cared for Briar. Deeply. Maybe even loved her. She pressed her hand to the space over her heart, feeling the steady beat under her ribs. Yes. She could picture happiness with Briar. She'd never really thought about happiness with another person. Not like that, anyway. Cordi had always assumed she would live with Edward and, she supposed, his future wife and children if he had any. She would be a maiden aunt, doting on his little ones in a way she had been denied. She rather liked the idea. She didn't really see herself having children of her own, but she liked the thought of caring for children in a way they were meant to be cared for. She could find work as a teacher to help the household and earn her keep.

Might she not have that with Briar?

The answer came swiftly. No. No, she could not. Another way Prim was right. If she chose Briar, her world would be these walls and the garden beyond. It would be Prim and her cruel games. There would not be children. There would only be Edenfield.

She flung her arm over her eyes. She hated Prim for being right. Hated her more for how hypocritical and wicked she was. How she made Cordi feel wicked in turn. How could Edward have loved a girl like that?

That answer to that riddle was easy enough to solve too. He hadn't known better. He had seen Prim on her best behavior. He had seen the Prim she had chosen to show him. Cordi had believed her friendly enough in those first days. And certainly beautiful. But now she had seen what lay hidden beneath that mask of cool refinement. And it was not beautiful.

It was cunning.

Feeling sorry for herself, however, was getting her nowhere. Cordi groaned as she sat up, flopping about on the bed and rolling till she sat upright against the pillows. She scratched at her scalp, the waves of her hair still slightly damp, the smell of lavender soothing. She shut her eyes and gave herself a talking-to.

She'd read through some of Prim's letters, nibbling at her food. It had been strange to see Prim's growing infatuation on the page. Her first letters brief and only vaguely curious. Posing questions as if the exchange of letters was both novel and something to be done practically and with careful examination. Eventually she warmed, became complimentary, though not overtly so. She drew in the margins and would often comment on her brother's flattery and kind words. Cordi could tell by the creases that those letters were favored, the ones Edward must have read many times. And these she blushed to read. There was nothing untoward, but they were personal, and reading them felt like betraying his trust. Spying. She told herself it was important, that she was looking for clues or an edge, but eventually she became engrossed in the story. A tragedy of lovers kept apart. Prim spoke of her confusion first, then her adoration, and then love.

It angered Cordi too. She had received short, cramped missives at the school, while Prim was worthy of sonnets, for all Cordi knew. Rationally, she knew postage was required to send letters to the Barrow and no such thing was necessary between Edward and Prim, but that did not ease the hurt. It also made Prim more human than Cordi wanted to readily admit. Made her barbs and thorns almost understandable.

Cordi resented it.

She needed the journal more than ever if just to prove how manipulative Prim really was. She pictured herself reading it, finding the truth, perhaps even leaving Prim a little note inside, since Prim thought herself so superior. And she so liked playing games with people. A note would be amusing. A taunt. The notion gave Cordi a little burst of pleasure. How furious Prim would be. How humiliated to be bested. But she deserved it. She deserved it for how cruel she had been to Briar. For poisoning Cordi. For whatever she had done to Edward.

What to do? She could not be caught again outside her room so soon and she didn't trust herself not to make mistakes when she was agitated, and she had already made so many mistakes.

Knock knock. "Cordi?"

The knocks were soft, hesitant, and the word was whispered so quietly, Cordi might have missed it. But she knew she was right. All thoughts of the journal, of her brother, slipped from her mind as she just as easily slipped from the bed, a moth to a flame.

She stood on one side of the door, temptation on the other. "Yes?"

Silence. Then a tremulous voice drifted through the wood. "Was she right? Are you going to leave?"

She unlocked the door, aware of the spot between her shoulder blades that had grown tight in anticipation. Before the door was even open, she was already reaching.

Briar sighed as she fell against Cordi, her face turned away, still denying the kiss Cordi knew they both wanted desperately. But it was enough to have Briar pressed against her, only their nightdresses separating them rather than silks and crinolines grown heavy with rain. There had been heat and warmth then, but not like this. Here, she could feel every line and every curve and the heat of Briar's skin beneath the thin fabric, and she made sure she missed nothing, her hands tracing the vertebrae before sweeping to the front, over ample hips and up to the curve of a breast.

To her credit, Briar's own hands weren't still, moving over Cordi with possession and promise. *Promise to stay and I'm yours,* they said. *Give me your promise and I'll give you everything.* Cordi groaned into Briar's hair, blood pounding, body aching. Briar, emboldened by Cordi's response, let her tongue slide over Cordi's ear, her breath sweet and hot and dizzying.

"Don't go," she begged, her voice deeper with desire, nails digging into Cordi's neck. Just a lick of pain. A claiming. And Cordi desperately hoped they would leave marks. "Please don't leave me."

As if she could. Cordi's arms enveloped her, crushing, delighting in the way Briar fit against her. But Briar wriggled in the embrace, unwilling to be a captive this time. Instead, she twisted them around, a stumbling, clumsy dance, and Cordi found her back against the doorjamb, half in the hall, half in her room. The light from the lamp near the table lit them in profile, casting their shadow onto the wall of the corridor.

In a haze, Cordi watched, seeing Briar's body sliding against her own, seeing her hands moving over Cordi's own curves—such as they were—and Briar's head dipping to kiss the space right above Cordi's heart. A searing heat. A brand.

That same mouth slid up till she found the neckline of Cordi's gown, tied with a ribbon. With a gentle tug of teeth, the bow fell away and the neckline gaped, and Cordi felt her tongue, hot and slick. Heard the rasp as it slid up her throat, halting at her chin.

Her head fell back, and she felt, rather than heard, Briar's delighted chuckle. This was not a Briar Cordi recognized. This was a girl who wanted power and control. Who was tired of her life being dictated and directed by others. Who was finally seizing the chance to be more than a pawn in a chess game. She was a queen. Not a princess—a queen. A goddess.

"You would not leave me," Briar breathed against Cordi's clavicle, her floral-scented breath making her dizzy. "She lies."

She lies.

Jane's words spoken in the dark. Here again, but whispered against Cordi's skin, carried on Briar's sweet breath. The ghost of them sent her shivering, with both fear and want.

Taking the shiver as encouragement, Briar shifted closer till Cordi felt the striking pad of the door in the hollow of her back, the hard metal and firm wood juxtaposed against the soft, swelling curves that held her in place. The lips that slipped across her breastbone might have been made of pure velvet, leaving hot, damp kisses as they passed from one side to the other. At the end, small, perfect teeth nipped gently at her skin, tugging playfully on the bone beneath.

"Say you won't leave me," Briar insisted, her voice darkening with promise, becoming something more like Prim's. Something like iron under all that velvet. Briar's hands had found the curve of Cordi's back and those nails of hers, tiny daggers, traced the scars under Cordi's gown.

Dig, Cordi found herself thinking.

"Briar," she pleaded. For mercy. For more.

Briar answered Cordi's plea with her own. "Please."

The word said so softly and at total odds with Briar's behavior broke something in Cordi. Gripping Briar's hips, she shoved and twisted, turning them till she was pressed against Briar's back, Briar's hands clutching the doorframe to keep her face from smashing into the wood. Cordi swept the long, thick curls to the side and her mouth latched on to the skin that was exposed, grazing with teeth, biting gently before soothing with her own tongue.

"My belladonna," Cordi whispered.

Briar bucked in her hold and gave a sharp intake of breath, caught by surprise. "*Yes.*"

Cordi's hands slipped around to the front, massaging the soft plane of Briar's belly, fascinated by the fuller shape of her without stays or corset, sweeping upward just to brush beneath her breasts, not quite touching. Something about the denial was nearly as addictive as her taste. Her scent was stronger, headier, and Cordi knew it for what it was. Briar shuddered against her, biting her lip so hard, the flesh turned white. She reached up, tugging Briar's lip free only to have Briar pull her finger into the wet cavern of her mouth, drawing on the digit.

With a muttered curse, Cordi filled her free hand with Briar's breast, lifting the heavy weight as Briar moaned around her finger before releasing her. Cordi slid her damp finger down Briar's throat and beneath the top of her gown, searching. Briar pressed back against her, offering little cries, seeking more of Cordi. And it was in Cordi's mind to give it to her, though part of her—the sane part of her that was nearly completely gone—knew they should not be so bold or reckless. The door wasn't even shut! They were halfway into the hall and—

Click.

The sound brought Briar up so fast, she nearly slammed her head into Cordi's skull. They stood panting, waiting in the near dark for any other sound. For anyone to make themselves known. But there was nothing. She leaned out into the hall, seeking the source of the sound. Had it been the closing of a door?

There was no point looking into the hall. All was dark. The moon had risen too high to be of any use through the front windows. She took a few cautious steps into the passage, her shadow growing huge on the wood panels. Squinting, she tried to see if any light came from the crack beneath Prim's door, but there was nothing. Perhaps it had only been a settling of the house.

But one look at Briar told her it had not. Where her face had been flushed with passion, her lips dark and swollen only a moment before, now they looked pale, her eyes nervously darting about. Cordi moved to her to usher her into the room, but Briar stood fast.

"I—I didn't mean to be so forward," she whispered, a breath of a sound. "I think I should go to bed."

It was on the tip of Cordi's tongue to ask her to stay. Briar was shaking, obviously frightened and in need of comfort. And Cordi was more than willing to provide it, but Briar stepped away, arms curling around her middle.

"Good night," she said, before fleeing down the hall. Cordi watched her disappear into the shadows and heard the faint opening and closing of her door. Cordi wanted to go after her. To beg. But for what? More time? More information? More flesh?

Cordi forced herself to lock the door. As much as she wanted fewer barriers between her and Briar, she knew it would be foolish to leave the door unbarred if Prim meant her harm.

Though if Briar had keys, it stood to reason Prim did as well.

Fantastic, she thought as she leaned her head against the wood. Just what she needed to be thinking about as she went to bed.

Letting out a frustrated breath, she pushed away from the door and went back to her bed.

She settled herself against the pillows again and groaned at her stupidity. At how easily she was distracted from her purpose.

What was it Prim had said in the salon? How Briar so easily brought Cordi to heel. The words snagged in Cordi's breast like a fishhook. And like any good fishhook, it had buried itself deep and Cordi knew she would not escape. She was well and truly caught in Prim's web and Briar's orbit.

As much as Cordi despised lies, she reviled this truth even more. Prim could read her. She might not know who Cordi was or what she had come for, but she knew enough, while her own motives remained a mystery to Cordi. She pulled her knees up and wrapped her arms around them, the short, damp strands of her hair cold against her heated skin. Disgust and disappointment at her behavior settled like a miasma around her, as toxic as the poison pumping through her body. She hadn't remembered any of Prim's lessons in chess if she let herself be so easily manipulated. Prim wanted her gone; that was clear enough. But it was more than that. It was almost like she wanted to prove a point.

I warned you what it means to give your heart away.

It had been a confession of sorts. She had spoken with familiarity. From experience. But it was nothing Cordi didn't already know. Her letters to Edward in her own hand were proof enough of her feelings, even if she urged caution and expressed genuine concerns. None of it implied she doubted Edward's own feelings. She had loved Edward and still did; otherwise, why keep his portrait? But the implication lay heavy that Edward had betrayed her, which did not sit well with Cordi. It didn't fit the passion of the letters, for one, and it certainly didn't coincide with the person her brother had always been. He had always wanted to look after those he loved.

She had seen other siblings at the Barrow, but few had had a bond like she and her brother did. Most of the older ones resented any familial responsibility toward younger siblings when there was already little enough food and love to go around. Sometimes she would see brothers and sisters unite, but mostly it was to take advantage of others. However, Edward had always tried to protect Cordi. Always.

He wouldn't have abandoned Prim. He simply wouldn't have.

And the Starlings believed it too. He had returned here. The only logical explanation was that Prim had hurt Edward as she had tried to hurt Cordi. Only the why eluded her.

If only Edward could have left her some clues . . . All she had were the letters from Prim.

She could still remember her closing words. Prim would have feared discovery, so of course she had never signed her name.

Your darling one, she'd written. Over and over.

Cordi sat bolt upright, her head snapping forward so quickly, the muscles spasmed in protest. She threw the covers off and all but fell to the floor in her haste. She flung herself down by the window seat and pried open her hiding space, reaching inside, scraping the delicate skin of her wrist on the wood. Threads on her skirt snapped as she yanked it free, feeling within for her own letters, the envelopes soft from so many handlings. They fell to the floor in a pile, the fox on top, staring up at her. The shadows thrown by her lamp seemed to narrow its gaze so it looked at her with smug satisfaction as if to say, *Ah. You've figured it out at last, have you?*

Her hands moved over the envelopes, seeking the right one, and she snatched it up.

The last letter she had received before Edward seemed to disappear from Farrow without a trace. The one that had not begun like any of the others.

My darling one.

Sure, but desperate to somehow be wrong, she tore open every envelope and read the salutation at the top of each page.

My Dearest Dee. My Dearest Dee. My Dearest Dee.

Cordi might well have been underwater, a ringing in her ears growing more and more pronounced till it was the only sound in the world. Somehow she had received a letter meant for Prim. A letter filled with promises. Edward was coming to take Prim away. To give them their happily ever after. He truly had chosen Prim over her.

A pain lanced through her heart, and she doubled over, covering her head with her arms as if she might protect herself from the onslaught of hornets again. But it was not her illness returning. It was heartbreak, sure and swift and the pain just as acute.

He had forgotten her. Left her despite his promises. She had come all this way to find him, thinking him missing, and he had—

With a gasp, she knew. Something *was* missing.

If she had the letter meant for Prim, where was the letter Edward had clearly meant to post for *her*?

She feared she knew.

Blindly Cordi gathered the letters from the floor, shoving them back into the folds of the skirt, save the last. She'd tried to deny it for so long, telling herself she would find him. That it was only a matter of time. But if Prim had suspected betrayal, she must have done something awful. Prim was not one to suffer insult. Nor was her mother one to suffer a man at all.

Slinking back to her bed, she dug the heels of her hands into her eyes, counting her breaths and praying to God as she had not done since she was little.

God did not answer. He had not answered her for a long time. Another abandonment.

A branch kept tapping at Cordi's window and she tried to shut it out, but the tapping persisted. Strange that Cordi couldn't hear any wind. Strange how rhythmic it was. Stranger still: there were no trees near the back of the house.

Turning to the glass, Cordi could vaguely make out her own reflection, a ghostly silhouette of a girl in white, floating untethered. But she could also see a vague shape in the upper corner of her window. Something bumping against the frame.

Easing from her bed, Cordi went to investigate, climbing up to the seat on her knees and easing the window open so she could lean out and see what it was. Maybe a nocturnal bird, pecking at its own reflection or—

One shoe.

Two shoes.

The ringing in her ears returned as Cordi's neck stretched back to see Stella lit by the moon, her arms limp at her sides, head hanging forward as she swayed back and forth from a rope tied around her neck.

It wasn't until Briar and Prim had both begun pounding on her locked door, calling her name, that Cordi had realized the ringing in her ears was really the sound of her own screaming.

Chapter 36

"WHY WOULD SHE DO SUCH a thing?" The words were broken by sobs that racked poor Briar's frame, a handkerchief clutched in her hand and pressed against a face already puffy and splotchy from crying. And as much as Cordi wanted to offer her a kind word, she found herself unable to move from where she stood on the patio, staring down at the shoes still tied to Stella's feet.

Nothing felt real. It was all some horrible dream. But when Cordi pinched her finger where the flesh was just beginning to knit back together after she had cut herself, the now familiar heat of pain and the fresh flow of blood that leaked from the wound told her she was very much awake. Dumbly, she wrapped her finger in her own handkerchief, still not wanting to believe.

She had still been screaming when Prim had unlocked her door, sending both sisters spilling inside, falling over one another. Briar had grabbed at Cordi, apparently thinking in a wild moment of fear she was going to leap from the window. After seeing Stella for herself, her own screams had joined Cordi's. Prim had run from the room to ring for Miss Eliot and Lady Evangeline.

It had been Miss Eliot and Faustine who pulled Stella back up to the rooftop balcony where she had tied the rope to a turret. The two had struggled down three flights of stairs with her poor body and laid her on the patio, panting behind their masks. Prim had dragged Briar from Cordi's room, snapping at Cordi to follow, and had shoved tiny glasses of brandy into their hands, making them drink and demanding they collect themselves. Then they had gathered outside, cloaks over their nightdresses, where all the servants already huddled, and Lady Evangeline had joined them moments later.

She knelt beside Stella's body, asking clipped questions of Miss Eliot, still trying to catch her breath, one hand pressed to her lower back. Prim ordered Sarah to fetch Miss Eliot and Faustine each a brandy, though Faustine looked so faint, Cordi thought the poor girl would need several. In all the time she had known her, Faustine had been smiling and laughing and exuberant. To see her so quiet and ready to bolt was disquieting.

"Who found her?"

Cordi heard the question and its answer from a great distance. Her name. Someone was calling her name. "Hmm?" she said, still not taking her eyes off the shoes.

"Cordelia." The voice was formal and quickly losing patience.

It took an effort to get her head to swivel on her neck. For Cordi to force her eyes up from the figure of Stella lying on the ground. It seemed to take forever before she was able to face her benefactress. "Ma'am?"

"What happened?" Lady Evangeline asked, unlikely for the first time.

Cordi shook her head, her mind blank, feeling strangely absent from her body and the situation. As if she knew that if she faced the reality, she might very well break. "I don't know. I was lying in bed. I heard a branch hitting my window. Over and over. They used to do that at school, you know? In the winter they would scratch the windows. I thought they were the hands of witches coming to steal me. Sometimes I wished they would. But it was only ever branches. I thought it was a branch. . . ."

She heard her voice trail off as she looked down and saw Stella's face for the first time in death. Her eye was open, bulging out of the socket, broken blood vessels cracking across the surface like shattered glass, the pupil so large, it had completely obliterated all color. Her beautiful hair was matted at the back and shiny in the pale light, torn free from the pins she used to coil it at her neck. Cordi realized she had been bleeding, though no blood flowed now. She must have hit her head as she—

"She tied the end of the rope to the turret, my lady," Miss Eliot said, stronger for the brandy. "Poor girl. I can't imagine what was in that head of hers to do such a thing. I know the poor mite had such a time before coming here. Scared of her own shadow." She cleared her throat and folded her hands. "The blame is mine, my lady. I should have paid her greater mind. I've no idea how she even got into the south wing!"

The keys. Stella had had the keys. Cordi had given them to her. *Oh God . . .*

"You've certainly nothing to blame yourself for, Eliot. The girl was obviously troubled." A heavy sigh. "Such a waste, too."

"Is there nothing to be done, my lady? She was such a devoted thing and—"

"No." Prim's voice was firm, her back straight and eyes dry, in total contrast with her sister, who still openly wept, her shoulders hunched. "Rule Three: What is reaped must first be sown. She cared so little for herself and her sisters to do such a thing. We cannot trust this act will not sully the soil. Rule Nine: She is called to the Garden in her time. This was not her time. Conditions mean it is unlikely she would even be capable of taking root."

Cordi could make no real sense of her speech, but it seemed as if Stella would be denied a proper burial because she had taken her own life. Was it akin to being excommunicated? Cordi had heard the furious, threat-filled sermons at the Barrow that spoke of fire and damnation for all who did not follow the word of God or uphold the values of the Church. But she had also seen how those same people who preached love and charity and righteousness walked through God's creation with nothing but hate and greed in their hearts.

It was true that Cordi had little understanding of what exactly the women of Edenfield believed in. Yet another mystery among many, but Cordi was certain of one thing: Stella had been a believer. Prim had said so herself! To hear her suggest that Stella, of all of them, had not practiced whatever faith or belief had brought the household together was monstrous. Stella had believed fervently in the gracious nature of Lady Evangeline and the rules laid forth. They all had to know that.

Cordi looked to the other servants, hoping someone whose voice carried more weight than hers did would speak up. Would say something! Yet they all remained silent. But Cordi could see eyes shifting to each other, looks passing quietly between them where words were obviously unwelcome. Faustine's jaw was set, her youthful face and brilliant eyes suddenly older, world-weary. Cordi did not miss the glare she threw in Prim's direction as the poised girl tutted over Briar, still unable to look at Stella's broken form.

Lady Evangeline spoke quietly to herself, lifting Stella's hands and bowing over them, splaying the dead girl's fingers and prodding at her nails. She flipped one over and bared the wrist, fingers tracing over dead skin, following the tracks of the cold veins. She frowned, the lines of her mouth drawing down, and she appeared older than she ever had, her expression one of disappointment.

Her examination finished, the mistress of the house gave her ruling. "There *is* nothing to be done, but that does not mean she is not welcome in the Garden." Prim opened her mouth to rebut, but her mother held up a hand. "Stella was a member of my house and she will be welcomed in the earth even if she cannot grow from it. She will feed her sisters with her sacrifice. Miss Eliot? Bring the cart around and—"

"Oh, please no!" Cordi cried, silencing everyone, even Briar's sobbing. "She hated the sound of a cart! She told me so. It was the thing that frightened her most. Please! I'll carry her!"

Lady Evangeline pressed her lips together and shook her head. "No, Cordelia. I think not. Nor will you be attending tomorrow. It is well and good that you cared for dear Stella, but she is beyond fear now. And I think it best if you three went to bed."

You three. She was being counted with Briar and Prim now. And it had not gone unnoticed by the others. Nobody wanted to look at her. Miss Eliot only kept her head bowed, her lips moving in what might have been a prayer. Faustine, Moira, and Sarah averted their eyes.

Prim's lips were set in a furious line, her eyes locked on the distance. Only Briar met her gaze. But the heat that had flared between them earlier was snuffed out in the face of such tragedy.

"Come along," Prim said stiffly, placing her arm around Briar and steering her to the door and inside. Cordi hesitated, but Lady Evangeline only nodded her head, dismissing her.

She looked once more to Stella, chin trembling. She wanted to say how sorry she was. To beg forgiveness of her friend. To ask her why. But something stopped her. Some slow, creeping realization.

Stella was dressed in her livery and shoes rather than her nightclothes. Her hair wasn't braided for bed. But she should have been in bed hours ago. More than that, the blow to her head must have been violent to do such damage. If she had jumped, why hadn't Cordi heard anything? The sound of her head hitting the wall? Or the slam of her shoe-clad feet against the window? The whole window should have shattered, but there had only been the gentle taps of her heels on the glass.

"Cordelia. To bed."

Digging her fingers into her thighs beneath her cloak, Cordi turned without another word, stepping over the threshold and into the darkened salon at the back of the house, pulling the door nearly closed behind her and drawing the curtains. Footsteps sounded overhead and Cordi imagined Briar staggering to her room, Prim consoling her. Prim would sit with her till she fell asleep, and Cordi was glad of it.

Especially as she pressed her ear to the crack she had left in the back door, straining to hear over the pounding of her heart.

"Off to bed with the rest of you." A shuffling of feet and the sound of receding footsteps.

Then: "I can't understand it, my lady. Not in the least."

There was a long stretch of silence before Lady Evangeline answered. "There has been a strangeness in the house for some time. An unsettling. I thought maybe the Flowers . . ." She stopped. "I begin to suspect an invasive species has rooted here." Another pause. "You don't believe Stella had a lover, do you?"

"*Stella?*" Miss Eliot's voice was incredulous. "I'd be more likely to suspect myself before I suspected such a thing of Stella. The girl couldn't even go past the gates. When Starling and his boy were here for the greenhouse, she wouldn't even step outside for the washing."

"Lovers don't have to be men," the Lady sighed, as if the topic was wearying.

"To be sure," Miss Eliot said, and Cordi was surprised to hear she didn't seem at all rattled by the thought. Cordi surmised that in a place like Edenfield, where men were met with more suspicion than the Devil himself, it was preferable. "Irene and Jane had each other. But Stella kept to herself. She seemed to take a liking to young Cordi, but I didn't get the impression she fancied her."

"What about the Flowers? The strain of relation, but being relegated to maid, perhaps?"

"If I may speak plainly, my lady?"

"Please."

"I know Misses Prim and Briar use the word *cloister* when they speak of servants, but with Stella it was true. She was like a little nun. Listened, abided, and took every word to heart. The planting was the only thing she didn't fear, I suspect. So if she felt anything for the Flowers, it was the love of an acolyte eager to please, not jealousy. And she both loved and feared her deities. Especially after Miss Prim . . . well . . ."

Cordi recalled Briar's remark on that first day about Prim leaping out and scaring Stella. "Yes, I spoke to her about frightening the girl. To her credit, Prim wasn't contrite at all. Which is exactly how I want her to be. Reservations are a weakness."

Miss Eliot said nothing, and Lady Evangeline obviously had not meant for her to, continuing with her own musings. "I have my keys and you have yours. I didn't want to check with the girls. Not tonight. But there aren't any keys in her pockets, and it troubles me how she gained access to this side of the house. We will need to search the ground below the windows thoroughly in the light."

Stella didn't have the keys Cordi had given her.

Someone had let her in. Or taken them from her after she'd let herself in. Someone who had no reservations about such things.

"Do you think Cordi an asset to this house, Miss Eliot?"

Cordi pressed her knuckles to her mouth at the question. At the low, disinterested voice and the underlying threat it seemed to suggest.

"I can't say much on the matter, my lady. She has a good attitude about work. She made Moira light up with her compliments on her cooking. Even heard her and Stella giggling one night, and I didn't think anyone could conjure a laugh from . . ." A cough, and the pain was fresh again. When Miss Eliot continued, Cordi thought the older woman sounded a bit choked up. "I was sorry to lose her hands so early, but I can hardly complain. The Flowers seem so fond of her. Miss Briar especially."

The Flowers. The Flowers mentioned over and over in the cross-stitch. They weren't the flowers growing on the grounds. They were Briar and Primrose. *They* were the Flowers of Edenfield. Poisonous blooms cultivated by their mother as some scientific triumph.

Lady Evangeline seemed pleased enough. "Very well. I'm relieved to hear it. Such an interesting specimen. Regardless, I still want her excused from the planting tomorrow. I don't expect she is ready for that. I'll retire now, Miss Eliot, and I suggest you get your own rest. Let everyone sleep in a bit later tomorrow. This has been a terrible shock."

"Yes, my lady."

It was some time before Cordi eased the door shut, fingers cramped from holding it so still. She moved through the darkness like a sleepwalker, heedless of the shadows that closed around her, swallowing her in their midst. She retreated to her room, locking the door while knowing full well it would not stop Prim if she wanted to come in.

She lay down in her luxurious bed, knowing that if sleep came, it would not be peaceful. Not while trying not to think of Stella's face or the gash on the back of her head. Cordi was sleeping next door to a murderer, and she couldn't deny it any longer. Prim had killed Stella. She would kill her too.

But worse than that were the words spoken so casually by Lady Evangeline. *The planting.* That's what she'd called it. And the final rule on the cross-stitch burned across the backs of Cordi's eyelids.

What is planted in the Garden, grows in the Garden.

Chapter 37

THE DAY DAWNED TOO BRIGHT for all the sorrow weighing on Cordi. She found a black dress in the wardrobe she thought suitable for mourning and slipped it on, struggling with the tiny pearl buttons along the back. She wanted to ask Briar for help but did not want to impose on Briar on such a day, even for something so innocent. Not when her thoughts could not be counted on to remain innocent.

She appreciated the dress's deep pockets. The room didn't feel safe. Nowhere felt safe, if she was honest. But Prim might not be so subtle in her snooping the next time. So Cordi shoved the final letter from Edward into one pocket along with the key to her room and the shears into another. She left the room unlocked as she went to breakfast, knowing it made no difference and unwilling to give Prim a reason to suspect she had a key herself.

Briar and Prim were seated in the floral room when she came down. The small table where they took their tea had been laid out for breakfast. Briar's eyes were red-rimmed from crying, dark-purple bruises beneath. She appeared brittle. Prim looked irritated, though paler than she had the day before, her own eyes shadowed by dark crescents. They both were wearing their hair down and white dresses rather than traditional black.

Her lips refused to make the shapes of the words *Good morning,* since there was simply nothing good at all about it. She nodded to both girls instead, taking her seat and trying not to scream or take up her knife and stab Prim in her pitiless heart.

Breakfast was a quiet, sullen affair. There was only the scrape of silverware on porcelain for some time. And though everything tasted of ash, Cordi ate because her stomach was empty and she knew she would need her strength. She would not be caught unawares like Stella. She was clever like her dear fox, she reminded herself. But she was running out of time. Indeed, she might be running out of time faster than she had anticipated.

"It seems you have come to us at rather a strange time, Cordi," Prim said, pushing blood sausages around on her plate.

Cordi steeled herself before she dared look up, schooling her features as she used to do in the Barrow. She needed to know her opponent. Prim had already gained too much ground. Cordi chewed thoughtfully, looking for cracks in Prim's own veneer. She had shaken that mask loose once. She could do it again.

"My condolences on yet another tragedy. I didn't know Irene, but I did know Stella and she was lovely. I can only imagine how difficult it is for the two of you."

Briar caught her lip with her teeth, biting so hard, Cordi thought she might draw blood. But Prim only continued looking disinterested, even taking another bite of food as if it was all inconsequential to her. "Lovely sentiments, but sentimentality is a weakness. If you allow people the privilege of your emotions—even well-intentioned people—you are giving them power over you. I've counseled Briar as much."

I bet you have, Cordi thought. Next to her, Briar bloomed so red, her purple bruises and amethyst eyes grew more pronounced. Cordi only shook her head solemnly, though her fist clenched in her lap as if it were wrapped around Prim's slim neck the way she had put the rope around Stella's. "I think our ability to love and care for each other is what makes us human."

A twitch. A fluttering of a muscle at the corner of Prim's mouth that she so delicately wiped with a pristine napkin. "You don't think animals have feelings? Isn't that why people are so fond of dogs or cats or even birds? What about plants? Do plants not feel?"

"Not in the same way."

Prim's eyes flashed. "Oh, but they do. Did you know that plants will rally around a dying companion? They will force-feed it. Urge it to keep growing. They will warn each other of danger, altering their very structure to avoid being eaten. Some plants will desperately try to bring their loved ones back from the dead! Are even successful. They know the seasons. Know when to sleep and when to wake. They will reroute their root systems to find a better source of water. Some are even dangerous."

"Poisonous plants, you mean?" Cordi said delicately.

Prim took a few sugar lumps from the crystal bowl and stirred them delicately into her tea before laying her spoon aside, the picture of elegance and refinement as she lifted her cup and took a careful sip. "I suppose. But poison alone doesn't imply intent. Some plants are a bit more devious than that." She lowered her cup, and it landed in the saucer with the faintest *clink*. "Take ivy! Ivy is very curious. It doesn't need much, but what it does need, it will take. It will latch on to something and twist and twine its way around to get what it wants, even if it means killing what helped it grow. Strangling the life out of anything that gets in its way. People think ivy is so innocent."

Cordi put her hand in her pocket, feeling for the comforting weight of the shears.

"But it survives, no matter the cost," Prim mused quietly, more to herself. "You see? Plants aren't that much different from people."

A test. A chess move. A game. That's all it was to Prim. Something to keep her amused. And she wanted to play with Cordi. Wanted to see if she was a worthy opponent, and Cordi was so very tired of losing. "By that logic, a solitary tree in a field is lonely. Left to fend for itself. Doesn't it need family? Friends? Love? If a tree needs these things, why don't people? Why is sentimentality a weakness for humans but a strength for plants?"

Prim sat unmoving, hands in her lap, though Cordi was sure she could hear the twist of fabric as if she were wringing her napkin. Finally she chuckled. "I do like you, Cordi. It still surprises me how much. But to answer your question, it is because people are liars. Didn't you know that?"

"I do," Cordi said with a smile. "Something we agree on."

Prim's smile was forced, the edges of her lips twitching again. "At last."

Briar laid her napkin on the table beside her plate, most of her food simply shifted around rather than eaten. "We need to get ready, Prim. Mother will want us there early."

"Perhaps you're right. Maybe we should go and prepare. Mother is already in such a mood. Irene. Jane. Stella. Marvelous how chaos brings with it such a change to routine. Which reminds me . . ."

From under the table, Prim produced a set of keys and held them out to Briar, dangling them on one finger. Cordi watched them sway back and forth, their faint *click-click* like the ticking of a clock. "I found your key ring. Don't let Mother know you lost it. She'll be even more furious, and you know how unbearable she is."

"My keys?" Confusion clouded Briar's features, already drawn and pained. "I lost them?"

"I suppose. I almost tripped upon them on the stairs last night. I do wish you'd be more careful with your things." She gave Cordi a wan smile as she stood up from the table. "I'm sorry you won't be joining us today. But I'm certain you'll find something to amuse yourself with. We may be a bit later than normal, seeing as how there are fewer hands now. Can't be helped, I suppose. And we'll all take dinner in our rooms tonight. Mother is insisting on quiet, solitary contemplation."

She swept from the room, leaving Cordi and Briar staring at each other helplessly. Briar held out her keys to Cordi, stricken. "I—I lost my keys. I shouldn't have done that. Stella. You don't think . . . ?"

Cordi did think, but not what Briar suspected. She leaned forward, itching to reach for her hand. "You did nothing wrong. Nothing has been your fault. It has nothing to do with your keys. Do you understand?" She opened her mouth to tell Briar the truth when Prim poked her head back into the room.

"Come along, dear. We'll need to color your cheeks. It won't do to have you looking so peaked."

Like a marionette summoned to life by its master, Briar rose from the table, her limbs loose, and half walked, half stumbled toward her sister, who held out her hand with the expression one might give a lost, bedraggled puppy. Cordi's own fingers fisted into her skirt as she watched Briar accept her sister's offering, seeing her shoulders ease as someone else took the weight of her sorrow.

Prim glanced over her shoulder and, though her lips never moved, Cordi could hear her voice as clearly as if she'd spoken aloud.

Oh dear, poor Cordi. Whenever will you learn to protect your queen?

Chapter 38

THERE WAS A BENEFIT TO having such thick pillows that went beyond their intended function. Cordi found they were perfect for screaming into.

After the disastrous breakfast during which she had been baited again and allowed Briar to suffer, Cordi had fled to her own room, where she had screamed and screamed into her pillows until her breath was gone.

Trapped. She was trapped in every sense of the word save one: the door was open. But she couldn't leave. Leaving would mean forsaking Edward. Leaving would mean abandoning Briar. Leaving would mean Prim won. Whether it was love or stupidity or pride that kept her in Edenfield, she had yet to decide. But no matter the reason, she was not leaving. Not yet.

She wondered where Jane was and hoped she had friends or family, but she doubted both. If she had had either, why would she have been in Edenfield? Had she stayed because she had nowhere else to go? Or had she stayed for Irene? Maybe both. But without one, the other no longer mattered.

Cordi sat in her window seat, staring out the windows and waiting. She needed rest—real rest—but she couldn't sleep. Not yet. She was tired of not knowing the next move Prim would make. She had played sloppily up until this point. Carelessly. Not thinking ahead. This time, she needed to be prepared.

She watched them gather on the back patio and file off down the stairs,

Lady Evangeline in the lead, the girls right behind, all in white, all with their hair down. They made a strange trio and nobody would have guessed they were family. Lady Evangeline with her straight, white-blond hair. Prim with her dark waves and Briar with her strawberry curls. It occurred to Cordi she had never seen a portrait of the girls' father. There probably wasn't one. She couldn't imagine Lady Evangeline allowing any to remain.

The staff came behind, bonnets on bowed heads, following the Lady and her Flowers. Cordi watched the procession as it passed through the maze, catching glimpses of hats and hair as they turned different corners. When they were out the other side, it took some time before they were again in Cordi's line of sight, and she wondered if she had lost them somehow. But no.

There they were again; this time, one of the staff pushed a wheelbarrow, a mound draped in white in its belly.

Stella.

No tears came. No screams of rage either. Her eyes and her throat were too raw, and she was too spent. Instead, a sharp, strange sense of calm settled over her. *Focus,* she demanded of herself. She would watch and see. And then she would learn.

The group set out toward the tree line, slipping through the thick trunks along what appeared to be a narrow path Cordi hadn't noticed before. She considered following, but if she was seen, she was done for. And there was a great deal of open grass between the garden and the trees. But she was alone in the house and she would not be idle.

Luckily, she had some reading to do.

Loath as she was to find any benefit in the upheaval caused by Stella's death, Cordi knew this might be her only chance to claim Prim's journal. But it would mean she had to hurry. She would cross to the other side of the house for the keys from beneath Demeter's stony glare in the study and hope one of them fit the lock on Prim's room.

She found a pair of gloves among the drawers and pulled them over her arms as she had done before. She did not see a mask but instead took a kerchief to tie around her face. She would do no harm to the other servants if she could keep from it. Nobody need be hurt on her account ever again.

Resolved to her plan, she stepped from the room and began to march down the hall, only to halt just outside Prim's door.

A sliver of light shone through the crack where it had been left ajar, as if it had been pulled closed but the latch had not quite caught. Such carelessness was not at all like Prim. Cordi could only guess Prim had been too distracted to notice. Or that it was a trap.

Or a taunt?

Cordi approached the door, half expecting all manner of demon to spill into the hallway and drag her away. She was no longer certain that such a thing was fanciful. Prim very well might have such powers. In which case, she was after not a diary but a witch's grimoire. After all, Faustine had called Prim a witch.

Prim and *Briar.*

Saw one and was put under a spell.

Gritting her teeth, Cordi pushed the door open, letting the light spill into the hall. Prim's room was pristine, everything put away just so, though the air was perhaps a bit close. And there, right on her bedside table, was the slim red volume like a bloody pool. Without another thought, Cordi rushed inside and snatched the book to her chest. No thunder crashed in the distance. No devils poured forth from the pages. It was only a book, the textured leather cover softened by use.

Back in her room, Cordi settled again into the window seat, where she could watch for the return of the household and feel the sun on her skin. She wanted a clear view and plenty of warning.

At first, the book seemed to yield nothing. It was all rather boring. There were no dates, so Cordi had no idea how often or for how long the book had been used, though entries seemed to go back for some time. Names were mentioned that Cordi had no knowledge of. Always women. *Annette. Pietra. Mary. Sophia. Beatrice.* They would appear and then be gone, sometimes seen only once. All staff, it would seem.

There were sketches. Some flowers drawn in the margins. A few scientific diagrams with parts of the plants labeled and annotated in the beautiful script she recognized from the letters Edward had so cherished. Several sketches were of Briar. How perfectly Prim could capture her belladonna's loveliness. She would have lingered over these pages, but she could not allow herself to get distracted.

On one page, she found the face of a man. It was crude, half-formed. As if the artist only half remembered the subject. But something about the shape of his eyes and the smile suggested under the mustache was familiar. It was Briar's smile. Or like enough. Their father, Cordi guessed. Prim had drawn their father the way she remembered him, with a tender expression. It disarmed Cordi, this glimpse into Prim's private thoughts and memories. One that she had obviously tried hard to get right, judging by the charcoal smudges and redrawn lines. She had wanted it to be accurate. She had cared enough. Possibly loved him enough.

The more Cordi learned about Prim and Edenfield, the less she understood. This became even more apparent as the journal began lapsing into points on botany and chemistry and anatomy that Cordi found increasingly difficult to follow. She wasn't learned in such sciences and could barely make sense of the writing, some of which was in Latin.

She rubbed her eyes and checked the sun's progress again. Still no one had emerged from the trees, and it was well past time for lunch, though Cordi was not hungry in the least. She needed answers, not food.

She forced her way through the next few entries. Studies on edible flowers. A charcoal rendering of the moss-covered statue by the pond. And then finally—

I have a secret. His name is Edward Beecher.

Cordi inhaled so loudly, she nearly gave herself a start as the silence of the room was broken. There was his name in the book in Prim's elegant hand.

He is an apprentice for the Starling man. They are building Mother's greenhouse. I have exchanged words with him! Mother will be furious if she discovers what I have done, but how exciting it is! How delightful to have such a sinful secret! I shall not even tell my dear Briar. I find I like having something all to myself and this is the first thing that is truly mine alone. My secret.

Edward. Repeated over and over till it filled an entire page! And on the following page, her own name combined with his. *Primrose Beecher.* Again and again and again till Cordi grew dizzy. Something a child might do if she fancied someone. Girls at the Barrow had done it often. Seeing how their name might look or sound with the surname of the object of their affection.

Cordi skimmed the next pages hastily, looking for signs. Anything. Anything she didn't already know. But there was no sense to the entries. The next pages were plants. Then a few studies of Edward, just quick sketches of him in various poses: working, wiping his brow, eyes closed in rest. A few pages cursing the weather and exclamations of how Prim would supposedly die if it didn't stop raining. Then an anatomical rendering of a heart, its chambers labeled clearly and with great precision. The word *love?* was circled over and over in a corner as if Prim had been trying to understand where the emotion might reside in the organ. She was logical and deliberate, and emotions seemed to confuse her because she could not clearly define their boundaries or origins. They defied the natural order of her world, especially an attraction to a man that went so utterly against her upbringing.

I am afraid.

This made Cordi pause. She could not imagine Prim as afraid. Briar had said on more than one occasion that Prim was the bravest person she knew. Yet here she was. Admitting to fear.

Is love meant to be so all-consuming as this? Am I whole only when we are together? I have always been half of a whole, but it has always been Briar, my sweet sister, who completed me. Yet I confess I have never felt as if that was enough. I do my duty. I do what I must. What Mother made me for. And while I cannot imagine a life without my dearest sister, I fear I shall wither and die here if I am parted from Edward. Nothing is as it was. I had purpose, if not joy. And now I know love and it is terrifying. Mother warned us of men, but she did not warn us of loving them. I suspect she did not know to fear it, having never known it herself. My dear Briar, what am I to do? I cannot keep you both.

This last line Cordi read again and again, her heart sinking like a stone into the well of her stomach. She might have written such herself. Was she not tormented by the same choice? Exactly the same choice? Were she and Prim so alike?

It might have made Cordi laugh if she hadn't turned the page and seen the hastily scrawled words that followed, splotches of ink and places where moisture had wetted the paper, blurring some of the letters:

Liar. LIAR. He loves HER not me. Liar liar liar liar liar. I'm a fool. A stupid fool! Liar liar loves her and means to use me to thieve to leave.

The more Cordi read, the more alarmed she became. Her mouth had gone completely dry but sweat beaded along her upper lip and had somehow gathered under her arms. She felt sick, the ramblings of a girl gone mad twisting and climbing across the page like the ivy Prim knew so much about. Here was Prim's fury unleashed, the carefully cultivated manners and propriety abandoned.

With trepidation, Cordi turned the page. The writing was clear. The images precise.

Logical Prim again. Plants, each carefully listed and illustrated with its components and uses. Mandrake. Belladonna. Iris. Willow. Others. A formula Cordi could not begin to understand took up nearly half a page. Each plant was meticulously drawn and labeled with the same care that had been taken on the portrait secreted in the attic. Whatever Prim had done, she had done with feeling.

As she read the following page, the book fell from her limp fingers to the window seat and Cordi put her hands to her mouth to hold back a scream.

He's alive. She recognized the words on the page, but her entire body had frozen in a state of shock. She had been prepared, she thought. Prepared to learn Edward was dead and buried somewhere on the grounds. Prepared to read how Prim had poisoned him the way she had Cordi and left him to suffer, screaming and writhing in agony.

Flipping the pages back and forth, Cordi tried to reconcile the words *He's alive* with what she read of the plants and their properties Prim had so carefully cataloged. Each seemed worse than the last. Hallucinations, rapid heartbeat, seizures, coma, respiratory failure . . .

Death.

Death. Alive.

A slow chill crept up from the soles of Cordi's feet, numbing her extremities before settling somewhere in her heart, threatening to freeze the organ. She flipped back to the anatomical heart Prim had drawn. Prim had wanted to know where love resided. Cordi scanned the picture, her fingers tracing along tubes and blood vessels, and tried to find the chamber where pain lived. Fear.

Rage.

Movement from the window caught her eye and she saw the white dresses emerging from the trees. She checked the sun's progress to find hours had passed. The company's slow crawl across the grass toward the garden suggested everyone was spent, and Cordi saw both Prim's and Briar's dresses soiled with dirt, their hands and arms black to their elbows. Both girls weaved a little on their feet, but Lady Evangeline looked radiant. Refreshed. Satisfied.

Knowing the book needed to be returned with haste, Cordi flipped through the next pages. Nothing indicative of what had happened to Edward. Comments on the weather. On Irene and Jane becoming ill. On Briar's incessant need for attention and her carelessness with her belongings. Cordi's arrival and even her illness, though no admission of guilt was written.

Chemical formulas again.

One page was a quickly rendered sketch in charcoal of some type of willow, its trunk bifurcated and peculiar. Fantastical and unexpected for an artist so talented at capturing reality. A pretty watercolor of a heart-shaped flower, purple and red, with teardrop leaves marking the bottom.

On the opposite page was another rough, incomplete sketch of a grove, statues all around.

It looked to be an outline for a bigger piece. Perhaps a planned landscape. A color study appeared in one corner, pinks and purples and greens; the shape of the manor loomed in the background, trees blocking most of it from view, but Cordi could make out the tops of the spires.

From her window, Cordi saw the last of the servants emerge from the dense forest.

What is planted in the Garden . . .

The Garden. This was what she was looking for. This was her next move in their game.

Chapter 39

THE HOUSE HAD NEVER BEEN so quiet. As day turned to dusk and then to evening, Cordi swore the wind even refused to blow. The calm before the storm, she might have said. But the storm gathered inside her, fueled by secrets and lies and half-truths and by all she had suffered.

After "the planting," both Prim and Briar had headed directly to their rooms. Cordi had listened to them pass in the hallway. She'd heard feet stop outside her door, hesitating before moving on. She could not be sure which of the girls it was—the one who yearned for her touch or the one who yearned for her death. She'd replaced Prim's journal exactly as she'd found it. She'd considered leaving the door open but instead closed it tight. It might give her away, but both options seemed risky. Either way, Prim had not come to confront her.

Only Faustine had arrived to deliver Cordi's meal on a tray and she was as subdued as she had been the night before, if not more. She didn't look at Cordi directly, even when Cordi tried to ask about Jane and Stella and the planting. She didn't know Faustine well, but she had run out of allies so very quickly. However, the pretty girl with the infectious giggle and willingness to chatter was gone. This new Faustine mumbled something about enough being enough before fleeing the room, leaving Cordi to eat alone.

Which was fine because she needed to prepare.

She ate quickly, tasting nothing, but scraping her bowl to the bottom. Her body was ravenous, and she was uncharacteristically thirsty. She drained her water pitcher, swallowing in great, greedy gulps and feeling better than she had in days. She supposed it was determination. Because she was determined, and she was not afraid any longer. She was too angry for fear.

Cordi pulled her treasures from her hiding spot and organized them. The letters she restacked and bound. The carvings Edward had made were piled together, save for the fox. She found stationery and a fine pen set in her vanity and she wrote her own letter. One to Briar.

The pen flew across the page, words coming almost too quickly for her pen to keep up. Confession after confession spilled forth, her heart laid bare upon the page. She imagined Prim writing in her journal, letting her feelings and thoughts flow freely through her fingers, words her tongue could not speak aloud. She and Prim were alike in this. In many ways. But she tried not to let the image linger, didn't want to hold such a mirror too close to her enemy for fear she might see herself reflected back.

Nothing was omitted. Edward's departure from the Barrow and the agony of loneliness and desperate hope. The abuses suffered at the hands of Clark and Mason, though her hand trembled to write the words and the phantom scent of onions lingered in her nostrils. The Starlings. Her flight and arrival at Edenfield and her deceptions. She told of Prim's lies, detailing the accounts from her journal. The poisoning and her firm suspicion it had been Prim who had killed Stella.

And she made promises. Promises only fools in love believe they can make. Promises made with the best intentions and which she very well might dance upon on her way to Hell.

She studied the letter, plucking the fox from where it rested on the vanity and holding it in her hand, running her thumb over its snout and down its back in a slow caress. Her mind eased and her shoulders relaxed. She could do this. She could play smart, but needed to rest before her next move. Cordi took the fox into the bed with her and fell asleep, cradling it in her palm beneath her pillow, next to the shears. She did not dream.

Cordi slunk from her room and down the hall. She listened carefully for any sound of movement, checking the narrow gaps below the doors for light. There was nothing. Both sisters seemed to be asleep. She stopped outside Briar's bedroom, still debating her decision, but she could not knowingly enter into danger or risk having to leave without telling Briar why.

She turned the knob, letting the door swing open smoothly on well-oiled hinges. The room was fragrant and sweet, the scent of water heavy in the air. Briar had likely had a long bath, and Cordi hoped it had helped ease her and offer some measure of comfort.

The moon outside was enough to illuminate the sleeping form in the bed, and in the silence Cordi could hear Briar's steady breathing. She was grateful there was no catch, that she had not cried herself to sleep. She hoped her belladonna would sleep till morning and wake rested.

Tiptoeing to the side of the bed, Cordi gave herself only a moment to commit her to memory, just in case. A wayward curl lay against Briar's cheek and Cordi resisted the urge to brush it away. Rather, she did what she'd come to do, placing her letter upon the pillow. She tucked the fox carving in as well, hoping Briar would understand that nothing would stop her from keeping her promise if she still had breath in her body.

And she prayed she would at the end of this.

Her eyes strayed to the table beside the bed and the paper there. Just a sketch, splotches of color along the side to remind the artist what colors to use. Cordi recognized it immediately. Recognized herself. It was the charcoal sketch Prim had made of her in the garden. Briar had kept it. Briar had kept *her.* In more ways than one.

It was enough. She leaned down and placed the whisper of a kiss against Briar's shining hair and silently said the words she knew to be true in her heart. Then she slipped out of the room, down the stairs, and out once more into the night.

Nobody had lit the lamps, their globes empty, wicks sleeping. Perhaps they were in mourning too. Or they knew Cordi was about and had chosen to help hide her wicked work. Yet, the darkness made no difference. It took her no time at all to navigate the maze, something guiding her steps without her having to think about the path. She instinctively knew where to go. Something willed her on, like a strange vibration she could feel rather than hear. A tuning fork that guided her forward and out of the maze and into the gardens beyond. The voices were silent, but Cordi felt their presence all the same. Silent, sleeping companions.

A path snaked through the tall grasses, trampled down by the cart and the feet of women earlier in the day, and she walked this easily to the edge of the woods. Cordi stood at the entrance between the trees, listening. Again, as before, the woods were abnormally silent. She expected the hoot of an owl or the rustling of some animals as they darted in and out of the undergrowth to avoid harm, but there was no sound at all. It made no sense. The forest went on for some distance. The woods should be teeming with life—deer, rabbits, foxes, and more. But it was all so still. Nothing stirred, but Cordi had the strong sense something watched and waited in the trees. And something called her, though she couldn't quite hear the voice. Or voices. It was just on the edge of hearing. If she closed her eyes it was clearer, but still out of range.

She looked back once more to the house, watching for signs of movement or a light floating out of the darkness, but Edenfield's manor remained as quiet and still as the forest beyond. With nothing left to do, Cordi took a deep breath and plunged headlong into the trees.

Her feet crunched in the dark over leaves and thin branches, but she managed to stay on a well-trodden path, the dirt packed hard, winding through the trees that pressed ever closer. A sound tickled the edge of her thoughts and Cordi angled her head to hear it better, but she still couldn't discern what it was. But she felt . . . something. She was being watched.

No. That was wrong. She wasn't being watched. But she was known. Something knew she was there.

Perhaps Lady Evangeline's curiosity had gone too far. What if she had created a carnivorous plant of greater scope? Something she fed the bodies of her fallen ladies or too-daring men, like flies to a Venus flytrap? Cordi tried not to imagine twisting vines wrapping themselves around her ankles and yanking her into the dark. She licked her lips and gripped the shears tightly.

The cool night air coiled around her, shrouding her in mist. It was refreshing, the moisture on her exposed skin. She felt tiny droplets on the backs of her hands, weaving into and across the roped scars. Beneath her feet, the soggy leaves were slick and the mud pulled at her heels. She inadvertently kicked the umbrella heads off mushrooms, hearing them roll away along the ground, and low-lying ferns dragged their fronds across her legs with a gentle *shush*. As strange—as *wrong*—as it felt in the woods, Cordi could not deny how wondrous and right it was as well. Part of her wanted to run to the safety of the house, but another part of her, a part that went beyond any need to find answers, longed to stay and sink into the earth where she stood. To let the soil cradle her and the rain bathe her and the wind caress her.

Of course, it was only fancy brought on by being in the forest at night. A strange dreamlike state born of her strange musings, but still . . .

Suddenly Cordi found herself stepping onto lush grass, the trees falling away behind her as if she had shed a heavy cloak. The moon was high above in an open sky, the tops of trees a black rim against navy. A grove. She'd wandered into a grove.

No. Not a grove. A graveyard.

Chapter 40

As she looked about, the shape of figures in various poses arranged in ever shrinking circles became clearer. Human forms draped in ivy, some reaching for the heavens, others with their arms outstretched as if ready to be embraced. So many statues out in the middle of the woods. As she passed through them, examining them as best she could in the dark, she was in awe of the honor given to each individual laid to rest there. For, obviously, this was where the women went to bury their "sisters." The statues were grave markers. So many. So, so many.

This was the Garden.

All this time, she had believed the Garden referenced the glorious lawns of Edenfield. The fountains overflowing with exotic greenery bathing in their sparkling waters. The orchards and the sunlight dappling through the leaves, creating an ever-shifting pattern on the grass below. And the flower beds so carefully and artfully arranged, the white stone path winding in and around so every plant might be adored and appreciated.

But the true Garden was here. A Garden of graves in honor of the women who served the Lady and her Flowers. Beneath the soil lay not seeds and bulbs, but skulls and bones.

All the names she had read in Prim's book. Annette. Beatrice. Sophia. Irene would be among them. And Stella. Stella would be here. Though she would not have a marker, not yet. Cordi followed the paths between the figures, searching for newly turned earth, hoping to pay the respects she had been denied earlier.

It was peaceful in the grove, quiet, and Cordi could easily understand why her friend had wanted to be buried there. Cordi felt at home. Home in a way she hadn't in some time.

She belonged with these figures, somehow. Those who had been planted. Those who grew in the Garden. Weaving through them, Cordi felt like she was dancing. She breathed in and spun with a laugh, grateful to be out of the forest and the closeness of the air, *here with her sisters.*

Her feet ground to a halt. Where had that thought come from? She had no sisters here or elsewhere. Cordi brushed her hair away from her face, feeling silly and strangely giddy. The air was so sweet. Sweet and familiar.

Briar's scent. And Prim's. That was what she smelled. It was everywhere, all around her. But the only plant growing was the ivy on the statues. Narrowing her eyes, Cordi stepped closer to one, its hand seeming to reach for her, squinting at it in the dark. They weren't statues at all, she realized, just ivy, shaped and twisted and given human form. Cordi had seen topiary before in the city.

Carefully manicured bushes, but not ivy. How odd.

She thought of what Prim had said about ivy. How it was deliberate and calculating. How it would take what it needed in order to survive. She shivered. But this ivy was foreign to her. Certainly not the sort that covered the manor house. She could just make out small flowers, their petals coiled around themselves, curled up for the night, ready to greet the morning. The smell came from them. The intoxicating scent made Cordi yearn for Briar, and she let loose a shaky breath, stirring the flower gently.

It opened. Slowly it unfurled as if awoken by her breath, the petals unfolding into the shape of a heart, teardrop leaves trembling as if disturbed by a breeze. But there was no breeze.

One flower opened and then another and another, till the entire figure was in full bloom, draped in flowers and greenery, coils and curls of vines flowing from floral scalps as hair. Each flower and leaf trembled lightly, giving the form a sense of movement, and Cordi peered even closer, stunned into silence. The flower was the same as the one she had seen before in Prim's watercolors, delicate and strange. Beneath the blossoms, the ivy peeked through, reminding Cordi of the blue veins running beneath the surface of her own skin. Cordi's mouth hung open in awe, dazzled by the fragrance and the so-lifelike form growing from the dirt. She half expected the plant to curtsy and begin to dance.

What she did not expect was the hand dashing out to wrap around her wrist.

Cordi was so surprised, she couldn't even utter a scream. The floral fingers gripped tightly around her wrist and pulled her closer, the figure's other arm swinging forward to clutch at Cordi's shoulder. As soon as the petals snagged at her cloak, she began to struggle, shocked into movement. But the plant held fast, squeezing her wrist, vines coiling up and over her exposed flesh. Cordi was panting, panicked, trying to get loose, but the flowers only trembled, unleashing more and more of their perfume till the air was saturated and all Cordi could taste was the flowers and the flavor she knew to be Briar's, for she'd sampled it before. Cordi heard the stirrings before she saw the others. More flowers opened. More figures began moving. Reaching. Some bent double, scratching at the ground that held them as if they might uproot themselves.

This was what became of those who did not survive the poison of the girls' breath. This was the planting. The true work of Edenfield. The Lady had cultivated her daughters, poisoning their blood till they were as beautiful and as deadly as the belladonna and foxglove. But she had not stopped there. Her loyal staff, those who looked to her for help, who succumbed to the poison either by accident or reward, were brought to the Garden. They were laid in the earth—all her specimens over the years—and they grew. Alive, but not human. Women once. Not anymore.

But what's planted in the Garden
Will grow where it is laid.

Cordi moaned in terror, and the thing holding her shook with the sound. Not in fear, but in delight. It wanted to hurt her. Wanted to make her pay. She knew it. Felt it in the tolling of that bell under her ribs she'd so long ignored.

She tore and scratched at the flowers along the head as she might eyes or hair, snapping stalks and vines and shredding petals, sending them floating to the ground below. A gaping hole was left, but her aggressor held tight. Cordi felt a scream lodge in her throat as she stared at the hollow where a face once belonged. It didn't need eyes to see her. It knew her. Recognized her as a sister. As a murderer.

She could hear the whispers in the secret language of the flowers. In the way plants spoke to each other. In the way they recognized their kin. She could hear and understand because she was linked to them through the poison that now ran in her veins. They only knew her as a twin toxin, scented her, blamed her. She had done this to them. A false goddess. A lying deity.

The once-woman would pull her in and pull her apart. Stella had been wrong to want such a fate. She could not have known; surely she could not have known! But if Cordi didn't get free, she would join her in the dirt. She felt the thin, whiplike ivy sliding up her legs and touching the bare skin of her thighs, trying to overpower her. And the horror of her situation—the memory of being held against her will—was enough to spur her into far greater violence. She was not a flower and she would not be plucked like one.

Cordi fumbled in her pocket and brought out the shears; opening them, she brought them down along the hand holding her wrist with a satisfying *snip!* And another. And another. With no mercy, no tears, she cut the offending hand away, yanking free of the once-woman's hold, feeling the vines around her legs and ankles snap free as she leapt aside. She weaved between them, feeling strange fingers grabbing for the hem of her skirt, her hair, but she ran.

She spared one last look behind her, saw the once-women writhe and dance beneath the moon, heard their silent screams of hate and regret and need. She plunged back into the woods, ignoring the path, only running. Undergrowth caught at her, twigs slicing her cheek and snagging in her cloak, but none with the intent of the floral maidens. Only trees. Only trees.

Cordi slipped down an embankment, nearly twisting her ankle on exposed roots before she scrambled up the other side, out of breath and shaking. She ran face-first into the long, waving branches of a willow, spitting out leaves and shoving them aside, wiping her face with the back of her hand. Under the willow's arching boughs, she stopped to catch her breath.

All those souls. On some level, she could hear them, their silent screams faint whispers teasing her inner ear. It wasn't supposed to be this way. Wasn't what they had been promised. Poisoned by lies and pride.

Macabre monuments to monstrous science. They remembered themselves. Knew who they had been and knew what they were. The planting had not granted them peace but rooted them in pain. All the women who had served so faithfully and believed they would be welcomed into paradise, tricked by a serpent who desired knowledge only they could offer. They had given their lives and the Lady had stolen their deaths.

Sheltered from the light of the moon, Cordi could not see her hands but felt them sticky with resin and pollen, the lifeblood of the once-women.

She swallowed as she touched a bit of tacky residue on her palm. If she were interred beneath the earth, would she too sprout roots and be born again as a shadow of herself?

It was a terrible thought for another day. She shoved the shears back into her pocket and looked about, trying to decide where she was.

In the distance, she could make out the spires of the manor, the slow, steady hand of dawn drawing them onto the midnight canvas in ever lightening shades of gray. She wasn't so lost after all. In fact, she was someplace familiar. The tree from Prim's quick sketch. The squat willow she stood beneath—it was the same tree. She recognized its bifurcated trunk, like arms stretching high, a thick knot between them that almost looked like a head.

And then she felt it. That knowledge. That call. Unable to stop herself, Cordi moved closer to the tree, eyeing the trunk. She pressed a hand against the bark, not afraid—not like before—and found it strangely warm. The knot drew her attention and she stared, the moon peeking through the vines and leaves just enough for her to discern what could be described as a face.

Chapter 41

BLINKING DID NOT CLEAR THE vision. And after what she had just seen in the grove, Cordi was not expecting it to. But still, she started as the tree moved. One of the long, branching fronds slipped over Cordi's wrist and looped back up again, settling into her palm. Not an act of violence like the once-women, but an offering. She closed her fingers around it and felt the tree shudder, its porcelain-pale leaves shaking as if it had given a ragged exhale.

Deeeeeeee . . .

Her lips quivered, at first unable to speak the name aloud. For to name it would be damning, regardless of whether she was wrong or right. If she was wrong, she was mad. But the notion that she was right? That was far, far worse.

"Ed . . ." she attempted, the name dying on her tongue before it was fully formed.

The tree shook and the frond grew taut, as if fingers were squeezing hers. The hand pressed against the tree flew to her mouth and muffled the animal cry of pain that burned her throat. Her face was hot and her very vision blurred in the growing light, black spots appearing, and she thought she might faint.

She must have fallen back, because she felt more of the fronds behind her, their supple stems gone rigid and helping to bolster her when she would have fallen. They gently supported her weight, steadying her until the spell passed and she could once again feel the earth solid beneath her feet. Cordi licked her suddenly dry lips, trying to focus on the frond still coiled over her wrist and hand. She brushed her thumb against the pale-green leaves, tracing their curves, noting the veins that ran just beneath the surface, darker and slightly raised.

Cordi looked up at the tree itself, at its frankly humanoid shape, at the bark's strange texture, remembering how warm it felt beneath her fingers, at the *face* caught in the wood. A face she knew by heart. But it was all wrong. *This* was all wrong. It was impossible.

Impossible was a word that had little meaning anymore.

Trapped inside? Yes. He was trapped. That was it, she told herself, her mind determined to make sense of a situation she had no explanation for. She lifted a hand again, fingers curling under a line of bark roughly where a cheek might be, ready to pull it away. Edward was trapped inside.

"Don't."

Cordi let loose a choked scream, her hand falling away as she whirled and pressed herself against the tree, retreating as far as she could. Behind the gently swaying branches of the peculiar willow, peering through them like a curtain, was Prim.

The tree that was not Edward—that *could not* be her brother—shuddered behind her, its branches dipping lower as if it might keep Prim out of its shade and away from Cordi.

Prim frowned. "Why are you so cruel?"

Cordi shook her head, the back of her head scratching against the bark behind her.

"I would have given you anything." Prim walked under the boughs, the branches brushing against her face, tangling in her hair, long and loose and unbrushed, strands wild around her shoulders. Her hands and arms still filthy. Cordi had never seen her disheveled. "Anything you asked. I gave you what was mine to keep."

Cordi couldn't move as Prim advanced, frozen against the trunk. "I don't know what you're talking about," she croaked.

But Prim ignored her, moving till she was right up against the tree and laid both her hands against it, her hand running down the bark in a caress, speaking as if Cordi weren't even there. "Such callous indifference. Betrayal. Just as Mother warned. But still I rewarded you because *I* at least meant it when I said the words you taught me. My darling. My Edward."

There was the groan and creak of heavy wood and Cordi leapt away before she could stop herself, the frond releasing her wrist even as leaves came away in her grip. The long, slender branch that had coiled around her skin retreated upward as if stung. Prim saw and cooed, cupping the protrusion at the top where Edward's face floated in the wood. It moved, leaning into her touch.

"You must be careful," she said to Cordi, eyes scanning the tree as if checking for any injuries. "You will hurt him. Isn't he beautiful? He was beautiful before too. You saw the painting. I know you did. And you loved him too. You saw him and you loved him. How could you not?" She laid her cheek in the crook between one of the raised limbs and the knot at the top of the tree and shut her eyes, her fingers moving in lazy patterns across the trunk, and she let out a happy sigh. "I can't blame you or her for loving him. But he is mine."

The tree stood still and tall, as if it were only a tree, but Cordi sensed it listening. Knew that it wasn't a tree at all. Knew in her heart.

"Edward." His name came readily that time, as if the truth had somehow eased its passage. As if to name a horror was to somehow make it less terrifying.

Prim nodded, her cheek scratching against the bark, her hair snagging in wisps in crevices. "Mother doesn't know about him. She never would have let me keep him. Just like she never would have given us her blessing. But we don't need it. Not this way. I can touch him this way as I could not before." She pressed back, standing straight again, gazing upward into that strange, distorted face with pure love and adoration. Rising on tiptoe, she pressed her lips to Edward's own, his slightly parted, a shallow crevice between them.

Cordi felt the contents of her stomach rise to the back of her throat and she bent over double, putting a hand over her mouth as she began to retch, swallowing with force as tears stung her eyes. Prim smoothed a hand down the dark dress she wore, its hem filthy and its skirts wrinkled as if she had slept in it, and fitfully. When she took a step forward, Cordi lurched back.

"Oh, don't be a goose," Prim sniffed. "I've no interest in harming you unless you make me. To do so would only wound Briar, and I'd cut off my own arm before I hurt her. And since you won't *leave*, you and I obviously need to have a chat, and you've so graciously afforded us privacy."

Still leaning forward, one hand wrapped around her middle while she forced herself not to be sick, Cordi sniffed wetly, wiping at her eyes and nose with a sleeve. "I don't understand."

"So you keep saying, though I believe you know a bit more than you let on. All that sneaking about you've been doing? I'll admit I've not been sure what to make of you beyond a source of entertainment. I thought for a while you were another of Father's bastards after a fortune. Or maybe a spy looking to steal Mother's work. But no. No, something else drives you on, our Cordi. Something more personal. Still, I'll afford you the benefit of the doubt for the sake of my sister. I went through so much to save you, after all."

Cordi had to admire Prim in that moment. Even in the pale light of dawn, her hair and dress a mess, she was still the picture of poise and cold nobility. But the way her face had softened when she had looked upon the tree . . . Upon Edward . . .

She again felt faint.

"You're familiar with Mr. Starling and I'll thank you not to deny it. So that will save us a bit of time. Mother hired him to build the greenhouse and to construct the arbors. Edward, as I'm sure you have also learned somehow, was Mr. Starling's apprentice. Mother was very clear that we were not to be in the garden on days when they were working, but," she said with a chuckle, "you know how well I suffer boredom."

She looked up at the gently swaying branches, moved by the wind rather than by intent, as if Edward's spirit or form had gone dormant and they were just standing within the shelter of a strange willow. But Prim's face again took on a gentleness Cordi barely recognized in the steady, proper young woman. "I saw him from the windows first. I was only curious, mind you. I'd seen men before. There was nothing particularly interesting about any of them. But I saw *him*! Whistling, of all things, and dreadfully off-key."

It was true. Edward had never had an ear for music and couldn't carry a tune if one had been handed to him in a bucket.

"I had to get closer. He saw me. The way he looked at me . . ." She held a hand over her heart. "I ran. I was *terrified*. Mother has always told of us of their viciousness. Their deceit. And I remember how much she hated my father, though I do not have the memories she wishes I did. I recall gifts of dolls and pats on the head and the smell of tobacco. Briar doesn't remember him at all. But Mother told us enough. Told us of how evil he was. How vile. How they all are. And we believed her. How could we not, with all the girls who came to us with stories of their own? Even with that, I had to see Edward again. I spied from the window. He watched me watch him, and he slipped something under one of the stones in the garden. It was a letter."

Her face was alight with memory, a blush on her cheeks burning away the icy exterior like the rising sun burning away the mist on the grove. She tilted her face up as if to receive a kiss and—much to Cordi's surprise—one of the branches, long and thin, lifted as if by invisible strings and brushed Prim's cheek. Prim sighed happily even as the branch drifted back down to join so many others enclosing them.

"It took me days to write back. And we corresponded like that, one letter at a time left under a stone, for the duration of his contract. I cannot tell you how my heart pounded with each letter I read. How I felt alive in ways I had never known! We met at the cottage for the first time. I was so frightened, but I had to speak to him. Even if it was just once. I didn't let him come near me. Ordered him to keep his distance, and he did."

Cordi could imagine it. Prim in one of her elegant dresses, hands folded beneath her breasts, beautiful and imperial. Edward had probably gone to his knees.

"But we spoke. He told me of his work and his plans to be a master craftsman and to carve and create beautiful things. He told me that his parents were dead and that he had a sister away at school. He told me I was fascinating and inspiring and beautiful.

"After, we met in secret. In the cottage where it was safe and open. Always at night. Sometimes one of us couldn't get away or the weather was foul, and those days were torturous. And finally, he asked me to marry him, even though we still had never touched. Even though I always made him stay well away from me. I even wore gloves to write his letters. And how could I tell him?"

Cordi could recall each time Briar had extended a hand as if to touch her and pulled back. Each momentary lapse that had her retreating if she inched too close. All before Cordi had been taken ill. All attempts to keep Cordi safe. She had revealed the truth only after Cordi was much the same as she was. Edward had never known. He had thought he was courting a beautiful, lonely girl. Not a deadly one. "You didn't tell him. You didn't tell him the truth. And he became sick."

But Prim only continued to ignore her, too caught up in her memories, as if somehow freed by speaking of her love and secrets aloud. "I wanted to believe we could be together. I knew we could if we were careful. If it was slow. I was careful. He was ill, true. But I nursed him to health again, just as I did you. They left him in our cottage to his pain and I went to him. His angel, he called me. His love. And I saved him. Made him better. Mother taught me so well. I learned my lessons at her knee. All of them, even if her warnings did not take root as they should have. Part of me wishes they had. The righteous part. The Primrose I was before Edward. Because he did deceive me, even after he promised he loved me."

She didn't know. She still didn't know.

"I was foolish. Even after I realized he had planned to use me, that he didn't want me. He wanted *her*."

"You—" Cordi's tongue felt thick and clumsy, and she gestured to the branches above her. She didn't have the words for what had happened, had no knowledge of how such a thing could even be possible, even after reading Prim's journal. "You did *this* to him?"

Prim continued as if she hadn't heard a word Cordi uttered. "He told me he loved me, promised we would be together. *Promised* me that we would never be parted. All the while scheming to be with *her*."

The tree rustled and the trunk groaned, and Cordi fancied the features in the bark twisted further, the knot trying to move stiffly, the ground shifting as if the tree was trying to rise from its roots. Agitated and desperate. This was her brother, or what was left of him. His consciousness? His soul? Like the once-women in the Garden, but different. Prim had made something unique with her fantastic and terrible knowledge.

Deeee . . . She . . . doesn't . . . hear. . . . Can't.

Cordi cupped her ear from behind even though the voice did not come from without, but within. Edward was speaking to her. In the way the flowers did. But Prim seemed to hear none of it.

Languages were not her forte.

"Prim. He's talking. Can't you hear him? He—"

But Cordi might as well have been speaking to herself. Prim ignored her as she danced around Edward's trunk, laughing, a cackling sound that had Cordi flinching at the edge of madness that had crept into her voice. "If it had been Briar, I might have allowed it. Her happiness for mine. I could have swallowed my pride and my longing if it was for her. But not for some *whore* out of that filthy city he came from!" Prim began to pace back and forth, slippered feet avoiding the roots that continued to roil as if they might tear straight from the ground. And Cordi realized she was witnessing a lovers' quarrel. An accusation and a denial, though neither was appealing to the other, but to her. "He mixed up the letters. I could *hear* my own heart breaking when I read what had been left for me. What had been meant for *her*! He was leaving." Prim reaching into the pocket of her skirt and withdrew a letter.

"Oh, Prim . . ." Cordi already knew how it would begin.

" 'My dearest Dee,' " Prim read, her voice pitched high, furious, holding back tears because she would probably die before she allowed them to fall. " 'Please forgive me for not writing. I hope I've not worried you. I'll tell you everything soon! I'm coming and we'll be together. Just like I pr—*promised*.' " Prim's voice broke on the word. At what she believed it meant, and Cordi's heart ached to hear it. " 'We're going to be so happy, and I'll have such a surprise for you! I miss you. All my love, Edward.' "

She crushed the letter in her fist, something Cordi guessed she had done many a time from the state of the paper. The tree that was Edward stood silent and watchful and rigid. The mist about their feet rose in wisps like tendrils of smoke. Silent, icy flames consuming them.

"Prim," Cordi whispered, both afraid of and sad for the wretched, heartbroken woman standing in the glade. What she had done was reprehensible.

Unforgivable. But Cordi couldn't help but feel sympathy for her. For what had been done to her. Jailed by what she had been told was love. Bitter and suspicious and broken by her hope for more. She had not known how to ask for the truth. How could she? When—for all she had known—her fears had been proven right? For there was the evidence of betrayal in her hands. Words written in the hand of the man she had loved, which—to her eyes—meant her mother had been right, had always been right, and she was a fool. Something Prim would not stomach to be. "Prim, you have it wrong."

Those violet eyes—dark in the just-before-dawn gloom—met hers, fire smoldering in their depths. Venom twisted Prim's beautiful, dark lips and she spat her next words, spittle flying, droplets landing on her chin. "Do not speak in that placating tone to me. What do you know of him? Of us? Nothing! You're another foundling like the rest. Broken little dolls that come here to be mended. A liar and a thief and worse. Not enough for you to steal my sister, but to try to steal Edward too? Who are you to tell me *anything*?"

Heat curled in Cordi's belly now. She was tired of lies and half-truths. Tired of running and being afraid and the crushing weight of want. "You spoiled little thing! I've every right to tell you you're wrong! Every right, because that letter was for *me*! The same way this one was for you!" She pulled the letter—Edward's final letter—from her pocket and held it out.

Prim snatched the letter, eyes moving over the words. Reading and rereading, confusion darkening her brow.

"He loved you! He was keeping his promise to you the same way he was keeping his promise to *me*! Don't you understand? *I'm Dee!* And Edward was no more in love with me than I am with him! He's my brother!"

The fronds on the tree shook in eagerness, and Cordi fancied she heard his voice as she had heard the once-women. *Yes. Yes.* But Prim was not so easily convinced. She was shaking her head. "No. That's . . . that can't be. You're lying. You're trying to confuse me!"

Cordi pulled out the few of her own letters she had brought with her and threw them onto the ground, the mist scattering. All in Edward's hand. All addressed to her at the Barrow. She pointed an accusing finger at them. "My brother. Not a lover. And I came looking for him, and you cannot stand there and tell me you would not have done the same for Briar!"

Prim dropped to her knees, the low-lying fog fleeing from her as if terrified, and she lifted the envelopes all addressed to Cordelia Beecher. The ripping sound of paper was the sound of a heart shattering. " 'Dearest Dee,' " Prim read, lifting her face, eyes pleading. Begging Cordi to take away the truth. Cordi could see it on her face.

Better to be avenged than to be wrong.

But it felt good and right to speak the truth, a fond smile on her face, picturing her brother. "He called me Dee. He said Cordelia was a name too big for such a little girl." A frond, long and covered in the pale leaves, landed on her head and she could almost feel his fingers. A gesture of affection from a big brother to his little sister.

Prim's mouth fell open and she clutched at her chest with both hands, the letter crushing against her heart. She folded over till her head hit the ground, her hair a shroud of mourning, and she screamed, the sound tearing through the dawn like a knife. She gasped, a hoarse rasp as if she might be choking, before she screamed again.

"That's quite enough, Primrose."

The imposing voice made Cordi's head snap up. Lady Evangeline glided through the grass and into the glade, brushing the branches away with an imperial wave of her hand. Her hair was braided down the back and she wore a long, white nightdress, tied at the collar, paired with a fur-lined cloak over the top. Prim still knelt on the ground, but she rotated her face up to her mother, peering through the hair plastered against splotchy cheeks. Lady Evangeline eyed her daughter with a look of disgust. "Get up, girl. I'll not have you howling like a wounded animal over a man. How dare you demean yourself in such a way? I taught you better."

Prim looked frightened and confused. As if she couldn't understand her mother's words.

"*Tsk.* Briar. Come help your sister to her feet."

Briar tiptoed in on bare feet, pushing through the fronds, shaking in what Cordi thought might be fear rather than cold. She must have run straight from her room, her dress hooked haphazardly, her eyes darting about the clearing, landing on each of the strange assembly in turn.

But she knelt in the dirt and dewy grass beside her sister, smoothed dark hair away from a pale face. Briar tugged a handkerchief from her dress and wiped at Prim's face, clearing away the mucus streaming from her nose and the spittle that had bubbled on her lips. "It's all right, Prim. I'm here. I'll help you."

Noooo . . .

Prim turned her head toward her sister, her eyes flat and hard. "Why?"

Briar licked her lips with her pink tongue, and for once, Cordi felt no rush of heat, but a sense of foreboding. "Come along, my sister. I need you to stand. Can you do that for me?"

Prim gave a low whine. An animal caught in a trap.

"Cordi, help me," Briar breathed.

And Cordi did. No matter what Prim had done to her, to Edward. She couldn't stand the sight of her writhing in agony on the ground, her mother without pity. Maybe she didn't deserve pity, but Cordi felt it nonetheless. She took one arm and Briar the other and, with some coaxing, managed to get Prim to her feet, though she sagged between them, all her strength gone.

Lady Evangeline stared hard at her daughter, then turned her gaze to the tree that was Edward. A chill ran up Cordi's spine at the look there. She had thought Lady Evangeline beautiful like the statue of Demeter, but that beauty was hard and cruel, and Cordi understood there was no love there. Only possession.

Another sound of displeasure. "After all the deliberate care I have taken over the years. My work. My creations. The careful order of things. And then suddenly—what? My house a mess. Full of weeds. And now I find betrayal?" She pointed a finger at Edward. "This perversion of the gift I gave you? And from *you*, Prim. I might have thought your sister weak, but not you."

On the other side of Prim, Briar hung her head and held tighter to her sister. "I gave you two *power.* No man could touch you. You belonged to yourselves. Independent women the likes of which the world would quake to see. And still I find you sniveling over something as common as a wounded heart. A drop of your blood could kill any man who dared try to wrong you, but you prostrate and shame yourself and call it love. Utterly disgusting.

"I'll not have it. Do you hear me? The both of you? I'll. Not. Have. It. Bad enough you shared my gift without proper consideration with *this* one," she said, gesturing with her chin to Cordi, "but to use *my* precious work to create this abomination?"

She circled the willow, studying the bifurcated trunk with something that might have been admiration if she could stop sneering. Prim had done something she had not, and somehow this both impressed and displeased the Lady of Edenfield. But displeasure won out and her lip curled in distaste as she looked into Edward's face and back to her daughter, still dazed and unable to support her own weight in her grief.

"The deceit. The gall. Well, since this was your doing, Primrose, *you* will be responsible for the felling."

Chapter 42

"THE WHAT?" CORDI DARED, HEART in her throat.

"The felling. Primrose is going to cut this thing down. If she would bring a serpent into my Eden just because it offered her knowledge, I would have her repent. But first I want samples of the bark and the leaves. Briar? You will collect these. Time you take more care with your training if your sister is going to be such a disappointment."

"You can't!" Cordi cried, and a jolt shot through Prim. Cordi met her eyes and saw some of the madness that had claimed her leach away, to be replaced by a glimmer of respect.

"I assure you, I can. And we are starting *over*," the Lady emphasized, looking each girl in the face. "The entire house. Only be grateful that at least there is more for the Garden."

Cordi was breaking under the combined weight of Prim and that stare. "What do you mean?"

The Lady of Edenfield gave a contemptuous laugh. "Do you think it is easy running a household like mine? To keep such secrets? One silly girl raving lunacy now and again is easily dismissed as fed off rumors. And I make sure those rumors never go entirely quiet but become no more than that. Let the sheep of Farrow and their children gossip about ghosts. But an entire house in mutiny? The others would likely have followed—and even if they hadn't, the risk was just too great."

"Oh, Mother," Briar said, her voice brittle. "You didn't."

"I did. The lot of them. We will be very busy planting today, girls. As for you . . ." she said, turning to Cordi with a weary sigh, "I can hardly blame you for the circumstances that have led to your immunity, as it were. On the contrary, it is rather fascinating. You're the first to have survived with long-term resistance. It will likely be permanent without treatment. So, I can offer you this."

She pulled a long glass tube from a pocket of her cloak and handed it to Cordi. The liquid inside was dark. "What is it?"

"An antidote. I diluted your blood and—well, it is all rather complicated. As it is, I only managed to make the one vial. I give you my word that it is perfectly safe. I'd not have gone through all this trouble just to plant you with the rest. But I give you the choice. You may stay here in Edenfield and continue on as you have as a companion to the girls. You'll help in the Garden. Have safety and comfort, as I promised. Or you can drink this and be gone. Banished from my Eden. It will make the story more convincing, in a way, for you to walk free and in such good health. It does get so tiresome to explain away the deaths and disappearances of this house. But I have been doing it for quite some time now. Accidents are so easily arranged."

Accidents. Briar had said as much before. Evangeline's parents? Her husband? The servants. How many others?

"But I warn you, Cordelia *Grey*," Lady Evangeline said, her tone indicative she knew full well how Cordi had lied. "If you utter a word of Edenfield beyond what I permit you to say, I will turn you in to the law. You entered my house under false pretenses, and someone is looking for you. Do not make the mistake of thinking I do not know how the world works simply because I choose not to engage in it. I know how heavy my name and my money can weigh and I will use them to protect what is mine."

Cordi believed her. How easy it would be for her too. She took in women with nowhere else to go, who had forsaken the world and its harsh cruelty. She was so careful to select those whom she might manipulate or frighten if she had to.

The liquid—a promise of freedom—sloshed around within the glass. Freedom. The thing she had always wanted. She could take Edward's earnings and start afresh. Away from this place and its secrets and horrors.

But she would have to leave Briar. She could never see her again. Touch her again. She would go the rest of her life dreaming of a poisonous girl with amethyst eyes locked in a tower.

And Edward was to be chopped down! Murdered!

Prim pulled free from her companions' hold. She straightened her back and swept her hair from her face and behind her shoulders. Cordi watched, fascinated, as the mask she wore—the cool and casual indifference—slid so easily into place. Like seeing her journal play out in real life. "I'm sorry, Mother. I do believe I got carried away. You're right. I was weak."

Lady Evangeline rolled her eyes. "Weakness is the least of your transgressions."

Prim gave a tight smile, then carefully took the vial from Cordi's hand and held it up to the light. "You're right again. And I see now what you've given us. But I don't understand how you created a cure for us. It's so remarkable."

A sniff of derision. "It isn't a cure. You should know better. You and Briar are unique. Your blood could not possibly be deprived of the toxins now. Cordelia would end up much the same after long exposure, but this will at least neutralize the poison in her blood. Such a thing would kill you or Briar."

"Ah. Well then . . ." Prim leaned to the side and kissed Briar's temple over the red curls, and with her thumb undid the stopper.

She raised the vial to her lips.

"No!" Cordi yelled at the same time Briar screamed. But it was too late.

Prim had thrown her head back and swallowed the contents, dropping the glass to the ground, where it rolled away. "Thank you, Mother," she said, moving toward Edward's trunk. Briar fell to her knees in the damp grass, hands to her mouth, her beautiful face twisted with horror. Cordi could only gape. The leaves shook above them, the branches trembling.

Lady Evangeline gawked in a most unladylike fashion. "You *stupid* girl! What have you done?"

Prim weaved and threw a hand out, catching herself on the tree. She chuckled as she sank to the ground, a humorless sound. "I told you. I see what you gave us now. Not a gift—a curse. You poisoned your children and called it love. You corrupted us and this place with your poison. Like a witch in one of the fairy stories Father used to read me." She laughed again. A drunken, delirious laugh of the damned. "He knew, didn't he? He knew what you were and tried to save us. That's why you did it, isn't it? He loved as you never could. He would have saved us from you."

She fell among the roots, clutching at handfuls of grass, and Edward's branches dipped down as if he might support her. Briar crawled to her sister through the dirt. "No, no, no, no, no." The one word, over and over. She reached her beloved sister and tried to lift her up, cradling her face. "You can't leave me, Prim. You can't leave me alone."

"Shh . . . You have love, Briar. *Real* love. Like I do." Prim smiled, and it was real. "Plant me here with my Edward. If he'll have me. Let me grow with him." And then she went limp, her head lolling in Briar's hold.

She was gone.

There was a groaning sound, like a tree ready to topple in the wind, and the branches around them swayed madly. Several knocked Cordi away, sending her reeling. Others reached for Briar and Lady Evangeline. Briar screamed as several tangled in her hair, yanking and pulling at the red strands, dragging her back. Cordi cried out and reached for her, but Briar was already thrashing, rolling free.

"Run!" Cordi yelled.

Briar stood, torn for a moment, and then dashed away, her pink dress visible between the trees as she fled toward the house.

Lady Evangeline was not so lucky. Though she struck out with her arms, flailing wildly, there was nothing she could do as the thin, whiplike stems wrapped around her throat and grew taut. She pulled at them, grabbing at leaves, tearing them with her nails, but the branches held, lifting her up till her toes grazed along the ground, seeking purchase. Cordi watched in horror as the Lady's struggles weakened, her face swelling, skin turning purple and mottled as what was now Edward pulled her close. The Lady quieted, unable to pull in another breath, but her eyes—bulging from her skull—seemed to drink Edward in, enthralled. Impressed.

There was the snap of a branch. But there wasn't.

It was the snap of a neck.

Chapter 43

THE SILENCE FOLLOWING THE CRACK of breaking bone was deafening. Cordi strained to hear anything beyond the phantom echo, but there was nothing.

Lady Evangeline hung suspended in the air, her head at a crooked angle, a protrusion of bone bulging through the skin on her neck. With a flick of fronds, her body tumbled to the ground, limp and lifeless, limbs splaying like a broken doll's. Cordi took halting steps toward her, knowing she was dead, but she no longer understood such seemingly simple concepts as dead or alive in this place. Edenfield had blurred the lines for her too many times.

Before she could reach the body, there was a great ripping sound, and Cordi fell to her knees, crawling backward across the forest floor, thinking somehow that with the Lady gone, all she had created in her hubris was falling apart. But instead, one of Edward's roots unearthed itself, and the tree—Edward—shook with extreme pain. Or incredible guilt. She couldn't be sure. Then, tenderly, his branches bowed, slender stems twisting and twining around Prim, her face peaceful, almost happy.

With great care, he dragged her body into the hole left by his roots, dirt and pebbles falling like a gentle rain. He pulled his beloved Prim into the grave he had carved for her before he settled again into the earth. The effort must have been enormous, because he did not move after, but his branches sagged and shook and Cordi felt his pain in her own limbs, in the parts of her that were now altered.

The sun climbed higher, dragging a lazy pink and golden dawn in its wake, driving the heaviest shadows from the forest. But a heavier shadow lay over Edenfield, its mistress and one of its daughters dead along with their servants. The true Garden was a graveyard, and now the house itself was a tomb.

Cordi crawled on hands and knees to nestle at the foot of Edward's trunk, resting her head on the thick root bowed over Prim. She curled up, her back to the lifeless body of Lady Evangeline so she would not have to see the mask of death or the striped flesh of her neck where the wiry stems had wrapped tight.

She lay like that for some time, knees drawn up and her damp, filthy cloak wrapped around her like a blanket. The bark was scratchy against her cheek, but warm. She wanted to cry, but tears would not come. She was too tired for tears. Too confused. Maybe even a bit frightened. But she had found Edward, and that was a comfort.

"I found you," Cordi repeated aloud, pushing up to sit among Edward's roots, head tilted up so she could see the sun filtering through the fronds, dappling his pale leaves, their dark veins blue and purple in the light. "And you should know Alice is quite cross with you for not saying good-bye. I promised to let you know. I promised, and we keep our promises, don't we?"

Her brother said nothing, but she thought she could feel him smile. Knew he would have rolled his eyes if he could. If he'd kept them.

She wondered if he could see her. She doubted it. Whatever senses he had now were not what they had been. Prim and Briar had described plants as social creatures. Explained how they spoke to and befriended one another. How they protected themselves. How they knew when to flower and when to sleep. Edward was like them now.

So was she.

She shut her eyes, watching the sun dance on the backs of her lids in bursts of color and shadow. "Are you . . . ?" Cordi let the question drift. She had meant to ask if he was happy, but how could he be? Trapped as he was? The woman he loved now buried beneath him?

Tears slid silently down her face and a frond gently brushed them away. Perhaps he *could* see her. Or he only sensed the water. She wasn't sure. But the slender branch lay on her shoulder, a comforting hand, and she kept her eyes shut, finding her brother in the quiet presence behind, above, and below her. Steady and strong as he had always been.

"What's planted in the Garden, will grow in the Garden." Opening her eyes, she rubbed at the moisture that had settled on her lower lashes with grubby hands, wiping her nose on her already filthy sleeve. "Will she grow here? With you?"

The breeze picked up then, lifting and spreading the long, twisting stems and rustling his leaves, so Cordi couldn't be sure of an answer. She could not hear his voice, his strength spent. But she hoped so. If that was what he wanted.

"What do I do now?"

She let herself shut her eyes again, lulled to near sleep by the wind through the leaves and the grasses. Birds called cheerfully from somewhere beyond the glade. She let herself be cradled among the roots and her breathing began to slow. It was then—caught somewhere between sleep and wakefulness—she felt the stirring beneath the earth. Without even becoming consciously aware of how she knew, she was certain it was the movement of worms. Could feel them burrowing through the soil, strengthening and nurturing it. She sensed water far below the ground, and her fingers splayed across the dirt as if she could reach for it. Her face angled again to the sun, searching for its light and warmth.

Dreamily, she raised her lids, listening to the call of her brother. Her sisters.

She stood, patting the trunk affectionately, eyes steady on the face she recognized even within the wood. "I'll be back. I promise."

She blew her brother a kiss that smelled of flowers.

Ignoring the cooling body of Lady Evangeline, she started back toward the house, a new purpose in mind.

She found Briar kneeling in her mother's study. Every drawer and every shelf had been emptied; every notebook and tome open upon the floor, Briar like a wilted, fallen flower amid the scattered papers and pages. She still wore her mud-spattered dress and Cordi could see her bare feet covered with earth, her nailbeds black, peeking out from under the soiled hem. Though Briar's eyes were rimmed with red, she was not crying. But her eyes were wild, her lips moving as she scanned page after page of cramped, looping handwriting.

"What are you doing?"

Briar jumped, falling back among the books stacked behind her and knocking them about, some pages fluttering from her hands and to the floor. When she saw it was Cordi standing there, she flushed red. She righted herself and reached for the pages again. "I'll find you a cure. I will."

Cordi watched Briar from just inside the doorway, her beautiful, poisonous flower, while she discarded the top page, laying it aside too carefully, too deliberately. As if it were a predator she must move cautiously around. As if she herself were not the most dangerous thing in that room. She didn't look up. "I may not have my mother's or Prim's skill, but I'll learn. I'll fix it."

"Briar . . ."

"I won't have you chained to me unwillingly!"

The ferocity of these words made Cordi gasp and step back. The girl she had come to know—to love—was not to be found in that face. Not a floral maiden, but a goddess once more, someone to be feared and respected in turn. A living, breathing Persephone. And even kneeling in a soiled dress, her hair in disarray, the skin of her face splotchy from sorrow, she sat ramrod straight and stared with righteous indignity.

"You are not to be caged, Cordi. Not you. Never you. You cannot thrive and grow and blossom here. Not without the very thing you want most. Not without your freedom." She began combing through the papers again.

Cordi looked at the walls around her. The walls that had been Prim's and Briar's and even Evangeline's world for so long. A beautiful prison full of light and shadow and life and death. And love. Their mother's: toxic and possessive. But there had been the love between sisters too. Something pure and adoring; even with Prim's growing envy and fear and her own warped sense of love, she had been unable to deny her sister's need for an affection she could not offer. Something she herself had wanted so desperately that she had stolen it and kept it the only way she knew how, even as it destroyed her.

She thought of Prim and her mother out in the grove. Of the women she'd glimpsed in the kitchen as she returned, gathered and slumped over at the breakfast table, their poisoned tea cold in their cups. Together. How Edward, even after what had been done to him, had tugged Prim close so she might stay beside him.

And here was Briar, haggard and desperate, but still disarmingly beautiful as she searched for hope. Not for herself, but for Cordi. Knowing if she found it—if she succeeded—she would be alone. She would wander the halls and the gardens till the color leached from her hair and eyes and her cheeks hollowed. There would be no more laughter. No more vibrant joy. Only desolation and madness.

Cordi walked into the room, her booted feet tracking mud across the expensive carpet, and she dropped to her knees in front of Briar, reaching her battered and scratched hands forward to take the pages Briar held so tightly. Briar didn't resist, but she didn't lift her head, leaving Cordi to stare at the crown of her strawberry hair, leaves and twigs tangled in the curls from her flight from the Garden.

She gathered Briar's hands in her own, her thumbs stroking across her delicate wrists, feeling the veins that moved both blood and poison through her beloved's body. The same toxin that ran in her own veins. But no matter how poisoned her heart, it belonged to this girl. And she had given it freely.

Love did not have to be a prison.

A drop of water landed on the back of Cordi's hand, sliding down along the fine hairs and cracks and leaving a pale path in the dirt and grime that coated her scarred skin. Another followed. "You wish to go," Briar said wetly, even as her fingers curled around Cordi's palms, betraying her words with her desire.

"Briar. Look at me."

Even with tears slipping down her cheeks, she had set her jaw so she managed to look both fragile and defiant. Afraid and alone for the first time and still looking for a way to set Cordi free.

"There is no cure," Cordi said plainly.

"There is! You heard Mother. There's no hope for me, but there is for you. We can find it and—"

"Shhh," Cordi hushed her, framing her face in her hands, brushing tears away and feeling the wayward curls on the back of Briar's neck. "There is no cure for love. You could draw every drop of poison from my heart, and it would still be yours."

Even as moisture gathered in the corners of her eyes, Briar lifted her chin, pushing Cordi's fingers deeper into the hair at the nape of her neck. There was again the resemblance to Prim's own determination. A knowing calculation. "You would grow to resent me. I couldn't bear that, Cordi. Watching your eyes turn cold and hard. Your world would be these walls and the Garden, and that's not enough. Not for you."

Cordi nodded. "You're right. It's not. But you are."

"For how long?" Briar asked doubtfully.

"I can't give you promises, Briar. I want to. I *desperately* want to promise you forever," she admitted, thinking of the promises Edward had meant and hadn't been allowed to keep. "But I'm here. And I love you."

Briar's cheeks flamed red, warming under Cordi's hands, and she looked away, face shuttering, before drawing Cordi's own hands down to hold them on her lap, reluctant to break their connection. "It's my fault. I should never have let myself want things not meant for me."

"Then you have far better control over your own heart than I do of mine, if you can bid it love or hate on command. I'm afraid I don't have such self-discipline, as many of my former teachers will tell you."

A snort of laughter that Briar immediately tried to smother with her hand. Cordi imagined she was horrified with herself for having the ability to laugh after all that had transpired that morning. But Cordi's heart was glad.

Briar took a deep breath. "What do we do now?"

We. Just the word made Cordi light-headed. She leaned forward till their foreheads rested together. "We live."

"Happily ever after?" Briar joked, her voice sad yet hopeful.

"Happily is a good start." Cordi angled her chin up and captured Briar's lips with her own, delighting as Briar's breath entered her mouth on a sigh. She pressed her back, toppling stacks of books pulled from shelves and stacked around Briar like a protective wall, listening to them tumble to the floor with solid thuds and skid across the hardwood. As she kissed her, Cordi thought of the walls they would continue to tear down.

She would not keep Briar trapped behind walls in pretty dresses and pretty lies. But she would keep her.

"My belladonna," she sighed into Briar's mouth.

A twitch of Briar's lips and a purr of delight. "Yours," she said, her voice husky and dark. "And you are *mine*."

As their clothes fell away, the air became saturated with the perfume of their flesh. And with each kiss and caress, each of them was emboldened till they were surging against the other, searching and demanding. Their breaths mingled and Cordi's head spun; no longer from the slow and steady poisoning of her blood, but from the touch of Briar's fingers and lips.

There was no part of the other they did not explore. No inch of skin left untouched or unloved, both of them desperate for contact. There was an urgency to their touches and they gave themselves over to it with total abandon, laughing and moaning in turn, their cries of pleasure and delight echoing through the house while the dead cooled downstairs.

After, as they lay in a tangle of limbs and silk, sweat cooling on their skin, the room smelled of ink, earth, and the sweet, cloying fragrance Cordi had always associated with the sisters but now knew would mark her as well. Briar lay with her nose pressed against Cordi's throat.

"I love you too," Briar whispered.

Cordi kissed the top of her head, fingers moving along Briar's scalp, tangling in her curls.

"I never wanted it to be this way. I wanted you, but—" Briar stopped herself short, sucking the words back as if to speak aloud would bring ruin upon them. But Cordi could feel the sudden heat of Briar's skin that had nothing to do with what they had just done and the hot splash of a tear on her collarbone.

Cordi hugged her tighter, pressing her closer, trying to absorb the hurt she knew only too well. Briar clung to her, wrapping herself around Cordi's body. Cordi thought of Prim, buried beneath Edward's roots, together as he had promised. Maybe some promises were forever.

As she held Briar, stroking her tangled hair and pressing kisses to her teary face till the tears slowed and the heat between them rose again, she fervently hoped some were.

Epilogue

BRIAR HUMMED AS THE TRIMMING shears danced in her hand, moving with practiced ease, intuition guiding her more than her eyes. She knew where to cut. Things always needed to be cut and weeded in order to flourish. Their mother had taught them that.

She supposed she should feel something. Some regret or ache at the loss of their mother. The mother the Garden had rejected. But she could only see the irony. The creator cast out of the Eden she had spent her entire life shaping. Her daughters had needed no serpents to lead them astray. They had done well enough on their own.

Distantly she heard the sound of high-pitched laughter and Cordi's answering voice, slightly muffled by her mask, but still distinct and music to her ears. As was the laughter of the children they so lovingly cared for now.

Briar heard the other voices too. But she ignored them. For now.

It had been Cordi's idea to open the house as an orphanage. Of course, precautions had to be taken. The forest was off-limits, now accessed only by a locked gate. The greenhouse was kept bolted and only she and Cordi kept the keys. The same was true of their wing of the house. But Briar no longer hid or kept to her rooms. *Our rooms,* she thought with a blush. No. Now she donned the masks she so lovingly embroidered and the long gloves and walked through her own home unafraid. She had gone to town. To the city!

And people might have stared at her and her beloved strangely—two women dressed in stylish clothing, masked and gloved, holding hands and sitting too close—but they had done it! They had been careful—Briar was always careful—but it had been so nice to see beyond the Garden.

Though she knew home was best. Home was where she was with Cordi. And Prim.

"There," she said, stroking the bright-amethyst, heart-shaped petals, pleased with the flower's growth. "You're coming along quite nicely. I'm very proud of you. If only you hadn't made such a fuss and been so rash. But you've always been stubborn."

The tree she sat beneath stood still as death, not even the wind moving its slender branches. She smiled up at the face in the bark, his features warped and misshapen, but still obvious. "Oh, Edward, please don't be cross with me. I can't bear it when anyone is cross with me. And you understand?"

The tree didn't stir.

"Of course you do." She patted a root, feeling it flinch beneath her touch, but choosing to ignore the slight. It was only fair.

But, really, what could she have been expected to do? Watch as her sister—the only person she had in the world—was taken from her by a man? Mother had always warned them of men! *Prim* had always warned her, shooing her into her rooms or out of sight whenever one was working on the estate. But she had seen Prim change. She had known her sister as well as she knew herself. Every turn of her head. Every dip of her chin. Every glance and breath. Briar knew them all. She had seen her sister change.

And she had seen why.

The boy that would have taken her beloved Prim from her. The boy who stole her heart!

She'd seen how they exchanged letters. Where they met in the cottage.

Had heard their whispered conversations and plans. Plans that didn't involve *her.* Seen and heard it all through the very roots that twisted them all together.

And she had waited.

It had been easy. Easy to plant doubt in Prim without even saying Edward's name or making her aware Briar knew anything. Easy to make subtle suggestions or beg her darling sister to read her their favorite poem about the tricky goblin men. So easy to steadily poison Prim against her own heart.

Edward had been easier still. Amazing how similar the sisters were in the dark in their twin cloaks without a moon to see by. How one might mistake one for the other with their hoods up and their breath so sweet. How so very easy it was to make people see what they wanted most to believe.

Just as Briar had done to Cordi.

To be fair, at first she thought she would just be like Edward. She'd seen Cordi touch the painting Prim was so sure she'd hidden. And the *jealousy* Briar felt! The rage! The humiliation! Cordi had to be punished. But after her devoted acolyte Stella had delivered Cordi's precious secret trove of letters and she'd realized who Cordi really was. Hers. All along.

Well, nobody could say she wasn't reasonable. She had made a mistake, so she would fix it! An apology of sorts. She knew, of course, that Prim and Mother would save her. If she wept just enough. If she begged just a little. Prim suspected, of course. She was right. Briar was not always kind to her toys. But her sister was as easily maneuvered as the rest. Easy enough to make Prim believe it was her fault through tiny, "innocent" comments and oh-so-carefully planted suggestions. A companion. Someone to love *her.*

Prim had had all the attention. Mother's. Edward's. Briar's. It was only fair that she got to keep Cordi to herself.

That had been easy too. Easy to leave Cordi clues and steer her right where she needed to be. Easy to drop her keys and flaunt Prim's journal. It wasn't manipulation. She didn't like to think of it like that. Men manipulated. That's what Mother said. She wasn't like that. She didn't manipulate. She only coaxed the pieces into place like on the chessboard. Prim was right: chess wasn't about the pieces; it was about knowing how people thought.

Stella . . . That was all rather regretful, but hardly Briar's fault that the girl had grown so impatient. She'd been so helpful too. Adjusting Cordi's tea. Alerting Briar when Cordi had slipped out that night. Bringing her the letters from Edward. So helpful. And all it had taken was a teensy offer of hope. What a girl like Stella would have given for the blessing of one of her revered Flowers. But then she'd seen her and Cordi that night in the dim light of the hallway. Her deity falling to lust, bestowing her favor upon another. She might have ruined all of it. She'd had leverage, something she had never had. And she couldn't be trusted after that.

Again the voices from the Garden tried to whisper, and Briar reached out through the bond and silenced them, daring them to speak again.

Prim was never strong with languages.

Cordi, however . . .

Briar sulked. She'd put it off so long. The voices of the children helped distract Cordi. And she herself was a lovely distraction, if she did say so herself, but Cordi would hear them again eventually. Soon, if the way she stirred in her sleep was an indication. And they had served their purpose.

The Garden needed tending. Better she see to the pruning quickly. Pull up any wicked, twisted roots that might burrow too deep. Some would consider it a mercy and that made her feel better. Still, Briar was pierced with a tiny twinge of guilt that made her frown.

"Oh, I *am* sorry, Prim. I'd no idea how it felt to love someone in such a way. But I'm still disappointed you thought you'd leave me." She sighed. "Well, it's all right, I suppose. We're *all* together now. Me and Cordi and you and Edward. And if you behave," she said, patting Edward's roots again, "maybe we can do something about your own predicament. We have Prim's journal. I'll be honest: it would be easier if Mother were still around, but I suppose that would also have made it impossible. Maybe it was for the best what you did."

Edward's boughs sagged in defeat, and Briar tutted.

"Now, don't pout so. Of course I wanted you and Prim to have each other. I just didn't want to be alone. So, that's that. It is done. And your sister is happy. Fulfilled and free and loved. Isn't that what you wanted?" She brightened. "You and I are like brother and sister now! In-laws, isn't that right? How charming for you to love my sister and your sister to love me. A family. A beautiful, healthy family. And Cordi *is* so happy here! Especially after what she suffered when you left her. But don't worry. I took care of that too. I gave Cordi exactly what she wanted and the revenge she deserved all in one breath."

Briar giggled at her own little joke.

On their trip to the city, she'd left Cordi in the rented rooms and gone to the meeting she'd arranged by letter. With her *generous* contribution to the school, Briar had been granted a position on the board, and she wanted to see how her charity was being spent. She'd had a lovely meeting with Mrs. Clark. They'd shared tea in her rooms and Briar had insisted on serving. The tea was her own brew, after all.

After that, she'd taken a brisk walk in the garden and peered into the classrooms at the children. They were all too thin, too pale. They needed clean country air. Cordi had been right about that too. The city was toxic to little souls. And the garden was even worse than Briar had imagined. More weeds than food grew in its silty, rocky soil. The gardener, hardly worthy of the name, passed out as he was in his little hovel, a bottle dangling limply in one hand.

She'd made that one a little more personal. She'd let him wake up first. She wondered what he saw when he opened his watery, red eyes. A pretty angel standing over him, offering him a kiss.

He was made to suffer as her Cordi had suffered.

And she made sure Edward knew it. She had done what he had not. Guilt worked so much better than fear.

Though, she thought, tapping the shears against Edward's roots, there was nothing very wrong with a little fear.

"You will be a good brother, won't you, Edward? You will behave yourself and keep our little secrets. For my sake as well as Cordi's?"

Edward stood still and silent, but Briar knew he was listening. Weighing his options. And what choice did he have, really? In time, she was sure he would see things her way as everyone typically did. And he would not snatch Cordi's happiness from her. Not when she was so incredibly happy. Not when she was home. Not where she was safe.

She heard Cordi's laugh again, and her heart stirred. Perhaps not as violent a lurch as it had been in the first weeks of infatuation, but it was pleasant. She was still happy. For now.

She laid her shears in the basket along with the cuttings she had taken. Most would be burned, for she couldn't risk the children hurting themselves. But some she would look at more closely, checking for nutrition and disease. It wouldn't do for her dear to be ill. She touched the delicate petals once more and chewed on her lip.

A peek wouldn't hurt, she decided.

Carefully, using her fingers rather than her little spade, she began pulling the moist, nutrient-dense soil away, careful not to snag any tender roots or do any damage. After a moment or so, she found what she was looking for and smiled affectionately.

Prim lay beneath the earth, her porcelain skin shot through with purple veins. Small threads of roots, nearly transparent, had split her flesh in places, spilling into the dirt below, reaching for the nurturing earth and water beneath. No rot or decay had touched her. In fact, she appeared to Briar more beautiful than ever, her lips and hair darker, richer, and her skin faintly luminous. As Briar watched, Prim's eyes snapped open, the twin amethysts staring, unseeing, above her.

Briar put a dirty finger to her own lips. "Shh. Go back to sleep. It's not *quite* time to wake up, sweet sister. Your Edward is here protecting you. Get some rest."

She scooped the dirt back into place, watching it fall over Prim's beloved face, blank and passive in her slumber. She patted it all down and wiped her hands before standing, looping her basket full of trimmings over her arm. With a beatific smile, she stroked the lovely toxic plant growing from between the thick roots of the tree.

"It's not yet harvest time."

Acknowledgments

I DID NOT CULTIVATE THIS GARDEN alone. There were many, many hands nurturing this book through the seasons so it would bloom.

To Jess Macy for screenshotting a mood board on a silly social media site and stumbling on it again at *just* the right time. Thank you for drafting me into the dream team.

To my indomitable agent, Marcy. For never pulling a punch. For being exactly who I needed. For making all this happen. For everything, but especially for believing in me.

To my outrageously cool editor, Kim, for all our unhinged texts, schemes, and sharing this journey with me. You are the most incredible champion, and thank you for loving my girls as much as I do. *Can I keep you?*

To the incredible team at Gallery! Jen Bergstrom, Aimée Bell, Sydney Morris, Kell Wilson, Danielle Mazzella di Bosco, Kathryn Kenney-Peterson, Nancy Tonik, and Caroline Pallotta. The enthusiasm and belief you have shown in me and my words has been beyond anything I had dreamed. To Marcela Bolívar for the beautiful cover art.

To Nathan Ballingrud for saying yes to that first coffee, talking shop, and explaining how publishing happens. I still don't really know, but that's okay. I'm so pleased to have kept you as a friend. Next coffee (or whiskey) is on me.

To Christopher Golden for answering every question and being the exception to the rule about never meeting your idols. Thank you for all the words you have written and for writing some with me. I will be forever grateful.

To my writing coven—Rae, Thea, Amanda, and Jess—for being there in the early days of this book and all the words that came after. For all the words we wrote together and all the words yet to come. You are all incredible mothers, brilliant writers, and some of the most amazing people I have ever known.

A special thank-you to Cortney Radocaj, Cordi's first champion (even though Prim is your favorite). Thank you for opening the door and holding my hand in the beginning.

To the Halloween people who have welcomed me as just another weird member of their weird family. Thank you for being wonderful and kind. Thank you to Josh Winning (my horror bestie!), Cynthia Pelayo, Johanna van Veen, Clay McLeod Chapman, and all the people who blurbed and were early readers.

Thank you to the readers, reviewers, bloggers, and vloggers who keep reading and promoting my words! I hope you keep sticking around. I have such horrors to show you.

To my parents, who made us readers. Thank you for every library sale, bookstore trip, and shared story. For my first copy of *Jane Eyre* and for letting me blast *The Phantom of the Opera* on repeat. For Dad, who made sure his children were morbid. For Mom, who tolerated her children being morbid.

For my sisters. I'm glad there are three of us. For balance, sure, but also for alibis and bail when one of us inevitably snaps. If Gondor calls for aid . . .

For my bestie best. Thank you for believing since the beginning, for being my cheerleader, and for every bougie coffee date and airport selfie. I'm glad you still surprise me, and I'm forever grateful for your friendship. Check another one off the bucket list.

For Natalya and Ronan. I'm glad that you love that your mom is weird and that you still think I'm cool. I will remind you of that in years to come. Love love.

And for Doug. Thank you for the life we've built, for the plans we're still making, and for helping my dreams come true. Thank you for being my very first reader. Don't worry, I'll eventually finish the project you like best. Till then—and always—I love you.

Keep reading for an excerpt
from Tanya Pell's latest book,

THIS B JUST WON'T DIE!

Available October 2026 from Gallery Books

One

If Barbra had to draw a pen across her boobs one more time, she was going to goddamn lose it.

"Could you make it out to Jack Daniel? Like the whiskey?" asked the aging Freddy Krueger, his face beaded with sweat as he fumbled to keep his cheap Spirit Halloween mask up. Barb could see the inside of the rubber, slick with moisture to match the sweat stains that had pooled under the guy's armpits, darkening the sweater's familiar red and green stripes to the color of mud.

Barb revealed her Hollywood smile, trying to picture parents who would name their child after what they had surely been drinking the night of conception. How many Margaritas and Captain Morgans were going to be in the crowd that day? "Sure! I think I'm familiar," she joked, careful to enunciate the vowels in an inconspicuous Midwestern accent rather than dragging them out in a Southern drawl. Something perfectly small-town American from any of the flyover states. "To Jack Daniel, like the whiskey," she teased with a wink, her Sharpie whipping across her breasts in their too-small bra, blown up to life-size on the glossy poster that lay on the table. With a flourish, she added her trademark heart, one hump bigger than the other, that always made her think of upside-down testicles, before signing her name: *Barbie*.

Another tiny piece of her chipped away.

She slid the poster to her table assistant and best friend to roll up. Scott was really what kept their booth—and her—going. "That'll be forty even, Freddy," he told the fan as Jack fished in his pocket. Scott took the money, handled the change if necessary (because fuck math), troubleshot the Square, sold the merch, and rolled up posters and slid prints into clear baggies so Barb's precious cleavage was protected. Barb was simply an automaton who signed her name and smiled pretty because that's all anybody wanted her to do anymore.

Scott would have her think differently. They'd been friends since *Mirror*, when she was the final girl and Scott was a nameless extra and worked in makeup. He'd been hilarious, keeping her laughing through the long days when her face was puffy from crying and reminding her to drink her water when she had a splitting headache from dehydration. He still did.

Twenty years as her best friend and still putting up with her shit.

He needed higher standards.

As like-the-whiskey Jack fumbled the mask back into place, hands encumbered by rubber clawed gloves, Leesa leaned in from Barb's other side, nearly falling out of the folding chair to reach her. "How the fuck do you keep this up?"

Careful to suppress the annoyance from both her voice and face, Barb turned the wattage down on her smile, only succeeding in making it feel brittle as she turned to her old costar. "Is your hand hurting or your pride?"

"Bitch," Leesa snapped without any real venom. If she were to strike, she would make it hurt. That was only meant as a warning as she tossed her tri-toned hair over her shoulder, ash and platinum streaks slicing through dark layers. Barb thought chunky skunk hair had gone out of fashion with young Christina Aguilera, but maybe Leesa hadn't gotten the memo. Or it had come back around and Barb was not up-to-date with what The Youth were doing?

Knowing Leesa Clover, it was whatever the clones at her current "wellness" clinic were sporting. She'd been a rowing instructor for years now, but was always chasing a new trend that promised peace and mindfulness and whatever other bullshit you could fit into an Instagram reel. She'd dragged Barb to a random seminar once, arguing that since Barb had always enjoyed meditation and yoga casually, she might progress into deeper practices. There were singing bowls and chakras and Chinese acupuncture and Korean skin care while all the staff had been white, blond Midwesterners wearing Lululemon in shades like "sandstorm" and "basic bitch beige." Barb had fancied she'd been able to see ring-lights burned into their irises. They all had high ponytails and names like Kasey, Kylie, Kyle, and Caley. Barb hadn't been able to tell them apart and she'd decided she had white-influencer face blindness. It had screamed *scam*. Or *cult*. She'd eyed the cucumber water with suspicion the entire weekend.

Regardless, Leesa had abandoned Hollywood and was probably better off for it. While Barb still groveled and tried her best to keep up in the rat race, Leesa had chosen to spend the past decade in pursuit of what she called a peaceful mind, free of performative expectations, while she choked down beef organ supplements and participated in primal screaming therapy, the only performance she screamed for anymore.

Yet here she was with Barb and the rest, honoring the anniversary of their first film. So much for a "peaceful mind." To be fair, Leesa was not someone Barb thought of as capable of peace. She was a one-woman army or possibly a missile designed to seek and destroy. Leesa was made for war. The trouble was, she had never quite cared whether she was fighting friend or foe, the concept of "friendly fire" moot. She had her good points, though Barb would probably need to be held at gunpoint to name five consecutively. They'd always been better frenemies than friends because she was a paradox that Barb could not wrap her brain around.

She was also a backstabbing bitch.

"No. Seriously. How do you do this on the regular? Sit here and smile and banter without going full nuke? Do you know the number of grown-ass men I have seen wearing black latex and rubber today? And not in a kinky way."

"It's kinky for some of them."

"That doesn't help!" Leesa continued, sulking. "This is crazy!" She gestured to the convention hall, which was an assault on the senses. Crocheted cryptids and reworked movie posters of everything from *Jaws* to *Abigail* that would glow under black light. Artists sat behind their tables, drawing away or scrolling through their phones while con-goers picked through kawaii stickers of Ghostface surrounded by hearts or Michael Myers holding a coffee. Candlemakers sold hand-poured candles in black jars with names like "Final Girl" or "Grave Dirt" or "Demon Song." Barb used to assume that Final Girl smelled like sweat and blood, but really they all always smelled overly sweet, like Froot Loops with notes of cinnamon.

Even in candle form, final girls had to be sugar and spice and everything nice.

Overhead, the lights were too bright, too loud, and too unflattering, giving the room a sickly yellow hue enhanced by the mustard walls and unfortunate carpet choice that looked like someone had sprayed the original beige with a hose filled with blood. It was like every horror convention.

A lot.

From the other side of Leesa, Vi tutted. "We're being good sports, Leesa. It's the anniversary. Try to have a little fun."

"They're making us pay for our own wine, Vi. They can suck my dick."

"Now, there's a mental picture I needed," Barb muttered, wishing Vi was next to her instead. Well, mostly . . . If Vi *was* beside her, Barb's insecurities might very well cripple her. Violet Crane was as stunning at forty as she had been at nineteen; possibly more so. She was tall and willowy and hadn't lost any of the grace and poise that had made her, if not a movie star, a successful runway model. With her dark ebony skin, perfect cheekbones, and coiled curls, she'd walked straight from the first *Mirror* set onto a catwalk. After meeting her playwright husband at a charity event, she'd become his muse and the next boards she'd walked had been those of Broadway.

Now Barb saw her seldom save for her immaculate Instagram grid filled with pictures of her sunlight-drenched brownstone, artistic angles of stage practice, selfies of her with her adoring husband, Jordan, or their gigantic Maine coon cat, Norma Desmond.

Even after all these years, she still marveled at the woman, a little starstruck. She wished they'd been closer on set, but Barb had always felt outclassed and awkward next to Vi, who made everything look effortless. It didn't matter that Barb was the star of the film or that "effortless" actually took *a lot* of effort. As she eyed Vi now, with her perfectly spiraled curls, red lips, and designer black sunglasses atop her head, Barb had to resist the urge to hide beneath the table. Thinking about it, she regretted the donut she'd had from the greenroom and every carb she'd had for the last decade and swiftly checked the corner of her mouth for any lingering frosting.

To keep from spiraling, she focused on playing nice. "The panel went well. Haven't done one of those in a while." She was usually at a signing table in a corner somewhere rather than onstage with Bill and the other famous horror monsters.

Leesa turned her head slowly like something possessed, meeting Barb's eyes with her own. Leesa did not *look* at anything. She *glared*. She *withered*. She *destroyed*. And now she smiled, making it all the worse. "You're shitting me."

"I mean," Barb offered, waffling between damage control and retreat, "that *we* haven't all been together in forever and the anniversary has brought us all back together."

Twenty years on from the original, ScareCon 2024 marked the first of several scheduled anniversary appearances. Twenty years—half!—of her life spent filling the shoes of Debbie Turner, the virginal teenage babysitter, even though Barb had not been either when she landed the role. And, like all good final girls, she'd been hunted by the same masked killer through multiple films—a black-clad, knife-or-glass-shard-wielding maniac known only as Mirror Man, who donned a dome-like mirrored mask, reflecting the faces of his victims. It was her big break, the six-film franchise that would crown her a scream queen.

And utterly destroy her chances of ever landing a serious role.

"If you're so eager to catch up, Barb, we could do dinner. The panel was the Bill Curry hour and you know it. You may have played second-string, but Vi and I had to dust ourselves off after that. I could feel myself being covered in cobwebs."

Vi bristled, but before she could respond, a man and his daughter approached her end of the table and her smile blossomed. The little girl looked up in awe, holding a creased Playbill from one of Vi's shows rather than a DVD of *Mirror*. The kid was probably too young to know what a DVD was anyway. Barb watched the way Vi folded her elegant hands, lotioned and oiled with collagen, her naked nails buffed to a shine and artfully shaped into perfect almonds. Vi never wore nail polish even during filming. She thought it was tacky.

Barb fought the urge to hide her pink-tipped fingers in her lap, counting to ten to ground herself rather than risk a look at her hand to check for a new wrinkle or freckle she could obsess into an age spot. Ever the serial fawner, she tried to find common ground with Leesa. "I get it, Leesa. I know they really want to see Bill. Not us."

Bill Curry was a horror icon. Not only the character he had portrayed successfully for years, but Bill himself. While most masked monsters became the bogeymen that audiences remembered, Bill had done the impossible and made himself just as famous as he was when he was faceless on-screen. He'd stalked Barb as Mirror Man through all six films and she loved him dearly. But it was hard not to hate him a little for the way he could move between worlds.

She'd tried for years to branch out. But the *Mirror* franchise had taken off and then one horror film bled into the next and, before she knew it, she was typecast. A scream queen. She wasn't a Jamie Lee Curtis or an Emily Blunt. She'd gotten stuck. Her thick, long blond hair, blue eyes, and small waist had wooed crowds who wanted a gory Barbie doll, but that hadn't been enough for casting agents and directors with more thought-provoking roles to fill. Directors didn't think she would be believable in dramas or even comedies after seeing her scream and flail as she ran, boobs bouncing so hard she actually ended up with stretch marks.

Now Barb was determined to give it one last real go while she could still see forty clearly in her rearview mirror. She was in good shape thanks to a weekly regime of Pilates, cycling, and strength training, had removed her implants (but sprung for a lift), had stopped going by Barbie—except at the cons—and was considering chopping off her trademark blond waves. In the last few years, she'd landed a few voice acting roles for video games and audiobooks and was putting herself out there again. These were the things she told her therapist so she could pretend she was doing a good job at being an adult, even if she knew the session would end with her in a Starbucks drive-through recounting all the ways she wasn't trying hard enough.

But her brief moment of optimism was cut short as she realized she had begun to slump in her chair. She quickly adjusted her posture and fell into her mental checklist, doing a full-body scan. Tummy sucked in, shoulders down, chin lifted so as not to risk showing folds. Relax the jaw to smooth any wrinkles. Were her lashes okay? Her nails chipped? Botox holding?

She shoved her hands under her thighs so she didn't start picking at her cuticles or reach for the compact she had in her bag. She did not need to check the mirror. She did not want to check the mirror. The mirror would not help. The mirror had never helped. Which was a funny thought when she was surrounded by her own face and the shiny, blood-splattered logo for the *Mirror* franchise.

Maybe the anniversary could mark a new beginning. Maybe she could move on now that there were no more films in the franchise. She could really try!

She only hoped she never had to be a final gir—

A high-pitched scream echoed through the room and Barb's heart stopped.

Two

The scream, followed by a maniacal laugh straight from a Halloween party playlist, had Barb massaging the back of her jaw, her inner ears ringing. The loudspeakers crackled as someone changed the audio channel from playback to a live mic somewhere.

"Hello, all you Halloween people, and thanks again for joining us for ScareCon 2024!" proclaimed a disembodied voice that rose and fell, pitching like an old radio personality.

"Oh, for the love of God," Leesa moaned, face contorting in annoyance.

"We'll be hosting our Scream Queen contest live on the main stage at the top of the hour! So warm up those pipes and get ready to scream for help!" A pause. "But don't expect any." The microphone jockey gave a prolonged cackle of laughter before snapping off.

Shit. She'd almost forgotten the contest. Which would have looked terrible considering she was the judge this year. She'd have to step back into Debbie Turner's shoes. *Barbie's* shoes, in a way. That's who they wanted, wasn't it? Barb would be surrounded on all sides by cosplayers brandishing cell phones while horror fans wearing fishnets, glittery bat earrings, and *Jade Daniels Is My Final Girl* T-shirts screamed at the top of their lungs.

Even now, she could hear dissonant wails from the bathrooms.

Contestants for these things always warmed up in the bathrooms. Barb wanted to tell them it was a terrible idea because bathroom acoustics—like their mirrors and surface sterility—were notorious liars. But they had to practice somewhere. She tapped a manicured nail on the table, wondering, not for the first time, what they imagined when they screamed. Did they try to channel their darkest fear and paint it across the backs of their eyelids? Did they scream into the void like so many women who came before them, wishing their screams had been heard? Did they consider their neck placement or did they go au naturel?

Scott nudged her thigh, pulling her from her reverie. They had a live one. Showtime. Barb slipped the mask on and turned the wattage up to full at the latest fan, jutting her chest out a little farther and pulling her shoulders down from her ears where tension was urging them higher. *They aren't earrings*, she told herself, hearing the voice of her favorite Peloton instructor in her head.

The man who approached looked to be in his late thirties, perhaps only a year or two younger than herself, and was sporting a screen-printed T-shirt with her screaming, terrified face on the front, a dark silhouette in the red-lit doorway in the background, light glinting off the curved mirror mask concealing his face and the shard of mirror he held in one gloved hand. The movie's tagline ran across the bottom in a serif font:

What will you see when you look in the mirror?

Barb hated that fucking question.

"I know her!" she said with a laugh and pointed before striking the same terrified pose as the shirt, practiced to perfection. It damn well better have been since she'd been doing the same face for almost twenty years. Beside her, she could feel Leesa prickle.

It all felt pretty gross to Barb, too, and she suddenly craved a Jack Daniel's. Preferably with pineapple juice and lemon rather than sweaty pit stains and rubber fingers.

"Wow," the guy said, face splitting into an eager grin. "I am such a huge fan!"

She poked her lips out and held her hands over her heart, batting her fake lashes; part of her genuinely touched, part of her wondering if it was her acting he appreciated or her cleavage. Two decades of the same words had left her jaded and she hated that. Hated that she could no longer fully appreciate fans, but regarded each one with suspicion and a measure of loathing. Her therapist said it was to be expected. That having never evolved from "scream queen" to "serious actress," she put unnecessary blame on those she believed had been culpable in keeping her in a box.

These people keep your name alive, she reminded herself before repeating her mantra for the eight-hundredth time that afternoon: *Be grateful. But don't be a victim. You are not a victim. Not on-screen. Not in life.*

She realized the guy in the screen-print shirt had asked her a question and she shook herself, sending her hair sliding over her shoulders. "I'm sorry. So loud in here. What was that?"

He had his hands in his pockets, a chain running from one belt loop back behind him to his wallet, and Barb knew instantly he had spent most of the year 2000 in Hot Topic. The jeans were faded and worn with soft, stained holes in the knees. Broad shoulders. Lean hips. He had a five-o'clock shadow over his cheeks and jaw, the stiff hairs just beginning to gray, and clear blue eyes. An alt kid who'd grown up and could have been on daytime television as a doctor or small-town sheriff.

"I heard that they're doing a whole docuseries that will include *Mirrors* and are considering a reboot. Any chance you're gonna be involved with either project?"

Ah, Reddit. "We'll see. I honestly think the fans find out about these things way faster than the actors do. I mean, I heard Sigourney Weaver didn't even know they were making *Aliens* until the script landed on her desk." She did not say that any reboot would most certainly not include her. Ever. Not in a million years.

She'd die first.

He bobbed his head. "Right on."

A silence stretched and Barbra pushed her tongue against her teeth, rolling the Sharpie between her fingers. "So, can I—"

"Right!" The man jerked as if shocked into remembering where he was and what he had been doing. He reached behind him and pulled out a silver Sharpie. "Actually, I wanted to snag a pic, and could you sign my shirt?"

"Sure!" Barbra stood, resisting the urge to check that her Spanx were in place while the man paid Scott for a photo. Rather than lean over the table, she opted to come around, taking the proffered silver marker and popping the cap. She twirled one finger, her pink nails filed to points, motioning for him to turn so she could sign the shoulder.

He obliged, and she laid her left palm between his shoulder blades, smoothing the fabric flat. She took a bit more care signing shirts and skin, knowing her swift signatures could look muddled and people paid for the real thing. She was especially careful with skin for those fans who came back hours later to proudly show her how they had permanently branded themselves with her name. As if they were all part of the same club.

She supposed they were.

Barb colored in her heart with the silver ink last before passing the pen back. "Thanks," he said, a faint blush on his cheeks. She was always floored by this response. Grown men reduced to shy boys around her. She didn't get it, but it helped chase off the intrusive thoughts for a few minutes before she started to question their eyesight or sanity.

"You're welcome. Lemme know if you hear about my next movie deal before I do," she whispered conspiratorially.

He gave a short laugh and scratched the back of his neck, right above where her hand had been. As he shoved the pen into his back pocket, he reached into the front with his opposite hand and pulled out his phone, handing it to Scott.

Barb stepped closer, tossing her hair over one shoulder, and smiled. The guy didn't put an arm around her, but stood with his head tilted in her direction, giving a thumbs-up, which was considerate. Some of the guys—and enough of the women—who paid for pictures with her would all but grope her butt or try to grab a handful of side-boob. Joke was on them. Her bra was padded more than a politician's pockets.

Scott held up the phone and centered them in frame. "One, two . . ." He took the shot, checking to make sure it was solid before handing it back. Likely also checking to make sure Leesa hadn't photobombed, middle fingers raised. Scott was professional. Customers didn't get blurry pics featuring petty costars. As the guy took his phone back, he passed Barb a business card.

She reached for it without thinking, glancing at the front of the heavy cardstock. Black with shimmery red veins of ink crawling from one edge of the card to the text on the other.

"Levi Connolly," she read aloud. "Levi like the jeans."

"Sorry?" he said with a chuckle.

Barb shook her head. "Nothing. You're a writer? You're working the con?"

He shrugged one shoulder, hands back in his front pockets, and nodded. "Unofficially. But took a break and had to come over and shoot my shot, ya know?"

She raised a brow. "Shoot your shot?"

His face flushed again and he slowly backed away. "It's no big deal. See ya around, Ms. Jacobs."

As she rounded the table, she flipped the card over. Email and cell. She snorted a laugh and flashed the card at Scott.

Scott grinned behind his glasses. "Give the man some credit for trying! And he could have used a line."

She gave a groan as she sat down. "What was the last one?"

Scott leaned back in his chair, arms crossed as he did when he was thinking, chin tucked against his chest in a way Barb would never allow herself to sit. She had enough of a shock anytime she accidentally opened the front-facing camera.

Snapping his fingers in front of his forehead, Scott tried to jog his memory like a magic trick. "It was from number five. God, what wa—OH!" *Abracadabra!* "'Baby, Mirror Man may want to collect your face, but I want you to sit on—'"

"Never mind!" Barbra interjected. "Forget I asked!" Some of the more colorful con attendees had jokes. Terrible, vulgar jokes that she knew they spent far too much time coming up with only to have Scott politely pull them away while flagging security. She'd kneed one in the balls once and her agent had ridden her ass so hard for it that she'd considered asking her why she didn't bother to pull Barb's hair too. Instead, she'd nodded, clenched her jaw, and promised it wouldn't happen again. Since then, she let others play the hero.

Final girls weren't heroes. Just survivors.

There seemed to be a lull, so Barbra sat back in her chair for a minute and stretched her arms over her head, stifling a yawn. "How are we doing?"

Scott scratched at his scalp as he did quick mental math, the heavy black leather cuff around his wrist dropping slightly to show a distinct tan line. His brown hair was still thick despite the number of times he ran a hand through it every day, his nervous habit meaning it would be streaked with greasepaint or prosthetic jelly when on a job. Today, though, it was clean and he smelled of the same deodorant he had worn for twenty years.

He was still hustling like the rest of them. Or like her, at least.

He'd watched his industry shift from prosthetics and spirit gum to CGI and compositing green screens. Scott had started in horror with blood and guts and now worked just as often with smoky eyes and rhinestones. She knew he missed filling wounds with maggots, but that was showbiz.

He still sculpted his horrors on a small scale and sold them at the cons and promoted his YouTube SFX makeup channel.

"Not bad, actually," he said. "Stickers are the big sell again. The hearse print is going fast this time. Maybe we commission new movie-poster concept art for signings. I'm almost sold out of my miniatures. Photos are down, but I suspect it is from people sneaking pics as they walk by. We can always go back to the pro-op, but not ideal."

Pro-op photos meant an hour of sweaty handshakes and gimmicky posing. By the end, Barb's back ached, her feet were sore, and she needed a scalding shower.

Worse were the times when there was no crowd at all.

"Yeah, I'll think about it," she sighed, reaching for her tumbler. It was empty.

"Refill?" He leaned in and stage-whispered, his breath smelling of coffee and tickling the hair by her ear, "Say yes and get me away from the bunny boiler!"

Barb had to stifle a laugh. It didn't matter that Leesa and Scott's inconvenienceship, an on-again, off-again hookup session on the set of the first film, was twenty years behind them; they still could hardly stand each other. Barb had never learned exactly what had happened, having only Scott's side of the story, which she was sure had a gap or two. It wouldn't matter. Leesa held on to grudges as if they were precious, and no amount of kumbaya-ing in a yurt could rid her of the habit.

"I am of the controversial opinion," she'd told Barb once over home-brewed kombucha that Barb had choked down, "that, while hatred is rooted in fear, it can actually help you blossom into a stronger, more resilient version of yourself. People mistake it for an energy exchange when really I'm merely mirroring the energy they try to force-feed me."

Barb knew a lot about mirroring.

Regardless, Scott believed Leesa was crazy. Or a demon. Barb would not be surprised if he packed holy water in his shaving kit when he knew she'd be around.

She smiled and handed Scott the pink cup. "Thanks. No—"

"No ice. Just ambivalent water. How dare you?"

"I'm sorry. You know everything."

"I do." His heavy hand squeezed her shoulder. "Hey, it's not over. Not for a final girl. That's the point. You're still standing in the end."

Barbra patted his hand. "I know."

"What am I?" he asked, cocking his head as if to make sure he could hear her.

"Right."

"And?"

"The best."

Squeezing her shoulder again, he took her empty cup and went around the booth, barely managing to push into the throng of Freddys, Michaels, and Mirror Men. Even the occasional Spider-Man or Darth Vader flitted about. There were always a handful of Ripleys, a rather outrageous number of Harley Quinns, and even the random Debbie Turner. Early in the con game, she'd made bingo boards to pass the time between customers, but eventually it became as repetitive as everything else and Barb began to resent it for that reason.

If it never changed, she never changed.

Or, more specifically, she wasn't supposed to.

She forced herself not to slouch again, refusing to let gravity have anything it did not earn. But she couldn't stop herself from seeing the prints of her face spread across the table. Five, ten, twenty years younger, thinner, brighter. Still mint from the box in some cases.

Barb hated that girl almost as much as she hated herself.